VISIBLE BY APPOINTMENT

I did my best to keep my face placid to hide a sudden wave of nervousness, and tried to feign nonchalance. "Hello. I'm here to see P. G. Holyfield."

The woman looked puzzled and reached for a book on her desk. "Do you have an appointment, sir?"

"No, I do not. But P. G. will want to see me. We met the other day at my aunt's party."

She looked back up at me. "I'm sorry, sir, but no one is permitted to see P. G. Holyfield without an appointment."

The nervousness drained out of me, and with a certain giddiness, words came flooding up to me from the hidden recesses of my brain. I didn't know what I had planned, but some corner of my mind assured me that it knew just what to say. I let the words flow. "No one?" I asked.

"No, sir." She shook her head.

"Doesn't that make it rather difficult to work here?"

"I'm sorry, sir?" She leaned her head to one side, as if that might make my words make more sense to her.

"If no one is allowed to see P. G. Holyfield without an appointment, then does everyone have to avert their eyes when P. G. Holyfield goes walking the hallways? Or do you have to have specific appointments for P. G. Holyfield to come, and to leave? Or to go to the bathroom?"

She blinked in confusion, then frowned at me. "Sir! Don't be ridiculous!"

"*I'm* being ridiculous? I'm not the one insisting that P. G. Holyfield is only visible by appointment."

"What?"

I pointed to the door behind her. "If you were to go through that door, would you be able to see P. G. Holyfield? Or would P. G. Holyfield be invisible?"

"What? Are you quite all right, sir?" She gave me a worried look.

"Would P. G. Holyfield be invisible?"

"No."

"So, P. G. Holyfield is in there?"

"Yes!"

"Thank you." I strode around the desk and moved to the door.

ALSO BY DOC COLEMAN

The Adventures of Crackle and Bang

The Perils of Prague

The Kindred of Kali

Other Titles

The Shining Cog and Other Steampunk Tales

Anthologies

The Way of the Gun, A Bushido Western Anthology

(Iron Kilt Productions)

Paradise Found, Tales from the Library

(Captain's Table Press)

Forgotten Lore Anthologies (eSpec Books)

A Cast of Crows

A Cry of Hounds

An Assembly of Monsters

Other Short Stories

The Gift

Welcome to Paradox

"A Walk in the Park", published in the Special Steampunk issue of Flagship

"The Cross of Columba", featured on The Ministry of Peculiar Occurrences
Tales from the Archives podcast

THE KINDRED OF KALI

Published in the United States of America by Swimming Cat Studios https://SwimmingCatStudios.com

Cover design, cover art, and interior illustrations by Scott E. Pond Designs, LLC (http://ScottPond.com) Edited by Leona Wisoker (http://LeonaWisoker.com)

Print ISBN: 978-0-9980151-5-6 EBook ISBN: 978-0-9980151-4-9

PRINTED IN THE UNITED STATES OF AMERICA

10 9 8 7 6 5 4 3 2 1

FIRST EDITION: First printing - August 2025

The Adventures of Crackle and Bang: Book Two

THE KINDRED OF KALI

DOC COLEMAN

SWIMMING CAT STUDIOS

Dedication

To my father, taken from us just a year past.
I grew up sitting across the kitchen table from you, reading your newspaper upside down. I answered the chemistry questions you asked, the ones that your students kept getting wrong.
I heard your rants on politics, taxes, and the stupidity that seemed rampant in the world.
Of all of it, I remember two things: Don't let obstacles stand in your way, and Think.
I took these things to heart, and thought my way through many a problem.
I miss you, Dad. There are so many things I wish I could talk about with you.

ACKNOWLEDGMENTS

I'd like to take a moment to express my thanks to the following people, without whom this book could not have come together:

Keetara Coleman - For supporting my writing, and doing the proofread, so this book can be its best.

Sara Lloyd - For asking all the right questions so I could make sure that I answered them in the text.

Shari Mosser - For helping me find the balance between period vocabulary and modern sensibility.

Scott Pond - For your amazing cover art that perfectly reflects a Crackle and Bang story.

Andrija Popovic - For helping make the book familiar to old readers and understandable to new readers.

Lori Ann Rutherford - For keeping my grammar and spelling in check.

Shanta Sand - For caring about my characters, and laughing at the right places.

Leona Wisoker - For helping me make this a better book. I may not have always agreed with your edits, but they helped me iron out the rough spots and make it a better story.

CHAPTER ONE
A DISTURBANCE IN AN INDIAN GARDEN

"You really didn't have to do this, Professor," I shouted, grabbing at my hat as we hit yet another bump in the road.

Professor Harmonious Crackle pressed up against me on the narrow bench and yelled over the sputtering of the engine, "Think nothing of it! We have all greatly enjoyed your company on the trip to India." His blue eyes shone as he glanced at me through the lenses of his goggles, and a wide grin split his face. While the professor was considerably older than I, he still had the appearance of a man in his late twenties. His clean-shaven face lacked any trace of lines or wrinkles. Wisps of his short, cropped blond hair squeezed out from beneath the brim of the top hat he clutched to his head. The strands remained bright and yellow and lacked any signs of graying as they fluttered in the wind. A second pair of goggles was strapped around the body of the hat.

I shook my head. "I meant that you could have simply left me at the port, Professor. You didn't need to come all this way." I gripped the edge of my seat as the driver swerved into oncoming lane to pass a mule cart, and dodged around a franticly honking lorry before returning to the proper lane. The driver shook his tanned fist at the other driver and promptly bounced us through a pothole in the unpaved road through the outskirts of Kanpur, India. I glanced over at my two companions, the professor in the middle of the bench seat, and his colleague, Miss Bang, on the other side. Neither seemed bothered by the rough ride or the driver's questionable skills. I swallowed before continuing. "I... I could have sent word to Aunt Phyllis. I'm sure she would have sent a carriage to collect me."

The professor chuckled. "Nonsense, old chap! We said we'd deliver you to your aunt, and we shall! Besides, I want to offer my condolences to your aunt on the loss of her brother. Reggie was a dear friend and one of my favorite students. His loss was a great tragedy." He gazed for a moment at the trees and bushes that lined the road as we shot by them. "But on the bright side, this gave us an opportunity to ride in a jitney! In all my years of travel, this was one thing I've never had the chance to do!" He crowed as he gave the seat in front of us an affectionate pat. The driver seemed to interpret the gesture as a request for additional speed. He opened the throttle, sending us bouncing down the rutted road through the Indian countryside.

While the professor may have been excited to hire this dubious transport to take us from the skyport, I was considerably less thrilled. The vehicle looked as if it had been assembled from scavenged parts bolted onto a discarded horse carriage. A buzzing diesel engine had been mounted at the front of the chassis, with the floorboard and most of the front seat on the left hand side cut away for the engine and the gears and chains that drove the front axle. The driver sat practically on top of the engine on what remained of the front seat. The exhaust wasn't properly fitted, so periodically we were enveloped by a cloud of black, foul-smelling smoke. Especially after hitting a bump or a pothole, which happened frequently.

"Have you been to India before, my lord?" Miss Bang called across the professor, somehow managing to look at ease while being bounced and jostled. Her long, dark hair was carefully tucked up into her wide-brimmed hat. She wore goggles against the wind and the sides of the hat were tied under her chin, providing additional protection from the wind and smoke. A long duster protected the rest of her clothing from the dust and debris of the road.

I clutched at the flimsy support for the tattered fabric roof as the ramshackle vehicle skidded around a turn, sending a pair of locals scrambling off the road. I gasped for breath before replying, "No. This is my first trip abroad. Prague was the first stop and Kanpur is the second. I've only seen my aunt when she's come to visit family back in England and I don't think I've ever met her husband. He's been posted out here for quite some time."

"I believe you mentioned he's in the military," she prodded.

"Yes, Miss Bang. Army, I believe. Assigned to the Colonial Defense troops..." I struggled to hold on as the jitney made a sudden left turn in front of another vehicle and threaded through a narrow gap in the trees lining the side of the road. We emerged into a large field in front of what appeared to be an English residence. Unfortunately, the field was currently covered with a wide assortment of carriages and vehicles. Our driver twisted the wheel this way and that, weaving his way through the parked vehicles and frightened carriage horses. Somehow, he managed to pilot our craft through the lot and brought it to a screeching stop in front of the main door of the building. More miraculously, he managed to do so without hitting anything.

"Well, wasn't that fun?" Professor Crackle laughed and pushed past me to drop to the ground beside the jitney, which looked horribly out of place next to the shining conveyances surrounding us.

I jumped to the grass and ran around to help Miss Bang down from her seat. Several grooms rushed to bring startled horses under control after our sudden entrance.

The professor calmly stripped off his goggles and strapped them onto his top hat above the other pair. The driver called to us in a fluid language, and Miss Bang responded to him in the same tongue. Miss Bang had mentioned the language's name several times as we approached the port, I had forgotten it, again, and was now too embarrassed to ask her once more.

The driver held out his hand and repeated his statement. Miss Bang reached into her reticule and handed the man a few coins. I walked over to join the professor, slapping the dust from my suit and regretting that I had refused Miss Bang's offer of a linen overcoat before we left the ship.

The professor studied the building as he absently struck at his white lab coat, failing to dislodge any significant amount of road dust. The house was a large, stone and brick building. Three stories of windows looked down at us, with the largest being on the first floor. Large columns framed the door with decorative stonework on either side. A large bay window looked out over the front yard, and the corners of the house were fashioned as turrets reaching up to pointed spires. The white painted sashes of the windows seemed to shine in the bright sunlight. In contrast, the dense vegetation seemed to come right up to the house at the base of each turret, making the house seem out of place.

"That is a sight for sore eyes, my friend," he said, pulling his coats open and perching his hands on his hips, exposing his blue checked waistcoat. "I can't remember the last time I laid eyes on good, old-fashioned English architecture." He looked around at the assorted vehicles and the lush vegetation growing at the fringes of the field. "Although it does seem a bit out of place here."

I pulled off my own hat and goggles. "I can't imagine Aunt Phyllis voluntarily living in anything except a proper English house. She is *very* particular."

With a scattering of gravel, the driver chivvied the jitney back into motion, dodging through the parked vehicles and back out onto the road. One of the grooms cursed at the retreating rattletrap, shaking his fist for good measure. I gave Miss Bang a look of concern, but she indicated with a wave of her hand that she was fine. She untied her hat and pulled her goggles off, sliding them into a pocket of her duster.

Looking at the house, she said, "Your aunt and uncle have a lovely home, Sir Richard."

It took me a moment to remember I was now Sir Richard Blasphemy. It still struck me as odd whenever anyone addressed me by my new title, it being completely unlike the horribly obscene name I'd suffered with for twenty-six years. I was slowly getting used to the much more socially acceptable title bestowed upon me in Prague less than a month ago.

Professor Crackle nodded. "And it appears your aunt has other guests today." He indicated the collection of vehicles on the lawn.

I felt a wave of nervousness at the professor's observation. It was bad enough that I was several weeks late for my visit with Aunt Phyllis, now to arrive in the middle of one of her parties? Aunt Phyllis did not forgive tardiness. She considered it a sign of poor planning. While the tragedy we encountered in Prague might mitigate my situation somewhat, my aunt was sure to be upset with me for not letting her know when I would arrive. And showing up with two uninvited guests in tow? I'm sure death would be preferable. Well, maybe that was a slight exaggeration.

"Perhaps this isn't the best time to come calling," I said.

"Pish and tosh!" the professor responded, "You're her nephew! I'm sure she'll be overjoyed to see you."

"That would make a change," I murmured.

"Shall we, my lord?" Miss Bang asked. She was right. No sense standing out in the sun and waiting.

"Very well," I said and led my companions up onto the step. I stepped up to the large wooden doors and faced down an ornate brass knocker. I stood there for several long seconds trying to come up with something to say to the person who answered the door. My mind stayed resolutely blank.

A soft "ahem" sounded behind me as Miss Bang cleared her throat. I sighed, and realized I had been holding my breath. With a shaky hand, I reached out and lifted the knocker, giving two solid knocks on the door.

For almost a minute, there was no sign of a response from inside the house. I wondered if the party was lively enough that no one had heard me knock. Right. Raucous noise at one of Aunt Phyllis' parties? I couldn't imagine any of her guests being so rambunctious.

A pair of loud clacks sounded from the door. A moment later, it cracked open, revealing an Indian man dressed in butler's livery. I blinked at the man, my mind gone blank once again.

"May I help you?" the butler asked, and his voice snapped me back to my senses. While the man's dark skin and features were clearly a product of the subcontinent, his accent was a flawless product of the English aristocracy.

"Ah, yes. I, uh, I mean, we. We're here to see Lady Phyllis Griffith-Holmes."

The butler looked at my companions in turn, straightening slightly as he looked at Miss Bang, and raising an eyebrow as he took in the professor and his dusty lab coat. He regarded me serenely and said, "The lady of the house is currently busy with a garden party and may not be available to see you. Whom may I say is calling?"

The old, familiar panic struck me when asked to provide my name. While I now had an acceptable alternative by giving my title instead, I had no idea if my aunt would know me by my new title. The professor's airship, the Argos, traveled fast. We might have outrun the news. Then again, I did have another alternative. "Please tell her that her nephew is here to see her."

The man arched his eyebrows at me and said haughtily, "Her nephew is already in attendance. Her ladyship does not have time to waste on imposters, sir." He closed the door, and I heard him shooting the bolt to lock it.

"Surely there must be some mistake," Miss Bang suggested.

"I say, my good man, come back here a moment," the professor called as he reached to pound on the door.

I turned and held up my hands to them. "Wait, wait. He's here. This is marvelous."

"My lord?"

For once, I got to see them looking confused while I knew what was going on. I couldn't help but break into a huge grin. "The butler said they're at a garden party. Everyone will be out back. This way!"

I led my companions off to one side of the house at a run and we pushed our way through a hedge, emerging into the gardens at the rear. The garden itself was much as I expected: a classic English design, with pathways, conversation alcoves, statuary, and a space large enough to play croquet. Several tables stood under awnings with a buffet laid out upon them. A string quartet played light music from a spot just far enough from the buffet to discourage the musicians from eating food intended for the guests.

What made me stop in my tracks was the people. Their clothes were a mixture of dark European suits and brightly coloured, embroidered Indian styles, and their hair and features also showed a variety of different ancestries. While I should have expected each of these things, I did not expect was the manner in which they were combined.

I remembered my professors telling us that the first British Raj was built on fear, and inevitably led to revolution. But the Eternal Empress, Queen Victoria, ended that with the formation of the second British Raj. She married her granddaughter, Princess Victoria, to Prince Victor Albert Jay Duleep Singh, the eldest son of Maharaja Duleep Singh of India, and declared an official policy of equality between the British and Indian peoples.

It was one thing to know of the blending of the two cultures, and quite another to see the product of that blending with one's own eyes. I saw women wearing saris whose skin tone was nearly as pale as any Scotsman, but whose features were clearly Indian. Another gentleman in a tasteful European suit had a classic Roman nose and dark brown skin. A trio of dark complexioned young women wearing brightly coloured day dresses decorated with local embroidery patterns talked with a pair of pale young men dressed in long jackets and tight pants.

Modern India had become a blend of British and Indian culture. Under the second Raj, power transferred back to Indian hands, but much of that was done through marriage to equally powerful British families. Many of the guests I saw were products of those marriages. I knew there were some people on both sides who frowned on the idea of mixing such different cultures, but the people I saw here were alive and vibrant.

They were stunning, and for a moment I forgot that I wasn't just looking at the people, but I was looking for someone in particular.

Unfortunately, while I was lost in wonder, the butler emerged from the back of the house and spotted us.

Accompanied by a pair of footmen, the head of the household servants rushed at us, calling for us to hold still. I dove into the crowd, with Miss Bang and Professor Crackle following close behind. I wove in and out among the surprised, and occasionally indignant, guests, using them to block the pursuing servants while I searched for my aunt or even better...

"Brother!" a familiar voice cried out. My heart jumped. He *was* here! A wide grin spread across my face.

"Bastard!" I shouted in return.

The quartet stopped playing and an older couple turned to stare at me, startled by my outburst. The woman clicked her tongue, and shook her head at me. The man bristled his white mustache and said, "I say! That's no language to use with ladies present."

"Sorry, must dash," I replied and pushed my way around them.

"Brother!" the call came again. I saw the flash of a raised arm in a red sleeve from behind a knot of about eight people. I started to move in that direction, but a pair of footmen restrained me by my arms and held me in place. Another footman seized Miss Bang by the arm, although she took her detainment in a calm manner. Professor

Crackle was not so sanguine. He struggled with the butler and another footman with indignant cries of "Unhand me!" and "How dare you accost me so!"

I cried out, "Bastard!" one last time, only to have the two footmen pick me up bodily in response. A young lieutenant with sun-bleached hair ran up to intercept them as they started to carry me away.

"Hold up, hold up!" the man shouted as he stopped in front of us. "You can let him go. He's family."

The two men placed me back upon my feet but retained a firm grip on my arms. One of them asked, "Are you sure, sir?"

The soldier laughed. "Yes, I am quite sure. You can let him go. I'll vouch for him." The footmen released my arms and stepped back. The soldier held his arms out to me.

"You glorious bastard," I said to him.

"Good to see you, too!"

With that my baby brother gathered me into a big hug.

"I had no idea you were in India!" I cried as I pounded his back.

"I was stationed here last year, after I got my commission. I wrote mother. Didn't she tell you?"

I pulled back and looked into my brother's brown eyes. "I must have been off at university at the time. I don't think she mentioned it. Then after graduation, everything was a rush to get my trip started."

He nodded. "Mother said they were sending you on a world tour. When did you get in?"

"Today, my friends just brought me out here from the skyport..."

The sound of an older woman clearing her throat stopped me in mid-sentence. It wasn't a loud sound, but it sent a chill down my back. The moment I feared most since leaving home had arrived at last. My brother and I quickly disengaged and I turned to face...

"Aunt Phyllis."

"Nephew." That single word crackled with contained fury and disdain. Voices of the people around us fell completely silent as my aunt regarded me with a cold, baleful eye. While she was only five foot four and slight of build, she projected displeasure into the air, giving her a formidable presence. Her grey-streaked hair and wrinkled face hinted at the storm contained within. "Is *this* how you announce yourself when you come to my house? Do I need to have *a word* with your mother about the behavior of her oldest son?"

"No, Aunt Phyllis, I didn't mean..."

My brother interrupted me. "I'm sorry, Aunt Phyllis, it was entirely my fault. I caught a glimpse of him walking through the crowd and I was so overwhelmed I lost my sense of decorum. It's been at least three years since we've seen each other and I'm afraid I couldn't contain my excitement."

Aunt Phyllis' hazel eyes slid from me to my brother, and I gasped slightly as I was freed from her piercing gaze. As she turned her attention to him, a strange transformation came over her face. Her eyes softened, and her lips turned up into something resembling... a smile?

"Oh, dear Willie. Of course you were excited to see your brother. How could you not be? You've got nothing to apologize for." She reached out and gently patted his cheek.

Aunt Phyllis' gaze swiveled back to me, her lips returned to their usual formation as a hard, straight line, and I became acutely aware I was standing with my mouth open in shock. I closed my jaw with a snap. Aunt Phyllis raised a single eyebrow at me. "And who are these persons you have brought into my garden?"

I turned, and saw Professor Crackle had ceased his struggles with the butler and the other footman and was waiting for a clue of how to proceed. I gestured to Miss Bang, who slipped her arm from the servant's grasp and approached. "Aunt Phyllis, if I might present Miss Titania Bang. Miss Bang, my aunt, the Lady Phyllis Griffith-Holmes."

Miss Bang glided into a perfect curtsy. "A pleasure to make your acquaintance, Lady Griffith-Holmes." The corner of my aunt's lips twitched upward slightly.

"And my other companion is Professor Harmonious Crackle. Professor Crackle, my aunt, Phyllis."

The hint of a smile on my aunt's face disappeared as the professor came forward and presented himself with a bow. The flourishing wrist movements as he doffed his top hat, and the way his blue checked vest clashed with his plaid pants and the incongruous lab coat on top of it all, made him look comical. Exactly the type of comedy my aunt never wanted at her gatherings.

The professor rose from his bow. "My lady. I knew your brother, Randolph. He was a dear friend. His loss is a blow to us all."

For once, I saw my aunt at a loss for words. A moment later she regained her composure. "Thank you, Professor Crackle, Miss Bang. I am not accustomed to receiving guests that arrive unannounced and un..."

The line of curious onlookers suddenly pulled back, and a slim young woman with rich brown skin walked up to Aunt Phyllis. Two large, dark men in matching suits trailed after her. Several Indian men and women bowed and walked backwards as the woman approached, so she was someone of importance. The men filled the space that opened up around the woman, making sure no one got too near. Their eyes were constantly in motion, sizing up any possible dangers. They stood with a relaxed stance, with no weapons visible, but somehow managed to both loom menacingly and blend in with the background. If this woman brought bodyguards to a simple garden party, she must be extremely important.

Her bright eyes lingered for a moment on Willie's face and a slight smile crossed her lips before she turned her gaze to myself and Aunt Phyllis. She was a tiny woman, roughly the size of Aunt Phyllis. My brother towered a head over both of them. Her long hair was gathered behind her in a long drape. She was dressed in Indian fashion in a closely fitted light blue blouse, with a long, pleated skirt attached to it. Both blouse and skirt were covered in intricate embroidery done in gold thread.

"Lady Griffith-Holmes?" the young woman asked. "Is there a problem? I heard shouting. Is everything all right?"

The pleasant mask sprung up over Aunt Phyllis' face again,

making her resemble a kindly old woman and not the specter who haunted my dreams since childhood. "Everything is fine, Maharani Chandrakanta. Nothing to worry about. My nephew finally arrived, somewhat later than expected. But no cause for alarm." Seeing a look of confusion on the maharani's face, Aunt Phyllis quickly added, "My other nephew. William's brother."

The young woman's face lit up. She extended her hand to me in greeting. I took the proffered appendage and kissed it lightly. "I have heard so much about you from Willie, but he absolutely refused to tell me your name," she said. "I'm so pleased to finally meet you."

"Oh dear," I said. "I hope I can manage to live down some of what you've heard." She laughed, a delightful sound, and I continued. "I'm afraid my given name is not appropriate for polite company, but I was recently honored under the name Sir Richard Blasphemy. I hope you will call me Richard. So very pleased to meet you, um, Maharani. That's a very pretty name."

She laughed. "Oh, that's not my name. Chandrakanta is my name. We have different noble titles here in India. My father is a maharaja, and I'm a maharani. It's not like you Europeans with all your different titles and levels. We use them much like you use 'lord' and 'lady'. A raja is a 'king', and a maharaja is a 'high king'. But we have several maharajas. You could say we have different levels of kings."

"So, a maharani is a queen? Or, I guess since you're his daughter, a princess?"

"Yes, more or less." The maharani looked sideways at me, narrowing her eyes slightly. "You said earlier, 'Richard' is not an appropriate name?"

Now it was my turn to laugh. "Richard is perfectly appropriate, but it isn't the name I was given at birth. I'm afraid it is rather a long story."

"One I'm sure can be addressed at a *much* later time," Aunt Phyllis interjected.

"Oh, it is quite all right, Lady Griffith-Holmes. I don't mind," the maharani said with a smile.

Aunt Phyllis bowed her head. "You are too gracious, Maharani." My aunt shot me a look of warning as she spoke.

I nodded. "I believe Aunt Phyllis is right. That tale should wait for another setting."

The maharani squeezed my hand before letting it go, "I hope we will have many opportunities to talk while you are here, Sir Richard."

"I think that would be delightful, Maharani."

The professor cleared his throat behind me.

I extended my arm to indicate my companions. "Please allow me to introduce my friends, who were kind enough to bring me here. Miss Titania Bang, and Professor Harmonious Crackle." Miss Bang executed another flawless curtsy and the professor tipped his top hat and bowed.

The princess looked at Miss Bang with curiosity. "Have we met somewhere before, Miss Bang?"

"I don't believe so, Maharani. I'm sure if we had I would remember the occasion."

The maharani tapped her lip with one manicured finger. "You seem very familiar." She threw her hand up in a surprisingly graceful gesture. "I'm sure it will come to me."

Aunt Phyllis frowned. "I'm sure there will be ample time to recollect such encounters later."

Miss Bang pulled off her duster and handed it to one of the footmen, revealing the tan day dress she wore underneath. She turned to me. "Sir Richard, would you be so kind as to introduce us to this officer?"

I threw an arm around my brother. "Miss Bang, Professor Crackle, allow me to present to you my brother, William Holmes."

Willie stood up straighter under my arm. "Second Lieutenant Holmes, at your service, ma'am, sir." He bowed his head to them.

"Maharani Chandrakanta, would you be so kind as to walk with me for a bit?" Aunt Phyllis asked. "I would so like to show you our hedge maze. It's very peaceful."

"Certainly, my lady. It would be my pleasure."

Aunt Phyllis shot me a look that promised that I would have plenty of explaining to do. She then gestured to the maharani. The maharani gave Willie a last glance before letting Aunt Phyllis sweep her away from the house and toward the hedge maze, the two body-guards trailing after. As they withdrew, the quartet resumed playing and conversation slowly resumed among the guests.

CHAPTER TWO
A PLURALITY OF P.G. HOLYFIELDS

When my parents sent me on this world tour as a reward for finishing my university studies, I knew I would see many of cultures with habits that would seem strange to me, and meet many aunts, uncles, and cousins who were likely to be equally strange. I didn't expect to encounter my own brother at my second stop, freshly commissioned and on his first assignment, but here he was, standing in my aunt's garden and grinning from ear to ear.

"You never mentioned having a brother, Sir Richard." Miss Bang glided forward and presented her hand to Willie.

"Well, I wasn't expecting to find him here waiting for me." I turned to my brother. "Last I heard, you were still in officer training school."

He kissed Miss Bang's hand and grinned. "Graduated almost a year ago. I'm not sure, but I think Uncle Malcolm pulled some strings and got me assigned here as an adjutant. It really is an amazing country."

"A year?" I said. "I'm so sorry! I must have been so deep in my own studies that nothing else got through my thick head."

Willie chuckled. "Oh, I understand. I don't hold it against you. You probably would have been bored to tears if you'd come, anyway."

Professor Crackle offered his hand to Willie, who gave it a firm shake. "Randolph's last name was Holmes. Are you boys brothers or cousins? Or are you honoring someone on your mother's side of the family?"

I shook my head. "It was our mother's way of getting back at Great-Grandfather. I told you about how he changed the family name when our father was a baby as an insult to society. When that didn't get the results he wanted, he stepped in when I was born and afflicted me with a name he had spent years crafting to be as obscene as possible."

The professor nodded. "Yes, I remember."

"Well," I said, "when mother was pregnant with Willie, Great-Grandfather tried to make trouble again. She put him in his place by telling him he had no right to name her child since it *wasn't* his grandchild. It caused a bit of a scandal at the time."

Willie picked up the story. "She was lying, of course. But, it meant I grew up as a Holmes and a lot of people thought I was the bastard of someone my mother refused to name. I didn't have to suffer through the problems my brother did, but I had my own dubious reputation to deal with."

"It earned you a nickname," I added.

"The mildest one in the house. Speaking of nicknames, how are you 'Sir Richard Blasphemy' now? I thought nicknames were explicitly forbidden in the will."

I sighed. "How much have you heard from Aunt Katerina about what happened in Prague?"

He sobered immediately. "Not a lot in the way of details. Someone tried to assassinate the Crown Prince. Uncle Randolph got caught up in it and was killed. She said something about you being part of the investigation. But nothing further."

The professor looked thoughtful. "It seems we made better time than the post, my boy." He clapped me on the shoulder. "You did send a letter to your aunt before we left, didn't you?"

I nodded and turned to Willie. "It is a bit of an involved story, but it seems at the end we uncovered an enemy agent in the Prince's Guard, and the prince found a loophole in Great-Grandfather's will. For my part in things, he made me a knight of the Royal Victorian Order-"

Willie grabbed my arm. "That's fantastic! But-"

"And he knighted me as Sir Richard-"

"BLASPHEMY!" A voice bellowed over the music of the string quartet.

We turned and saw a group of military men making their way over to us, led by a barrel-chested colonel who pushed past the other guests at the garden party and got a number of dirty looks in return. The colonel raised his arm with a small wave and shouted, "Blasphemy!" again. A very pink, balding lieutenant-colonel puffed after him, flanked by several lesser ranks.

"Willie," I began, but before I could continue, the brace of soldiers were upon us.

"Blasphemy, I thought it was you! It had to be you," the colonel declared without preamble. "I just got the dispatch this morning about that business in Prague. Had a picture of you with the Crown Prince. Isn't that right, Griffith?" He playfully smacked the arm of the balding man, who had just caught up, and nearly sent him sprawling. The man leaned over his knees and struggled to catch his breath.

"Actually, sir," he gasped, but the colonel plowed on.

"Holmes, you seem to be on good terms with our guests. Please, introduce us." The colonel threw out his chest and looked pointedly at my brother.

"Yes, sir. Colonel, if I might present to you my brother, and his traveling companions, Miss Titania Bang and Professor Harmonious Crackle. Brother, Miss Bang, Professor, allow me to introduce you to our regimental commander, Colonel Gordon Ticking."

My hand was quickly engulfed by both of the colonel's hands

and vigorously pumped. "Sir Richard Blasphemy," I said as I tried to retrieve my limb.

"I knew it, I knew it!" he chortled. He smiled broadly under his bushy imperial mustache, which connected to the sideburns on either side of his head. "We don't get many heroes in this part of the world, but a man of adventure will always stand out among lesser men. Good to have you here, Blasphemy!" He slapped me heavily on the shoulder. "Men like us need to stick together."

My brother continued his introductions when the colonel finally paused. "This is my uncle, and our host, Lieutenant-Colonel Jeremy Griffith, our regimental chief of staff." The bald man shook hands all around.

"So good to finally meet you, Uncle Jeremy," I said. He smiled and patted my hand, still out of breath from his dash across the lawn after the colonel. He carried a few more pounds than any of the other soldiers, but his bright red uniform was tailored to fit him.

"The photograph with the dispatch," Uncle Jeremy said between breaths. "Very good likeness of you and the Crown Prince."

William next indicated a middle-aged man standing on the other side of Colonel Ticking. "Captain Lathrop Preston, the company commander."

"Very glad to make your acquaintance, sir!" He grinned broadly and shook our hands. Captain Preston looked as if he had just stepped out of a British Army recruiting poster. He was fit, with a square jaw, piercing blue eyes, and a friendly smile under his neatly trimmed mustache.

"And this is Lieutenant Maurice Renault, and Colour Sergeant Geoffrey Banks." The former was a small, clean shaven man who barely looked old enough to be in uniform. The latter was a solidly built black man with a slight beard. Criss-crossing white sashes over his crimson coat marked him as a senior enlisted man. The sergeant bowed, but did not attempt to shake hands. Professor Crackle made a point of proffering his hand to him, which made the sergeant's eyes widen in surprise. When the professor repeated the offer the man shook hands with a wide grin.

"I thought they were changing the rank to Staff Sergeant," the professor said.

The Sergeant Banks shook his head. "No, sir," he said in a deep voice. "Not yet at least. I wish they would. Some folks don't seem to understand that saying 'Coloured Sergeant' isn't quite right."

Introductions completed, the colonel stepped forward and put his arm around me, sweeping me along toward the buffet. "Did the troubles bring you here, or was it something else, Lord Blasphemy?"

The professor kept pace beside us. "Troubles, Colonel, what troubles?" he asked.

Miss Bang offered her arm to the lieutenant-colonel, who took it gratefully, and they proceeded along behind us at a more sedate pace. Willie talked briefly to the other soldiers and they nodded and moved off to mingle among the other guests while my brother followed after us.

Colonel Ticking gestured with his other hand as he answered. "Oh, the typical. Unrest among the natives. India has never taken well to industrialization. They flock to the factories for work, then an accident happens and they take to the streets complaining the machines are unsafe. Any excuse to shirk, if you ask me. They don't really want to work. They're looking for a handout from the crown. But what can you do, eh?"

I carefully schooled my expression to appear non-committal. His comment was rude, but I didn't want to get into a row with Willie and Uncle Jeremy's commander after I had just met him. "I thought those issues had been settled ages ago with the return of control to local authorities," I said as I sidled up to the buffet tables and grabbed a plate. Aunt Phyllis had laid out an impressive spread of food. A footman was manning the carving station at one end, serving up slices from a large ham. There were also several dishes that appeared to be chunks of chicken in a variety of sauces, as well as small pastries and finger sandwiches. I steered away from the heavily sauced items and loaded my plate with an assortment of finger foods.

"They were, my boy, for the most part," Professor Crackle answered as I filled my plate. "That was when the old colonial authority was dissolved and local power reverted to the Indian nobility. Of course, the occupation left its mark on Indian society, and the new Raj has become one of the most culturally diverse governments in the Empire." Professor Crackle looked up at Colonel Ticking. "And, of course, the Industrial Safety Act should have resolved any remaining issues, once the new mandated safeguards were implemented and businessmen were no longer allowed to ruthlessly exploit labor in the outlying territories."

"Oh, indeed, Professor. The current difficulties are not a problem of the Eternal Empress, may she live forever! The British Crown's policies are clear. No, it is strictly a local issue."

The professor frowned. "If the policies are clear, how is there a problem, Colonel?"

"I'm afraid the resumption of local government hasn't been everything one might have hoped for. Some officials have been slow to implement measures, or to take action when violations have been reported. There are rumors some officials are easily swayed through bribery or political favors."

"That sounds very serious, indeed, Colonel," Professor Crackle said, still frowning.

The colonel shrugged. "That isn't for me to decide. My job is to protect the safety of the empire, from whatever threats may arise." Ticking smiled and popped a savory from a tray directly into his mouth.

Willie plucked at my elbow and nodded off to one side. I let him lead me a few steps away to a shaded spot out of the hot sun.

"So, what was the loophole?" he began without preamble.

"What?"

He looked askance at me. "You said the prince found a loophole in Great-Grandfather's will. What was it?"

"Oh! Apparently Great-Grandfather never considered the possibility Father or I might gain titles by any method other than inheritance. Since there was no proviso for it, the terms of the will don't apply to any new titles we may gain in our own right. The lower ranks in the Royal Victorian Order just add the honoree's name to the order's rolls, but the rank of Knight Commander restyles the recipient's name. Usually one adds 'Sir' or 'Dame' to the front of their given name, but there's no restriction on how the new name is styled. By declaring me a Knight Commander, the prince was free to dub me with any name he pleased. So he did."

"And Richard Blasphemy?"

I shrugged. "Apparently the prince has a sense of humor. Who knew?" I sighed. "He could have dubbed me 'Sir Silly Git' or 'Sir Mumbly Peg' if he wanted to. Honestly, I wouldn't have put up a fight if he had. The only thing I've ever wanted to do with my given name is give it back."

Willie laughed, then looked thoughtful. "When I opted for a life of calling people 'sir,' I never expected my brother to be one of them."

I leaned closer to him. "How bad is it?"

"The military?" He looked at me quizzically.

"No. Aunt Phyllis."

He laughed again. "Well, it hasn't been that bad for me. Army discipline and all. She actually softens up a bit if you don't give her anything to complain about."

"You mean if you're perfect all the time," I scoffed.

"I guess it might seem that way. She was always a by the book person. But she and Uncle Jeremy have done their best to help me along in my career."

"Sounds like you've managed to charm her. I don't think I've ever seen Aunt Phyllis smile before. I was afraid her face might crack."

He laughed. "She's not that bad, really. Mind you, she was a terror when we were boys. I think you just need to get to know her. This visit should be really good for you. She's given me a lot of sound advice. She has a keen mind for political insights. Rather better than Uncle Jeremy."

"I think I know what you mean. When Uncle Randolph died..." I paused as I remembered the moment it all hit me, a few days before we left Prague. My uncle tried to give me the benefits of his experience, and I hadn't listened, and now it was all gone. "When he lectured me, I didn't want to hear it. I thought he was trying to get me to conform to what the family wanted. Then after he was gone, I realized how much was actually meant to help me. Every now and then I wonder how much good advice I missed because I wasn't paying attention."

My brother gripped my arm and we stood there for a moment in silence.

I changed the subject. "What's the story with you and the maharani?"

"What? What do you mean?" His face took on a blank "at attention" expression, but he looked at me sideways. A classic attempt to hide something.

I gave him a shake. "You can't fool me. I saw the way she looked at you. And she's heard so much about me from you? Come on. What gives?"

His face tightened, looking very much like he was trying to suppress a grin, or a grimace of embarrassment. "She's someone who has become a very special..." He hesitated, obviously searching for a safe explanation, and finally settling on... "Friend." From the looks they exchanged, I was pretty sure I already understood the nature of their relationship.

I eyed Willie suspiciously. "I suspect we'll be seeing a lot of your lady 'friend' while I'm here."

He shook his head. "It's not like that. I'm the colonel's adjutant. I do a lot of liaison work with her father, Maharaja Rajender Yadav." Willie gestured, bringing his right hand in front of him. "He's the local governor. She's his heir, so she's training to run the government someday." He repeated his gesture with his left, and his two hands coming together in the middle. "We work together."

"And she just happens to be at our aunt's garden party?"

"That was Aunt Phyllis' idea. I have no idea if she's planning something or if she wants to curry favor with the local potentate." He spread his hands.

"Since when does Aunt Phyllis not have a plan?" I replied. "Don't worry. I won't make trouble for you. Although I reserve the right to twit you about it from time to time. Big brother's privilege."

"Like I could stop you." He grinned.

I laughed. I grabbed him by the shoulders. "God, I've missed you, Willie. I don't think we've had a chance to share a dozen words since I started university. It's been good talking to you."

"It has, brother."

"But I'm afraid I must ask you to excuse me for now. I've just realized we left Professor Crackle talking politics with your colonel, and I can't see any good out of letting that go on for too long. I'd best get back and find something shiny to distract the professor with."

"I'll come with you."

I held up a hand. "No, that's all right. I've monopolized enough of your time already. Go, mingle. Rescue your lady friend from Aunt Phyllis. We'll talk more later."

I took my leave quickly. Poor Willie. He'd gotten himself involved with the maharaja's daughter. I was sure of it. I hoped he enjoyed the affair while it lasted, and their romance wouldn't land them into any trouble. The lady would no doubt marry for reasons of state, and he would sadly be put aside.

Strolling among the party guests, I found I could see over the heads of most of them. I tried to catch a glimpse of the professor or Colonel Ticking. They were similar in height to myself, especially with the professor's top hat, and should have been relatively easier to spot, but they had moved away from the buffet, and I was unable to locate either of them. As chance would have it, I came upon the familiar form of Miss Bang. Her silhouette and long dark hair were unmistakable, although it appeared she had changed out of her day dress for more colourful local attire.

"Ah, there you are, Miss Bang. So good to see a friendly face in the crowd. What prompted you to change your dress?" I said as I came up behind her.

She turned to me with a polite smile. I felt the colour drain from my face. In addition to her change of clothes, her face had turned a rich brown shade in my absence. "It is no longer 'Miss', sir,"she said, now speaking with an Indian accent. "I married recently. I am now Mrs. Basumatary."

I blinked at her in confusion. "Has the sun turned you brown so quickly? Wait. Married? You got married? We've only been to this party for an hour or so..."

She looked similarly confused. "My husband and I were married two months ago, sir. We have only recently returned from our honeymoon." She tilted her head as she considered me. "I'm sorry, sir, but have we met?"

I gaped at the woman as my mind tried to make sense of our conversation, when rescue came unexpectedly from a very different corner.

"Kashvi!" Miss Bang cried as she charged up to grasp hands with her darker self.

"Titania!" the woman jumped with joy. "Is it really you? When did you arrive in Kanpur?"

"Just this morning. What are you doing here? I thought you were still living in Delhi."

"Ranjeet and I moved here two years ago to help expand father's business into the south. Oh, Titania, it is so good to see you again!" The two women embraced each other.

As they separated, Miss Bang, the real one, turned to me. "Sir Richard! Harmonious and I wondered where you had gotten off to."

The other woman said, "This poor gentleman mistook me for you, Titania."

"You have a twin sister?" I asked.

Miss Bang laughed, and the other woman giggled. "Not exactly. Let me introduce you. Sir Richard, this is my cousin, Miss Kashvi Bhang." She pronounced the name differently from her own, with a softer sound at the beginning. "Kashvi, this is the latest addition to our crew, Sir Richard Blasphemy."

"Oh! It isn't Bhang anymore," the darker woman corrected, "I got married!" She displayed a pair of rings on her left hand. "It's Basumatary now."

Miss Bang hugged her cousin again. "Oh, that is wonderful! Is he here? I must meet him."

Not Miss Bang's face sagged. "Unfortunately, no. He's on a business trip, inspecting some fields we are thinking of investing in. I am here with my brother." She frowned at the last part.

"And a good thing, too, or there is no telling what kind of trouble she'd be getting into." An Indian gentleman in a European suit stepped up beside Miss Ba... Mrs. Basumatry. He was slightly shorter than myself and stood without slouching in the slightest. He glared at us with dark eyes, as if measuring us with his gaze and being disappointed at the results. A hint of a smirk teased the corner of his lips. His dark hair was plastered into place with a generous amount of hair oil. Or that could have been sweat, as the suit he was wearing appeared to be wool, which would have him roasting in this hot weather. He stalked into our presence with an air of authority, or superiority, and favored Miss Bang with a scowl of disapproval. "I see the Griffiths haven't been very exclusive with their guest list."

Miss Bang sobered. I started toward the irritating man, my fist clenched, but Miss Bang put a hand up to stop me. "So glad to see you, too, Ranjeet," she said. "I see time has not improved your disposition."

"My disposition improves remarkably with the quality of my company, so you will just have to live with what you deserve. Have you come sniffing around for another handout?"

Miss Bang bristled, but her cousin interposed herself between them. "Don't let him provoke you, Titania, it only proves his point," she whispered.

I, however, was under no such restriction. "That is no way to address a lady, sir! I insist you apologize to Miss Bang at once!"

"And whom might you be, to tell me how I should address my own family?" He tried to draw himself up straighter and look more imposing, but he ended up looking like a small boy trying to be tall.

I stood my ground and replied in a matter-of-fact tone. "I am Sir Richard Blasphemy, recently knighted for foiling an attempt on the life of the Crown Prince. My aunt and uncle are hosting this party." He blinked at that, and went back on his heels a bit. "I don't think Lady Phyllis would take well to hearing how a lady under her hospitality has been treated by another of her guests. But if you insist, I will be more than happy to convey your rude behavior to her."

I don't know which made more of an impact on him, the suggestion I had rubbed shoulders with the Eternal Empress' heir, or the threat of my aunt's displeasure. In any case, the man deflated slightly. He lowered his head and in a low voice murmured, "I apologize, Titania. I should not have brought up old arguments at a social gathering."

Miss Bang nodded gracefully. "Thank you, Ranjeet."

He straightened and addressed his sister more forcefully, "Come along, Kashvi, we are needed elsewhere." He turned and strode away from us without waiting for a response.

Her cousin dipped her head. "I'm sure we'll find an opportunity to talk later, Titania. A pleasure to meet you, Sir Richard." She stepped forward and grabbed Miss Bang's hands, adding in a low tone, "Please, come visit me in a day or two. He'll be out most of the day."

"Kashvi, now!" Ranjeet called from several feet away. She released her cousin's hands, bobbed a brief curtsy to me, which surprised me a bit, and scurried after her brother. Miss Bang waited as her cousins moved among the other guests. Once she lost sight of them, she looked at the card her cousin slipped into her hand, and then tucked it into her reticule.

"Who was that?" I asked.

She sighed. "Ranjeet Bhang, Kashvi's brother, and another of my cousins. He's never really approved of my side of the family. He claims that when our grandfather married my grandmother he married beneath caste."

"Caste?" I asked.

"It's the class system that has been dominant in India, my lord. Different families belong to different castes or classes. So much so that people of certain castes can only take jobs that are traditional for their caste, and can only marry to families of the same caste," Miss Bang explained.

"That sounds barbaric!" I said.

She shook her head. "To be honest, my lord, England isn't so much different. You wouldn't expect a nobleman's daughter to marry a farm worker, for instance. In fact, I imagine that Ranjeet would say that England is more barbaric than India because it is more common for the classes to intermarry."

"And he thinks your grandmother was lower class?"

Miss Bang nodded. "Technically the English are outside of the class system, which is why people of all castes can marry into British families if they see fit. But Ranjeet decided he didn't like us, so he chooses to believe we're beneath him."

"I hope you'll forgive me for saying he seems to be a bit of an ass."

"No need for forgiveness, my lord. He is."

"I must say, your cousin, Kashvi, I believe it is? She bears a remarkable resemblance to you."

She smiled. "Yes. That sometimes happens with cousins and other close relatives. We grew up almost as sisters. My parents did research in India for a while when I was a child. Kashvi and I used to have great fun pretending to be twins. Or each other."

"You lived in India as a child?" I asked. "Was that when you learned to speak..." I tried in vain to remember the name of the language again.

"Hindi?" Miss Bang provided. "Yes. And Farsi. And a I got started on Arabic, but I was never really fluent."

Unsure of what to say to that, I changed the subject. "So, what's her brother's problem?"

"When Ranjeet and Kashvi's father was in his teens, our grandfather's first wife died. Grandfather then fell in love with, and married, a British woman. When Uncle Ravish, Ranjeet and Kashvi's father, was old enough to take over the family business, my grandparents retired and moved to England, where my father was raised. In order to fit in better, they changed their name from Bhang to Bang. It wasn't an issue for my uncle, but Ranjeet," She sighed and shook her head. "He decided that Grandfather's second marriage was an affront to our Indian heritage. He never accepted our side of the family, even when we lived here. When my parents died, I wrote to my uncle for financial help, as my grandparents had died the year before and I had no support. Debts ate up what little estate my parents had left me. But he had just expanded the family business. While they could have used my scientific background, they didn't have the funds at the time to get me to India. Fortunately, I found a research position with Professor Crackle."

"And your cousin still sees you as a pauper, does he?"

"He is *very* opinionated."

Miss Bang hooked a hand on my arm, and led me across the lawn. "But enough of such things. This is a party, and your aunt has collected a number of interesting guests. Shall we go meet them?"

We strolled into the party and mingled for a while. Aunt Phyllis' guests seemed to be a cross-section of the social elite of the area. Socialites, dignitaries, captains of industry, a very promising young doctor, and of course, the local colonial military. Most of them were quite pleasant.

Most of them.

We finally found Professor Crackle in conversation with a young couple. The couple were arguing heatedly in angry voices and jabbing fingers at each other. Professor Crackle appeared to be trying to calm them down to no success. Upon catching sight of us, he waved us over. "I'm so glad I found you! You simply must meet P. G. Holyfield!" He had his familiar child-in-a-candy-store grin.

As we approached, I asked, "The reclusive P. G. Holyfield of Holyfield Industries?" I looked at the man, a bearded gentleman in a brown suit that looked like it had seen better days. He seemed a bit young to be the inventor who sparked a world spanning enterprise. I directed my gaze to the woman, who was a young blonde wearing a sundress. Neither of them seemed to fit the bill, but P.G. Holyfield was very mysterious. Perhaps I was misjudging. I looked at the professor. "Which one is P.G.?"

"I AM!" they both cried at the same time. Their accents marked them as Americans.

"What has you both so upset?" Miss Bang asked.

The man replied, "The company received an invitation for P. G. Holyfield. One invitation. I came, so *she* shouldn't be here."

"The invitation came to my office, so you had no business even knowing about it." The woman responded, giving the man a shove.

I looked to the professor.

"They're both P. G. Holyfield!" he replied. He indicated the woman. "This is..."

"Patricia Gladys Holyfield," she supplied and offered her hand to myself and Miss Bang.

"Peter Gordon Holyfield," the man interjected, and likewise shook our hands.

"Are you..." I began.

"Cousins," Peter growled, looking at Patricia. He then continued more politely. "It's a family business."

The woman broke in. "All of the major positions in the company are run by members of the family. The ones that are the most successful..."

"Get promoted, and a bigger share of the will," her cousin interrupted.

Miss Bang looked at the couple quizzically. "Whose will?"

"Old man Holyfield," Patricia replied. "Patrick Gail Holyfield. The founder of the company."

"If he ever actually dies," the man grumbled.

The professor stared at Peter, his eyes wide. "He's not dead?"

Peter's frowned, looking much like he'd bitten into something sour. "No, he holds on, year after year. Awfully damn spry, too. He keeps popping up where you least expect him to."

"That's amazing!" A wide smile spread across Professor Crackle's face and his eyes glowed.

"It's a royal pain in the ass," Mr. Holyfield countered, and then stalked off towards the house, making a beeline for a bar that had been set up as far away from the musicians as possible.

"Please forgive my cousin," Patricia said. "He gets very frustrated by it all."

I nodded. "I understand what it's like to have an unusual family."

She smiled. "He's not a bad guy, really. I guess all the competition gets to us all after a while. The old man wanted to keep the business in the family, but he also wanted it to prosper, and make sure we never became the idle rich. I don't think he ever thought about the toll it would take on us."

"Did you ever ask him?" Miss Bang asked.

She shrugged. "We never see him anymore. He pops up from time to time to talk to someone, but never to a member of the family."

Before anyone could say anything more, screams broke out over near the house.

CHAPTER THREE
ATTACK OF THE KINDRED

We dashed towards the commotion, leaving the Holyfields behind, and soon found ourselves dodging well dressed men and women fleeing the other way. The other, perhaps more reasonable, guests were putting as much distance between themselves and the source of the screams as they could. A moment later, I understood why.

On the veranda of the house, framed by the shattered ruins of the rear door, stood three veiled women, draped in colourful patterned fabrics. Unlike the saris worn by many of the guests, which flowed down to the ground, these women's skirts had been gathered up and pulled between their legs before being tucked into a sturdy belt. A series of metal bands were fastened to their arms, which were painted or tattooed with dark lines winding down to their hands and fingers. Veils hung across their noses and obscured the lower portions of their faces, but did not cover their eyes, which were full of anger and passion beneath carefully sculpted brows. The overall effect was both beautiful and dangerous.

Each woman had a monstrous device strapped to her back. It

resembled a metal spine with three mechanical arms branching out on each side of the device. A chugging steam engine sat atop the device, providing power to the extremities. Pistons on a framework down the outside of each leg bore the weight of the artificial skeleton. Each hand, both metal and flesh, gripped a sword.

Blood dripped from the blades of the women on either side, as the trio advanced with a dancing motion, swaying from side to side as they brandished their blades. The steam engines increased their pace, and the mechanical arms hissed and popped and clanked as they moved.

A similar clank and hiss echoed from either side of us, two more identically clad women stepped out from each side of the house. With escape through or around the house blocked off by the sword wielding women, the guests moved deeper into the garden, looking for another exit. Professor Crackle rushed towards the house, and was quickly joined by the soldiers, who spread out in a defensive line and drew their swords. The enlisted men armed themselves with an assortment of improvised weapons. Miss Bang and I stood our ground and let the others push past us. The women halted several meters away, their flesh and mechanical arms spread out in a lethal halo.

The one in the center called out in a loud voice. "We are the Kindred of Kali! Too long have the invaders occupied our shores. The Divine Mother has been generous, granting time for the British interlopers to see the error of their ways and withdraw from our land, restoring freedom to Her children. But you have been blinded by your worship of the False Mother, the so-called Eternal Empress, Victoria."

Gasps of shock came from many of the British guests present. Few were brave enough to name the Eternal Empress, as superstition said that would bring her attention. And none would talk of her so contemptuously.

"Kali sends a warning. The time of liberation draws near. If you would spare yourself Her wrath, Englishmen, then gather your children unto you, and leave this land before it is too late. Or prostrate yourself before the Divine Mother and beg for her to accept you as one of her own. But do not wait too long. For the day is coming when the Divine Mother WILL cleanse the invaders from this land!"

The Kindred spokeswoman clashed her swords together. One of the soldiers flinched at the noise.

"Among you are those who have turned from Kali and embraced the invader. Who have groveled at the feet of the False Mother and put your brothers and sisters in chains in their factories. Who have embraced the invader's ways and turned from your own people. You beg for their scraps. You pledge yourselves in service to their arrogance. It is you we have come for, traitors to Kali. Your doom is at hand."

As one, the women raised their arms, their mechanical arms rising as well with an ominous snap. The Kindred advanced again.

"That is about enough of that!" Colonel Ticking's battlefield roar stopped the Kindred in their tracks. Uncle Jeremy swallowed nervously, but held his ground a half pace to the colonel's right.

"Gentlemen, protect the civilians," Colonel Ticking bellowed.

The soldiers advanced, interposing themselves between the Kindred and the guests, who were trying to withdraw deeper into the gardens. While the soldiers outnumbered the Kindred, they didn't look confident as they eyed the array of blades each woman carried.

The professor stepped up behind the line of soldiers. "Now just a moment here..." he began.

The colonel inhaled deeply and announced, "I am Colonel Ticking of the 4th Madras Infantry. These people are under the Regiment's protection. I advise you to put down your weapons and submit yourself to the Crown's justice. If you cooperate, I will plead with the courts for leniency."

The woman spat. "We are not subject to your false justice! Sita!" She gestured with one arm, and the woman to her right danced forward, arms and blades flashing. I watched her advance and realized the motions of her arms directly correlated with the patterns the blades in her mechanical hands traced though the air. Even the placement of her feet and the sway of her hips adjusted the power in the pistons running alongside her legs, keeping her balanced and upright.

"Stop her!" Ticking barked.

"What?" the professor cried.

Captain Preston sprang forward to meet the woman and she spun into a flurry of motion, her mechanical arms carving a complicated pattern of death in the air. The officer continued to advance, his own sword becoming a blur as he attempted to parry all eight of the woman's weapons. He held his own at first, sweeping the blades together and limiting his opponent's ability to bring her swords to bear. For a brief moment it looked like he was gaining the upper hand and driving her back, but then one of the mechanical arms dropped under cover of the rest, and lunged for the captain.

Captain Preston cried out as the blade caught him in the leg, then grunted as the other swords slipped past his guard, piercing him again and again. He crumpled to the ground. Sergeant Banks, armed with only a large serving spoon snatched from one of the buffet tables, rushed to intercept the woman, but Professor Crackle interposed himself between them. The woman in front of them pulled her blades from Captain Preston's body, and took a defensive pose, waiting for the sergeant's attack.

"Wait, wait, wait!" The professor placed his empty hand on the Sergeant's arm. "Let's not add your name to the casualty list, just yet."

"But she killed Captain Preston!" Banks grumbled to the professor.

"Yes, my good man," he replied, "but it will do neither of us any good to have her kill you, too. Let me try."

Colonel Ticking called out, "Banks! Get that civilian out of there."

The sergeant reached for the professor, but he shook his head and took a step closer to the Kindred. He turned to their leader. "Consider your message delivered, but we will not permit you to harm anyone else. Leave now before you provoke any further response."

"Banks!" the colonel yelled again.

The woman replied with a cruel laugh. "And why should we withdraw when we have the upper hand? We are the Kindred of Kali! The Divine Mother works through us. You cannot stand against her will."

Sergeant Banks pulled at Professor Crackle's sleeve, but the professor just ignored him. "Perhaps. Perhaps not. But I think you'll find me rather more difficult to get rid of." The professor stepped forward again. He didn't seem the least bit worried about the armed woman in front of him.

Colonel Ticking screamed at Professor Crackle, "Dammit man! Get out of there!"

The leader's brows knitted together and a flush touched her cheeks above the edge of her veil as she screamed. "Sita, kill him!"

With a flick of the wrists to shake the captain's blood from her blades, the swordswoman danced forward again, edging around the professor like a hunter stalking their prey.

"No, Harmonious!" Miss Bang cried and started forward, but the colonel put an arm out and commanded her to stay back.

She stepped back to my side, and I put a hand out to her. "He'll be fine," I said.

"I know," she replied, "but I hate when he does this. I'm always afraid that he'll run into something that he can't handle."

Professor Crackle jumped and hopped, circling his opponent in turn as she advanced, always staying just ahead of her whirling blades. He made no offensive moves, but made her chase after him in the space between the lines of Kindred and soldiers.

"Banks, get back here," Colonel Ticking called out, and Sergeant Banks rejoined the line of soldiers.

Sita reversed direction, trying to catch Professor Crackle off guard. He skipped back and continued to remain just out of reach her strikes. Her moves became less graceful, and she grunted as she lunged at him with her many blades.

"He's wearing her out..." I whispered, but Miss Bang raised a hand to keep me from saying anything further. I didn't think anyone could hear me from this distance, but she was right. It wouldn't do for the attackers to know he had his own wellspring of energy and couldn't tire.

The professor's opponent lunged and spun with increased ferocity as she redoubled her efforts to make contact with Professor Crackle. The hem of his frock coat was in tatters, as it took the brunt of her attacks as he continued to dodge and sidestep just out of her reach. Each near miss sliced off another strip of fabric but never quite found flesh.

The woman was now panting heavily and grunting with each attack. Despite the assistance of the steam engine on her back, she was tiring quickly.

Then the pattern changed. The professor continued dodging, but there was something different in his movements. He was letting her get closer and starting to push her blades out of the way instead of dodging them completely.

I heard gasps behind me as one blade grazed along the professor's face and knocked his glasses askew, but didn't so much as scratch his cheek. I looked back to see group of men and women staring raptly at the battle as it unfolded. "Take cover!" I called to them, and motioned for them to move farther into the garden, but they didn't seem to see or hear me.

The professor reached up to straighten his glasses, and Sita struck, catching him across his forearm with a blade wielded by one of the mechanical arms.

"Ow!" Professor Crackle yelped.

He peered at the cuts in his jacket and shirt, and at the unblemished skin beneath it. The woman paused in surprise. He looked back up at her and admonished, "Do be careful, you could hurt someone!"

Miss Bang shook her head and quietly said, "Now we'll have to tell Manqoba that he's ruined another suit."

The woman reared back with all her blades to stab him repeatedly in one mighty blow, but he was already in motion. He stepped inside her guard and dealt her two swift punches to the face. He followed up with a kick to her midriff which sent her sprawling onto her back. The professor stepped over and swiftly yanked several hoses free from the harness on her back. Bright red fluid fountained from the ends of the hoses, and from the device, and the mechanical arms flopped to the ground, laying inert. Sita pulled against the weight, but without the hydraulic assistance from the engine, she was unable to move her arms. Not even enough to release herself from the device. She continue to strain and curse, held down by the weight of her own apparatus.

"I would advise you to surrender. The Crown will be more lenient if you cooperate," the professor told the woman leading the raiders.

She stared at him, her eyes narrowing over her veil as she positively shook with fury. The leader screamed in defiance as she charged at Professor Crackle herself. Her attack had none of the grace of Sita's fighting style, but was a straight on driving attack. The professor backpedaled away from her. The soldiers pulled back their defensive line as the woman advanced, and Miss Bang and I scrambled to get out of the way, leaving a wide path for the two combatants.

A few gentlemen who stayed nearby, either out of curiosity or a desire to seem brave, squawked at her sudden advance and ran to join the guests who had retreated deeper into the yard. I noticed one of them sought refuge in the hedge maze before I turned my attention back to the onrushing Kindred.

Fast as the professor was, the furious insurgent was faster, her steam-assisted strides eating up ground. She quickly caught up to him and launched a series of savage cuts at his arms and legs. He jumped as her blows struck, letting out small exclamations of pain as each strike landed and flinching away from the blows. She rained cuts down on him with her mechanical arms, slicing his suit to ribbons, but never marking his flesh.

I glanced at the other Kindred. While they still presented menacing figures, their posture lacked the confidence they had when they had entered. I got the feeling that things were not proceeding as planned.

She halted, staring at him incredulously, unable to believe the professor had not already fallen to her onslaught. She dropped the sword in her left hand to the ground and raised the one in her right, gripping it with both hands in an overhead strike.

The professor raised his hand to block the blow, catching the falling blade on his flat palm. The blade flashed as the blow descended, met Professor Crackle's upraised hand... and bounced.

The world rang.

A throbbing vibration filled the air, the ground, our very bodies from the impact of that blow. A wave of pressure spread out from the point of impact. The professor and his attacker were pushed apart by the wave, each sliding across the grass. Several of the soldiers staggered backwards. The insurgents seemed more shaken than any of the rest of us as they were rocked back on their heels and had to regain their balance. Some guests were knocked off of their feet, despite being farther away from the conflict. I looked to Miss Bang, but she seemed as confused as I as the vibrations died down. Apparently this was not a trick the professor had used before. Even he looked surprised.

The Kindred were the first to recover from the shock. The leader shouted something in a language that wasn't English, and her compatriots spun and retreated. She paused long enough to run the sword still clutched in her hand through Sita's prone body before escaping through the house.

"Don't let them get away!" the colonel yelled.

The soldiers took off after the fleeing women, running flat out to prevent their escape, except for the colonel, who grabbed Uncle

Jeremy, and ordered him to see the guests were rounded up and all accounted for.

Miss Bang and I approached the professor. He turned to us and said, "That was a mite strange, don't you think?"

Miss Bang's face went white. "Harmonious, you're bleeding."

He looked at his hand, where a thin line of blood ran from the tip of his middle finger to the base of his palm.

"Surely it is more remarkable he isn't bleeding more?" I said. "He took more than a dozen hits. His suit is in tatters. That is barely a scratch."

Miss Bang called out loudly, "I need a vessel, quickly! A tumbler, a water glass, something clean!" She searched for a table or a tray which hadn't been overturned in the fray. Now that the attackers had departed some of the more curious of my aunt's guests were slowly returning from the deeper portions of the garden. Responding to Miss Bang's call, one of the servants detached himself from the group and ran to the bar that still stood off to one side of the porch. Miss Bang rushed to meet him.

Professor Crackle replied, "It is important, my boy. You see, I haven't bled in over a hundred... well, since the accident. In all that time, nothing has pierced my skin." The professor peered at his own hand in curiosity. "I thought we had tried everything. I mean, some attempts were particularly creative, but this seems to be something completely new."

Miss Bang was suddenly at the professor's elbow, holding an empty tumbler. She held up Professor Crackle's bleeding hand and scraped the glass up the length of his palm, squeezing the blood into the glass. She glanced briefly at me and added, "This is the first chance I've had to collect a sample of Harmonious' blood."

As she gathered the blood into the glass, the cut closed and disappeared before my eyes. The skin appeared in moments as if it had never been damage.

Miss Bang looked at the smear of blood as a drop trickled to the bottom of the glass. "I need a laboratory, *now*." She shifted her gaze to me. "Do your aunt and uncle have any scientific hobbies? Chemistry? Botany? Astronomy? Brewing? *Anything*."

"I, ah, I don't think so. I can go find one of them..."

She interrupted, "There is no time. I'll have to improvise." She gathered her skirts in her free hand and dashed for the house, leaving us to scramble after her.

We entered through the shattered French doors and found Miss Bang prowling down a hallway, poking her head in each doorway. "Where is the pantry? The kitchens?"

"If Aunt Phyllis had any say in the construction of the house, they'll be downstairs. There should be a staircase by the dining room."

Professor Crackle opened a nearby door, and found a set of stairs heading down to the floor below. A rich scent of roasting meat and curry wafted up to me. "Down here, my dear!" the professor called. Miss Bang pushed by him and flew down the stairwell. We followed, and found her in a drab room filled with cabinets across the hall from the main kitchen. Three Indian serving women were also there, and Miss Bang was giving them orders in a fluid tongue I didn't know.

The women threw open the doors of the cabinets, pulled out a variety of glassware pieces, and placed them on the table in front of Miss Bang. One woman brought a candelabra in from an adjoining room and lit it. They also produced several highly polished silver trays in an assortment of sizes.

"Why don't we go back to the ship? The Argos has a full laboratory." I asked as I tried to keep out of the way of Miss Bang's small army of impromptu lab assistants.

Miss Bang answered before the professor could. "We don't know how long we will have the sample. Harmonious can eat and excrete normally, but he doesn't actually get hungry, or have to eat. We've never had a blood sample from him to work with. It could be as Eternal as he is, or it could be normal blood, or it could turn to dust any second!"

"Why would it turn to dust?'

Professor Crackle took me by the elbow and steered me to a spot out of the way. "We've developed many theories to explain my condition over the years. One of them is that I am somehow suspended in time. While I am able to experience events, build new memories, and such, my physical form is tied to the state it was at a particular moment, and it keeps trying to revert to that state. If it is a localized phenomenon, centered around my person, then once a sample of tissue is away from the rest of me, theoretically time will catch up with it, and it will age proportionately to the amount of time since the accident. The sample could potentially age over a century in an instant. Thus, turning to dust."

"That sounds gruesome."

He grimaced. "Yes, it does. And if that theory proves out, it would likely mean that curing my condition would be a death sentence."

"That's horrible!"

"Honestly, it doesn't bother me so much as another possibility. It could be the very molecules of my body are linked together in a particular pattern. Right now, the pattern is incomplete because I am missing some blood. Specifically, that amount of blood," he said, pointing to the tumbler that was now at the center of an assembly of glasses, bottles, candles and silver trays. Miss Bang had several of the servants holding pieces of the device in particular locations and was making small adjustments to the way each piece was positioned.

"Past incidents have shown I can be damaged, but my body always regenerates," he added.

I recalled when the professor had been crushed under a boulder at the bottom of an airshaft in Prague. When we pulled him out, I could hear his bones crack and snap as they fit back together and life flooded back into him. I shuddered at the memory.

"What we don't know," the professor continued, "is if the regeneration process repairs the damage, or if it physically pulls the displaced matter from wherever it happens to be. If the latter, then the missing blood will physically re-integrate with me. Frankly, old chap, I'm a bit worried about how that re-integration will actually take place."

"Is there any way we can help?" I asked, indicating Miss Bang and her makeshift lab equipment being assembled before our eyes.

"Not unless she asks for our help. She's a very skilled scientist, and we would only get in her way. I know enough biology to know I would only slow things down if I tried to help. Believe me, I'd much rather be over there looking at her results. The waiting is killing me."

"What is she building, Professor?"

"I believe she's constructing an improvised microscope, using the curvature of the glass and droplets of water to act as a lens to magnify the images. See, she's put a smear of blood on the bottom of a small bottle, and she's reflecting light up through it and through that shot glass to let her examine my blood. The goal is to try to see what is happening on a cellular level, but that may be difficult with makeshift equipment like this."

Miss Bang bent over the aforementioned bottle, which was upended on top of a small silver tray, and held a shot glass to her eye as she raised and lowered her head, to bring it into focus. She adjusted the placement of another silver platter to reflect light from the candles down onto the tray on the table.

"What does she hope to learn by examining your blood?"

"Well, for one thing, if there is anything present in my blood that isn't present in a normal person's blood. If there are factors present in my body that aren't in yours, for instance, it may be a clue to help us to understand my unusual abil..."

The Professor's explanation was cut short by a cry from Miss Bang. She pounded the table with her free hand. "Shit!" she spat, sagging as the bottle toppled over and rolled on the tray. There was no trace of red on the bottom of the bottle. And the tumbler that had contained Professor Crackle's blood was completely empty.

"Did you see anything, Titania?" the professor asked as he stepped closer to her.

She sighed and motioned for the kitchen helpers to put down the items they had been holding for her. "I had it, Harmonious. I finally had it in focus and was able to see some of the cells, and then it just... disappeared! The smear, the sample, they vanished."

"Drat. I had hoped this would have proved the key to making some progress on your research. But at least we know what we need to do now." The professor drew himself up. "We must recover that sword."

CHAPTER FOUR
AN EXAMINATION OF A REVOLUTIONARY

We emerged from the house into a flurry of activity. Colonel Ticking had taken charge of the servants and was using them and his soldiers to corral the guests and verify everyone's identity. The bodies of the casualties were laid out in neat rows in the yard. In addition to the corpses of Captain Preston and the Kindred Sita, there were two footmen who had been slain inside the house, and several men in livery. Drivers who had been killed among the cars out front.

At one corner of the veranda, a considerable group of guests waited to be seen by the doctor we had met earlier, who was trying his best to treat them with what was on hand. The injuries were mostly from collisions and falls as people pushed to stay out of the way of the fighting. Cries of pain, grief, and shock surrounded us. Two young women clutched each other for support as they bawled wordlessly. Two of the house servants tried to comfort a third who was keening loudly over the body of one of the footmen.

Uncle Jeremy franticly rushed from group to group, scanning the faces of the guests, obviously looking for someone in particular, but not finding them. He grabbed one of the servants and spoke firmly with him, but got a negative answer to his question. My uncle yelled at the servant and sent him rushing back into the house.

I was about to approach my uncle and ask if I could help, when Professor Crackle charged up to Ticking. "Colonel, what the devil do you think you're doing? You've moved the bodies, you've got your men running around and trampling all kinds of evidence. There's no way anyone is going to be able to make any sense out of what happened here. You've destroyed the investigation before it can even begin."

The colonel looked down on Professor Crackle and visibly puffed up. "Sir," he replied archly, "I *am* the authorities in this case. This was clearly an attack against Her Eternal Majesty's Government, and therefore an Army matter to deal with. This gathering is filled with VIPs, and we must ensure their safety. We already have several individuals not accounted for, including the hostess. If you will excuse me, *sir*, I am very busy."

The professor took a deep breath to continue arguing, but Miss Bang took his arm. "The damage is done, Harmonious. At this point we'd be better off assisting with locating the missing guests." She steered him back towards the house and added, "And in the process we can look for clues that the soldiers missed."

The professor grunted, but didn't argue as we walked back to the house.

Miss Bang turned to me. "My lord, you must be worried for your aunt." I looked at her and gaped like a gasping fish. While I was concerned that my aunt was missing, I'd only just found out about the fact. It was all a bit of a shock. "Do you have any idea where she might have hidden herself?"

I shrugged, unsure what I could say that would be helpful. "Honestly, I don't know my aunt all that well. Before now, I've only seen her when she was visiting family in England, so I can't begin to guess where her favorite haunts might be here. Uncle Jeremy would have a much better idea than I, and he was rather distraught earlier."

The professor looked thoughtful. "If she went for a walk, she could have slipped out before our unwelcome visitors arrived. Otherwise she would have walked right into them." His eyes bulged at that thought. "Didn't the soldiers go chasing after them? Why are they back here bossing guests around?" With that he charged up the stairs and through the shattered porch doors and into the house proper.

Miss Bang and I followed behind him, as servants dodged out of our way into sitting rooms and salons, until we emerged in the foyer. Pools of blood stained the carpet in two places where the servants had tried to fend off the intruders and were cut down. The door had been hacked apart, leaving a ragged hole in the front of the building. We found the professor on the front step having an energetic discussion with Sergeant Banks.

"Sir, I'm sorry, but no one is permitted to leave the premises." The black non-commissioned officer had his hands out to either side, and was trying to keep the professor from defending the front steps. "Please go back inside. The colonel insists that everyone stay until all guests are accounted for."

"I know that, young man. But I'm concerned about the Kindred of Kali. They came this way to make their escape, and you and your lot were chasing after them. What happened? Where did they go?"

The sergeant noticed the arrival of Miss Bang and myself and raised a hand to forestall our exit. I anticipated his instructions. "We know, Colour Sergeant," I said, "you need to keep everyone inside. Trust me, if you answer the professor's questions as well as you can, we'll not cause you any more trouble, and we'll take the professor with us."

He looked at us, and back to the professor. He opened his mouth to argue, but sighed instead. "All right. You wanted to know where those women went?"

The professor nodded. "Yes! You and your cohort were chasing the Kindred out here. Where did they go? What happened, young man?"

"We chased them out to the front of the house right enough, but those things on their backs let them out-distance us. They weren't so much running as jumping with each stride. Some of them ran right over the carriages."

He turned and pointed to the vehicles parked on the front lawn. There wasn't a single one that wasn't damaged in some way. Several had large dents on their hoods or trunks as if a heavy weight had been dropped on them, and some of those showed signs of having broken axles. I noticed that the horse drawn carriages were all abandoned. The horses had been cut free and run off. A couple of carriages had been toppled in the process, and some of the automobiles were strewn on top of each other as if they'd been thrown like a child's toy.

Sergeant Banks shook his head. "There's gonna be hell to pay when some of these nobs see what happened to their high priced rides."

"They simply outran you, Sergeant?" Miss Bang asked.

"No, ma'am. There was a wagon parked at the end of the lot. Those women jumped up onto the bed and it took off. Big industrial model, with one of those heavy diesel engines like we get in some of our new military equipment."

"How could you tell it was a diesel engine?" I asked.

"When it started up, it belched up a big cloud of black smoke. Even with the Eternal Empress', may she live forever, clean air initiatives, those diesels still cough out a ton of smoke. Diesel's got a distinctive smell, too. I was in motor pool when I was a corporal. I remember the smell. And it sounded just like the tanks we got in last month."

"So they got away with the sword?" Professor Crackle shouted and stomped his foot. "And you let them?"

The colour sergeant put his hands on his hips, and bit his lips. His brow furrowed and it was clear that he was doing his best to suppress his thoughts at the professor's accusation.

"Don't blame the sergeant, Harmonious. It isn't his fault. Someone has access to considerable resources," Miss Bang said.

The professor nodded, his anger flowing away in a rush. "That's true. That's true. It wouldn't be easy to get a hold of military grade engines, or to steal a vehicle from an authorized user. And those arm devices, the Ministry of Technological Security would never approve those for public use. So who made them?"

"And on that note," the sergeant said, squaring his shoulders, "I've answered your questions. I don't know anything about the MoTS. I've told you all I can. I need you to rejoin the other guests now. The last thing I need is to get into trouble for letting you lot roam around." He gestured at the remains of the front door. "Please?"

"Thank you, Colour Sergeant," I told him. "Come on, Professor, time to rejoin the others." I tugged on the professor's elbow, and a chunk of his sleeve came off in my hand.

"Yes, quite right. They may have gotten away with the sword, but we may be able to figure out where they went. We need to examine the clues we have left."

I looked at him askance. "What clues, Professor? They got away, and the soldiers have disturbed the crime scenes. No offense, Colour Sergeant, you were acting under orders."

"None taken, sir." He gestured to the ravaged door again, urging us to retreat through it.

"You're forgetting one thing, my lord." Miss Bang smiled as she stepped back into the foyer. "Thanks to Harmonious, they left one of their number behind."

"More importantly, they left her arm device behind. We can use that to figure out where they've taken the sword!" the professor crowed. We followed him through the house, out onto the back lawn, and over to where the casualties were laid out.

Tablecloths had been draped over the bodies. Several of the cloths were stained with blood as a gruesome reminder of what lay beneath. I imagined Aunt Phyllis having some choice words with whomever grabbed her best tablecloths for this purpose. They might end up wishing they were under the cloths instead of spreading them.

The professor peeled back one covering to reveal the body of the Indian woman who had attacked him. She appeared to be a young, athletic woman with finely sculpted features. In another setting I would have thought her beautiful, and probably embarrassed myself trying to get to know her. I wondered what had driven her to this end. Her clothes were well made, and looked expensive to me. She wore an embroidered top with a long sash pinned over it. A bloody stain over her heart indicated where her leader had stabbed her as she lay helpless on the ground. Now, freed of the metal arms that she had worn, she looked like she could have been another of the guests at the party.

"Blast it, it's gone!" Professor Crackle exclaimed.

Miss Bang knelt next to the body. "Don't be silly, Harmonious. Naturally, they would have removed the harness before moving the body. This poor woman was pinned by the weight of it once you pulled out her hydraulic feeds. The device would have made the body too heavy to shift." Someone had removed the veil across her face, and Miss Bang reached down and caressed the woman's cheek. "Poor girl. What did you get mixed up in?" Miss Bang looked curiously at the woman, and moved her hair aside so she could see the woman's earrings clearly. "These look... familiar."

"I'm not being silly, Titania. The woman fell right over there." The professor gestured to a space on the lawn that was conspicuously empty. "I thought they had moved the weapons when they moved the bodies. And obviously they did, as we're not tripping over this woman's swords everywhere, but where did they move them to?"

I touched the professor on the arm to draw his attention. "Let me see if I can find Willie or my uncle, Professor. One of them might be able to tell me where they secured the weapons."

"Yes, a good idea, my boy. Go see if you can find someone to tell us where all the equipment has gone. We'll remain here and examine the body. There may be additional clues to help us determine who she was and where the others might have gone." The Professor bent over the body and lifted one of the woman's hands to look more closely at a highly detailed pattern stained onto her hands and arms. Miss Bang continued to examine the woman's jewelry.

I turned away from my friends and searched for the red uniforms of the military. A soldier was assisting the doctor on the veranda with treating the injured, but he appeared to be a private I had not met. On the grass a few yards away, an officer struggled to be heard over the complaints of several irate gentlemen. Several male servants were trying to assist him in taking a census of the guests, but they were drowned out by the angry shouts of the men.

"How dare you hold us here like prisoners! I have important business in town. I demand you release us at once!" a fat, sweating man yelled.

Next to him a small Indian man in an embroidered suit added his voice, "Is this the kind of protection the British Army provides? You let thugs ransack the houses of your own officers and slaughter innocent people? How are you going to protect us from these criminals?"

A chorus of similar shouts erupted from the other men, so that none of them could be heard clearly.

While I didn't cherish inserting myself into that mess, there was no sign of Willie or my uncle. Even Colonel Ticking seemed to have disappeared. If could give the officer a brief respite from their complains, I might get him to help me in locating my family. I moved up behind the officer and considered what I could do to help bring order from the chaos before me. I could just imagine what Aunt Phyllis would say about such behavior at one of her parties.

Maybe that was the answer.

I sidled up next to the officer and fixed the gentlemen in front of me with a disapproving stare for a moment. I drew in a breath, then said in a loud, arch tone, "What is the meaning of this behavior? Is THIS how the nobles of the Empire behave in a crisis? You squabble like ill-behaved children? You prevent those who are here to ensure your safety from doing their jobs? Someone attacked this house, my family's house. Brave men gave their *lives* in your defense, and you complain that it isn't enough. How can you even stand with the weight of the shame you have brought down upon yourselves? Now go sit down and behave like gentlemen of the

Empire. Cooperate with these soldiers, and let them get their jobs done."

As the complaints died down, my voice dropped lower, until I ended at a normal speaking tone and finished to complete silence. The men turned away slowly, with a whipped-dog look on their faces that I knew so well from the many times I'd worn it myself. The servants helping to conduct the census directed them off to a waiting area where some chairs had been set up.

I turned to the officer.

"I... thank you, sir. I appreciate your assistance," he said before I could address him.

"You are welcome, ah..." I stumbled now, trying to recall his name.

"Lieutenant Maurice Renault," he supplied, pronouncing the rank oddly, sounding like loo-ten-ant. He quickly corrected himself. "I'm sorry, I should say lef-ten-ant. I'm Canadian, my lord, and it seems we've learned some bad habits from the Americans over the years. The colonel keeps insisting I pronounce it correctly, but I slip at times."

"I shall be quite happy to keep that among us, if you'll refrain from telling my aunt that I'm doing impersonations of her. I hope you might be able to help me, Lieutenant Renault. I'm looking for my uncle, Lieutenant-Colonel Griffith, or my brother, Lieutenant Holmes. Do you know where I might find either of them?"

"I believe the Lieutenant-Colonel is in the house, sir, trying to make sure all the servants are accounted for. I think Lieutenant Holmes is off rounding up stragglers."

"Thank you, Lieutenant Renault. I wonder if you might be able to answer one more question for me. Professor Crackle noticed that the swords and the device his attacker was wearing have gone missing. Do you know where they might have been taken?"

The lieutenant rubbed his chin. "I'm not sure, sir. Colonel Ticking wanted them secured, but I don't know where he had them taken."

"I see. Thank you again, Lieutenant. I'll inform the professor." I turned to go, but he stepped in front of me.

"I'm sorry, sir, I'm going to have to ask you to stay with the other guests for now. We can't have people wandering all over while we're trying to account for everyone." The lieutenant lifted a handful of papers and started flipping through them with a slight frown on his face. "Let me just mark your name off the list and you can go sit with the guests that are accounted for."

"You won't find my name on your list, Lieutenant. My aunt and uncle weren't expecting me to arrive today. They knew I was due to arrive soon, but not the date, so we weren't actually invited to the party. Technically, I'm not a guest. I'm family." I went to leave and he jumped in front of me again.

"But, sir..."

"Look, we won't be wandering around. Professor Crackle urgently needs to discuss something with my uncle. We'll be in the house talking to him. Sergeant Banks will be sure to see that we don't slip out the front. It will be fine." I started to walk around him, but he placed an arm across my chest.

"Sir, I really must insist..."

I put my hands on the outside of each of his arms, and slowly turned him around as I spoke. "I get it, Lieutenant. You have a duty to perform, and you want to execute it with the utmost dispatch. But while you're distracted with me, you've got a bunch of unidentified guests who are going to wander off if you can't keep them in line. What will your colonel say if something were to happen to one of them on your watch? Especially while you're keeping me from helping the professor?"

I turned him and pointed to the group of argumentative gentlemen that the servants had ushered off a few minutes ago. Some of them had sat down quietly, but several had stood up again and started to wander towards the garden, and two seemed to have worked up a fresh head of anger and were making a bee line for Lieutenant Renault. He stepped forward to forestall their fresh arguments, and I took off across the lawn to meet up with Miss Bang and the professor. I heard him call after me, but I pretended I couldn't hear. The simple mathematics of the situation would play in my favor. He could chase after me, or deal with the growing number of irate guests who were starting to get their voices back after the dressing down I gave them. He could only control one situation; the question was, which would he choose?

As I hoped, he chose to deal with the people who wanted to yell at him. Or they chose to deal with him.

Professor Crackle and Miss Bang were still examining the body of the woman who attacked the professor when I got back to them. Miss Bang looked up from studying the woman's hands as I walked up. "It doesn't make sense, Harmonious. What would drive such women to become part of a rebellion?"

"That is a very good question, my dear." Professor Crackle was taking a close look at the wound in the woman's chest. "There has to be some motivation for her behavior, and her companions. While their politics may be based in their own religious doctrine, there has to be some kind of personal motivation for these women to take up arms. If we can determine what that is, it might be a significant clue in tracking the rest of them down."

"Did you find something, Professor?" I stopped a little short of them to avoid getting too good a look at the woman's wound.

"What? Oh, it's you, my boy. No, no I didn't, but Titania found something very unusual indeed." He tilted his head and considered. "Or perhaps, what she found is something completely unexpected. It seems our assailants, or at least this one, isn't exactly your run of the mill dissident."

"There are typical revolutionaries, Professor?" I asked, surprised at the very idea.

Miss Bang leaned back and addressed me. "Indeed there are, Sir Richard. Most persons who take part in rebellions tend to be from the poorer end of the middle class. They tend to be educated enough to be willing to fight for an ideology, but poor enough that they have very little to lose. Those with more education tend to provide strategy, and those who are more desperate are more willing to use violence to achieve their ends."

"So, which type is this woman?" As usual, their explanations were losing me.

The professor looked at me over the top of his glasses. "Neither. That's why it is interesting."

Miss Bang pointed to the woman's necklace and earrings. "This subject shows none of the typical signs of poverty. Her jewelry is well made and appears to be on the expensive side. Her clothes are high quality fabrics, in good condition, and freshly laundered. While she is obviously very athletic, her hands and feet don't show any signs of labor. No calluses. No scars. In fact, they show signs of professional care, although her nails are trimmed rather shorter than is typical for a fashionable lady. All this evidence indicates she was a member of a privileged class, someone with considerable personal assets. This is not the sort of person who typically becomes a revolutionary, much less someone who would fight on the front lines."

"There are no rich revolutionaries?" I asked.

The professor shook his head. "Not generally, my boy. Usually the wealthy or the nobility are defending the status quo. Typically from behind a brace of bodyguards. Or they're the ones behind uprising, using the people to gain more power. As a rule, the wealthy don't voluntarily put themselves in positions of danger. Not unless they feel their safety is assured."

"So, either way, not the kind of person you'd see crossing swords with the military?" I nodded, finally understanding why they were interested.

"I'd be less surprised if she was on the guest list, instead of crashing the party," Professor Crackle said as he cleaned his glasses with a strip of fabric that used to be part of his left sleeve.

I looked at the professor. "You think she was a guest?"

He waved his hands, one of them still holding his glasses. "No, no, no, my boy. Not at all. But based on what we've seen here, I would not be surprised if she was familiar to some of the guests. I wonder if we could get them to come over and see if anyone recognizes her." He put his glasses back on and peered at the cluster of guests on the other side of the lawn.

"I don't think this would be a good time for that, Professor. The Lieutenant is having enough problems corralling the guests. I don't think looking at a corpse would improve their disposition."

"Did he tell you where they moved the weapons? The arms and the swords?" The professor replied, suddenly very eager.

"Um, no. He didn't know. But he thought my uncle had gone into the house to account for the servants, and my brother is off trying to find the rest of the guests."

"Drat." The professor was unusually agitated.

Miss Bang stood in a single flowing movement. "Harmonious, given the situation, there are only two places they would have reasonably taken the woman's harness: into the house, or through the house to one of the vehicles out front. We might as well go back inside and see if Sir Richard's uncle can tell us where the weapons were taken."

"That's just what I was about to do," I added.

"Excellent! Come along!" Professor Crackle turned and strode toward the house at a brisk walk that was practically a run.

"Let us hope that we find your uncle before Harmonious runs into Colonel Ticking again," Miss Bang sighed, and we followed at a more sedate pace.

CHAPTER FIVE

THE MURDER IN THE MAZE

"Get a hold of yourself, man!" Colonel Ticking bellowed as we stepped into the main hall to find him facing off against my uncle at the foot of the stairs. He pulled his arm back and swung at Uncle Jeremy, connecting solidly with his jaw and knocking him onto his back. I rushed to kneel next to my uncle. He was dazed from the blow. His cheek had a raised red mark in the shape of a hand.

"Colonel Ticking! That was completely uncalled for!" Professor Crackle interposed himself between the colonel and my uncle. Two of the maids gasped as they looked down from the top of the stairs. They appeared shocked at the uproar, but were too confused to take action. Another maid peeked around the corner from the stairs down to the kitchens and looked worried.

"The man was hysterical. I had to do something," Ticking said defensively. He was visibly agitated, snorting and clenching and unclenching his fists in the attempt to bring his temper under control.

Miss Bang knelt on the other side of my uncle and examined his injury. She said something to the kitchen maid and the woman ran off. She talked softly to my uncle.

The professor continued his argument. "That is no excuse for striking a junior officer, Colonel! And it isn't helping us to find the culprits who attacked this house. There are dangerous insurrectionists out there and we need to be after them as soon as possible."

Colonel Ticking scowled. "I have the matter well in hand, sir. Now, if you will rejoin the other guests..."

"Well in hand?" the professor shouted incredulously. "When you are assaulting your officers in their own homes? Having your men hide the evidence of the attack? Letting the assailants escape without mounting pursuit?" The professor's face was bright red.

The colonel's face gained a similar crimson. "How dare you, sir! I am in charge of this investigation, I do not need the constant interference of self-righteous dilettantes such as yourself. Now will you rejoin the guests, or must I have you restrained?"

My uncle grunted and shook his head. Miss Bang and I helped him into a sitting position. "Are you all right, Uncle Jeremy?" I asked. "Take it easy. What was going on? Why did the colonel strike you?"

My uncle looked at me in a daze for a moment as he tried to make sense of my words. Then his eyes cleared and he gripped my arm. "She's gone! They took her!"

The colonel thrust a hand at my uncle. "See, he's fine. No harm done."

I ignored the colonel. "Hold on, Uncle. Who is gone?"

"Phyllis! They took my wife!" His eyes went wide in panic and he broke out in a cold sweat. I understood why the colonel said he was hysterical.

"Not again. Pull yourself together man!" Colonel Ticking barked.

Miss Bang tried to soothe him. "We'll find her, Lieutenant-Colonel. We won't stop until we do. Why do you think she was taken?"

Tears spilled down my uncle's face. "We can't find her. Not anywhere. We've searched the house. She's not among the guests. She's gone."

The colonel snapped his fingers at my uncle. "Snap out of it, man!"

Professor Crackle shouted at the senior officer, "Colonel! That is rude under the best of circumstances, and completely uncalled for here. This man has just suffered a severe shock. The least you can afford him is some time to process it."

Colonel Ticking raised a pudgy finger at the professor. "I am not going to be lectured on proper behavior by some scruffy vagabond! If need be, I will have you restrained, sir!"

"We'll find her, never fear." Miss Bang said to my uncle under the raging argument between the professor and the colonel. She looked over my uncle at me. "Sir Richard, do you remember where your aunt was going when you last saw her? Perhaps we can retrace her steps."

I looked up at the professor and the colonel as I racked my brain. They shouted back and forth at each other, making it difficult for me to remember. "I think..." I said, "I think the last time I saw her, she was going to show the maharani around the hedge maze."

The colonel and Professor Crackle both went silent and stared down at me where I knelt beside my uncle.

"The hedge maze!" they shouted and ran onto the back porch. Miss Bang and I helped Uncle Jeremy back onto his feet, and he immediately lurched after them, one hand held to his bruised cheek.

We followed them out onto the veranda, where the colonel was shouting orders and the other soldiers were scrambling toward the maze. Except for Lieutenant Renault, who was trying to keep the guests in one place while checking their names off the guest list. This was made more difficult with the fresh commotion. The professor ran full tilt for the hedge, and quickly outpaced some of the soldiers. Several gentlemen tried to follow after them to see what was going on, and Lieutenant Renault had to run after them and turn them back.

Uncle Jeremy staggered down the steps to the garden. I rushed after him and grabbed his arm. "No, Uncle. Let the others search the maze. You sit down and rest."

He gave one long exhalation, and slumped like the sigh had let all the air out of him. He nodded. "I suppose you're right, Nephew. I've already had more running about than I'm used to. I'm just so worried about Phyllis."

"You know she can take care of herself, Uncle." We both sat down on the top step.

The kitchen maid that Miss Bang had sent off came out of the house and handed Miss Bang a compress. Miss Bang brought it over and pressed it gently against Uncle Jeremy's cheek. "Here. Hold this. It should help reduce the swelling."

He nodded and pressed the moist cloth against his face.

I tipped my head to the maze. "That thing is huge. It will take quite a while to search it all." The professor had already disappeared into the hedge. I could hear him and the soldiers calling to each other. Then suddenly there was a pair of hard strikes, like something crashing into foliage. I saw the top of a section of bush collapse inward. "Or, perhaps not."

Uncle Jeremy hid his face in his hands. "Phyllis will be furious."

There was more shouting and crashing as the searchers hacked their way through the maze. Colonel Ticking started walking in the direction of the maze. As he passed by Lieutenant Renault, the lieutenant fell into step next to him and began reporting on the inventory of the guests, flipping back and forth through his papers, but the colonel clearly didn't want to hear any of it. He stopped and berated the younger man, pointing back toward the house. Both of them stood still for a second when the colonel finished and then they looked at the hedge maze.

The shouting had stopped.

Miss Bang stood. "I think they found something." She hurried down the stairs.

"Wait here, Uncle," I said, and followed Miss Bang onto the lawn.

A soldier emerged from the maze and beckoned to the colonel.

Colonel Ticking broke into a trot and Miss Bang and I trailed him to the entrance of the maze where he was talking with the soldier.

The colonel held up a hand to us. "That's as far as you go. We'll handle things from there."

Miss Bang nodded. "Of course, Colonel. I simply thought I could take Professor Crackle off your hands. Once Harmonious gets an idea into his head, I'm the only one who has a chance to shift him."

Colonel Ticking glanced over at me.

I nodded. "It's true, Colonel. Once the professor sets himself on something, only Miss Bang can make him stop." He looked skeptical and tapped his chin. "Would I lie to you? A knight of the realm?"

That apparently decided him, as he dove into the maze and didn't say any more about it.

A private led us down a twisted path and through several cuts the soldiers had hacked into the hedge. We passed a couple more soldiers and emerged into a widened section of the maze, a conversation nook with a bench and a pair of small tables.

And two bodies.

The space had been a nice spot in the midst of the hedge maze. A stone bench where someone might rest for a moment in their explorations, or where friends might sit and talk for a while. A pair of wrought iron tables where tea could be laid stood close to hand. Two towers of flowering plants to break up the green of the hedge and provide something pretty to look at stood on either side of a small fountain, adding a peaceful atmosphere and providing a gentle trickling to cover the sound of quiet conversation and foil an eavesdropper.

Now the fountain pumped out a pinkish liquid, and blood was splattered across the ground. One of the towers of floral arrangements had been truncated halfway up and the shattered remains of the pottery were partially to be seen under the top half of the body of a young, muscular man. The other half of the man lay at the foot of the bench, intestines strewn about on the paving stones, and a pool of blood draining off into the grass. A second man's body was embedded into the foliage behind the bench, his face and chest slashed open and their contents spilled out upon the ground. Blood stained the top of the bench in an odd pattern.

"Don't you see! That's proof they were here and survived the attack!" The professor pointed furiously to the portion of the bench that was free of stains. Willie stood blocking the professor, trying to keep him from examining the scene more closely.

"Sir, you can't be here. Please!" My brother's face was twisted with conflict. He was doing his duty, but he looked to me like he desperately wanted to be doing something else. Or be ill.

"All right, Lieutenant. Who are these persons?" the colonel bellowed as he strode up to where Willie was trying to hold the professor back. He indicated the two bodies with a gesture that seemed almost dismissive.

Willie drew himself upright to attention, but stopped short when the professor tried to move past him. He shot his arm back out to block the professor's path as he replied, "The princess, er, the maharani's bodyguard, sir. They were last seen with her and my aunt, but there is no indication that either of them were here when the attack happened."

Professor Crackle stamped his foot. "You haven't listened to a word I've said! They were here and left *after* the attack."

"What makes you so sure, Harmonious?" Miss Bang asked in a soothing voice as she moved to his other side.

The professor let out a labored sigh. "That is a void." He pointed to the bench again, at the portion of it that was not stained with blood. "The two ladies were sitting right there when these poor men were killed. Their bodies blocked the splatter of blood. The maharani and Lady Griffith-Holmes survived the attack and left afterwards. Look, there's a bloody footprint." This time he pointed to a paving stone in the path with a bloody mark on it that resembled the outline of a woman's shoe. "Your aunt and the maharani fled from here. The question is, were they kidnapped, or did they flee ahead of their attacker? We need to follow the trail while there is still time."

"That's it. I'm done with humoring you..." the colonel began, but Miss Bang cut him off.

"He's right, Colonel. The ladies must have been sitting here when the men were cut down. This man fell at their feet." She squatted down and peered at the scene, being careful to avoid touching any of the gore spread about. "You can see from the way the intestines are pushed aside that they spilled out on someone's foot, and they hastily stood up and moved away." She pointed at another paving stone. "There are a couple more bloody footprints there. Both the left shoe. The closeness of the strides would indicate the person was not moving quickly. I would say the evidence is pretty conclusive that at least one of the women was captured."

"Well spotted, my dear," the professor said.

She looked up at me. "I'm afraid it is most likely your aunt, my lord."

The colonel now frowned at Miss Bang. "This is no place for a lady. I'm going to have to ask you to leave, miss."

Miss Bang stood up. "Certainly, Colonel." She reached a hand out to the professor. "Come, Harmonious. I need you to escort me back to the house. This scene is just too horrible to bear," she said in a tone that indicated boredom rather than horror.

The professor blinked at her. "Titania, we need to follow the trail while there is time."

"No, Harmonious, we need to go back to the house. The colonel has soldiers who can follow the trail. There are more of them, and they are better organized. We are of more use going back and figuring out what we can do if the trail is a dead end. Come, we'd best leave before I become faint. You should come along, too, Sir Richard. If I swoon, Harmonious will need you to help carry me." She placed the back of her hand against her forehead dramatically.

"Yes, off you go!" the colonel agreed, seeming oblivious to the fact that Miss Bang didn't seem the least disturbed by the surroundings.

"But..." the professor started, but Miss Bang gave him a look. He sighed and carefully stepped over the slain bodyguard.

Colonel Ticking smiled as if he had won a victory and thrust his chest out. "Go with them, Lieutenant Holmes. See that they don't get lost."

"But, sir," Willie started to protest.

"That's an order, Lieutenant. With your aunt one of the missing, you're too close to this. Take them back to the house, and see if Banks can get one of the cars started. We'll continue the investigation here, but I need you to get reinforcements from the base, and to inform the civil authorities of what happened."

"I... I... Yes, sir."

We marched back out through the maze, my brother leading, then myself, and the professor and Miss Bang bringing up the rear. I think Professor Crackle would have lagged farther behind, or separated from us and gone searching on his own had Miss Bang not maintained a firm grip on his arm. As it was, she half-dragged him along as they walked, even though he was supposed to be supporting her.

The way Willie navigated the maze showed that he was very familiar with its layout. Every time we came to a place where the soldiers had cut through the hedge he took a second to mentally review the options, and then picked the quicker route. Only once did he lead us through a cut.

When we emerged from the hedge and there was less chance of being overheard, Miss Bang began talking again. "Harmonious, I know you got caught up in all the excitement, and we need to locate the two missing ladies, but *you* have a more important concern."

"I do? Oh! Yes! I do!" Miss Bang released his arm and the professor ran past me and matched pace with my brother. "Lieutenant Holmes, we were wondering where your colonel had the swords and arm device from that one girl stored. I am quite sure that if I could examine them I could find some clue as to who made them. This would give us a lead on who the Kindred of Kali are and where we can find them."

"I... I don't know, Professor. I was searching for the maharani.

Um, and the other guests. I don't know where they were stowed." I could tell my brother was worried by the way his shoulders bunched as we walked across the lawn toward the main house.

"Surely you can find out, my good man? It could be very important to understand where they are getting their technology." The professor gestured emphatically, once again caught up in the excitement to examine the new weapons.

Willie shook his head. "I understand that, sir, but it is going to have to wait until I get back. I have to carry out the colonel's orders first."

Miss Bang and I caught up to them. "Then you should take us with you, Lieutenant," she said. "You'll need corroborating witnesses when you talk to the civil authorities. Harmonious and I can fill that role for you. And you, my lord, if you're willing to come along."

I nodded. "I think that might be a good idea, if only so I can help stand you up, old man." I clapped my brother on the back. "You look like you've had one shock too many."

He looked at me. "I don't know what you mean."

I shoved him back toward the house. "The scene back there was ghastly. Now two people you care about are missing, and you want to go look for them. Make sure they're all right. I know what that's like. But right now, none of that matters. You can't help them if you're filled with worry. Others will do the searching. You need to trust them and focus on the task at hand. You've got a job to do, and we're coming along to help you do it."

While Willie and the professor helped Sergeant Banks search for a working vehicle to commandeer, Miss Bang and I filled Uncle Jeremy in on the situation. He was dismayed to find out that Aunt Phyllis and the maharani were missing, but he managed to keep from descending into hysterics. We asked him if he knew where the steam harness had been taken, but he had no idea. He had been searching when Colonel Ticking had it moved. He promised he'd let us know once he found out.

The rumble of an engine from the front of the house told us Willie and the professor had managed to find a working vehicle among the wreckage. We left my uncle and moved on to the front yard, where the sergeant was carefully turning around an expensive looking sedan so it could exit the crowded lot.

There was still no sign of the horses that had been cut loose. I suspected that some of them ran home to their stables, while others scattered to the countryside. It seemed odd that the Kindred had shown more concern for equine lives than human ones. The carriages they had pulled sat off to one side of the yard, looking somewhat forlorn. A few were on their sides, or had been damaged, but most of them seemed intact.

Several other vehicles sat with their bonnets raised, engines exposed to the sun. Some of the bonnets were removed completely from the automobiles. Parts from a number of engines lay strewn across the grass, some crushed and bent, but others had simply been tossed aside. The vehicle that Sergeant Banks was driving was missing its bonnet, which I spotted nearby with a huge dent in it.

"Come along!" shouted the professor. "We managed to get one of them started after pulling together pieces of three different engines. Some of these machines are absolutely fascinating."

"How?" I asked. "I mean, where did you get the tools so quickly?"

"Colonel's staff car," Willie answered, wiping his hands with a small cloth. "All our staff cars have tool kits for emergency repairs. We were just lucky that the damage to the colonel's car still let us get to it."

The professor nodded. "And while I still haven't been able to rebuild the harmonic spanner, I do still have a few odds and ends handy." He held up a small tool, shook it, and then dropped it into his pocket.

"You carry tools in your pockets?" I asked.

"That's what pockets are for, my boy!" he said as he walked toward the car.

Miss Bang and I rushed to join them at the sedan. Once the sergeant had finished turning the vehicle about so that its nose pointed to the one lane that lead out to the road, Willie helped him out of the driver's seat and got behind the wheel himself. Professor Crackle climbed into the seat next to him, and I helped Miss Bang into the wide back seat. "Sergeant, let the colonel know that I've commandeered a vehicle to report to the maharaja as ordered." He looked back at us and added, "No need to mention the passengers."

"Yes, sir!" The sergeant saluted and headed into the house to deliver his report.

"Do you know how to drive this silly thing, Willie?" I asked.

"I do. It's part of basic training now. The Eternal Empress, may she live forever, is phasing out horse cavalry for mechanized infantry. Now hold on."

He gunned the engine and we sped out onto the country road. The suspension on the sedan was much superior to that of the jitney that ferried us out to my uncle's house, but it was still the same unpaved road, full of ruts and potholes. We bounced and rattled down the road at an alarming speed, Willie twisting the wheel to dodge back and forth across the road and around other vehicles. Their protestations to this behavior quickly faded as we sped down the road.

"Don't you think we're going a bit fast, brother?" I cried after being jounced into the roof of the sedan as he plowed across a large pothole.

"It would be best if we arrived in one piece, Lieutenant," Miss Bang added.

"We are in a bit of a hurry," he responded.

"Most exhilarating!" the professor chimed in, grinning from ear to ear.

We hit another pothole and bounced sideways across the road, into the path of an oncoming lorry. Willie turned the wheel sharply, but instead of sliding back to our side of the road we skidded, spreading gravel out in a fan behind us. The lorry leaned on his horn. Willie twisted the wheel the other way and our wheels found traction again with a jolt, bouncing us out of the way of the oncoming vehicle, but not quite fast enough. The lorry tore one of the side mirrors off and scraped down the side of the sedan. The driver quickly pulled his vehicle over to the side of the road, but my brother drove on.

Miss Bang leaned onto the front seat. "If we break an axle or crash we won't be going *anywhere* in a hurry, Lieutenant."

We rattled along for a moment before the car slowed to a more reasonable pace. "I believe you may have a point, Miss," my brother said meekly.

We proceeded in relative silence for a while before turning onto a side road. "This isn't the way back to the city, my good man," the professor noted.

"No. We're going to the base first. I'll get the guard at the gate to summon reinforcements. Then we'll be off to tell the maharaja what happened to his daughter."

CHAPTER SIX

THE PALACE GARDENER

The stop at the base proved to be short. Willie brought the sedan to a sliding stop in front of the guard booth at the gate, a tall stone fortification that broke up a length of chain linked fencing, with a second fence about a dozen feet inside it. Our entrance left us staring down the barrels of at least six rifles, two of them lightning rifles, being wielded by several soldiers wearing khaki uniforms. One of the guards stepped toward us, his bayonet fixed to his rifle. He wore his peaked pith helmet low over his eyes, and his jacket was starting to show sweat stains from being stationed in the heat.

The guard challenged us, demanding we state our business. Willie replied with a military personnel number, and identified himself as Colonel Ticking's adjutant. One of the other men relayed Willie's identification number to another guard inside the gatehouse, and a short while later a voice called out, "It checks!" The soldiers lowered their weapons, but remained ready.

Willie motioned the man who had approached us to step closer and gave him orders to pass to the officer of the day: muster reinforcements and medical staff to be deployed at Lieutenant-Colonel Griffith's home immediately.

No sooner had the guard acknowledged the order than Willie gunned the engine, spun the automobile around and headed us back to the main road.

The drive into Kanpur proper was less harrowing than the trip to the base. This was mostly because the we ran into a higher level of traffic that prevented my brother from gaining much speed as he navigated through the crowded streets of the small city. He wove his way through crowds of pedestrians; carts drawn by horses, donkeys, and goats; and a smattering of jitneys and lorries.

As he wove through the streets, we quickly left behind dusty markets and moderate residences for lavish parks and rich houses. These gave way to government buildings and civil monuments. Not long after that, we beheld the maharaja's palace.

The outer walls showed the property's past as an ancient fortification. In several places they bore clear battle scars, where they had been damaged and repaired with newer materials. Some of these repairs were already starting to crumble with age, while others appeared to be very recent.

Willie drove up to a pair of massive gates manned by men in the dun coloured uniform of the maharaja's guard. The uniforms were very different from the British Imperial troops. Each man wore a turban wrapped around a helmet with a spike pushing up through the top. Both jacket and pants were cotton, and the lower legs were wrapped tightly, causing the pants to blouse out above the knees.

The guards recognized Wille's name and permitted us to pass into an elaborate courtyard and park. The walls were covered with geometric designs done in intricate tile-work that was very old, but well maintained. The palace itself rose above us, with rows of windows overlooking the courtyard, and tall towers rising higher still. Trees and small plots of decorative plants were spread about the edges of the courtyard, bringing a coolness to the air while leaving most of the space free for vehicle traffic. Across from the gate was a large archway, where more guards stood on duty.

As Professor Crackle exited the car, another guardsman stepped forward, his gun at the ready as he gave the professor a serious looking over. I wasn't surprised. The arms and legs of the professor's suit were nothing but tatters from the earlier sword fight with the Kindred. Willie raised his hands in a placating gesture and slowly approached the man and spoke to him. They conversed quietly and made several gestures to the professor, and to Miss Bang and myself. Finally, the man nodded and directed us to a nearby archway and a secondary entrance, but he never let his eyes leave the professor.

An officer wearing a purple sash met us inside. He gave the professor another once over, frowning. He took our names, writing them down in a ledger. He strode to a nearby desk, saying, "His Majesty is very busy today, and is not seeing petitioners. I might be able to make an appointment for you in a week or two."

Willie shook his head. "I'm sorry, but that won't do. I have an urgent message for the maharaja from Colonel Ticking, the commander of the British Colonial Forces. It really is important that I deliver it soon."

The man nodded. "Very well, but you may be in for a bit of a wait." He led us to a room in a functionary's office and told to remain here while word was sent ahead.

When we were left alone, I turned to Wille. "I thought you said they knew you. Shouldn't they have taken you right in to see him?"

Professor Crackle answered instead while showing great interest in a collection of small statues arrayed upon a nearby table. "Don't be silly, my boy. The maharaja is a busy man. He's a ruling lord in his own right, even if he owes allegiance to larger powers here in India and to the Empire. It takes a lot of work to run even a small dominion. I think Kanpur is roughly equivalent to one of the larger counties back home in England. Maybe even larger. And a maharaja is a king in his own right, even if he is part of a larger nation or empire.

Anyway, even if he's not actively working, that doesn't necessarily mean he's ready at any given moment to receive visitors."

Willie nodded. "If this had been a scheduled visit, I would have been shown right in. Perhaps wait a minute or two while some other business was concluded before seeing him. But showing up unannounced? Then it depends on how busy he is and how willing he is to see me. And if the man who passed the message along conveys the sense of urgency." He sighed. "Part of military life. Hurry up and wait."

Miss Bang sat down on a chair, settling in to wait as long as necessary. "Lieutenant Holmes, have you encountered these Kindred of Kali before?"

He spread his hands. "I haven't, but there always seems to be a fair amount of unrest somewhere on the subcontinent. Mostly it is complaints about unsafe working conditions, long hours in the factories, and low pay. Honestly, I don't blame them. From what little I've heard, there are a lot of safety and welfare violations still going on in the factories. But those are civil matters, so we're forbidden to interfere. We only get called in to keep the peace when the local authorities aren't up to it."

The professor turned back to face us. "I thought those issues had been cleared up years ago. The Safe Industry Initiative and the Labour Practices Act."

"They were supposed to be," Willie said. "New factories are required to comply before they can open, but there's been a major problem getting the pre-existing facilities updated."

Miss Bang leaned forward. "So, the factories that caused the problems in the first place are still causing problems?"

"Exactly. There've been a number of temporary shutdowns, but they never last. The factories employ so many people, if they're shut down for too long, entire communities suffer. People are starving, economies come close to collapse, and the next thing we know there are riots to reopen the factories." Willie frowned. "There never seems to be any progress on getting any of the problems fixed."

The professor picked up a statuette and looked at it closely. A strip of cloth from his sleeve pulled free and fluttered to the floor as he spoke. "It sounds like these companies are playing the people off against the law to avoid modernizing their factories. Criminal greed at its worst. Why hasn't the Crown gotten involved?"

Willie shrugged. "Above my pay grade, Professor. If it were my choice, the Crown would have put a stop to it a long time ago. If there's a reason why they shouldn't do something, no one's talking about it. My best guess is that it's being treated as a bunch of local issues for those authorities to deal with. Not like a national problem. Things have been getting better, but the progress is too slow."

"You sound like you're very invested, Willie," I said.

Willie gestured with both hands. "I work with these people. They are good people." He jabbed a finger at me. "They shouldn't be treated like this. I mean, they're part of the Empire. They should be treated like any other citizens. It's not right." He shook his head and turned away from me.

Professor Crackle set down the statue with a thump. He turned back to us. "Very good, Lieutenant! With an attitude like that you should go far."

Willie turned back to us. "Thank you, Professor Crackle, but I feel quite helpless. Unless we get orders to intervene, there is very little I can do." He spread his hands for a moment, then clasped them behind his back.

At that moment the door opened, and a man in a long, colourful tunic that reached past his knees stepped in and told us to follow him. From the quality of the fabric, and the gold embroidery along his collar, I guessed him to be some sort of important functionary.

We followed the man down a long hallway walking past a number of offices and business spaces. While the decor was lavish, it seemed cold, official. As we stepped into a different section of the palace, the halls became warmer, more personal. The walls were decorated with paintings of various Indian figures. Some were portraits, either of a person or a family. Others were scenes of land-scapes, or battles.

The man led us outside, into a private garden in a large court-yard. Two large men in uniform stood inside the door leading out to the courtyard. Their turbans were purple and white, and they each wore a wide purple sash underneath their belts. Each was armed with a sword and halberd.

The garden was filled with tall trees and exotic plants. Well, they seemed exotic to me. I suppose they might have been commonplace if I knew anything about the local flora. The effect was like stepping into a small jungle. We followed a path that wound around through the courtyard. In its own way it was like the hedge maze on a much smaller scale.

We stopped when we came to a man in rich silk robes. He stood next to a man in a dirty white singlet and pants, who was down on his knees digging at the base of a large bush with a trowel. Our guide bowed and backed away, retreating the way he came.

The robed man frowned at us. He had dusky skin and a pointed beard with a touch of grey at the tip. His face was thin and had a drawn look.

The gardener continued his digging, oblivious to our presence.

We waited, but the man in the robes now had his attention focused on the gardener and his trowel work.

Professor Crackle stepped forward and opened his mouth to speak, but Willie held a hand in front of him and motioned for silence.

We stood there and stared at each other. Miss Bang pulled out a fan, flipped it open with a snap, and cooled herself with slow beats.

The gardener finished his work sculpting the earth around the roots of the bush. He gave the soil a final pat to hold it in place, dropped the trowel into a bucket, and clambered to his feet. He slapped his hands together to knock the dirt from them, and then turned to face us. He had a warm brown complexion, and as he saw us a broad smile crossed his face. "William! I didn't expect to see you today. I thought you were at that party for Chandra. I was sure it was this afternoon."

Willie bowed low. "I was, Maharaja Yadav. Unfortunately, I have grave news. There was an attack at the party. A group calling themselves the 'Kindred of Kali' stormed the house. Several women, each wearing some kind of steam-powered assembly to give them a number of mechanical arms."

The professor stepped forward and added, "A steam-driven pneumatic exoskeleton with muscle synchronization."

The bearded man managed to scowl more fiercely. "You will not speak unless addressed first!" he snapped.

The maharaja turned to the man and chided him. "Oh, shush, Sankar. These are serious matters; we don't have time to stand on protocol."

"I'm afraid it is even more serious, Your Highness." Willie gulped before he continued. "Your daughter's bodyguard was killed in the attack, and we believe that she has been kidnapped, along with Lady Phyllis Griffith-Holmes."

The maharaja's face turned hard. "She is still alive?"

Willie nodded. "We think so, Your Highness. Colonel Ticking has his men searching for signs of her. We know the main group of attackers eluded us, but they were a distraction. We don't know if the maharani and Lady Griffith-Holmes were captured, or if they managed to escape and are in hiding. The colonel dispatched me to inform you of the situation."

"Then come and give me every detail. Sankar, I want you to hear this, and then get your spies out scouring the streets for every whisper. And these people are?" He gestured at us.

"Witnesses to the attack, Your Highness," Willie said. He gestured to the professor. "Professor Harmonious Crackle is a scientist, and he defeated one of the attackers in combat."

The maharaja gave the professor's sleeves a dubious look.

"My suit did not fare nearly as well as I did, Your Highness," the professor explained.

"So it would seem."

Willie continued introductions. "Miss Bang, his companion..."

"Colleague, Your Highness," Miss Bang interjected. "I am a scientist in my own right."

"... and my brother." Here he hesitated.

"Sir Richard Blasphemy, Your Highness," I provided.

The maharaja gestured with his hands and we parted. He walked past us, Sankar following in his wake. The four of us trailing behind. The maharaja spoke a few words to one of the guards as we passed into the palace proper and the guardsman ran on ahead of us, while the other one secured the garden door and brought up the rear of our small procession.

We followed the maharaja into a comfortable room nearby. He had us sit, and instructed Willie to recount the events of the attack. As Willie described the sudden appearance and the demands of the Kindred, several servants entered the room. They were quiet and effective. One of them brought a basin where the maharaja washed his hands and face. Two more set up a valet and a lavishly decorated screen depicting a battle charge by a man with blue skin. Fresh robes were laid out on the valet. After washing up, the maharaja went behind the screen and changed out of his grubby gardening clothes and into silk robes. One last servant approached Professor Crackle and presented him with a plain linen robe, which the professor donned with thanks.

Sankar paced as my brother gave his report. He snorted and scoffed frequently, but did not otherwise interrupt Willie's tale. He did make it clear that he was very skeptical of the report.

As Willie described the grisly death of Captain Preston and the way the professor disabled the Kindred, the maharaja emerged from behind the screen, looking much more regal in his robes. He waved for Willie to stop, the addressed the professor.

"You appear to be specially blessed, sir. How is it these Kindred were unable to hurt you?"

"I wish I knew, Your Highness. I have a condition that has a number of side effects that some might call beneficial. One of them is that I have seemingly impenetrable skin." Sankar scoffed again. "Except..."

"Except?" The maharaja pursed his lips. "There *is* something that can harm you?"

"After I disarmed the one Kindred, their leader attacked me. She struck me with a sword that managed to leave a cut across my hand."

"That is putting it mildly, Harmonious," Miss Bang added. "The blow barely managed to scratch you, but it sent out a shock wave I'll not soon forget. I would hazard that we now have an idea what happens when an impenetrable object meets an unstoppable force."

Sankar couldn't take it anymore. "Maharaja, please! This is preposterous. These people are wasting your time with fanciful tales! A man with magic skin that cannot be cut except with a special sword? This must be some sort of ploy. If your daughter truly has been kidnapped, these persons must be in league with the kidnappers. Perhaps they are meant to stall for time to allow the kidnappers to make good their escape?" He paused and looked at us with a positively feral grin. "Let me put them to the question, Your Highness. I'm sure after a few hours I'll be able to get a reasonable account out of them."

"Sankar! Now you are being ridiculous." The maharaja frowned at his advisor. "My daughter is missing, and these people are trying to help us. This is no time for theatrics. William knows that we are not savages, and I don't think these people will fall for your acting. In any case, this is not a matter to challenge the Eternal Empress over."

Sankar and my brother both murmured, "May she live forever."

The professor cleared his throat. "I beg Your Highness' pardon, but if there is doubt about the veracity of our account, it is easy enough to test." He held out a hand. "Try to cut me."

"What trick is this?" Sankar growled. "What do you think to gain by having us shed your blood?"

"I said that you could try. I should be very surprised if you succeed." He stood there with his hand outstretched. "But if you did succeed, it would help me greatly to understand my condition."

Sankar started to speak again, but the maharaja cut him off. "Enough of this. I will not have this squabbling. Guard!" The man who followed us from the garden entered the room and drew himself to attention. His eyes were alert for trouble. "If you must have proof, let us get it over with." To the guard he said, "Hand me a blade."

The man quickly laid the hilt of a small knife in the maharaja's palm. The maharaja then handed the blade to Sankar. "Go ahead and cut him."

"Your Highness?" Sankar looked at the blade in his hand with surprise and hesitated.

Professor Crackle took a step forward. "Please, go ahead. I assure you I'll be fine."

The advisor grabbed the professor's hand and pulled his arm forward. "You asked for this!" He slashed the edge of the blade across the professor's palm.

Professor Crackle smiled.

Sankar and the maharaja stared at the professor's unblemished hand. To his credit, the only sign of the guard's reaction was the sudden shift of his gaze from the professor's palm to his face.

Sankar slashed the professor's hand again. And again.

He dug the point of the knife into the professor's arm and twisted it. Then he pulled the blade away and stared at the perfectly clean tip.

The maharaja uttered an oath under his breath.

"This is a conjurer's trick! Did you slip the guard a fake knife? Or a dull one perhaps?" Sankar said, and brought the blade across the palm of his left hand, raising a bloody line. He dropped the knife and stared at his hand as his blood welled up and spilled over, spattering onto the floor.

Miss Bang sprang into action, her hand darting inside the professor's robe and pulling out an oversized handkerchief from his pocket. The guard stepped between the maharaja and Miss Bang, pushing his lord back several feet. Miss Bang snapped out the handkerchief and wrapped it around Sankar's hand in a quick improvised bandage. The guard stood his ground and watched.

The maharaja shouted and the room erupted in a flurry of activity. I didn't understand a word he said, but servants ran in, then ran off, then one of them returned moments later with an Indian man in a dark linen suit flanked by two more guards. With a gesture, the guard standing in front of the maharaja indicated for the new guards to take up positions next to the door.

The man in the suit carried a large case with him, which he set on a nearby chair and opened. He must have been a physician, as he stripped his coat off and pulled out gauze and tools from his case. He examined the cut on Sankar's hand, carefully peeling back soaked handkerchief and re-packing the wound with gauze.

"I should take him to my offices and treat him there. The wound is deep, and there may be additional damage," the man said. "By your leave, Maharaja."

"No," Sankar said.

"You are injured, Sankar," the maharaja said.

H nodded. "Yes, but my duty is here. As skeptical as I am of this report, I need to hear the rest of it. This wound will remind me that not all is as it seems. Doctor, can you bandage my hand for now, and I will come to you as soon as we are finished here."

The doctor had the advisor sit, pulled sterile wrappings from his case, and re-bandaged Sankar's hand.

The entire time this happened, the guard kept his place in front of the maharaja.

As the doctor worked on Sankar's hand, Professor Crackle apologized profusely. "I'm so very sorry, Your Highness. I would never have suggested he try if I thought he would turn the blade on himself. I take full responsibility."

"No," Sankar replied. "I do not understand how a blade that cuts my skin harmlessly slides off of your own, but I will own my own actions. This wound is my folly, Mr..."

"Professor Crackle, sir. Harmonious Crackle."

The maharaja peered out from behind his guard. "Sankar, are you ready to listen to what these people have to say? I still need your brain to find my daughter." The bearded man nodded. "Good. Now, William, continue your tale and be quick about it. We've lost too much time already." The maharaja patted his guard on the shoulder. The guard picked up his knife from the floor and took up a position to the side of the maharaja.

The doctor finished his work and left, and my brother continued his recitation, recounting how the Kindred fled, crushing the guest's vehicles, and escaping on a waiting lorry. In the aftermath, both the maharani and Lady Griffith-Holmes were missing, and the maharani's bodyguards were found dead in the hedge maze, but no trace of the ladies. "At that point, the colonel dispatched me to bring you the news while our men continued the search."

Professor Crackled added, "The ladies survived the attack, Your Highness, but we're not sure if they were able to escape or were captured."

The maharaja frowned and nodded. "Thank you for bringing me the news, William. I will put half of my personal guard on the trail of these monsters. Let us pray that she is returned to me unharmed. Please, let your colonel know that my men will be by presently to take over the investigation."

Willie nodded. "Yes, Your Highness. I hope we can resolve this soon."

Miss Bang spoke up, "If I may offer an observation that may help in recovering your daughter, Your Highness? These Kindred of Kali do not seem to be very typical of revolutionaries. The woman that the professor subdued was from a background of wealth or authority. Upper class. Privileged. She wore fine jewelry and her hands were manicured. Normally in a revolution, one sees embittered workers among the fighters, not persons of means."

"The leaders of revolutions often come from more educated classes," Sankar pointed out.

"They do," Miss Bang agreed, "but they rarely put themselves on the front lines. Much less have a front line composed solely of leaders. Whomever these women are, I think they are playing a deeper game than anyone suspects. Also, they claimed the attack was to strike down Indians who had embraced European ways. Typical nationalist causes usually don't hunt down so called 'traitors' until after they've taken power. This doesn't fit the pattern of a rebellion."

The maharaja rubbed his chin for a moment, then said, "Thank you for your thoughts, miss. I'm sure Sankar will consider their implications in his analysis."

"I beg your pardon, Your Highness," the professor interjected. "I know we haven't really met, but my friends and I have some prior experience in this type of investigation, and I'd like to offer our services in helping to recover your daughter."

The maharaja started shaking his head before the professor finished speaking. "I appreciate the offer, but it is completely unnecessary. While Sankar is sometimes overly dramatic, he has an excellent spy network, and is *usually* an excellent advisor." The maharaja turned and gave his advisor a sidelong look. "He will not require your assistance." He turned back to us. "You may go."

The professor pled his case again, "But we have special skills, Your Highness. Scientific knowledge in a variety of disciplines!"

"Then should we find ourselves in need of your skills, Sankar will call upon you." The wounded man started to protest, but the maharaja talked over him. "He *will* call upon you. But, I suspect that will not be necessary. Now, there is much work to do to deal with this situation. If you will excuse us." He gestured toward the door.

The professor opened his mouth again, but Miss Bang took him by the arm and quietly said "Not now, Harmonious."

We bowed our way out of the maharaja's presence, and a servant led us back to the yard where our borrowed car sat waiting.

The drive back to the estate was considerably more subdued. I think we were out of the city proper before the professor finally spoke. He sat up in the front passenger seat and looked over to my brother and asked, "Who, exactly, was that man?"

"What?" Willie replied, his attention on the road.

"The man with the maharaja. The one who cut himself. Who is he?"

Willie sighed. "He is Sankar Chatterjee, the chief advisor to the maharaja. He's been playing politics as long as I've been alive. Usually he's pretty accurate in his assessments, but the maharaja is right, he does have a tendency to be dramatic. I've seen him use it to trick people into telling him their plans, but I don't think he's ever seen anything as fantastic as what we've lived through today, though."

"Does he normally threaten to torture people he doesn't believe, Lieutenant?" Miss Bang asked, and sat up to put her hand on the back of the professor's seat.

"Not that I recall. I guess he thought he was calling your bluff. That he expected you to back down and change your story." After a moment, Willie added, "How did you do the trick with the knife, professor?"

"Trick? What trick?"

"The thing where you kept the knife from cutting you. For that matter, how did you manage to keep from being slashed to ribbons earlier? I didn't really think about it until just now. I saw it, but I don't get why you're not all cut up."

I leaned forward and patted my brother on the shoulder. "Oh, Willie. You're about to learn that the trick is... there is no trick."

"What?"

The professor shot me a glance over his shoulder. "What your brother is trying to say is that I didn't actually do anything. It isn't really something that I'm very comfortable sharing with people. I'd appreciate it if you wouldn't go talking to anyone about it."

"I apologize, Professor. I don't mean to pry, it's just... I've never seen anything like it."

"Suffice it to say that a number of years ago, I was in an accident. I'm still not exactly sure what happened, but my body was changed. One of the side effects is that it isn't possible to pierce my skin anymore."

Willie was quiet for a time. "But, Professor, didn't that one woman manage to cut your hand?"

The professor nodded. "Yes, she did. And we'd very much like to find her so that we can figure out how she did that. It might hold the answer to a cure to my condition."

"I know a regiment full of men who would love to have that particular condition."

"No, my friend. It may sound like something desirable, but the downsides are quite significant." I don't think I'd ever heard Professor Crackle sound more serious.

"Downsides?"

"Yes. Things I'd rather not talk about."

"I'm sorry, Professor," Willie said. After a moment he added, "Should we have told the maharaja about the fact that the one woman was able to harm you? Wouldn't that be important to the investigation?"

The professor sighed heavily. "Perhaps, Lieutenant. But I fear it would have wasted more time, and I don't think the information would be useful to the maharaja's men. It doesn't make the Kindred any more dangerous, except possibly to me. And it would just have raised more questions about our account of events. I have had previous encounters with functionaries of various governments, and in my experience, it is best not to burden them with information they cannot or will not use."

CHAPTER SEVEN

THE COLONEL'S BARGAIN

When we arrived back at the house, the front lawn looked a bit less like a battlefield and a significantly more like a military encampment. While ruined vehicles were still littered about, most of the horse-drawn carriages had been removed. In their place were two military lorries. Several of the automobiles had disappeared as well. I hoped that they had been repaired and their owners had left in them.

Several soldiers stood on the front steps nailing boards over the open doorway.

We exited the car and Willie told us to wait before running up to the soldiers. They stopped their pounding and held a brief conversation with Willie before pointing off to the left side of the house. Willie returned and said, "We're going to have to use the servants' entrance until the door is repaired."

He led us around the corner of the house, down a few steps, then through a door into the lower part of the house. We passed a pantry, a storeroom, and finally ran into people in the kitchens. The atmosphere in the room was subdued. An older woman was talking to two younger maids sitting in a corner. It was obvious that all three had been crying, but it wasn't clear who was comforting whom. Several housemaids were busy cleaning up after the party, but they were working quietly, throwing themselves into their tasks rather than dealing with the emotions around them.

Miss Bang recommended that we go upstairs and find out what was going on without her, and then she joined the trio in the corner, kneeling and talking to them quietly.

Willie led us up the stairs to the main level and more pounding. When the three Kindred had broken through the front door, they'd gone straight through the house and broken through the glass doors to the veranda while more of their number went around either side of the house. Another group of soldiers was putting up planks over those shattered doors. My brother led us out through a smaller dining room that also opened onto the veranda. More soldiers were in the garden, cleaning away the tables and decorations from the party. A pair of footmen were trying to tell them where things needed to be placed, but their hearts didn't seem to be in it. And the soldiers didn't seem to be listening anyway.

"Madness! Utter madness! They've cleared away all the evidence. Destroyed it all. How are we ever going to find anything if these ham-fisted imbeciles keep destroying all the evidence!" the professor screamed at the soldiers. Some of the soldiers cast an indifferent glance at the professor, but otherwise they just ignored him.

"There's no use yelling at them, Professor," I told him. "They're soldiers, following orders. They're doing their jobs."

"Then who do I get to yell at?" the professor yelled in reply, stamping his foot for emphasis. "Who's ruining everything?"

I looked at Willie.

Willie called to one of the men on the cleanup detail. "Corporal Thomas!"

A young, blond soldier in khaki battle dress uniform with two stripes on his sleeves ran over to my brother. "Yes, sir!"

"Thomas, where is Colonel Ticking?"

"I believe he and the Lieutenant-Colonel are in the house, sir. We were told that if we found anything out of the ordinary we should take it to the library."

"Thank you, Corporal. Has... has there been any sign of the maharani or Lady Phyllis?"

"Not that I'm aware of, sir."

"As you were." Willie turned back to us. "They're in the library. Follow me."

Willie led us through the house at a fast walk. Without breaking stride, he opened a door at the front of the house and waked into the room. We followed him into a plush salon whose walls were lined with bookshelves. Uncle Jeremy and Colonel Ticking sat on a pair of overstuffed leather chairs, an open bottle of brandy on the table in front of them. Each of them held glasses in their hands, although the colonel's glass has much less brandy in it. Uncle Jeremy was leaning on one hand and his face was screwed up as if he had been crying.

The colonel started at the intrusion, sitting up in his chair. "Is that how you enter a room, Lieutenant Holmes?"

Willie stopped in his tracks. "Um, I... I'm sorry, Colonel. I was anxious to find out if there was any news about Lady Phyllis, and the... I, I'm afraid I let my fears get away with me."

The colonel snorted. "I shall expect you to keep yourself and your fears in check in the future, Lieutenant. But I do understand your concerns. Even more seasoned soldiers like your uncle are having difficulty keeping their emotions in check on a day like today." He clapped Uncle Jeremy on the shoulder. A gesture that seemed odd to me after the way he'd treated my uncle earlier.

"Sir?" Willy swallowed. "Was there any sign of the ladies?"

Instead of another rebuke, the colonel shook his head. "We followed traces of blood through the maze to a place where a heavy lorry had been driven up onto the lawn. One of the men found a bracelet next to the tire tracks which looks like something that the princess might have been wearing. It certainly didn't look like your aunt's style. The blood trail stopped there. The tire tracks led to an access road. I'm afraid, gentlemen, that your aunt has indeed been kidnapped. I'm sorry we couldn't have done more." He sipped from his brandy.

"Do more?" blurted out the professor as he stamped his foot. "Could you at least have done less? Less tramping about and destroying evidence?" He waved his arms as he paced back and forth. "Every time we turn around, you've had your men run off with some important clue or other. Or made them gather up materials that should be examined in place and chuck them in the dust bin!" He raised his voice and shook his hands above his head. "How can you expect to find the people behind this attack when you're doing everything in your power to obliterate every trace?"

The colonel's face turned a bright red. He slammed down his empty brandy glass and stood up. "Now see here, young man! I don't know what nonsense they have you teach in whatever school gave a wet behind the ears pup like you a professorship, but *this* is India!" He pointed a finger at the professor and used it to punctuate each of his points. "Here, *I* represent the Empire. This is an Imperial investigation, and I will conduct it as I see fit to do so. I don't need the advice of some over-educated fool who's never done an honest day's work in his life. I don't care if you mean well by it, boy, I have had it up to here with you trying to insinuate yourself into this investigation. Should I, by some unimaginable turn of events, find myself needing the advice of a self-important jackanapes such as yourself, I shall contact you forthwith. But until that moment you will keep your sizable nose out of this investigation, or I shall have you thrown into a cell for interfering with the Crown. Do I make myself clear, sir?" Colonel Ticking leaned toward the professor.

The professor drew himself up and shook a finger at the enraged officer. "Now just one minute, Colonel!" he began.

Ticking yelled, "Guard!" in a voice that felt like it would shake the room. A moment later, a private dashed into the room and snapped to attention.

The colonel looked hard at Professor Crackle. "Do I make myself clear?"

"Colonel, if you would just..."

Colonel Ticking stood up straight, and said in a manner of fact voice. "Private Lester, arrest this man. Have him secured in irons and taken back to the base under guard. He is to be placed in solitary confinement."

"Yes, sir!" the private quickly stepped over to Professor Crackle and took him by the arm.

The professor threw his hands up in front of him. "All right, Colonel, you've made your point!"

Ticking held up a hand to the private, who paused, still holding the professor's arm. "Do I make myself clear?"

The professor looked like he had bit into something sour. "Yes. Yes, you have, Colonel Ticking. But if you could just let me look at the harness the woman was wearing. I have technical expertise..."

"Private." The man pulled the professor around to escort him out the door.

"No, Colonel, please!" The professor tried to squirm away from the private's grasp without success.

The colonel signaled the private to wait another moment, and pointed a finger at Professor Crackle. "What are you going to do?"

The professor deflated with a sigh, his shoulders sagging and eyes downcast. He replied dejectedly. "I will keep out of your investigation, Colonel, unless I am specifically invited to consult with you."

The colonel smiled. "And?"

Professor Crackle's brows knotted for a moment. Then he added, "I will refrain from making further comments on your methods." He shrank in on himself further.

A self-satisfied grin split the colonel's face. He said, "Private Lester, on second thought, I think we can permit the professor his freedom for now. Providing he keeps to the terms of his parole. But if you see any evidence of him interfering with my investigation of the kidnapping, you are to arrest him immediately. Understood?"

The private snapped to attention again. "Yes, sir!"

"Good. Now find me a driver. I need to return to the base." The private saluted and left the room, closing the door behind him, as the colonel turned back to my uncle. "Jeremy, I've got plenty of work to do back at the office. You, however, are off duty for the next couple of days. You need a rest, and to set your house back in order. Hopefully, I'll have this sorted by then. And you," he said, turning to Willie, "will stay here with him, and see that he is fit for duty when he returns. And yourself as well."

Willie drew himself up but didn't quite snap to attention. "Yes, sir."

The colonel stepped over to me. "I'm sorry that your visit has been marred by all this unpleasantness, Lord Blasphemy. I would have liked to have you work beside me, but after having to make such an issue with your companion, well, I'm sure you understand. I hope once this is over you'll have time to talk." He held out his hand to me. "A pleasure to see you, Blasphemy!"

He pumped my hand energetically, then strode out of the room without looking back.

The colonel's exit seemed to take the air out of the room for a moment. We blinked an looked at each other as if to say "now what?"

My uncle broke the silence with a whimpered, "I'm so sorry."

I crossed over and knelt by Uncle Jeremy. "You've got nothing to be sorry about, Uncle. None of this is your fault."

"But it has all gone wrong. We had such big plans for your visit, and now Phyllis is missing and I don't know if I can manage without her." He seemed to be on the verge of tears.

"Don't worry, Uncle. We'll get it sorted out. Just take it easy." I patted him on the knee.

"Half the staff are dead, Nephew. And I wouldn't be surprised if the rest of them quit. The house is in shambles. And Phyllis is gone.

Taken. I was in my own home and I couldn't even protect her." Now he was crying.

Willie joined us with the professor close behind. "It's not nearly that bad, Uncle. The men who were killed was a tragic loss, but it wasn't half the staff. And the rest of them are standing by you. I don't think they'll leave. We'll help you, Uncle Jeremy. I'll get some of the men from the base to help fill in."

"Don't be silly, Lieutenant. You can't do that," Professor Crackle chided. "That would be a gross abuse of your position. You and your uncle would be up on charges. But I believe *I* can help. Colonel Griffith, my butler travels with me on my airship. I can loan him to you while we're here, and I may be able to get some additional volunteers from among my crew to help out. My men could help repair your doors and secure your home. It's the least we can do, given the circumstances."

Uncle Jeremy gaped for a moment, his eyes bright and wet. "You would do that for us?"

"Oh, certainly. Miss Bang and I will stay here to make sure that everything goes smoothly. You needn't worry about a thing, I assure you." He gave Uncle Jeremy a broad, somewhat overeager smile. "In fact, since I've nothing else to do at the moment, if I could borrow one of your men to drive me back to the port, Lieutenant, I'll see about getting our bags moved here and arrange for the volunteers to help out. I suspect it won't really be the style of service that you're used to, but they're all good men and they'll work with a will."

Willie frowned slightly. "Isn't that the kind of personal service you just warned me against, Professor?"

"Oh, I'll drive if you like, I just need a guide. I'm not used to navigation this close to the ground. It's so inconvenient for spotting landmarks, and there are all these buildings sitting in your way." The professor looked expectantly at Willie.

"No, I meant the use of the car." My brother rolled his eyes upward and sighed. "Very well, I'll ask Corporal Thomas. He's driven VIPs to the skyport before. Come along, Professor. Let's get this sorted."

Professor Crackle followed Willie to the door but stopped to look back at us. "Don't worry, I'll be back in a jiffy. You won't even know I'm gone." With that he disappeared through the door, leaving me alone with Uncle Jeremy for the first time.

"So, um... Uncle," I said. Not knowing what to follow that with, I moved to the seat that the colonel had vacated.

"We were so looking forward to your visit, Nephew. Phyllis has been telling me stories of you since you were a boy. I've been wanting to meet you for myself."

"A-aunt Phyllis told you stories about me?" I cleared my throat. "I'm afraid I wasn't really around when she talked about you. As I recall I was usually off being punished for something or other."

He chuckled and then sniffed and dabbed at his eyes. "Yes. You were quite a scamp as a boy, weren't you? Always getting into some mischief or other. Your aunt was always so proud of you."

"*Proud?*"

"Yes."

"*Aunt Phyllis?*"

He chuckled again. "Yes."

"Are you sure you're not thinking of another of her sisters?"

"No. It was definitely my Phyllis." His lips widened into a small smile. "She's been very proud of you for a long time."

I gaped at my uncle. "But she was always punishing me!"

He laughed. "If she hadn't punished you, how would you know what you did was wrong?"

"What?"

Uncle Jeremy blinked his eyes a couple times as he explained, "She was always impressed that you always got into new trouble. Never the same thing twice." He smiled again.

I struggled to process the information. "You're saying that she was forced to punish me so I could *learn* from the experience?"

He nodded. "Yes. And you did." He took a sip of brandy from the glass in his hand. "That is part of parenting." He sighed. "Regrettably, we were never able to have children of our own."

I sat back and blinked at him in disbelief. "She terrorized me, Uncle. I *dreaded* her visits. I spent all my time avoiding her so she wouldn't be able to punish me again. *Nothing* I did was ever good enough for her!"

"Oh, don't be silly, boy." Uncle Jeremy patted my knee. "You did plenty that made her proud of you. You just did a wee bit more that she had to punish you for." He held his finger and thumb up before his eye in a squeezing motion to illustrate. "You'll see. When we get her back, I'll have her tell you herself."

"That would be something," I said.

My uncle squeezed my hand, then released it. "Thank you, Nephew. Talking like this has helped me tremendously. Phyllis wouldn't give up. I shan't give up either. We will get her back."

The door reopened and Willie came in. "Well, Professor Crackle is off for now. How have you two been getting along?"

"Uncle Jeremy has been trying to tell me that Aunt Phyllis is proud of me." I still couldn't believe the words when they came from my own mouth.

Willie dropped himself into an armchair. "Well, you always have been her favorite."

"*What?*"

"Well, you have," Willie insisted. "She always asked after you. Wanted to know what you were up to."

Uncle Jeremy added, "Now, William, you know your aunt doesn't play favorites."

Willie shook his head. "I know she *tries* to be scrupulously fair and not show favoritism, but that doesn't mean she doesn't have her favorite nephew. And, honestly, it doesn't bother me. You were always the smart one, brother. That's why I didn't try for University. I knew I wouldn't be able to hack it. Officer school was bad enough." He leaned to one side in his chair.

I sat back in my chair and stared at the two of them. "I can't believe we're talking about the same woman. I need a drink." I reached for the bottle of brandy on the table and a glass.

"Pour me one, too," Willie said, retrieving a fresh glass from a small bar tucked up against the wall. I realized that the glass I poured for myself was the same one that Colonel Ticking had been drinking from. I considered asking Willie for a fresh glass, but right at the moment, I didn't care, and I wasn't willing to waste perfectly good brandy. He held his glass out and I poured.

Uncle Jeremy raised his glass. "To Phyllis' safe return." We all drank. "As much as I hate that this happened, I am so glad to have you boys here."

"It's the least we can do, Uncle," said Willie.

"Well, at the very least, it's what we're allowed to do," I replied.

"Oh, don't you start now, brother," Willie said looking at me over his glass. "Your friend, the professor, nearly got himself locked up with that kind of talk."

"I know that I wouldn't have survived Prague if it hadn't been for Professor Crackle and Miss Bang. They're both brilliant. They could be a great help if he'd just let them. They deal with situations like this all the time." I sat back in my seat and looked at Willie. "I noticed that you didn't tell the colonel that the maharaja is turning the investigation over to his personal guard."

Willie shrugged. "He knows it's going to be a civilian investigation, eventually. Besides, one of the first things I learned as his adjutant is that it is a bad idea to try to correct him when he's yelling at someone."

"Speaking of the maharaja's guard, where are they? I would have expected them to have shown up by now." Uncle Jeremy look around as if he half expected them to walk through the door at any moment.

Willie sipped his brandy. "They are here, Uncle. They showed up while I was trying to get the professor's transport sorted. Lieutenant Renault is dealing with them as the officer in charge."

I sat forward. "Shouldn't we go out and talk with them? Give our account of things?"

"They'll find us when they want us," Uncle Jeremy replied. "I've been on the fringes of a local investigation before, back when I was stationed in Assam. I wouldn't expect the native authorities to be any less stubborn than Colonel Ticking."

"Is this really how the Empire runs?" It seemed very haphazard to me.

Uncle Jeremy shook his head. "This is India, Nephew. We made some stupid mistakes when we came to this country, and however civil the Indian people are, they haven't forgotten. Or forgiven. Well, some have, but most simply moved on and they focus on dealing with life now, not dwelling on the past. But they haven't forgotten it either. I suppose they hope we've learned to do better. I hope we have."

"What happened to all the guests, Uncle?" Willie asked.

He shrugged. "Colonel Ticking sent them home. Fortunately, they were all accounted for, except for the maharani. The only casualties among the guests were Captain Preston and the maharani's bodyguards. The other injuries were relatively minor. I think two of them were taken to hospital or their own physicians, just to make sure. Once we were sure they were safe, there wasn't any reason to hold them. We all saw the attack in the garden, and no one saw the attack in the maze."

I nodded. "I guess that makes sense. It isn't like you don't know who all of them are." I remembered one of the professor's questions from earlier. "What happened with the harness with all the arms?"

Willie pointed at me. "Now don't you start, or I'm going to have to lock up my own brother."

I held a hand up to him. "Professor Crackle promised to keep out of the official investigation, not me. And no one has threatened me with arrest for having a little curiosity. Besides, if we don't tell the professor what happened to the damned thing, sooner or later he'll be peeking into every cupboard looking for it the whole time he's here."

"Is your friend really that bad?" Willie asked.

"Let's say that he understands the value of perseverance from a very unique perspective."

Uncle Jeremy shook his head. "Then you can safely tell him that Colonel Ticking had the apparatus and the swords moved back to the base. He won't get to look at them without Ticking's approval, and at this point the only thing that would compel him to grant that, short of hell freezing over, would be a direct order from the Eternal Empress."

"May she live forever," they said in unison as they raised their glasses. They sipped their drinks and relaxed back into their seats.

"That does sound a bit unlikely," I replied. "Where has Miss Bang been all this time?"

"I saw her talking to the house staff," Willie said. "I think she's helping them deal with their grief. Some of them worked with Singh, the butler, for years. And I think one of the footmen who was killed was courting one of the housemaids. When did your friend learn Hindi?"

I shrugged. "She said that she had family in India and spent some time here in her childhood. I guess she learned it then."

"That probably explains why she's doing so well with them. I imagine she knows the culture better than someone who only studied it." My brother sipped his brandy.

"She is an amazing woman."

"Do I detect a bit of a crush on the woman, Nephew?" My uncle grinned at me.

"What? Oh, no. No, no. Trust me, the lady's heart lies elsewhere." I thought of the bond between Miss Bang and the professor, and how neither of them could admit it to the other. "She is brilliant and beautiful, but as far as I'm concerned, she's just a good friend."

"Are you sure, brother?"

"Quite sure. Any illusions I might have had on that score were buried in Prague."

CHAPTER EIGHT

A PLAN IN THE HATCHING

An hour or so later the maharaja's guard got around to questioning us. They seemed very bored with the process. They were wrapping up their questions when Private Thomas returned with Professor Crackle, Manqoba, about half a dozen Riggers, and a lorry full of baggage and equipment.

This caused a frenzy of activity, as the maharaja's guardsmen had to question all the newcomers and inspect all the baggage and equipment before allowing anyone or anything to enter the house.

The Riggers, as the ship's engineering and repair crew were named, looked like a bunch of rowdy sailors, which, to be fair, they were at times. Rather a lot of the time, really. They dressed in a variety of soiled leather, canvas, and cotton. They explained that they were workmen, brought in to clear up the damage, and they were quickly cleared, and started unloading the lorry for inspection.

Miss Bang appeared with the older Indian woman she talked to when we passed through the kitchens. "My lord," she said, "Do you know, Mrs. Hudson, here, your aunt's housekeeper?"

"No, I'm afraid we haven't met before. How do you do, Mrs. Hudson?" I replied.

She gave me a slight curtsey in response. "I have seen better days, your lordship. But I have hope to see them again."

"A commendable attitude, ma'am," I said.

Miss Bang nodded. "Mrs. Hudson and her housekeepers will be taking charge of the luggage and seeing us set up in our rooms. Oh," she stopped, looking at the guardsmen by the lorry. "Goodness! What do they think they are doing now?"

One group of guards started questioning the professor and Manqoba and a second team began inspecting the luggage and equipment. They opened each of the bags and pulled out all their contents, often simply dumping it on the ground and poking through it.

Miss Bang and I crossed over to him. "What do you gentlemen think you are doing with our clothes? Have you no decency? These things were all cleaned and pressed and now that you've thrown them on the ground they have to be re-laundered!"

The guard in charge of the team sneered at her and gave a short, rude sounding reply in Hindi.

Miss Bang responded with a scathing retort in the same language, which caught the guard by surprise. His face first showed shock that she knew his language, then fear that he had angered the wrong person, and finally submission, as he apologized to her and shouted orders to the other guards, who stopped dumping out bags and began treating our clothes with more respect.

In the meantime, Mrs. Hudson arrived with a brace of housemaids. They spread out blankets on the ground, and quickly gathered and folded the clothing and placed it on the blankets in two piles. A pair of women placed the clothing in one pile into baskets, while the other women took clothing from the other pile and repacked them into the bags, which were then taken into the house.

In the end the housemaids took over the clothing inspection. They would pull out each garment and hold it up for a guardsman to view. The guard would look at it and nod, and the woman would hand it off to the next maid who would fold it and pack it into a different bag.

Things weren't going nearly as easily with the interviews of the professor and Manqoba.

The professor's butler was an intimidating figure. He stood over six feet tall, was well muscled, and of such a dark complexion that "black" seemed inadequate to describe it. Despite his gentle demeanor, he possessed an air of lethality that I still found unnerving at times. Manqoba wore his usual butler's livery, which for him included an animal pelt worn over one shoulder and a leather kilt. He seemed more like a panther pretending to be a house cat than a respected servant.

The pair of guardsmen who questioned him looked unsure of what to make of him. He spoke calmly and politely in response to every question, but they flinched each time he moved. His bright white smile did little to put them at ease. Manqoba's answers were short and to the point, but the Guardsmen kept peppering him with questions, as if they intended to trick him into making a mistake or provoke him into action, which they wouldn't want either.

Similarly, the guards took quite a long time interviewing Professor Crackle. In this case, the delay was mostly because each of the professor's answers became long angry diatribes on the inefficiency of political functionaries. By the time they finally, grudgingly, accepted that neither the professor nor his butler was a threat, the baggage had been inspected and carried inside.

The other equipment was a different matter. When the guardsmen began unpacking those cases they, became very excited. The first case they opened was full of carpentry tools. Saws, hammers, chisels, awls, gouges, and other, more exotic tools whose names and uses were beyond me. This caused great excitement, presumably because they saw them as potential weapons and not as tools. Miss Bang and one of the Riggers tried to explain that the tools were for repairing the shattered doors, but none of the guards were inclined to listen, even when Miss Bang explained in Hindi. The guard Miss Bang cowed earlier had disappeared. The process stalled until one of the surviving footmen joined the conversation. He explained the situation, using almost exactly the same words as Miss Bang had, and the guardsmen abruptly lost interest and moved on to the next crate. Miss Bang was furious.

The next crate was full of laboratory equipment: microscopes, test tubes, beakers, flasks, and all other sorts of things that Miss Bang could have dearly used earlier when she was trying to examine Professor Crackle's blood. Miss Bang nearly had a fit when they started tossing items out on the lawn without even looking. She enlisted the footman to speak for her and dressed the Guardsmen down in English about the careless way they were flinging around expensive equipment and breaking glassware. Together they managed to convince the Guardsmen that the broken glassware they were creating was more dangerous than any of the laboratory equipment. The guards handed the pieces off to the cleared Riggers instead, who laid it aside until the case was empty, then stowed the items back in their places and hauled it inside.

"I can't believe how rude and brutish these inspectors are!" Miss Bang seethed.

The footman who had been helping shook his head. "These aren't the inspectors, ma'am. They were here earlier and questioned all the guests. They left when they released the last visitor. These men are the security detail left behind. They were told to keep the area secure and make sure none of the servants got up to any mischief."

Miss Bang frowned. "How do you know this?"

"I heard the inspector give the order as they were getting back into their cars," he replied. "He said the family was inside and all the guests had gone, so they should make sure we," he pointed to himself, "don't cause any trouble. The word he used wasn't polite."

"So they thought we were all servants?" I asked.

"Yes, sir."

"No one should be treated like that," Miss Bang said.

When we finally re-entered the house, Uncle Jeremy took us upstairs, with Mrs. Hudson trailing along behind. "You know," he said, "Phyllis always insisted that we dress for dinner. But given the day that we've had, and everything..."

"I think that's a capital idea!" the professor said. "It would do us all a world of good to clean up and change into fresh clothes."

Given that the professor was wearing a borrowed robe and the tattered remains of his suit, a new set of clothes did indeed seem to be in order for him.

"Professor Crackle," Willie said, "Uncle Jeremy and I are already wearing our dress uniforms. We're already 'dressed'."

"Well, perhaps tonight we shall be a bit more casual than usual, but I think we can all do with a chance to freshen up, don't you agree?"

Uncle Jeremy nodded. "I don't think Phylis would mind."

Mrs. Hudson showed us to our assigned rooms. My clothes were not unpacked, but someone had laid out a formal suit for me. Normally Manqoba did this sort of thing, but it couldn't have been him. He was still busy downstairs. One of the housemaids must have anticipated the need and made sure the clothes were easily available.

I cleaned up in the bathroom adjoining my room and changed into the clothes laid out for me. At which point I was sure that Manqoba had nothing to do with the selection of my clothing. When I went to put the shirt on, I found that it was too small, and the sleeves were at least an inch too short. It was obviously one of the professor's shirts that had gotten mixed into my luggage. While each piece was neatly folded, they were repacked with no real attempt at order. I opened my bag, pulling all the clothing out to find a suitable shirt of my own. And then I had to go thorough all the pouches to find my brushes and cuff links.

I came downstairs to find that I was the last to arrive. Uncle Jeremy and Willie had changed out of their dress uniforms and were in civilian clothing. Miss Bang had changed into a stunning black gown that complimented her dark hair. Most surprising of all was Professor Crackle, who for once was appropriately dressed in classic black evening wear. He even wore a white tie and waistcoat, although I noticed that he kept constantly fiddling with his cuffs.

Manqoba handed me a drink and told me that dinner would be ready in a few minutes. The black-skinned butler also looked different. Instead of his usual shoulder pelt and kilt, he was wearing more traditional livery, including trousers and dress shoes. "You're looking very handsome tonight, Manqoba."

"Thank you, sir. I thought it best to conform to the house's dress code to make the others more comfortable."

"Very thoughtful of you, Manqoba."

"Thank you, sir."

I joined the others as they relaxed in the lounge.

"This is casual?" I asked, grinning.

Miss Bang smiled. "There is no 'dressing casual' for women, my lord."

My uncle nodded. "I suspect my wife would agree with you, Miss Bang."

The professor gestured at himself. "This was all I could find. The rest of my clothing has gone missing."

"It may have been among the things that required laundering. We can look into it later, Harmonious," Miss Bang said. "In the meantime, it does look good on you."

The professor smiled. "Thank you, my dear."

"We were beginning to wonder what had happened to you, Sir Richard," Miss Bang said.

"My apologies for my tardiness. The inspectors weren't being very careful in going through our baggage and somehow I ended up with one of the professor's shirts by mistake. I had to go find one of my own."

"Is that what happened?" the professor asked. "I was trying to figure out how they had managed to stretch the sleeves of my shirt." He held up one sleeve where the cuff half swallowed his hand. "I'd never encountered textiles with this much elasticity in the weave."

"We'll get it all sorted out tonight after dinner, Professor," I said.

As if on cue, Manqoba materialized and informed us that dinner was served.

Dinner was a delicious roast chicken and vegetables. The plates were served steaming from the sideboard and it filled the room with the most enticing aromas. The chicken smelled slightly of lemon and had a peppery taste to it. The vegetables I didn't recognize, but instead of being boiled, they'd been braised in different sauces and put off a spicy aroma that made my mouth water. Dessert was something called gulab jamun, small spheres of fried dough soaked in a light syrup.

The service for dinner was somewhat unusual, though. While Manqoba seemed to work well with the two remaining footmen, several of the Riggers assisted as well. Mostly they carried dishes up from the kitchen to the sideboard and cleared away dirty plates. The footmen tried to keep them from interacting with us at the table, but the Riggers wouldn't have any of it. They'd either give them a gentle push out of the way, or feint to draw them out of position. While the Riggers were surprisingly well behaved, they certainly did not look the part. They were still dressed in their normal clothing, a hodge-podge mixture of cotton and canvas with leather reinforcements that were well weathered and stained from much use. But I did notice that their hands were surprisingly clean. Indeed, I noticed as one rigger was clearing my dishes away before the desert was served, his hands were a bright pink, and looked like they'd been recently scrubbed.

After dinner, Uncle Jeremy invited Miss Bang to join us in the library, there not being any other women for her to join in the drawing room. He said, "I'm sure that if Phyllis were here, she would enjoy chatting with you, but for tonight I'm afraid that you'll have to deal with us." Uncle Jeremy nodded to her and added for the rest of us, "I think that for tonight we can dispense with the cigars, gentlemen."

"No problem, Lieutenant-Colonel. Nasty habit, that," the professor muttered and sipped his wine.

"I should be happy to join you, Lieutenant-Colonel Griffith. Thank you for the invitation," Miss Bang replied.

My uncle stood up and offered Miss Bang his arm. They proceeded out of the dining room and we followed them to the library.

"Would you care for a bit of an aperitif, Miss Bang?" my uncle asked, crossing to a table with various decanters on it.

"A brandy, if you don't mind," she replied, and he poured her a snifter of dark liquid from a crystal decanter.

"I would not have thought that brandy was quite your style, Miss Bang," I said.

Miss Bang grinned at my uncle as she took the glass. "I endeavor to be open to trying new things, my lord. I believe that for tonight I shall be an unofficial gentleman, so, as brandy is considered a gentleman's drink, it seems appropriate."

We laughed and accepted our own snifters from my uncle. Miss Bang and the professor sat down on opposite ends of a settee, while Willie and I sat in a pair of armchairs opposite them. I took a sip from my glass and after a moment to appreciate the burn as it went down, I said, "It is a crying shame that Colonel Ticking had all the physical evidence taken away. You know, like the arm device that one girl was wearing, and her weapons. I'm sure the professor would be able to assist if he had something to examine, but now it's all behind lock and key at the base."

Professor Crackle stood up again, and paced near one of the bookshelves. "Exactly, my boy! I can't believe he took everything! What does he think he's going do with it all?" The professor gestured to punctuate his words and nearly slopped his brandy out onto the carpet.

"It is evidence, Professor," my brother said. "The colonel does have a responsibility to preserve evidence for the investigation."

The professor snorted. "What investigation? By whom? As far as I know, Colonel Ticking doesn't have any technical skills. Does he have any investigative officers under his command?" Willie shook his head "I don't understand what he's planning to do with the equipment."

"Well," I suggested, "perhaps he's planning on holding it for the MoTS?"

The professor scoffed. "The Ministry of Technological Security? Those ham-fisted idiots? He'd be better off giving it to a precocious kindergarten class." When Willie raised his eyebrow at the professor, he hastily added, "That is a criticism of the incompetence of the MoTS."

"Well," Uncle Jeremy set the bottle of brandy down on the table and sat in his armchair next to Miss Bang. "I can set your minds at ease on that score. The Technological Security types are supposed to judge new discoveries to see if they're safe enough to release to the general public. This is technology that someone has made into a weapon. It is *already* categorically unsafe. No, no. The MoTS won't get their hands on this." He sipped from his glass. "That lot will go straight to military security. If we ever hear of any of this again, it will be in the form of some new weapon deployed to the troops. Most likely, we won't hear of it again." He leaned back in his armchair. "Well, perhaps you might, William. If your career takes you to the right place. But I imagine it will all be state secrets very soon."

"Don't you think that's a little short sighted?" Miss Bang asked. "We could still learn a lot from such devices and be able to turn them to peaceful uses. Labor saving devices. Possibly prosthetics and life-enhancing products."

Uncle Jeremy shook his head. "Our prime concern is the safety of the Empire and all her citizens, Miss. If the Eternal Empress…"

"May she live forever," Willie and Uncle Jeremy said in unison.

My uncle continued, "If she, in her wisdom decides such technologies are better off forgotten, it is not for us to second guess her. Once a technology has been made into a weapon, there is no doubt that it can and will be done again. History has shown that the potential peaceful uses of science rarely outweigh the damage done by its misuse."

The professor paced. "But if more minds could study such weapons, don't you think that it would allow us to make better defenses? By keeping them secret, doesn't that make us more vulnerable for the next weapon?"

Uncle Jeremy cleared his throat. "I've heard this argument before, Professor. But the decision has been made for us already. I'm afraid there's no point debating." He sighed. "I'm sorry, I'm afraid I'm feeling a bit tired. I do appreciate you all being here and helping, but I think I'll be turning in now. Things will look better in the morning."

He stood, and we all rose as well. "Please, stay. Enjoy your evening," he said.

Miss Bang took a step towards him. "I know that I'm not family to you, Lieutenant-Colonel Griffith, but it would seem that no one else appropriate is here." She took another step and hugged him. When she released him she added, "You seemed to need that."

Tears welled in his eyes. "Thank you, Miss Bang. I did." He sighed. "Well, good night, all. I will see you at breakfast."

"No duty tomorrow, Uncle Jeremy," Willie said. "You may want to sleep in."

"You're a little too young to be giving advice to an old soldier, William." Uncle Jeremy clapped my brother on the shoulder as he left the room.

We stood and looked at each other for a moment.

"Shall we sit?" I asked, and we resumed our seats. The professor prowled along the bookshelves, looking at the titles of the books.

We sat in uneasy silence for a minute.

Willie cleared his throat and asked, "I know you were planning this trip for a while. Did you have anything specific to do while you're here, brother?"

I could tell that my brother was trying to steer the conversation towards something he hoped would be a nice, safe neutral topic. Unfortunately for him, that wasn't where I wanted to go.

"Well, I imagine that in the next few days we'll be busy trying to track down the people who took your friend and Aunt Phyllis," I said.

He looked at me over his drink. "That's not funny."

"Nor was it intended to be."

"You were told to keep out of the investigation." He scowled at me.

"No. Professor Crackle was told to keep out of Colonel Ticking's investigation," I said. "He also offered his and Miss Bang's services to the maharaja, but they were refused. My aunt has been kidnapped, and as a noble of the realm, I have every right to conduct my own investigation into the matter, provided I don't interfere with any official ongoing investigation. But I spoke out of turn, a moment ago. Miss Bang, Professor Crackle, would you be willing to lend your skills and wits to furthering my search?"

Professor Crackle shoved a book back into the bookcase, crossed to me, and shook my hand. "I shall be very happy to do so, my boy!"

Miss Bang lifted her brandy. "My pleasure, my lord." She sipped.

"Are you serious?" Willie asked. His brow furrowed and I thought how much he looked like our father when he got angry.

"I would have asked you, too, but you're under orders to take care of Uncle Jeremy for the next day or two. I wouldn't want you to get in trouble with your command."

"You *are* serious!" He pounded the arm of his chair and the action caused what was left of his brandy to jump into the air.

"Willie, we've spent the whole day being run around by different officials who have wasted time and made every mistake in the book. We've got to do something if we're going to have a chance of recovering Aunt Phyllis and your friend, the maharani. I've worked with the professor and Miss Bang. I know that their methods may seem a bit unorthodox at times, but they get results. I'm sure that they're the best hope the ladies have of coming home safe."

Willie shook his head. "I don't know. I want to do something to get Chandra... I mean, Aunt Phyllis back, but going behind the colonel's back..."

I tried to appease my brother's concerns. "We're just going to run down a few leads. If we find something, you can pass it on to the colonel. If we don't find anything, then our time will be wasted, not his."

Miss Bang reached across and touched Willie's knee. "Please let us do this, Lieutenant. It's one of the few ways we can help out."

He sighed. "Very well. But leave me out of it. And stay out of trouble."

"Are you sure?" I asked.

"Yes! No." He groaned. "No, I'm not sure, but you're right. If I help you out, I'll be disobeying orders. As much as I'd like to help out, this is the life I signed up for. To put duty first." He stood. "It's just that this... this is so unlike you, brother. Showing up late, that's you. Arriving uninvited, that's you."

"I had no way to know there was a party going on!"

He nodded, but went on. "Arriving with people we've never met before, no offense meant, Miss, Professor. That's you all over it."

"You left out having the door shut in my face and having to climb in through the hedge," I said.

Willie grimaced. "Yes, there's that, too. But you've always tried to avoid trouble, and it has always come hot on your heels."

"And now I'm facing it, when it would be easy to stand to one side and let someone else deal with it."

He nodded.

"Well, Prague opened my eyes to a lot of things. Maybe when this is done I can tell you about some of it."

He shook his head slowly. "You never used to be this bold."

"I'm not." I snorted. "But like you, I've learned there are times when you have to do things you don't want to."

"I look forward to hearing those stories. But I think right now, I'm better off knowing as little as possible of what you're planning." He put his snifter down on the table next to his chair. "I thought I understood why you hated all the demands that the family put on you."

I laughed. "You were the only one who ever saw my side of things."

He nodded. "I find I'm glad that you're willing to take this on for Aunt Phyllis. For the family. I wish you luck."

"Thanks," I said, feeling for the first time that I didn't really know what I was getting myself into.

Willie stood, and I rose as well. "Well, I will give you some privacy to make your plans."

"Goodnight, Lieutenant," Miss Bang replied.

"Goodnight, my friend." The professor raised his glass.

"See you tomorrow, Willie."

We watched as he left and closed the door behind him.

"Well done, my boy!" Professor Crackle said. "I hadn't realized how strongly you felt about your aunt."

I shook my head. "It's more for Willie. Aunt Phyllis always terrified me. Now Willie and my uncle tell me I'm her favorite. I don't know what to make of that, but Willie is my brother. He is a close friend of the maharani. Very close. It's going to drive him crazy not knowing that she's all right. If I don't do something, for Willie or Aunt Phyllis, I know I'm going to regret it later."

Miss Bang turned to me. "What is your plan for us to proceed, my lord?"

"Actually, Miss Bang, I was hoping that you and the professor could come up with something."

The professor rubbed his hands together. "Well, my boy, we'll need to get into that military base and find out where they are keeping that exoskeleton. There has to be some clue as to who made it and where we can find them."

"I'm sure you're right, Professor, but getting on the base isn't possible. We're going to have to abandon that angle for now." The professor looked disappointed. I turned to Miss Bang. "Do you have any ideas, Miss Bang?"

She considered the question for a moment. "They call themselves the 'Kindred of Kali'. They're not positioning themselves as patriots, but as religious figures. Perhaps if we inquire with the local temples, they might be able to tell us something about them."

"So, we should see if we can find a temple of Kali?"

"No, my lord. I think tomorrow morning we should go and pay a visit to my cousin."

CHAPTER NINE

A VISIT WITH MRS. BASUMATRY

In the morning, after an excellent breakfast, we discovered that we'd overlooked one problem in our planning the night before: transportation.

While there were still plenty of vehicles at the house, none of them were in a working state. The sedan we borrowed yesterday afternoon was missing. The owner of the vehicle sent a pair of servants early in the morning to reclaim it. Manqoba told us they said their master would be very angry about the damage to his property. He informed them that we weren't responsible for the damage, but they were not interested.

Most of the horse-driven carriages were gone. Fresh horses and harnesses were sufficient to allow the owners to reclaim them. While some vehicles were reclaimed by their owners, damaged automobiles still littered the lawn. Even Uncle Jeremy's staff car had been towed off for repairs.

By the time we realized we needed transport, the cook had already taken the house's horse carriage to do the shopping in the local village and there was no longer a working vehicle on the premises. Rather than elect to wait an unknown amount of time for her return, Professor Crackle proposed we head into town to hire a vehicle for the day.

Miss Bang talked to the staff and found out there was a bus service of sorts. She got directions, and we followed them out to a smaller road adjoining my uncle's property. We waited next to a carved post which indicated the bus stop. After about twenty minutes, a horse-drawn wagon with a flat bed and several rows of benches nailed onto it came along. The benches were crammed with all manner of people. Indian men and women in dark European suits and colourful Indian outfits, all the way down to two men in loose white pajamas that were already sweat stained and who stood on the back step and hung onto the cart. The three of us stuck out rather conspicuously as the only light-skinned persons there.

Miss Bang talked to the driver and paid for our passage. A pair of women on the front bench scooted over, making room for Miss Bang. She climbed up next to them and thanked them for making space for her. I looked at the men in the second row, and they avoided my gaze, staring straight ahead. Professor Crackle didn't waste a moment. He ran to the rear of the wagon, jumped onto the back step, and grabbed a handhold. Having little choice in the matter, I followed, one of the laborer's giving me a hand up with a large, broken-toothed smile and a burst of noxious breath. I nodded to the man and tried to keep from gagging at his breath.

The bus took off and we rattled along down the road, feeling every bump and jostle. The professor seemed to think the whole thing was a grand adventure, but I found that it reminded me rather depressingly of the time I ended up riding home from a party in a dog cart. In this particular case the dog cart came out on the more favorable side because I had been sufficiently inebriated that I still don't remember the actual trip. Just the smell of the dogs.

The wagon rattled along for most of an hour without stopping. The two farm workers slipped from the bus without even asking for it to stop. With them went the smell of sweat and dirt and honest labour. For a minute I thought this would freshen the air, but I soon realized why the trip reminded me of that dog cart. Someone on the bus smelled of wet dog.

No one else took notice of the farm hand's departure, and there were no other stops as we traveled to the center of a village. Once we stopped, the other passengers disembarked and quickly scattered, going about their business. Miss Bang stepped down from the wagon carefully, still maintaining a conversation with her seat mates. The other ladies bid her good day, and she turned to where the professor and I were slapping dust from our trouser legs.

"We are in luck, gentlemen," she said. "While this village doesn't have a place to rent a jitney or automobile, I am told that down this street we *can* rent a carriage and driver for the day. Shall we go see what is available?"

We walked down the length of the street, passing a green grocer, two butchers, a bookseller, and a carpenter with several examples of furniture on display on the sidewalk, but we didn't see any sign of a stable or carriage house. We turned around and were walking back to the town square, when we spied a man dozing in the back of a small wagon attached to a swaybacked horse. The professor stopped, rapped on the side rail, and said, "I beg your pardon, my good sir, but I'm hoping that you can help us."

The man blinked and propped himself up on one elbow. "Yes? How can old Bijoy be of service?"

The professor nodded and said, "We were told that somewhere on this street we could rent a carriage for the day, but we can't seem to find the correct shop. Could you tell us where we need to go?"

The man sat up, suddenly wide awake. "Me. That is me!" He patted his chest with one hand and grinned. "Bijoy is carriage for hire!"

I eyed the dirty, flat bed wagon with some misgivings. As it lacked any kind of passenger seating, the wagon could only be classified as a carriage in the broadest sense of the term. "Is there another vehicle available?" It looked like a past cargo had been manure, or some other farm waste.

"No. Only Bijoy." The old man sounded almost sad as he said it. He patted the wagon next to where he sat. "Is good carriage. Very smooth. Good ride. Take you wherever you need to go." He got up and climbed onto the front seat of the small wagon. The horse turned his grey muzzle to the man and shook his head. His dull grey coat indicated he was well past his prime. "Come, come. We go. I take you where you need to go." The driver waved us into the wagon.

"Excellent!" Professor Crackle immediately scrambled into the back of the wagon and turned around to help Miss Bang up.

I gave the wagon a dubious look. "Are you sure about this, Professor?"

"Certainly, my boy. Climb aboard!"

I dusted off the end of the bed, but it didn't make a significant difference in the cleanliness of the surface. It gave me a new appreciation of our earlier bus ride. Reluctantly, I pulled myself into the wagon, just as the driver twitched the reins and the horse set off at a walk down the street.

Miss Bang gave the odd man the address, and he nodded and shook the reins to encourage more speed. We trotted through the village and closer to the taller buildings of the city proper. We ambled back and forth through the maze of neighborhoods. It seemed like we were getting lost, but the driver assured us he knew exactly where he was going, which actually didn't reassure me at all.

The wagon finally stopped in front of a well-maintained townhouse in what appeared to be a comfortable neighborhood. The house was two stories tall, with a gabled roof. Unlike the townhouses of London, it didn't entirely fill the property, sharing a wall with its neighbors. Instead, there was a small alley between each building. The front lawn was covered with flowers in bloom and two large trees provided shade from the sun.

The professor jumped out of the wagon, and went to talk to the driver as I climbed down and helped Miss Bang disembark. He told the old man, "We will likely be inside for a couple of hours..." At which point the driver dropped his reins and crawled into the back of the wagon and curled up to sleep. The professor blinked in surprise. "I guess you're prepared to wait."

The horse shook his head, stepped over to the verge, and began chewing grass from the edge of the front lawn. I followed Miss Bang up to the front door, brushing dirt from my pants as I went. Professor Crackle joined me.

Miss Bang knocked on the door, and it was answered by a small Indian woman who eyed the three of us warily. She wore a white blouse with short sleeves and a drab sari. "Yes?" she said, her voice matching her somewhat gloomy appearance.

"Good morning," Miss Bang said cheerfully. "Could you please inform Mrs. Basumatry that her cousin, Miss Titania Bang, is here to see her?"

The woman cast a dubious eye at the professor and myself.

Miss Bang added, "I am accompanied by my colleague, Professor Harmonious Crackle, and our friend, Sir Richard Blasphemy."

The woman seemed even less reassured by this additional introduction. She frowned and told us, "Mr. Bhang left instructions that Mrs. Basumatry is not to have visitors while he is out."

Miss Bang's face lost its warmth. "Please inform Mrs. Basumatry that we are here. We shall await her pleasure."

The woman stared at us for a moment, scowling. She closed the door and left us waiting on the doorstep.

Professor Crackle pushed his top hat slightly back on this head. "Titania, I get the feeling that your cousin... Mr. Bhang? He's not very fond of visitors, is he?"

She sighed. "He's very controlling. As the eldest male of the family present, he takes precedence over Kashvi, unless her husband is present. As such, he lords it over her as much as he can. I had hoped that he would grow out of it, but it appears that he has not."

"Does that mean this was a wasted trip?" I asked.

"Nonsense, my boy!" the professor began, when the door was suddenly thrown open. A dark young woman in a brightly coloured dress erupted through it and flung herself at Miss Bang.

"Kashvi!" Miss Bang cried as she hugged her cousin.

"Titania!" her darker-skinned duplicate replied. "Oh, it is so good to see you! I wasn't expecting you so soon, but I am so glad you came!" She saw the professor and myself, standing there on the step and broke into a mischievous grin. "And you brought your husbands. How wonderful!"

"Kashvi!" Miss Bang scolded. "These gentlemen are my friends, not my husbands!"

Her cousin giggled. "Are you sure?"

"Kashvi!"

Mrs. Basumatry laughed. "I'm sorry, Titania. I couldn't resist. You should have seen your face." She hid a grin behind her hand. "I apologize. Please, Titania, gentlemen, do come in and visit for a while."

The woman who had answered the door re-appeared and said, "Mr. Bhang said visitors were not allowed while he was away."

Mrs. Basumatry shot the woman a scolding look. "Mr. Bhang is a guest, Indira, *not* the master. These people are my friends and they are welcome in this house. You will show them every courtesy, and you will not discuss their visit with Mr. Bhang, or you will no longer be a part of this household."

Indira cast her eyes down in submission. "Yes, mistress."

Kashvi turned back to us, her face happy and shining once more. "Please, come in! I so want to hear what you've been doing."

We were led into a sitting room, where Indira meekly served us tea, scones, and a pastry of nuts and honey between thin layers of dough. The ladies did most of the talking, while Professor Crackle and I simply sat and smiled, adding a detail here and there for stories we were familiar with. I said very little while they swapped stories covering the last six years.

At last Miss Bang brought the conversation around to the information we were interested in. "Kashvi, have you heard of the group that attacked the party yesterday? The ones calling themselves the Kindred of Kali?"

"NO!" she said in a rush as she leaned forward and grabbed Miss Bang's hand. "Weren't they just terrible! Striking down that poor man and wrecking all those automobiles and carriages. I had never heard of them before, and suddenly, there they were." She looked at each of us, hoping that we had gossip to share.

Professor Crackle cleared his throat. "We were thinking much on the subject last night, my good lady, and we were wondering if there might be a connection between these Kindred and a local church."

Kashvi gave him a puzzled look. "What church would associate with such terrible persons?"

"I think what the professor means is, are there any churches that worship Kali in the area?" I suggested.

Miss Bang shook her head. "My lord, the dominant religion in India is Hinduism, which is a belief with many gods and goddesses."

Kashvi nodded. "Kali-Ma is a loving goddess. She watches over us and cares for us as her children. These people have made a twisted mockery of her to justify their attacks against the English and our own people. Just like the Thugs. They claimed to worship Kali-Ma and suddenly the English all thought that everyone who worships Kali-Ma was a criminal." She shook her head. "I don't know any person of true faith who would entertain such thoughts for a moment. I suppose this may not make much sense to you gentlemen. You are not Hindu, and I have heard that the English are Christian and have but one *deva* and do not understand those who have more. Your beliefs are so different from ours. But surely, Titania, you understand."

"I do, and I agree with you. But, the goddess has her vengeful side. I believe someone is playing upon that and other popular fears. I think Harmonious meant to ask," Miss Bang glanced in his direction briefly, "if there might be a nearby temple to Kali-Ma that may have given them support, not knowing what kind of people they were?"

"Oh, we do not have any of the great temples here. Not to Kali-Ma. Kanpur is growing, but the city is too small for that, and in this part of India there aren't many *mandir* dedicated to the *Mahavidyas*.

We do have *mandir* to Shiva, Vishnu, and Brahma, and some are quite large, but nothing dedicated to Kali-Ma. But as a major *devi*, she does have a presence in just about every *mandir*. She is not neglected."

I cleared my throat. "Pardon me. As you said, your ways aren't familiar to me. What is a *mandir*? And the *Mahavi...*"

Miss Bang interrupted as a I struggled with the unfamiliar word. "The *Mahavidyas*, my lord, are a collection of ten major goddesses in one style of Hindu belief. The majority of Hindu belief is that the *deva*, the gods if you will, are aspects of the universal whole, the Supreme God, and the *devi*, the goddesses, are supporting aspects. But there is another sect that believes the divine power flows through the *devi* and the *Mahavidyas* are those sources of power from which the *deva* spring."

"Oh," I said. "And a *mandir*?"

Kashvi answered, "It is where the gods live. A house for the god it is dedicated to."

This I understood. "So it's a church? A holy place, but on a smaller scale than a temple?"

Kashvi nodded, then her eyes got a faraway look for a few moments. "Although... I think there may be a small shrine to Kali-Ma at the edge of the poor district. I remember Mrs. Singh telling me about the priest there. A very holy man. He was from a wealthy family, but he walked away from them, to become a priest and minister to the poor. I remember she said he was very persuasive at fundraising."

"That does indeed sound like the sort of thing we are looking for," the professor replied. "Can you tell us where it is?"

She tapped her lip as she thought about it. "No, I do not think I can describe how to get there. I am sorry." Then her face brightened. "But I could take you there. I don't know the street names, but I know the way."

I spoke up. "I'm not sure that would be a good idea, Mrs. Basumatry. Our current transportation is a hired wagon, and it isn't exactly the cleanest, or the most comfortable."

She looked at me in surprise. "You hired Bijoy?"

"Yes, do you know him?" the professor asked.

She laughed. "Everyone in this area knows Bijoy. But I don't know anyone who actually hired him before."

"Is that a problem?" I asked.

She shrugged. "I don't know. We've never seen him working before. No one even knows how he manages to keep that poor horse alive. Some people have been speculating on who might be supporting him, but no one knows. Perhaps this will be what he needs to get him off of that cart and earning a proper living." She stood, and the professor and I stood as well. "But if we will be riding with Bijoy, I shall need to change into a different dress. As you say, one that doesn't show the dirt as much. Please, sit. I won't be long. Riding with Bijoy!" She walked off, laughing.

"Somehow, I don't think I find it too reassuring when one's host laughs about one's transport," I said.

"Oh, don't worry about it, my boy," the professor said as he slapped me on the shoulder. "It can't be too bad, or she wouldn't be going with us. Besides, we seem to be doing a public service."

"Or Kashvi is desperate to get out of the house for a while," Miss Bang finished.

A few minutes later our hostess returned wearing a dun traveling dress and carrying a pair of cushions. "Indira!" she called to her servant. "I'll be going out for a while, but I should be back before my brother returns from his business."

The small woman appeared at the door to the sitting room and said, "Are you sure this is wise, mistress?" She cast a dark look at the professor, Miss Bang, and myself.

"Don't be such a stick in the mud, Indira," Kashvi said. "We're just going for a little ride. We should be back in no time."

Indira withheld any further criticism she had, and we went back to the front step. The horse was patiently cropping the grass from the verge by the street.

"What happened to Bijoy?" Kashvi asked.

"I'm pretty sure he's still there," I said and we approached the wagon to find him still curled up in the back, softly snoring.

I rapped on the side of the wagon and the old man woke with a start. He blinked up at us, and suddenly was wide awake and climbing to his feet. "Oh, yes, sir, lady. Ladies. How can Bijoy help?"

Kashvi laughed quietly to herself. Professor Crackle spoke to the old man. "Time to head out, my good man! Look alive!"

Miss Bang continued, "We're going to a local shrine. My cousin," she gestured to Mrs. Basumatry, "will provide you with directions."

"Yes, lady. Ladies," Bijoy said as he climbed back into the driver's seat.

Professor Crackle and I handed the ladies into the cart, and Kashvi set the cushions out for her and Miss Bang to sit upon. She sat down next to him and said, "You're driving a wagon, now, Bijoy? Weren't you working as a gardener not too long ago?"

He bobbed his head up and down. "Bijoy work many jobs. Many jobs. Gardener. Driver. Stable hand. Always there is work to be done."

The professor and I climbed into the back of the wagon. Miss Bang's cousin told the cart-man, "Start driving, and take the next left up the street." Bijoy reached past Miss Bang to release the handbrake, then shook the reins, clicked his tongue at the horse, and we set off.

We drove through the length of the neighborhood, the houses all very similar to each other, but each with distinct features, such as exterior patterns done in colored tile, or the occasional gabled window. As we progressed, the quality of the homes changed. The houses were not decorated in quite as much detail, or showed signs of disrepair that needed to be attended to. Unlike our previous journeys, where we had cut sharply across bands of differing levels of prosperity, this time we were following a slow decline into the poorer sections of the city.

We finally got to a street where Bijoy stopped the wagon, pulled the handbrake, and refused to go any further. "Bad. Bad neighborhood. They hurt poor Bijoy."

Mrs. Basumatry seemed unperturbed by his refusal. "We're almost there. It is just down the street. We can walk from here."

We climbed down from the wagon, and the professor handed Miss Bang's cousin down. I came around to likewise help Miss Bang down from her seat, when she suddenly swung out of my grasp and landed hard on the street, knocking the wind out of her. As I bent down to make sure that she was unharmed, I could see that part of her dress had been caught in the cart's brake and that caused her to trip. I released the brake and pulled the folds of her dress out of the mechanism before the cart-man engaged it again.

"Are you all right, Titania? Are you hurt?" The professor said as he and Mrs. Basumatry appeared at my side as I helped Miss Bang back to her feet.

"I think so, Harmonious." She stumbled slightly as she put weight on one foot. "I just need a moment to set myself to rights. It's nothing, really. Go go ahead on without me. I'll catch up in a moment."

"Are you sure?" her cousin asked. "We can wait."

"No, please, go on," Miss Bang repeated. "I insist."

"I'll stay with her," I volunteered. "I'll make sure that she's all right."

"Very well." The professor looked a little worried, but he didn't seem inclined to protest. "Take all the time you need."

Bijoy and I helped Miss Bang to the back of the wagon and I sat her on the end of it as the professor and Mrs. Basumatry walked reluctantly down the street with a few backward glances.

"Now," I said. "What have you done to that ankle?"

"I think it is only a sprain, my lord. Let me tighten up my boot laces and I believe I'll have enough support to walk." She lifted her wounded leg up and laid it along the bed of the wagon. Pulling her long skirts back and tucking them underneath her, she began loosening the laces of her boot.

I looked at Bijoy, who bit his lower lip and peered over the wagon at the professor and Mrs. Basumatry. He shot nervous glances at the surrounding buildings.

"We should go," the driver said. "Very bad neighborhood."

"In good time," I said, and likewise looked after the professor and Mrs. Basumatry.

My head swam for a moment, as looking at the professor and Mrs. Basumatry walking down the street I had the feeling that Miss Bang was both next to me and walking with the professor at the same time. It passed as soon as it came, as I realized that Mrs. Basumatry moved differently from her cousin, despite their physical similarity.

The professor and Mrs. Basumatry knocked on the doors of a building perhaps halfway down the block. The building seemed to be as old as the rest of the neighborhood, or even slightly older, but was in considerably better condition. The building was on a flat space at the bottom of the hill, and the road widened here, to create a small square.

As I watched, a robed man emerged and spoke with them.

I glanced back at Miss Bang as she ministered to her ankle. "Is there anything I can do to help?"

She had settled her foot more firmly into the boot and was now proceeding to lace it back up. "Thank you, my lord, but I don't think so. It doesn't seem that bad. I should be fine as long as I don't overdo it."

There were shouts down the street, and I looked up again to see angry men in dirty work clothes pouring out of the buildings on both sides of the street. They surrounded the professor and Mrs. Basumatry, several of them brandishing short clubs or other tools. I started to run to their aid, but Miss Bang grabbed my arm and held fast. "Wait," she hissed.

Bijoy scrambled over the side of the wagon and dove behind us to cower. I think he might have run off, were it not for the horse and cart, his sole means of livelihood. I think he would have turned the cart and rode off except that would have drawn attention from the crowd. The horse was strangely calm, as it it was used to this sort of noise and activity.

As we watched, men took hold of the professor and Miss Bang's cousin and held them fast. More men poured from the adjoining buildings. The robed man raised his voice again, and a space cleared in front of the shrine. From within the building came a metallic sound, and then the double doors of the shrine opened and one of the Kindred of Kali stepped out into the street.

This one wasn't brandishing swords, but she still looked fearsome. She glared from behind the veil that hid her identity. The men in the street prostrated themselves before the woman, except for the ones holding Professor Crackle and Mrs. Basumatry. To her credit, Miss Bang's cousin kept her face placid, unreadable. With a crunch of steel shoes and the hiss of steam-driven pistons, the Kindred stepped forward to look at them.

Miss Bang slipped off the end of the wagon, wincing, and pulled me down beside her. "We're too conspicuous here with everyone making obeisance," she whispered in my ear.

Bijoy crouched next to us and nodded vigorously. "We should go! We go now, yes?"

We peeked around the corner of the cart and saw the Kindred order the men to take the professor and Mrs. Basumatry into the shrine. The captors hustled their prisoners into the building, with the Kindred and the priest following. As the men in the streets rose from their position of reverence, they took up a chant that echoed down the street. "Kali-Ma! Kali-Ma! Kali-Ma!"

CHAPTER TEN

A CLASH OF AVATARS

The crowd chanted for a few minutes after the departure of the priest and the Kindred before finally dispersing back into the surrounding buildings. A handful of men remained in the street. They stationed themselves in front of the shrine's door. Standing guard.

"What do we do?" I asked Miss Bang.

Bijoy answered for her, saying, "We should go. Is too dangerous here."

She ignored him and took a moment to finish retying her boot before answering. "There are too many of them for us to take on alone. We need reinforcements." Her calm tone gave me hope. After all, she was the expert and had gotten out of many similar scrapes.

Bijoy nodded and whispered. "Yes! Go! Get help!"

I glanced at the driver, then looked at Miss Bang. "Agreed. Should we go to the colonel, or the maharaja?"

"Neither, I'm afraid," Miss Bang replied. "I suspect both of them would be more concerned with recovering the maharani and wouldn't actually give us any support. And if Colonel Ticking helped, I suspect he'd throw Harmonious in a cell."

"The Riggers?" I guessed.

"Yes. And Tinka. We'll need Tinka."

I looked at Miss Bang and wondered what she was thinking. Tinka was the head of the Riggers and a talented engineer, but she also suffered from crippling social anxiety due to a being born with two extra arms.

I glanced back at the men standing guard. "I thought she was dead set against leaving the ship."

"She is. I'm going to have to be more persuasive." She reached out an arm and grabbed Bijoy. "I need you to take me to the port."

"Yes, yes, I take you far away from here. Let us go now!"

Miss Bang held him in place for a moment more. "I need you to stay here, my lord."

"*What?*" I yelped, then repeated in a whisper, "What?"

"Someone has to stay here and watch so we'll know if they move Professor Crackle and my cousin to a different location. I can't leave Bijoy, I need him to navigate through the city. I could stay, but that would mean you'd have to make sure Tinka comes to help. Do you think you can convince her to come, Sir Richard?"

I considered the request. Either Tinka would immediately accept the plan, or she'd dig her heels in. And once she made that decision, I couldn't imagine anything shaking her from it. "Not if she doesn't want to."

"Then I have to go to the ship. And back to your aunt's house to gather the men there. And that means I need you to stay here and watch to see if they move the prisoners."

"But what do I do if they do move them? Or if they go out another entrance. I can't see the whole building from here."

"If they move, follow them. Do your best to leave some kind of trail. Grab a rock and scratch an arrow on the front of a building. We mustn't lose them."

"How long will you be gone?"

"It will take time to get to the port, get ready, and get back here. Perhaps an hour?"

"An hour?" Bijoy flinched and Miss Bang shushed me for my sudden outburst. We looked back down the street, but the men were talking among themselves and didn't seem to have noticed.

"It will take as long as it takes, my lord," Miss Bang whispered at me through gritted teeth. "There is nothing I can do to speed the process except to leave *now*."

"Yes, let us leave now, miss!" the driver interjected.

She shot him a rebuking look and continued. "You'll need to stay out of sight until we return. Can you do that?"

I looked at the men in front of the shrine. There were four of them, but they didn't seem to be particularly attentive. They made a show of guarding the entryway and postured for each other. They behaved more like gang members than faithful followers defending a holy place. Perhaps it was as Mrs. Basumatry had said: that they were warping belief in Kali for their own violent ends.

I glanced at the buildings and spotted an alley that appeared to be rather disused.

"I think so. Let me move over to the alley across the street. If I can get there without them seeing me, I think I should be able to stay hidden well enough."

"Very well. As soon as you go, we'll get the wagon turned around and go get help."

I shifted around them to peek out at the men down the street. They were milling about, making small conversation. As a guard force, they weren't very effective. Hopefully they would prove equally inattentive. I waited for a moment when their attention was away from the cart and sprinted across the street to the alley, laying myself flat against the wall of the building.

There was no sound of alarm from the men. I peeked out around the corner of the alley. They continued to mill around in front of the shrine. I signed to Miss Bang that I was ready.

She released Bijoy, who came out from around the back of the wagon and nervously climbed up into the seat at the front of the cart. Miss Bang crawled into the bed, keeping herself as low as she could.

The cart-man grabbed the reins, released the brake, and turned the cart around in the narrow street, urging the horse up to a trot as soon as it was facing away from the shrine. The wagon thundered away from me, quickly disappearing.

A couple of the men in front of the shrine looked up the street at the sound of the cart turning. One of them even took a couple steps in their direction, but the other one stopped him. He gestured dismissively, and said something that made both men laugh.

I settled in to wait. The alley itself was dirty and filled with all manner of refuse and oddly shaped junk. It looked as if someone had tossed or stored a few large items in the alley, and over time they'd been covered with hay, branches, and other detritus, which now were half decayed.

I paced back and forth in the space, going deeper into the alley to keep to the shadows, and coming back to the entrance to keep a watch on the shrine. I was nervous, frightened, and bored all at the same time. The Kali-worshipers were not having a better time of it. They had each other to talk to, but soon showed signs of boredom. Shortly, they were all leaning against the wall, making small talk, and trying to pass the time.

As we each waited for someone to do something significant, the afternoon dragged on. One of the men ran off and returned with food which he shared with the others, while I grew steadily hungrier and sweatier in the heat of the day. There was little traffic on the street. Each time someone came by, I ducked back into the alley. No one seemed to notice me.

Men in ones and twos would come down the street. Some were ignored, others would talk briefly to the men outside the shrine before running off on their own errands. Women who passed down the street were always in twos and threes. They would cross to the other side of the street and avoid the men, who called after them and laughed as they hurried away.

Finally, the sky began to darken, and I wondered how much longer it was going to take for Miss Bang to return.

As the last sliver of light faded from the sky, small lights appeared in the streets. Men with torches came out of the neighboring buildings in ones and twos. Some appeared from alleyways, which made me more nervous about my own position.

They didn't approach the shrine directly, but gathered nearby, as if they knew that something was about to happen and wanted a good spot to watch the event.

The crowd grew, and still no sign of Miss Bang and the Riggers. I became increasingly worried.

That worry grew to a near panic when two men came out of the temple and pried up a pair of stones set in the middle of the street uncovering two deep holes. More men followed with a pair of wooden posts, which they slotted down into the holes. I could tell that the post holes were significantly deeper than the thickness of the stones covering them. Other men came out and stacked piles of kindling around the bases of each pole. I did not like the way events were developing.

The final stacks of kindling were laid, and the men grew quiet. They stood, watching the door to the shrine, waiting for something to begin.

A chill passed through me as I heard someone approaching from the other end of the street. The clop of hooves, and the slow grind of wheels on the cobbled stones. Were there footsteps as well?

I shot a look down the dark alley and tried to remember how it looked under the light of day. I remember there being a way through, but I wasn't sure if I could navigate it without running into the debris if I was spotted. The buildings to either side blocked the moonlight and accustomed as my eyes were to the assembled torches, the alley seemed to be pitch black.

I glanced back up the street, away from the torch bearing crowd, and could barely make out a group of shady figures walking down the street behind a small wagon. More moonlight penetrated to the street, and I could make them out as slightly lighter forms in the darkness. The figure driving the wagon was short, but was taller than Bijoy, and was wrapped in a cloak that hid all features. Burly shapes carrying a variety of weapons filed in behind and lined up on either side of the wagon.

The double doors were flung wide and the robed man exited the shrine, followed by more men who dragged out Professor Crackle and Mrs. Basumatry and secured them to the two posts.

This man must have been the priest that we came here looking for. His robes were lavishly decorated and had the look of silk. His hair was clean and carefully brushed back from his face. He stood tall and straight and moved with an upper class bearing. All these things made him stand out from the sweaty, dirty, followers that surrounded him.

The priest turned to the crowd and began to talk to them in Hindi, his voice projecting loud and strong over the shuffling and occasional cheers of the men. I had no idea what he was saying, but whatever it was, they were eating it up. He would yell to them, and they would cheer back. He was obviously stirring them up into a frenzy.

In the midst of the cheering and screaming of the crowd, the Kindred woman emerged from the shrine again. Upon seeing her, the men chanted "Kali-Ma! Kali-Ma!" and thrust their torches in the air to the rhythm of their cries. The veiled woman raised her arms, all eight of them, encouraging them to shout louder as she paced back and forth in front of the shrine. I could hear the pistons hissing and popping and the metal braces crunching on the ground with each step as an odd counterpoint to the shouts of the men.

As the cheering reached a deafening stage, the cloaked figure on the wagon stood up. One of the men moved forward and took a position next to the nervous horse and hoisted something that glowed around the edges, like a shuttered lantern with the panels closed.

The Kindred turned her hands to the crowd, signaling for silence, and the chanting stopped abruptly. But before the woman could address them, another voice called out in Hindi, followed in English with, "Who dares call the name of Kali-Ma?"

I recognized that voice. It was Miss Bang!

The Kindred turned and squinted into the darkness. "The Kindred of Kali need not answer to you, stranger in the dark." She gestured to the professor and Miss Basumatry with one set of hands. "These fools dared to question the will of the goddess, and now they will feel her wrath for their temerity. Flee while you can. Or we will add *you* to the fire."

A shutter opened on a lantern in the cart, backlighting the cloaked figure. "Is this how you speak to a true daughter of Kali, false Kindred?" The cloak parted and four swords glided out from under the cloth, followed by the flesh and blood arms that held them. The arms were painted indigo, with red and white streaks along their length. They spread wide, framing either side of the figure.

The crowd was stunned. Many men stepped back, only to be stopped by the bodies behind them. Some prostrated themselves. Even the priest seemed shocked.

"No!" the Kindred cried as she unsheathed her own swords, "this is a trick. Be not deceived! Capture the false avatar!"

The cloak dropped from the figure, and the man at the front of the cart unshuttered his lantern, illuminating the four armed figure standing on the seat of the cart. I grinned as I recognized Tinka, the lead Rigger from the Argos. When I first met her, she seemed a mere slip of a girl, but I soon learned that she was a tough, talented, and strong woman. Now she stood transformed into a figure of wrath and glory.

Bracelets, metal bands, and bright paint covered each of her four arms. Likewise, anklets pooled at the top of her bare feet. She was painted in indigo from head to toe, and was almost naked, covered only in strips of white gauze that held down her breasts and a breech-clout girding her loins. Dye changed her strawberry blond hair to black, and a bright red color covered her lips. She grimaced at the Kindred, her face a fearsome sight.

"I will show you which of us is false!" Miss Bang's voice cried again. Tinka ran along the length of the horses's back, and flipped forward to land on her feet facing the Kindred, swords out and on guard. It was an utterly beautiful maneuver, full of grace and coordination the mechanical Kindred could not hope to match. The horse shied, but two men from the group of Riggers stepped forward and calmed it quickly.

My heart leapt as the Kindred woman screamed and charged, looking less like a woman and more like a hedge of blades. Tinka parried the charge, dodging to the side and slipping behind her steam powered opponent. The eight-armed woman whirled and lashed out with the blades on her right side, but Tinka simply ducked under the swords and struck out with a single weapon, nicking her opponent's leg.

The two women set to battle, their swords chiming off each other. It was a terrifying thing to behold. Tinka moved like a wild thing. My jaw dropped as I tried to follower her. I had never seen anyone move like that. She seemed everywhere and nowhere at once, striking and tumbling and parrying at the same time, like a living whirlwind.

Some of the men turned and fled. The sight of two avatars of Kali battling for supremacy in front of them was too much for them to take. Or perhaps they feared what would happen to them should the Kindred lose?

A few took it into their heads to come to the Kindred's aid. They stepped forward, but quickly checked themselves before walking into reach of the battle. The Riggers moved out of the shadows, slipping around to either side of the battle, and interposing themselves between the crowd and the fighting. The few who had stepped forward thought better of it and moved back to join their friends. The locals outnumbered the Riggers, but none of them were willing to take on the larger men.

A loud clang momentarily interrupted the ringing of blade on blade when Tinka's blade struck the joint of a steel arm instead of the sword. The sudden change in the battle rhythm made the combatants hesitate for a brief moment. Tinka recovered first, and she nearly ended the fight right there with a strike to the Kindred's stomach which the other woman barely managed to block.

The tempo of the combat changed. Instead of a constant ringing as the combatants parried each other's blows, a new cadence became apparent. *Ring, ring, ring,* clang! *Ring, ring, ring,* clang!

Tinka targeted the same joint on the Kindred's arm as she cycled through a series of blows over and over again. Tinka's four arms could move independently, while her opponent's steam-powered arms were limited to set patterns defined by the position of her flesh appendages. Tinka used that predictability to her advantage, striking in ways that forced the Kindred to put her damaged mechanical arm where Tinka could hit it again. *Clang!*

The Indian woman saw what Tinka was doing, and she tried to disengage and regain control of the encounter. Unfortunately for her, Tinka was faster, and kept pressing her advantage. The pair circled around each other in the street, Tinka pushing the other woman back and continuing her same assault on that same joint. *Clang! Clang! Clang!*

"Stop her!" the Kindred called as she retreated from Tinka's assault. Sweat drenched her face and plastered her clothing to her body. She panted from the sustained effort. She was tiring already, despite the assistance of the apparatus she wore. A single stumble, and the heavy harness would pin her to the ground, ending the fight.

The priest yelled to his followers in Hindi. By his gestures he urged them to get into the fight and attack Tinka. A few obeyed, and small fights broke out as the Riggers engaged those brave enough to tangle with them. The clash of metal on metal was joined by the thud and scream of club meeting flesh.

A dozen Riggers held their ground, their opponents falling before them as the motley crew of sailors defended the back of their leader. While some of the priest's followers ran off into the night, others of the faithful took the place of the fallen and the crew were slowly beginning to be pushed back.

A man in a dirty tunic and trews rushed screaming between two

Riggers who were engaged with other foes and charged at Tinka. She cut him down with a backhand slash from one of her lower arms, but that moment of distraction permitted the Kindred to regroup. The Kindred charged again, her undamaged set of arms lashing out in a fan of edges from ankle to head height.

Tinka leapt into the air, jumping to meet the Kindred's strike. She blocked the Kindred's blades with her own, and let the power of her opponent's strike push her away. She flew through the air, hit the ground, and rolled to her feet, guard up.

Pistons hissing, the Kindred charged again, all arms raised in an overhead strike that rained razor sharp steel down upon Tinka.

Tinka spun away from the blows and struck out with a single blade. Another clang sounded, but this time the joint parted, sword and forearm falling away as a single piece and rolling across the street to stop by the mouth of the alley where I watched.

The Kindred screamed again, this time in tones of fear rather than rage. She stumbled toward the shrine, hydraulic fluid bleeding out through severed hoses. One by one, her other swords rattled to the ground as she tore at the straps that bound her body to the device, the mechanical arms doing strange gyrations as she worked. One of the Riggers tried to stop her, to knock her down, but she pushed him away, sending him rolling along the street. She staggered through the doors of the shrine before the device failed completely. The woman released the last strap, and fell out of her harness, crawling away into the shrine. The empty harness stood there, just inside the shrine, slowly leaning forward as the hydraulic fluid continued to pour out on the floor, robbing the device of the strength to stand upright.

Tinka stood and panted for a moment, in sole possession of this section of the street. She turned to the dwindling crowd of onlookers, who stared back at her with wide eyes, not sure what she would do next. Tinka raised her blades over her head and screamed, a wordless cry of pure defiance.

This seemed to have the desired effect, as the remaining men turned and ran. The priest snatched torches from the hands of two of the fleeing men and thrust one of them into the kindling beneath the professor's feet. He stuffed the second torch underneath Mrs. Basumatry, who began screaming. The priest then ran through the entrance to the shrine, and closed the doors behind him.

Grabbing the severed forearm from the front of the alley, the sword still firm in its grip, I looked up to see a tall figure dressed in black step out of the darkness behind Mrs. Basumatry and kick away the kindling that was beginning to catch at her feet. She continued screaming as the man moved closer to release her bonds.

Miss Bang and the few Riggers who held themselves in reserve moved forward, bringing the lanterns with them. Those who had been in combat gathered around Mrs. Basumatry and the professor, kicking the burning kindling farther away from them, and cutting their bonds. A couple of the crewmen ran to the door of the shrine and kicked it, to no effect. They hefted their weapons, large metal spanners, and pounded on the door a few times, but it appeared to have been barred on the inside.

Miss Bang ran up to the posts and shined her lantern on the professor and her cousin. "Harmonious? Kashvi? Are you harmed?" she cried.

I carefully approached Tinka, who stood panting heavily. While I had never seen anyone fight as fiercely as Tinka had just done, I had seen other fighters go into a state where they were consumed by the fight, and could no longer tell friend from foe. I wanted to be sure that she was herself again. Keeping well back, I called to her. "Tinka? Are you all right?"

She startled at first; but I breathed a sigh of relief when she recognized me. She motioned for me to come over with one of her blades and I moved closer. As I approached, one of her knees buckled and I rushed forward to catch her. I wrapped my free arm around her, careful to avoid the blades she still gripped in each hand. She threw one of her upper arms over my shoulder, and I helped her stand up straight.

"Are you hurt?" I asked.

She sighed, her breath warm on my chest. "No," she panted. "Just knackered. Ah... I haven't had a workout like that... in I don't know how long. The crew trains with me." She paused to swallow. "But it don't get that intense."

I glanced up to see Miss Bang comforting her cousin, who stopped screaming when she realized she wasn't actually on fire. The shadowy figure stood next to Professor Crackle now, who rubbed his wrists after having his bonds removed. With the light of the lantern directly on him, I recognized the figure as Manqoba, dressed all in black.

I started to move toward them, but Tinka was rooted to the spot, holding on to me. "Tinka? Let's go see how they're getting on."

She roused slightly. "Huh?"

"Let's go see how they're getting on. Miss Bang and the professor."

She leaned into my chest for a moment, then raised her head, the paint on her face and lips smeared across her cheek, and a large amount of it staining my shirt. "Oh. Alright."

We turned and walked to join the others. Tinka leaned on me as we went, still trying to recover her energy spent on the fight.

Miss Bang comforted her cousin and assured her that she was safe, while the professor took a moment to shrug his shoulders and stretch his back before standing up straight. The old fire back in his eyes, he told the Riggers who had freed him to pull one of the poles from the ground and use it as a battering ram. Four of the men made quick work pulling the post from its slot. Several more helped to level it and they began striking the door with a resounding noise.

"Quickly," Professor Crackle cried, "We mustn't let them escape!" The crew redoubled their efforts.

As the post struck the door with another loud boom, I asked Miss Bang, "Isn't that going to attract a lot of attention?"

She shook her head. "No more than the noise that has already been made here tonight. I suspect that anyone who wasn't here earlier is just going to stay away until the noise stops."

With that, the Riggers broke through the door to the shrine and poured into the building. The professor followed on their heels.

Kashvi let out a squeak as the doors banged open, and Miss Bang hugged her cousin. Tinka clung to me for support, no longer buoyed up by adrenaline. "Should we go after him?" I asked Miss Bang.

"No," Miss Bang shook her head. "The Riggers will keep him out of too much trouble. And unless there are more Kindred in the temple, he shouldn't run into anything they can't handle."

"There aren't," said Mrs. Basumatry. "I... I heard them talking while they held us." She paused and swallowed. "They sent word to their leader that we'd been captured. The woman with all the arms was there as a messenger. She... she told the priest to get rid of us. That the site was compromised and it was best to cut all ties. She said their leader wanted it done quickly and quietly, but the priest disagreed." Her eyes widened. "He thought he could use our deaths to stir up more support for their cause."

"And he won that argument?" Miss Bang seemed surprised.

"No. The Kindred just suddenly decided to go along with his plan anyway. She said if a riot broke out, it wouldn't matter as long as we were killed."

"These Kindred of Kali don't seem to be very well coordinated." I observed.

Mrs. Basumatry sighed. "From what I heard, they squabble a lot."

"Did you hear anything about where they took Aunt Phyllis, um, I mean Lady Griffith-Holmes and Maharani Chandrakanta?" I asked.

Kashvi shook her head. "No. They said that they had enough valuable hostages and didn't need any more."

"Well," Miss Bang said, "we now know they have at least one more base of operations."

A couple of Riggers returned from the shrine, with Professor Crackle behind them. The professor did not look happy.

"They got away. There must have been a vehicle waiting. They didn't even leave the exoskeleton behind. There was a bloody trail of hydraulic fluid that lead us right to a loading dock." He shrugged and dropped his hands helplessly.

"Probably the vehicle the Kindred arrived in," I suggested. "But I'm surprised that they could drag it through the building like that."

"I'm sure you're right. I think they managed to drag it with a winch. Most likely one attached to the truck. But in any account, it is gone now and we don't have anything to..." He broke off, looking at Tinka and I standing together. "What have you got there, my boy?"

I hefted the metal forearm, the hand still grasping the sword tightly. "Tinka found a way to ah... disarm the Kindred." Tinka vibrated against me. Laughing. "I picked it up when it came off in the fight."

Tinka nodded. "Yep. A few good whacks in one spot and they're 'armless." She sputtered, laughing at her own joke.

The professor came over and took the arm from me like it was a sacred object . "Absolutely brilliant, Tinka! Well done! Now we have something we can examine for clues. There must be something here. Some clue to tell us who made the machines the Kindred have been using. And if we know who made them, that should lead us to who bought them."

"Professor, shouldn't we inform the authorities about what we've learned here?" I asked.

"No!" Professor Crackle flinched away from me and clutched the arm protectively, as if I'd tried to take it away from him. "No. Not until we have fully examined it. We don't want to distract them with unverified information."

"We can discuss that later, Harmonious. For now, we've made enough of a fuss and we need to get going. We are several hours late in returning Kashvi to her home." Miss Bang squeezed her cousin gently.

"Oh, no!" Kashvi exclaimed. "Ranjeet is sure to have thrown a fit."

"You were almost burned at the stake, and you're worried about how your brother will react?" I asked.

Kashvi and Miss Bang looked at me. Together they said, "You don't know Ranjeet."

Miss Bang turned to Kashvi. "I'm sorry to have gotten you into all this trouble, cousin. I had no idea this would happen."

Kashvi shook her head and said, "No, it was not your fault, Titania. I *wanted* to go. While I think I have had enough of adventures for now, I do not regret anything." She raised her chin proudly for a moment, then dropped her eyes a bit as she raised a finger. "Except perhaps the fire. I could have done without the fire."

"Well, Mrs. Basumatry, let's get you home before we do anything else," I said.

We returned to the wagon, where Tinka handed her blades off to a couple of the Riggers. I then saw that the crew were gathering up the discarded weapons and piling them into a second horse cart parked several yards further back along the street.

When I looked into our wagon, I discovered Bijoy lying bound in the back. "Why is he tied up?" I asked as I draped Tinka's cloak over her shoulders.

"He insisted on it," Miss Bang said. "He wouldn't let us use the wagon unless he came along, but he was too afraid to drive it because he thought he'd turn and run. He insisted we tie him up."

I looked at Bijoy. "Did you really want to be tied up?"

He nodded.

"But why?"

He shrugged his shoulders. "If you win, I am free. If you lose, I tell them you tie me up and take my cart. Bijoy just poor victim of events."

"Really?" I said.

The old man stared up at me from the bed of the cart and said nothing. "Should we untie him now?" I asked Miss Bang. Bijoy nodded vigorously.

"Yes, it should be fine. We're leaving here anyway."

I untied Bijoy and he rubbed his wrists and ankles, thanking me, then climbed into his seat.

Miss Bang and her cousin climbed into the bed, with the professor right behind, still clutching the severed arm of the Kindred harness. Tinka's knee bucked when she went to get into the cart and she nearly fell, so I picked her up and set her in the cart. She insisted I climb up next to her, which seemed odd to me, but I pulled myself up into the back of the cart and scooted next to her. Tinka promptly crawled into my lap and huddled against my chest, surprising me further. Bijoy set the cart in motion and we settled in for the journey back to Mrs. Basumatry's house.

CHAPTER ELEVEN
A QUESTION OF TRUST

Mr. Bhang was livid when we returned his sister.

Ranjeet stormed out of the house wearing a long white nightshirt as we pulled up in front of it. The housekeeper, Indira, trailed out of the house in his wake, a plain robe wrapped tightly around her body.

"How dare you! How dare you!" he raged at us. "You come into my house without my knowledge and steal my sister away into the night. I should have you up on charges for kidnapping! The lot of you." He glared at the Riggers, but they ignored him and waited while we dealt with him.

I noticed lights in a few of the neighboring houses as people heard the noise. A few curtains also twitched aside as the occupants looked out to see who was making such racket in the night.

Mrs. Basumatry stood up in the horse cart and matched her brother's ire. "Ranjeet, it is *not* your house! It is my husband's house and you are a guest. I went with them of my own free will!" Two of the Riggers stepped up to the side of the wagon and raised their hands to help her down. She took their hands and they caught her just under her shoulders. She stepped over the rail and they deposited her lightly on the ground. "Oh, thank you."

They tugged their caps at her.

Ranjeet rushed up to the two large crewmen and tried to push them away from Kashvi, but only managed to slap them ineffectively on the chest. "Get away from my sister, you dirty brutes! How dare you put your hands on her! This is just like you British! You think you can come here and take what you want. Well, I won't have it in my house!"

Kashvi corrected her brother again. "It is *not* your house. Ranjeet, stop being an ass."

He turned on her. "I am your brother! You do not talk to me like this. How dare you go gallivanting off, embarrassing the family like this! Go to your room! I will have more to say to you when I am done with these people."

Mrs. Basumatry rolled her eyes at her brother and waved to the rest of us. "Goodnight, Titania. Thank you so much for coming over and visiting. I hope you will be able to stop by again, although next time we'll have to pass on the outing."

"Into the house, woman!" her brother snapped.

She snorted and turned her back on him.

"And as for you," Mr. Bhang said, turning on Miss Bang, who raised an eyebrow as he pointed at her. "You keep away from us. You won't be getting any money from us, so don't even try."

Kashvi walked across the lawn, gathered up Indira by the door and went into the house as Miss Bang calmly addressed her other cousin. "Ranjeet, I have not asked you or Kashvi for money, nor do I have any intention of doing so."

The door to the house closed, and for a brief moment, in the evening air, we could hear the click as Mrs. Basumatry locked the door behind her.

"Hah!" her cousin scoffed, unaware that his sister had shut him out of the house. "What else does a penniless orphan like you do but beg for money? I have had enough of your interference with the family. Taking my sister off and endangering her as part of whatever scheme you're up to."

Miss Bang shook her head.

"And you!" Now Ranjeet was pointing at Professor Crackle and myself. I'm not sure how he spotted me sitting in the wagon, covered with a shapeless ball that was the exhausted Tinka covering my lap, but he managed to single me out for his ire. "You so-called English nobles! Go back to England and leave our Indian girls alone!" He spat at us.

"Now see here, my good man," the professor started as he stood up in the cart, but Miss Bang grabbed his arm.

"It's no good, Harmonious. He won't listen."

As if to prove her point, Mr. Bhang started screaming again. "Don't you tell me to listen! You're not going to come into my country, into my house, lay waste to it, and then try to lecture me on civilized behavior! My people were building cities when your ancestors were still dressing in furs like savages!"

"Let's go," Miss Bang said as the professor sat back down. Bijoy shook the reins and we moved down the street to turn the carts around. Mr. Bhang continued to scream dire imprecations at us, but seemed to lose some steam when we ignored him. By the time we had turned the wagons and returned to pass the house, he was pounding on the front door.

"Kashvi! Indira! Open this door! Unlock this door immediately, do you hear me? Kashvi!" He continued to pound on the door, but the lights inside the house went out, leaving him stranded outside.

Bijoy clucked to the horse and shook the reins again, and we picked up speed.

As we left the neighborhood, I could faintly hear him calling, "I'm still out here, you know! Hello? Let me in!"

When we returned to my aunt's house, it was obvious that the Riggers were busy before Miss Bang called them away to rescue the professor and her cousin. An oil lantern hung on a metal hook planted in the front yard, lighting the front of the house. Some of the vehicles were missing, presumably retrieved by their owners. The remaining ones had been moved to the edges of the yard where they were no longer in the way. It was now relatively easy to navigate to the front door where a temporary wall with a simple door now replaced the damaged entryway.

Bijoy dropped us off at the front step. Tinka had fallen asleep in my lap on the trip back. One of the Riggers came and gently picked her up so I could slip off the back of the cart. He then held her up for me to take her back.

"Um, would you mind terribly taking her into the house? I'm sure we can find a bed for her." I asked.

He shook his head. "Sorry, Mr. B, but she wouldn't like that. She chose you to look after her. She'd be very upset if I were to butt in."

"And you don't want her to be angry at you?"

He snorted softly. "No, mate. I don't want her to be angry at *you*."

"Oh," I said. He waited patiently while that thought processed through my mind for a few seconds. Then he handed her back to me.

Once Tinka was nestled in my arms, he raised a hand and tugged his forelock. "Good night, Mr. B," he said and turned, following the rest of the Riggers to see about putting the house's wagon away and tending the horses.

Professor Crackle handed a coin to the driver and asked for him to return the next morning. Bijoy looked at the coin in his hand for a long moment, then closed his hand around it as if he was afraid it might vanish. He promised he would return very promptly in the morning, and that he'd very much be at our service.

I carried Tinka up the steps as Miss Bang opened the door to the house. I stepped over the threshold and carried her into the house. As we stood in the foyer, Manqoba called out a pair of names, and two of the housemaids appeared. When they saw Tinka in my arms, they both smiled. I was glad she was bundled up in a cloak and her extra arms weren't apparent. Manqoba told them to prepare a second bed in Miss Bang's room and they hurried up the stairs.

Manqoba attempted to take Tinka from me, but she wouldn't have it. While she wasn't fully wake, she held on to me, two hands gripping my shirt front. After a couple attempts to get her to release me, he patted her hands and settled for leading me up to Miss Bang's room, where a pallet bed was laid out by the window and the maids just finished making the bed. They pulled back the sheets and I slid Tinka between them. When I tried to stand, I found that she still held onto my shirt front.

"Tinka," I said, "you're safe now. The fight is done, and you're among friends. You can relax and sleep now." I pried at her fingers with a little gentle pressure and I was able to get her to release her grip after the fourth repetition.

I looked down at the stains on my shirt as I stood and stepped back, while the maids tucked the blankets around her. "I'm afraid she will stain the sheets," I said. "She still has paint on her face and arms."

"Do not worry, sir," the older of the two maids answered. She looked up at me and smiled, her dark eyes bright and glowing. "We will take care of her. It is our honor."

"Ah... Thank you."

Manqoba appeared at my shoulder. "I understand that you've had an extremely long and harrowing day, my lord. If you would like, I can arrange for some refreshments downstairs in the private dining room."

"Thank you, Manqoba, that would be excellent."

"Then I will see you downstairs, my lord."

After changing out of my soiled clothes and washing off some of the paint that had rubbed off of Tinka, I made my way downstairs and found the private dining room. This room was considerably smaller than the main one, which stretched along the back of the house. Miss Bang and the professor were already there when I arrived. The professor, still in his scorched clothes from earlier, sat at one end of the table, examining the mechanical forearm. As I sat down, he managed to pry the sword from the grip of the metal hand. He produced a small case from one of the many pockets in his vest and opened it up on the table, displaying a number of tools within. He pulled a tool out and tried to use it to open the casing on the arm. It looked oddly grisly, as the severed tubes running from the device still leaked drops of red hydraulic fluid, making the tablecloth appear to be stained with blood.

"Professor? Perhaps it might not be the best idea to work on that forearm down here?" I asked. "Especially not on top of my aunt's linens."

"Yes, it is a fascinating piece of workmanship," he replied. "The skill with which these seams are joined is amazing." He didn't even look up from his work, but dropped the device in his hand on the table and applied a new tool to the seam.

I placed my hand on his shoulder. "Professor, as fascinating as it may be, you shouldn't be doing that here."

"I think there's a catch inside that holds it shut. I just need to figure out how to open it." He picked up the arm and looked closely at the seams around the severed elbow.

I looked at Miss Bang.

She shrugged. "I tried. He seems wholly engrossed with the object."

"Why did he bring it back down here?" I asked her.

She shook her head. "He didn't. As near as I can tell, when we went upstairs, he came in here and started trying to examine it."

I got up and pulled on the professor's shoulders, forcing him to stand up and look at me. "If Willie walks in and sees this he'll have no choice but to confiscate it and hand it over to the colonel," I said speaking slowly and emphasizing each word.

His eyes drifted back to the metal arm until I said "colonel". That word made him blink. He blinked at me several times, as if his mind was trying to catch up on the conversation.

"I'm sorry, my boy, what did you say?"

"I said, Professor, that if my brother comes in here and sees you playing with that arm, he will be duty bound to confiscate it and turn it over to Colonel Ticking. If you want to hold on to this piece of evidence, you need to keep it in your room, out of sight."

"Oh, yes. Yes. Excellent point. I think I shall go ahead and retire to my room." He grabbed the arm in one hand and picked up the tools in the other without bothering to close the case. As he started for the door, small tools rained down on the floor.

"Harmonious, hold up a moment." Miss Bang rose from her seat, picked up a pair of implements left on the table, and collected the tools scattered on the floor. She took the case from him and carefully slotted the scattered tools back into their places before closing the case and handing it back to him.

I picked up the sword from the table. "You'll need to hide this, too, Professor, or Willie will be wondering what we've been up to."

"Ah, of course." His free hand wandered back and forth between trying to take the tools from Miss Bang and trying to take the sword from me.

Miss Bang reached out and took his hand with her free one. "Harmonious, why don't you let Manqoba take these upstairs. He'll be able to do so without running into Lieutenant Holmes in the hallways. Besides, you've had a harrowing day. Come and sit with us and take dinner. There will be plenty of time to work with the arm later."

"But... but..."

"No need to worry, sir. I will take excellent care of your equipment," Manqoba said as he gently pried the metal arm from the professor's fingers. He approached so silently I hadn't even been aware he was there until he spoke. Somehow, he'd even found a moment to change back into his butler's livery. He cradled the tool case against the mechanical arm and took the sword from me. "I will return momentarily, sir. Please sit. A light repast is being prepared."

Miss Bang guided the professor over to the table and made him sit down next to her at the end away from the hydraulic fluid stains. I crossed and sat on the opposite side of the table.

"I waited for hours, Miss Bang," I said. "I thought you were going to gather reinforcements and be right back. What took so long?"

"I do apologize for that, Sir Richard. Tinka proved considerably more recalcitrant than I expected. It took a lot of time to convince her, but we needed her for the plan to work."

"How did you know she'd be able to beat the Kindred woman?"

"I didn't, my lord. She wasn't supposed to fight at all. We needed her as a distraction to keep the crowd at bay long enough for Manqoba to get into place. I figured that if they were impressed with the Kindred, they'd think twice once they saw a real woman with four arms. They needed to be kept guessing while Manqoba freed the prisoners. I didn't expect Tinka to actually cross swords with the Kindred!"

"It's just as well that she did," the professor said. "Otherwise we would be out of leads."

"She could have been killed, Harmonious! If another Kindred had been there, they would have cut her to ribbons."

"But she wasn't, my dear. Tinka acquitted herself quite well."

"She fought like a demon, Professor," I said. "I don't think I've ever seen someone move so fast in all my life." I looked to Miss Bang. "But if she wasn't supposed to fight, why was she so reluctant to come?"

"She didn't want to be seen, my lord. She is very sensitive about her appearance. While she's comfortable with everyone on board, now." The look she gave me was a bit pointed. "She still has considerable anxiety about being seen by outsiders. In the end she only agreed because I promised that she'd be disguised and that no one would recognize her."

"Is that why she was painted up so much?"

Miss Bang shook her head. "I'm afraid that was the household staff's idea."

"The household staff? You mean the housemaids here?" I asked.

Miss Bang didn't answer as two housemaids came in bearing trays. They set them on the sideboard and uncovered them, allowing the smells of food to waft into the room. The two women left as quietly as they came.

I leaned toward Miss Bang. "Those women?"

She nodded. "Yes. Tinka came into the building to roust the rest of her crew, but then the housemaids saw her. They called her 'blessed child' and were fawning all over her. They would have kept Tinka here, but we told them that we needed her to put a scare into some bad men. They jumped straight into action, and produced the entire costume and painted her up as an avatar of Kali."

"Is, is that where the whole 'daughter of Kali' thing came from?"

"Yes. It was their idea." She nodded

"Do you think we can trust them?" I looked nervously to the door.

"Why wouldn't we be able to trust them, my boy?" the professor asked.

"If they're Kali worshipers, doesn't that make them the enemy? Wouldn't they side with the Kindred?"

Miss Bang gave me a look that reminded me of most of my school-teachers. "Kali is a major deity in the Hindu religion, my lord. While there aren't many temples dedicated to her, she is present and revered in almost every temple. She is considered both a goddess and a force of nature."

"But isn't she the goddess of destruction?" I said.

"And of creation. And time, my lord. To certain schools of philosophy, Kali literally *is* the universe."

"Then why did we seek out a Kali temple?" I asked.

"Because, my boy, whomever these Kindred people are, they're using the widespread belief in Kali to turn otherwise innocent people

to their cause. That's an abomination whatever faith one holds dear."
The professor looked at me over the top of his glasses. "Haven't you
ever seen someone twist religious belief and try to use it for their own
ends?"

I swallowed. Unsure of how to answer his question, I plowed on.
"We're using our fake avatar of Kali to fight their fake avatar of Kali?"

Miss Bang shook her head. "Not exactly. Kali is the creator of the
universe. Everyone is a daughter or son of Kali, strictly speaking.
That certainly includes Tinka."

"I'm not sure people will see it that way."

"Then we shall make sure no one else finds out, my lord. Please. I
trust the staff, and the chicken and curry they brought up smells delicious. Shall we?" Miss Bang stood up and the professor and I
followed suit. We helped ourselves from the sideboard and returned
to the table to eat.

The food *was* delicious.

It consisted of chunks of baked chicken, rice, and three different
curry sauces. Some delightfully tasty flat bread, an assortment of
Indian pastry, and a variety of candied nuts.

We were still eating when my brother poked his head in.

"There you are! I've been wondering what you've been up to all
day," he said. "Uncle Jeremy hasn't been much for company today. It
has been maddeningly quiet. I ended up napping most of the afternoon. When I got up, it seemed like all your crewmen had pulled up
stakes and left." He went to the sideboard and helped himself to a
plate of the waiting curry. "Where've you been?"

"Um..." I started, unsure of what to tell him.

"We paid a visit to my cousin, Mrs. Basumatry." Miss Bang said.
"She took us out to see some of the local temples and shrines. I'm
afraid we kept her out quite a bit later than we had intended. Her
brother was most cross."

"That's it? Visiting and sight-seeing? You've been gone absolutely
all day."

"Well, Mrs. Basumatry is a charming hostess," I said. I looked around in a panic while I tired to think of what else to tell him, and saw the stains in the tablecloth at the far end of the table! "And uh, the professor has a huge interest in history." While Willie's back was still turned, I picked up my mostly empty plate and moved it down the table, trying to cover the stains with it. The stain was too large to cover with a single plate. I turned to Miss Bang and threw my hand out for something else to use. Miss Bang plucked the professor's plate out from in front of him and handed it to me. "Once he gets stuck into something, the hours just seem to fly by."

"What?" the professor said. "Oh. Oh, yes. I guess I do tend to lose track of time when I find something of interest. For instance, the architecture of the area is surprisingly advanced for its age." I put the other plate at the far end of the table and slid back into my seat, trying to look as if I hadn't moved at all. The professor, somewhat confused at having his plate snatched out from in front of him, lowered his hand to the table, still holding his fork.

Miss Bang put her hand over the professor's. "Another time, Harmonious. I don't think Lieutenant Holmes really wants to discuss comparative architecture."

"Oh? Well, another time, then, Lieutenant." At Miss Bang's urging, the professor put his fork down on the table.

Willie pulled up a chair and sat down. "No, I mean you, brother. History was never your subject. Weren't you incredibly bored all day?" He began eating, shoveling food into his mouth.

My mind leapt back to the hours I spent keeping a watch upon the shrine and hiding out in the alley. I hesitated for a moment, then said, "Actually, I think I've learned a lot from traveling with the professor and Miss Bang. They certainly have a way of explaining things that is much more interesting than anything my teachers or professors ever said. They have a way of making information seem more relevant and... immediate."

"Why thank you, my boy! High praise indeed," the professor said.

"Very kind of you to say so, my lord."

My brother stared at me.

"Are you all right, Willie?" I asked.

"You have changed."

"Well, haven't we all? Lots of things have happened since we last saw each other."

He shook his head. "No, I don't mean that. I mean, you *never* really liked school. You only went to University because Father insisted. You even said that the only reason you studied kinesthesiology was because it was more about doing than about book learning."

"Kinesiology. And I was bloody well wrong about that. There was tons of book learning."

Miss Bang sat up. "You studied kinesiology, my lord? The science of human motion?"

"Yes. That's what my degrees are in."

"Then you're a fellow colleague! A scientist, like us." Professor Crackle grinned broadly.

"I guess so. I never really thought about it." I paused for a moment, then shook my head. "We're getting off track. You were saying, Willie. How have I changed?"

He stopped for a moment to swallow. "I never thought that you would have turned into a man who appreciates knowledge for its own sake."

"I'm not sure how to take that." I frowned at my brother.

"No, no. It's a good thing. Really."

"I've learned that a lot of things have more practical applications that I ever dreamed when I was a boy. I guess I've got a lot of catching up to do."

Willie looked at me, and his lips bent into a slight grin. "I don't think you're catching up. I think you're finding your stride. I can't wait to see what you'll do next." He put his fork down on his empty plate and stood up. "Well, it is late. I guess I had better turn in for the night. I suppose you'll be doing more sightseeing tomorrow?"

Miss Bang answered for us. "Quite possibly. I think we've had a full enough day that we'll sleep on it and discuss our plans in the morning."

"I see. Well, good night." Willie turned to the door.

I went after him, following him into the hall. "Willie, I... I was hoping that I could ask you a favor."

He paused. "Sure, what do you need?"

I hesitated. "Do you think... I mean." I sighed. "Can you get me a gun?"

"What?"

"A pistol. Can you get me a pistol? All this stuff with the Kindred of Kali and the attack yesterday. I'm a bit concerned. I don't know when they're going to strike again. I thought it might be a good idea to have some protection along. Just in case."

He turned back to me. "Are you sure about this, brother?"

"Yes," I nodded. "I've given it a lot of thought."

He shook his head slightly. "I can't get you a military pistol, you know. They're all rigorously accounted for."

"I know that, but if there was some place where one could purchase a pistol, I figure you'd know better than I. And I need someone to show me how to take care of the thing."

"How to take care of it?" He cocked his head at me. "How to clean it? Have you ever even held a pistol, brother? I remember you were always a bit rubbish at hunting."

I nodded. "I have held a pistol. I have shot one. I know what I'm doing. It was a bit of a special circumstance." I waved my hand ambiguously and did not elaborate.

"Were you in a duel?" He furrowed his brows at me.

"Not exactly. Look." I put my hand on his shoulder. "If I can show you that I know how to handle a pistol safely, do you think you can get me one and show me how to maintain it?"

Willie thought for a moment, rubbing his chin with one hand. "That sounds fair. Let me talk to Uncle Jeremy in the morning. I think he has a few of his own pistols. There's a spot at the back of the property where he sometimes goes to shoot targets. If you can delay your excursions until the afternoon, we can head out to the range in the morning. Show me that you can handle a gun, and I'll help convince Uncle Jeremy to let you borrow one of his pistols while you're here. Good?"

I clapped him on the shoulder. "Perfect. Thank you, Willie."

"But if you're rubbish, you can forget it. Agreed?"

I grinned. "Agreed. I think you're in for a surprise."

"We'll see. Good night."

"Good night, Willie."

CHAPTER TWELVE
THE PROOF IN THE PISTOL

After breakfast the next morning, Willie grabbed me, and we set off across the yard. He had a case tucked up under his arm.

"How far are we going?" I asked.

"Quite a ways. When I said that it was at the back of the property, I wasn't kidding. Aunt Phyllis didn't want it anywhere near the house."

"Well, I can't say I blame her. Wouldn't want the noise or the concern of a stray bullet hitting the house. I guess when we get her back, she'll probably insist that he get rid of it."

"Or she'll take up shooting as well."

I looked at my brother. "Aunt Phyllis has never needed a weapon to dole out injuries."

He laughed.

We finally came to the back of the property and Uncle Jeremy's target range. It consisted of three six-foot-tall earthen berms forming the backstop and sides of the range, with three wooden targets set up at the far end. The targets were roughly man-shaped, with concentric circles of white and red paint centered on the point where the heart would be on a man. On the opposite side of the range, there was a low stone wall. Willie placed his case down upon the wall and opened it up to reveal three pistols inside. One was a simple revolver. The other two were semi-automatic pistols, like the one I had used in Prague. One pistol was considerably heavier, and took larger caliber ammunition.

Willie hefted the revolver, rotated the cylinder out to the loading position, and began dropping rounds into each chamber. "We'll start with the revolver. It's pretty simple as guns go. Easy to maintain. Very little that can go wrong."

I gave him a hard look. "You're expecting me to mess this up."

He held a hand up defensively. "No, no. It's a good, reliable weapon. You said you don't know about maintaining a gun, so I thought we'd start with the simplest gun first. That's all."

"Really."

"Come on. Let's see you shoot. Do you need me to show you anything about the gun?" He placed the revolver down on the wall. I waited until he withdrew his arm and then reached for it. The pistol was heavy. I hefted it, keeping the barrel pointed downrange. The balance seemed off. It felt barrel heavy. The metal of the cylinder was cold against my extended index finger. I adjusted my grip so my finger was clear of the cylinder and laid across the trigger guard. Cocking the hammer, I lifted the gun to shoulder height.

"OK. What's my target?"

"Left hand target. Aim for the center of mass."

"Not the bullseye on the heart?"

"Let's start with the center of mass and work up."

"Very well."

I pushed my hand forward and squeezed off a single shot. Then I dropped my hand to the wall and put the revolver down.

"Giving up?" Willie said.

"You said center of mass. I hit the center of mass."

"Look, go ahead and shoot the rest of the rounds. I need to see how well you group your shots. Then we'll go see how well you hit the target. You never go downrange while there's a loaded gun on the firing line."

"Very well." I picked up the revolver and cocked it again. I pointed the gun at the target and squeezed off five more rounds in quick succession. I rotated the cylinder out and shook out the spent brass onto the top of the wall. Snapping the cylinder back into place, I put it back down on the wall, the barrel angled at the right-hand berm.

"Well, you do seem familiar with your weapon. Let's go see how well you did."

We walked around the wall to the left side and strode down the range. As we went, Willie peered downrange to try to make out holes in the target. The farther we went, the more he sped up, until he broke into a run.

When I caught up to him, he was bending close to the target, rubbing his fingers along the edge of six fresh holes arranged vertically in the center of the figure. "Unbelievable."

"Yes. I'm still getting used to it."

Willie shook his head. "If this is what you can do with an unfamiliar gun..." He let out a low whistle.

I shook my head. "No, no. That's not what I meant."

He looked at me. "How long have you been training?"

I shrugged. "I haven't. I shot a pistol in Prague. And then once on the way here. It just... comes to me. I think about where I want the bullet to go, and it goes there."

Willie shook his head. "But this isn't possible." He pointed to the target. "The revolver isn't accurate at this range. You shouldn't be able to place your shots this precisely."

"The first shot pulled to the left. I compensated so the others lined up with it. I didn't really think about it, I just... did it."

His mouth worked a few times, but Willie didn't say anything.

"Let's go try the other two. I don't really like the revolver. It feels too front heavy," I said.

We walked back to the wall at the other end of the range. Willie put the now cooled revolver back into the case and pulled out another weapon. "This is a .45. It is a heavier pistol, but it has more stopping power."

"What does that mean?"

"It puts a bigger hole in your target. Between shock, damage, and blood loss, your target is more likely to go down on the first shot. Especially if you can place your shots like you just did." He gave me an odd look. "Are you sure you never considered a career in the Army?"

"Definitely not. I've never been one for taking orders."

"I guess that's true." He handed me the pistol. "Here, you load this one."

"I've never loaded one of these," I admitted. "The ones I used before were loaded by someone else."

"Then you'll have no bad habits to unlearn." He held up a magazine. "This is the magazine. It holds eight rounds. But even when the magazine is out of the gun, you must assume the gun is loaded. If there was a round in the chamber when the magazine was ejected, it will still be there, and the gun will be able to fire."

"Right. So, what do I do?"

He handed me the magazine. "There is a spring inside to push the cartridges up so the next one can be pulled into the chamber." He pointed to the top of the magazine, where the metal of the outside casing pulled away to show a grooved metal piece underneath. He pushed on the groove with his finger and it dipped a bit. "See? This opening faces forward in the gun when the magazine is loaded, so to put ammunition in, you need to line the bullet up along the groove, push down, and slide it back into the magazine."

"I line it up with the groove and push it back?" I placed a round on top of the magazine, putting the ridge at the back of the cartridge up against the place where the metal started to slope away.

"Yes. Give it a push and slide it back."

I pushed down with my thumb and pushed on the front of the round. It slid back into place.

"Good. Now do that seven more times. As the spring compresses, it gets harder to push the new round in, but you should be able to do it." He watched as I slotted the remaining rounds into the magazine. The last round almost slipped out of my hand as I tried to slide it into the magazine, but I got it loaded.

"Right. It will get easier with practice." He took the magazine back from me. "Before inserting the magazine, you want to clear the chamber, always assuming there is already a bullet in there."

"How do I do that?"

"Pull the slide. Be careful, the spring is pretty strong, too. Grab the back of the slide with your left hand and pull it back as far as it will go." I picked up the gun and did as he instructed, pulling the slide back and holding it open at the end of its range of motion.

"This isn't very easy."

"Just let it go." I did and the top of the pistol snapped back into place. "If there had been a round in the chamber, pulling back the slide would have ejected it. For now, just know that you can pull it back and let it go to clear the chamber. That's called racking the slide. Now before I give you this magazine, you see that switch on the side?" He pointed to a small lever on the side of the body.

"The safety?"

"Yes. Engage it, and you won't be able to pull the trigger. But don't trust it. On some models of gun it can slip back easily enough, or if the gun has seen lots of use, the safety may be worn down enough it doesn't hold."

"Then why have it?"

"Because when it works, it helps prevent accidents."

"I guess that makes sense."

"Engage the safety." I did so. "Right. Now take this magazine and push it all the way up into the grip. It will snap in. Slap it up in there to make sure it is seated properly."

I did as he said, hearing a slight click as the magazine slid all the way into the pistol.

"Now disengage the safety and pull the slide back again to chamber the round."

I flipped the safety to the firing position, then pulled the slide back and let it spring forward.

"That is now a live weapon," Willie said as he took a step back to stand behind me and off to one side. "Aim for the center target this time. Let's see what you can do."

"Am I still shooting for center of mass?"

"You tell me. You're the gun savant."

"Let me go for the bullseye this time," I said. The .45 felt heavy but was better balanced in my hand. I remembered what Willie had said about it making larger holes. "Eight shots. A ring around the edge with the last one in the center."

"What?" said Willie, but I was already firing and the noise of the gun drowned out any comments. With my last shot, the red bullseye on the center target popped out and fell to the ground. The slide on the gun also caught in the fully open position. My ears rang. This gun was much louder than the revolver, and the air was filled with the smell of burnt gunpowder.

"Did something go wrong?" I asked, looking down at the pistol.

"No. They're made to do that when the magazine is empty." He showed me the lever to release the magazine. I ejected the spent magazine and caught it in my left hand. I put the pistol and the magazine down on the wall.

Willie pointed to the top of the magazine. "See that ridge right there?" He indicated a point at the front end of the magazine, at the end of the groove that the round sits on. "That bit pushes a lever inside the gun that makes it lock open. You can rack the slide to release it." He also pointed out a small lever that could be used to lock or unlock the gun.

As we were walking downrange Willie asked, "How did you like the .45?"

"It seems a little heavy. It packs quite a kick. And it is louder than I expected."

"Yes, sorry about that. I should have found some earplugs before we headed out here this morning." He pointed to the large hole in the target. "But it doesn't seem to have affected your accuracy."

"True. But I remember hearing something about how rate of fire is an important consideration."

"It is."

"With only eight shots in a magazine, I'd have to reload more often. If we got mobbed, that would be a problem."

Willie shook his head. "There's no time to reload a magazine in real combat. You want to carry extra loaded magazines with you. You can swap out magazines quickly, but you need to find a secure space to reload. If you get mobbed, your best bet is to shoot them while they're far enough away from you. If you're lucky, they'll slow down, and you can run away."

I looked at my brother. "I'm surprised to hear you say that."

"Don't be. It's good advice. We teach soldiers how to stand and take a charge, but we also teach officers to know when taking the charge will get your men killed for nothing. If a large group is charging you, your best bet is to make them slow down, and then put as much distance between you as possible. If the mob doesn't slow down, they'll run you over and trample you. You might survive that, but you definitely won't escape without a scratch. The more even the sides are, the easier it will be to take the charge."

"I never really thought about it like that."

He gave me a sad look. "Neither do most of the soldiers. If you can shoot like this when push comes to shove, take out as many kneecaps as you can, and run."

"You've learned a lot about guns in the military, haven't you?" I said.

He nodded. "I've learned about the weapons that we use in combat. And I've picked up some from some of the lads who've made a hobby of it. A lot of chaps in uniform take up gun collecting as a hobby."

"Did you ever fire a lighting rifle?"

He shook his head. "Not so lucky. Those are reserved for special detail. But we do have a few of them at the base, and I have heard them being fired. Those are noisy."

"I know."

He gave me a sidelong look. "When did you ever see a lightning rifle fired?"

"I haven't," I said, "but when I was in Prague I was there when the Crown Prince was attacked. I picked up one of his bodyguard's lighting pistols and shot the assassin." The memory of the smell of burning flesh from firing that weapon at close range came back to me. I could just imagine the devastation the larger version could cause.

My brother stopped in his tracks.

"You fired a lightning pistol? You realize that it is unheard of a civilian to get a hold of one of those?" He seemed shocked.

I nodded. "It was... gruesome. Perhaps we can talk about that later. What do you think of my shooting?" I said as we arrived at the row of targets.

The center target now had a heptagonal hole instead of a bullseye, a portion of a bullet hole at each vertex and a ragged tear along the sides where the weathered wood splintered. Willie walked behind the target and picked up the piece broken off the bullseye. He whistled as he stood. "I don't believe it." He held up the piece of wood. There was a single bullet hole in the center. The exact center.

I felt the hairs stand up on my arms and the back of my neck. A coldness spread down my body, and I shivered lightly. "If it is any consolation, I have chills," I said.

"Not so much, no."

"Fair enough."

We walked back to the top of the range.

The last pistol was a 9mm. It looked very similar to the weapon Lord Scaleslea's guards had in Prague. The balance felt much nicer than the other two guns. It fit better in my hand. The word "Armolt" was stamped along the side of the slide.

I pointed to the name. "Is this the manufacturer?"

He nodded. "Yes, a relatively new pistol maker out of Cornwall. One of the soldiers under Uncle Jeremy's command was the son of one of the partners. The boy was wounded in the line of duty, and the father gave this gun to our uncle as a thank you for bringing him home alive."

Willie handed me the magazine.

"How many in this one?" I asked.

"Seventeen rounds. You've got a larger magazine, but smaller bullets. I've seen a man get hit with a 9mm and still keep fighting. You might be better off with the .45."

I started loading bullets into the magazine. "That depends on where I hit them, doesn't it?"

"Well, yes, but you can't always be sure of hitting where you want to."

I arched an eyebrow at him.

He rolled his eyes. "Most people can't be sure of hitting where they want to. And you're still shooting at stationary targets. A moving target is a very different thing."

"Like shooting skeet?"

"Yes, that's one example. Wait. Have you shot skeet?"

"Ask Miss Bang to tell you about it when all this is over. It was an interesting experiment." I pushed the last bullet into the magazine. It wasn't as difficult as loading the .45-caliber ammunition. I inserted the magazine into the gun with a quick slap.

"Not bad, but don't get too cocky," Willie said. "Aim at the right-hand target."

I lifted the pistol and squeezed off three quick shots. Dropped the gun slightly and fired four more times. Dropped it again and shot two more times.

I ejected the magazine and placed it on the wall. The holes on the back of the magazine indicated there were still seven rounds in it. I kept the gun pointed downrange. "There's still a round in there, right?"

"Yes. You have to eject it."

"I pull the slide?"

"Yes."

I pulled the slide, and the round bounced out and away from me. "I think this one will work for me." I put the gun down on the wall.

"What did you do this time?"

"Let's go see."

We walked downrange and examined the right-hand target. There were three holes in the head of the target in a line about where a person's eyes would be. There were four more holes in the bullseye, and two holes lower down, approximately where a man's knees would be.

"Right. I'll talk to Uncle Jeremy about letting you borrow the gun while you're here. I'll put together some of the things you'll need and tonight I'll show you how to strip it and clean it."

"Thank you, Willie."

"You can thank me by helping to pick up the spent brass. And find that last bullet."

CHAPTER THIRTEEN
AN ENCOUNTER WITH P.G. HOLYFIELD

The professor and Miss Bang were waiting for us on the back porch of the house when we came walking back from the range. While Miss Bang sat in a rattan chair in the shade, the professor paced up and down the porch until we drew close. I noted that Professor Crackle was still in the clothes he had been wearing the day before.

"I hope you enjoyed your constitutional, my boy. Titania insisted that we wait until you came back." I got the distinct feeling that if she hadn't done so, they would both have been gone a while ago.

"More sight-seeing?" Willie asked.

The professor opened his mouth, but Miss Bang spoke before he could say anything. "Something like that, Lieutenant. There is a lot of rich history here. It took us a while to figure out what we wanted to see next. We didn't want for Sir Richard to miss out on our excursion."

My brother shook his head. "I'm still not used to people calling you 'Sir Richard'."

"Neither am I," I replied.

"Well, enjoy your trip," Willie said as he entered the building. "I'll go check in on Uncle Jeremy."

"We'll see you later," I called after him. We watched as he went into the house. When he was out of sight, I continued in a hushed tone. "You found something, Professor?"

"Yes, my boy. I believe I have." He reached into his pocket and pulled out a small piece of metal, holding it up victoriously before him.

I looked it over carefully. "And what is this?"

"A clue!" He practically giggled. "A lead to whomever made those exoskeletons." He pointed to one side of the oddly shaped piece. "See, right there."

I took the item from him and looked where he indicated. Something seemed to be stamped into the side of the oddly shaped part. "I can't make it out."

The professor handed me a jeweler's loupe. I held it up to one eye and examined the item again. Pressed into the side of the part, on a very small scale, was a small gear with a star overlaid upon it. I looked up. "Holyfield Industries?"

"Yes! Precisely! Holyfield Industries manufactured this part. Now all we have to do is get them to tell us who they have been selling these pieces to."

"But, Professor, Holyfield Industries has factories all over the world. There is no telling where this part was made. Even if it was made at a factory near here, there's no reason why they would even tell us who they sold them to. It's not like we have any authority to make them tell us anything."

"True. But we have one advantage in getting the information."

"And that would be?"

"We know P. G. Holyfield," he said with glee.

I looked to Miss Bang. She made the slightest of shrugs with her shoulders, and then turned to follow the professor through the house to Bijoy's waiting cart.

The Holyfield Industries factory was on the western edge of the town, next to the river. It was a huge building covered in sheet metal and windows, dominated by two brick smokestacks that belched thick ribbons of white smoke. Waves of heat rippled off the building, more from the machines inside than from the relentless sunshine. A smell of hot steel and brick tinged the air, but we were far enough away to be spared other scents. While the doors to the factory stood wide open, we didn't see much activity. We heard machines working inside, but there was very little traffic into or out of the building. Presumably all the factory workers were at their stations, working.

Another building showed considerably more activity. This was a smaller, three story building made of brick. People were coming in and out of the entrance. Some loitered nearby, talking or smoking. Others entered and left the premises. A few more crossed from the main building to the factory floor.

The professor pointed to the smaller building. "That would be the administration building. That's where we'll find our answers."

"Are you sure about this, Professor?" I asked.

"Of course, my boy. What could go wrong?"

Miss Bang didn't say anything, but squared her shoulders and followed the professor. I sighed and followed along in their wake.

We crossed over to the brick building and entered through the main doors. We found a cramped lobby inside with a pair of benches along each side and a large desk blocking the path to a pair of double doors. On one wall, in the space between the benches and the desk was a large framed portrait of an old man in a wheelchair with a plaid blanket across his lap. His face was pale and covered in age spots, and his thinning hair was grey. Small tufts of black hair showed at the edges of his eyebrows and along the sides of his grey beard. His face was lined with age, but the portrait still had a fierce energy to it. The brass plaque underneath read "Our Founder, P. G. Holyfield".

The benches were mostly filled with businessmen, both Indian and European, who looked like they'd been waiting for a while. An older white man had fallen asleep on on end of the bench and was snoring. The other occupants of the benches looked up at us as we stepped in with a mixture of looks of exhaustion, hope, and disappointment when they realized that we were not whomever they had been waiting for.

A bored-looking Indian man with slicked down hair and a bushy mustache sat behind the desk. He slouched in his wrinkled suit and shuffled through a sheaf of papers. He had the air of someone trying to look busy without actually doing any work. He didn't even look in our direction as we entered, but idly poked in his papers and scratched the stubble on his cheek.

The professor rushed up to the desk. "Good afternoon, my good man! We need to speak with P. G. Holyfield."

The man tapped a book on the top of the desk. "All visitors must sign in." He didn't bother to look up. He went back to shuffling his papers.

"You don't understand, my good man, it is vitally important that we talk with P. G. Holyfield immediately."

Now the man did look up. He frowned at the professor and tapped the book again. "*All* visitors must sign in." He went back to his papers.

"It is very important..." the professor began, but was interrupted by the receptionist, who smacked the visitor book with each word. "All. Visitors. Must. Sign. In. No. Exceptions." The man glared at the professor.

Miss Bang gently nudged Professor Crackle aside, picked up a pen, and wrote our names on the next three lines of the book. As she put the pen back, she said, "We're here to see P. G. Holyfield, thank you."

The man turned the book around, studied the lines that Miss Bang had written, and stared at each of us in turn. He then put the book back in its place and reached for another book buried under the papers on his desk. "Do you have an appointment?"

"No, we don't," the professor said, "but this is a…"

The receptionist dropped the book he had just dug out onto the top of the pile of papers. "P. G. Holyfield doesn't see anyone without an appointment." He looked back down at his desk, ignoring us.

The professor opened his mouth to argue the point, but Miss Bang put a hand on his arm to silence him. "Can we make an appointment?"

The man gave her a dark look and picked up the book. He opened it and began flipping pages, glancing at each one for a second before flipping on to the next one. And the next one. And the next one. And the next. The man finally stopped on a page and pointed to a line. "There is an opening on August 23rd…"

"August!" cried the professor.

The man continued, "… of next year, at 5:30 in the morning. Would you like to schedule for then?"

"You mean to tell me that both P. G. Holyfields are booked solid for the next fourteen months?" The professor was indignant.

"Mr. Holyfield is a very busy man."

"What about Miss Holyfield?" Miss Bang asked.

The man closed the book and dug under some papers before producing a second, identical volume. He began the same procedure of leafing through pages of appointments.

"This is ridiculous!" The professor exclaimed, then rounded the desk and barged through the doors beyond.

"You can't go back there! Sir! No one is allowed back there!" the receptionist yelled as he chased after the professor.

I looked at Miss Bang. "I guess we'll have to find P. G. Holyfield for ourselves," she said.

I followed her through the door and in the opposite direction of Professor Crackle and the incensed receptionist.

A quick examination of the first floor of the office building showed it to be populated with low-level workers. We passed row after row of clerks who hardly looked up as we went, while stern-faced portraits of P. G. Holyfield looked down from each of the walls. We quickly located a stairwell and ascended to the second floor, taking us away from the calls of the receptionist trying to corral Professor Crackle and eject him from the building.

The second floor was divided into several large rooms filled with rows of desks under the watchful gaze of more of the founder's pictures. Here we saw employees passing back and forth various bits of paperwork which I presumed involved the running of the plant. We didn't see anything that might be an executive's office, so we returned to the stairwell and ascended to the third floor.

On the third floor was a short hallway with a door on each end. The doors were labeled identically. Each one said, "P. G. Holyfield", and below that, "Private. No admittance."

"Shall we try the left, or the right?" I asked.

"Both," Miss Bang replied. "You take that door. I'll take this one."

Miss Bang strode confidently away from me down the hallway. I turned and approached my door with less aplomb.

Behind the door were two rows of desks on either side of a central aisle. Portraits of the founder kept watch here from either side, each looking over a row of desks. At the end of the aisle, a single, larger desk stood in front of a door labeled "Private". Each desk was occupied by a clerk of some sort, most of them women. They didn't seem to take notice of me as I walked down the aisle, but focused on the paperwork in front of them. The only one who did acknowledge my presence was the woman sitting at the lone desk at the end. She was an attractive Indian woman dressed in a plain, simple, and very businesslike dark vest and jacket. As I approached, she look up and asked, "Can I help you, sir?"

I did my best to keep my face placid to hide a sudden wave of nervousness, and tried to feign nonchalance. "Hello. I'm here to see P. G. Holyfield."

The woman looked puzzled and reached for a book on her desk. "Do you have an appointment, sir?"

"No, I do not. But P. G. will want to see me. We met the other day at my aunt's party."

She looked back up at me. "I'm sorry, sir, but no one is permitted to see P. G. Holyfield without an appointment."

The nervousness drained out of me, and with a certain giddiness, words came flooding up to me from the hidden recesses of my brain. I didn't know what I had planned, but some corner of my mind assured me that it knew just what to say. I let the words flow. "No one?" I asked.

"No, sir." She shook her head.

"Doesn't that make it rather difficult to work here?"

"I'm sorry, sir?" She leaned her head to one side, as if that might make my words make more sense to her.

"If no one is allowed to see P. G. Holyfield without an appointment, then does everyone have to avert their eyes when P. G. Holyfield goes walking the hallways? Or do you have to have specific appointments for P. G. Holyfield to come, and to leave? Or to go to the bathroom?"

She blinked in confusion, then frowned at me. "Sir! Don't be ridiculous!"

"*I'm* being ridiculous? I'm not the one insisting that P. G. Holyfield is only visible by appointment."

"What?"

I pointed to the door behind her. "If you were to go through that door, would you be able to see P. G. Holyfield? Or would P. G. Holyfield be invisible?"

"What? Are you quite all right, sir?" She gave me a worried look.

"Would P. G. Holyfield be invisible?"

"No."

"So, P. G. Holyfield is in there?"

"Yes!"

"Thank you." I strode around the desk and moved to the door.

The woman scrambled to her feet and rushed to the door ahead of me. "Sir, you can't go in there!"

"I can't? Is the door jammed? Is it broken? Is P. G. Holyfield trapped?"

"What? No." She looked confused again. That meant I was getting somewhere.

"Then it's a fake door. It's really a wall, it's just painted to look like a door, right?" I reached out and knocked on the door.

"Sir, please!" She grabbed my hand. "You mustn't disturb Miss Holyfield. She's a very busy person."

I looked down at her. "How do you know?"

She leaned away from me. "I'm sorry?"

"How do you know she's a busy person if you never see her? Do you make an appointment to watch her be busy?"

"Sir, I..." Her answer was mercifully cut short when the door opened, and Patricia Gladys Holyfield stood there in the doorway staring at the two of us.

"What is going on out here?" she asked.

"Patricia! So good to see you. We met the night before last. Sir Richard Blasphemy." I shook her hand.

"Oh, yes. Sir Richard. I remember you. I was hoping to talk to you. But what are you doing here?"

"I needed to talk to you about something. Can I come in, so your staff can get back to work?" I gestured with one hand at the room behind me, where I was sure heads were suddenly re-focusing on the work before them after watching the little scene I played out with the secretary.

"Ah, yes." She tapped her secretary on the shoulder. "Thank you, Marda, I'll take care of this." The young woman went back to her desk and Miss Holyfield opened the door wider and let me step inside.

The office was elegantly furnished with two stuffed leather armchairs facing a large mahogany desk. A bar sat underneath the window to the left side of the room, and a couch faced it on the right.

"Have a seat, Sir Richard. What can I do for you?" she said as she crossed the room and sat behind her desk.

"I'd like your help tracking down some information dealing with the attack on my aunt's party the other day."

"I don't understand. In what way can I help?"

"My friend, Professor Crackle, was able to disassemble a portion of one of the devices the Kindred of Kali were wearing. Inside of it, he found a part that bears the Holyfield gear and star logo. We're hoping that you can help us identify the part and who might have purchased a quantity of them to construct those devices."

"You want to try to track down these, these... insurgents from a part?" She shook her head. "You realize that's practically impossible. We manufacture thousands of different parts and ship them all over the world. Even if this particular part was made at this facility, there's no way of tracking how many times it might have been sold and re-sold before being put into one of those machines. And that's assuming the part was purchased and not stolen."

"Admittedly, it is a bit of a long shot. But at the moment, it is the best lead we have."

"I don't think we can afford the time it would take to do the records search, Sir Richard. We do have a lot of work going on in this plant."

"Could you at least take a look? These Kindred of Kali could strike again, and if we can help the authorities track them down it could make the difference in people's lives."

She looked at me dubiously. "Do you know which part number it is?"

"Part number?"

"Every product that Holyfield Industries makes is stamped some-where with a part number. If you have that we can look at how many sales there are for that particular piece. That would give us a better idea of how hard it will be to track down."

"Oh. Actually, Professor Crackle has the part with him. If we could get him up here, we can find the part number."

"He didn't come with you? I'm afraid this has all the makings of a wasted trip, Sir Richard. I'm booked solid today and tomorrow. I really shouldn't be taking this time to talk to you now. I've so much work to make up from taking the time off to attend your aunt's party, and that took much longer than expected." She sighed and rubbed her forehead. "On days like this I feel like I can't take the pressure of putting the business first. Some days I wish I could have a normal life. Retire from business. Maybe get married. Raise a family." She dropped her hand and looked at me, a touch of color rising to her cheeks. "I'm sorry. I shouldn't be pouring my heart out to you like that. It's just..." She stopped.

"You don't have anyone else you can talk to about it?" I ventured. She nodded.

"I understand. Sometimes it is easier to talk to a stranger about what is troubling you. Because they don't really know you it feels safe to say what you feel. You can speak and it won't come back to you, and yet you don't know if they'll really understand what you're going through. I come from a strange family myself. Some things you just live with because no one else understands."

"Yes. It's like that. Sometimes there is someone else in the family I can talk to, but Peter... he's never been very empathetic."

"I'm sorry."

"No, *I'm* sorry for bringing it up." She wiped at her eyes. "But I'm afraid you should have brought your friend the professor with you..."

"Oh, he's here. He's downstairs somewhere. I suspect he's still being chased by your receptionist. Or security might have caught him and expelled him from the building."

"Why would they do that?"

"The professor really doesn't take 'No' for an answer. And this whole place is set up so no one can ever see you. It's like they're guarding you. Making sure that you never see anyone."

She jerked and gave me a wary look. "My people are following standard policy."

"Don't you make the policy? I was under the impression that you and your cousin ran this facility."

She stared at me for a long, long moment. Her lips twitched as if she was about to say something, but decided against it.

"Let me see if I can get someone to locate your friend, this professor," she said at last, standing and walking past me towards the door. I looked at my hands, considering if I had gone a bit too far.

"Well, it's about time!" said a voice behind me.

I turned around. Next to the door sat an ancient man in a wheelchair. His pale skin was covered with deep wrinkles and age spots, and his thinning hair was completely white. A patchy beard covered his chin. A plaid blanket covered his lap. I hadn't heard the door open or close, but there was no sign of Patricia.

"I've been trying to get through for ages. I was about to give it up and go back to my book," he said.

"I'm sorry, sir, you are?" I let the question dangle in the air.

"P. G. Holyfield. The original article. The founder of this enterprise."

The old man rolled his wheelchair over next to the armchair where I sat. He gave me a curious look. "Do I know you from somewhere, son? Have we met before?"

I shook my head. "I'm sure if we'd met, I'd remember, sir."

He snorted. "Never mind. Memory sometimes plays tricks on me. But your face does look familiar. It'll come to me. Anyway, I know who you are, son. I've been reading up on the things you did in Prague. Impressive stuff. I wanted to meet you in person. I think you've got potential, son. I can always use a man with your kind of potential."

"I'm sorry, Mr. Holyfield. Are you offering me a job?"

"No, no. Too early for that. I wanted to meet you. Let you know

I've got my eye on you. But every now and then I have a need for some... unorthodox assistance. Someone who doesn't necessarily play by the rules, but still knows how to come up on the right side of the law. If you could help me out in one of those situations, I might be willing to do you a favor."

"A favor?"

"Favors are worth more than money to men such as we are," he said, and the look he gave me certainly made it seem like he expected me to know what he meant. I wasn't about to correct him.

"No offense, Mr. Holyfield, but you don't seem like the kind of man who does many favors for other people."

A smile crossed his lips, then disappeared. "What makes you say that?"

"The way you work your family, sir. Patricia was just telling me how stressful the work was. How sometimes she wishes she could lead a normal life and raise a family. You've got them imprisoned here. Shut away from the world. They seem to be doing an awful lot for you, but it doesn't seem like you're doing them any favors."

The old man snorted. "Don't be ridiculous. I'm not about to hurt my family. They are my life, in a very literal sense. As long as there is one P. G. Holyfield around, I will continue. I will do what I must to make sure the name continues. But I can't have my children sitting around spending my wealth and waiting for the chance to breed. They need to do something for themselves. Something to give their lives meaning. I've given them that, too."

"Even if it kills them? Do you have to have them all under your thumb to make sure your family name continues? They won't all be cut out for business. Not under the pressure that you've created. Can't you let a few of them seek other lives?"

"Ha. What would they do without me?"

"Live? Discover their own special talents? Be happy?"

Mr. Holyfield's brows furrowed and he gave me a hard stare. "This isn't really your business, son. Why is this so important to you?"

I shrugged. "Because I understand what they're going through. Patricia told me what she felt, and I knew what she meant, because I'm going through the same thing. Family duty is heavy on expectations and rules for behavior, but very light on rewards. I had to lose an uncle to realize there are reasons for those obligations. And consequences. How I meet that duty now is my choice."

P. G. grunted.

I continued. "You asked what would they do if you let them create families of their own? Well, what wouldn't they do? I would imagine most of them will stay with your company. It's the only life they've ever known. But if you give them the chance some may try something else for a while and come back, they'll be happier for it, knowing it was their choice. And they'll do better once it is their decision. Or they might succeed on their own. Isn't that what you want for your family? For them to succeed? Why not let the ones who really want something else go find it?"

Mr. Holyfield rubbed his beard and gave me a measuring look. "Well... maybe. As long as their children have the right name, maybe I could spare one or two. But they *have* to *do* something. I've seen too many children of wealthy families sit back and squander all the privileges they've been given. I'm not going to allow that in my family. They can't sit back and spend my money. God knows some of them are absolutely awful at business. I could certainly get along without *them*. I've been tempted to cut a couple of them loose in the past, but I wasn't sure what they'd do." He stroked his beard again. "Let me think about it. I'm not about to change anything until I give it more thought." He tapped his chin. "Some very serious thought."

"That's all I'm asking, sir," I said, and then remembered that I did have an additional ask. "Mr. Holyfield, since you are here, can you help us track down the Kindred of Kali? They're very dangerous. They're threatening to drive the British out of India. They endanger your family as well."

He shook his head slowly. "I don't know anything about this

group. I've never heard of them. What do you think I can do to help you?"

"They wear these metal spines that give them extra arms to fight with. We found a part in one of them that is made by your company. If you could help us find out who bought this part, we may be able to figure out where they are and stop them. They've... They've kidnapped my aunt, sir, and the daughter of the local maharaja."

He snorted. "They're not playing around, are they? Perhaps we may be able to do something." He wheeled himself over to the desk, grabbed a pen, and wrote a note. "Do me a favor, son. Go call my granddaughter back in here, would you?"

I rose from the chair and crossed to the door. Opening it, I peered out at the office. "Miss Holyfield? Patricia?" The secretary turned around and gave me a curious look. "Patricia?"

"Yes?" a voice said from behind me.

I turned. Miss Holyfield stood next to her desk giving me a curious look. Right where the old man's wheelchair had been when I turned my back. My skin tingled, and the room suddenly felt very cold. How could she have disappeared and returned so quickly? The thought sent another chill down my spine.

Miss Holyfield blinked at me. "We... we met the other day, didn't we? At that garden party where those horrible people attacked?"

"Yes, Miss Holyfield. We discussed all that when I first came in to see you." I looked around the room. There was no sign of the old man. Or of any other exit. "Where did Mr. Holyfield go?" My voice didn't quite break.

She gave a bitter laugh. "My cousin? He never comes into my offices."

"No," I shook my head. "The old man in the wheelchair. The original P. G. Holyfield."

The colour drained from her face. She stumbled and sat down heavily in her chair. "He was here? Grandfather Patrick was here?" She looked down at the desk and picked up the note. Then she dropped it as if it was something horrible and pushed back from the desk. "He was." Her eyes were wide and her hands shook as she held them up to her face.

"Are you all right, Miss Holyfield?"

"I'm... I'm sorry. Ah... What, what did you say your name was?"

"I'm Sir Richard Blasphemy."

"Oh, yes. Of course. I'm sorry, it's just..." She put her hand to her forehead. "Sometimes. Sometimes I forget things. When it happens it's very... disconcerting."

I agreed. This was very disconcerting. I had no idea what was going on with this young woman and her grandfather. I suspected it was something event the professor couldn't explain. Instead of voicing my own fears, I said, "I'm sorry. Do you need a moment?"

"No. Thank you. It usually helps to sort of push through it." She looked down at the note again. "You wanted our help with something? Where did we leave that?"

"You were going to ask one of your staff to go find Professor Crackle. The gentleman in the top hat with two pairs of goggles on it. He has the part we need to trace. You were going to check your records to see if anyone in this area has received a shipment of those parts." I hoped that she wouldn't realize that I was stretching the truth. Or how much.

She blinked. "Are you sure? That would take a lot of resources to do the search..." She cut off as she looked down at the note again. She swallowed. "Yes. Yes, we can make the time to do this. Let me see if we can locate your friend." She rose and went through the door. I could hear her talking to the secretary as I stood, alone in the office.

I stepped over to the desk and looked at the note. It was only two lines.

Give him what he wants. It's an investment.
P. G.

I couldn't help but wonder what kind of favor P. G. Holyfield was going to want in return.

CHAPTER FOURTEEN

A BIT OF LOCAL EXPERTISE

The professor and Miss Bang were soon located downstairs in a security office. It seems that Miss Bang had very little luck with Peter Holyfield, who was outraged at the invasion of his office and sent for security immediately. When they returned with her in custody, another security team had managed to corral the professor and take him into custody as well.

When Professor Crackle produced the piece from the arm, one of Patricia's staff was able to read the part number, and the staff pulled the shipment records from the factory within minutes. Miss Holyfield expressed surprised at how quickly her people were able to find and retrieve the information once they had the part number. It seemed that the filing system was much more efficient than she had been led to believe. Or perhaps her staff usually wasn't particularly efficient?

Fortunately, the part wasn't one that was particularly in demand. There were only two sizable shipments that had included that particular piece. One was to a factory in Australia, but the other was a shipment to a local warehouse.

Armed with the address and the name of the company that placed the order, we thanked Miss Holyfield and left her offices.

As we exited the building, I said, "Professor, I ran into P. G. Holyfield while I was in there…"

"Yes, my boy, that's why we came. And she was most helpful."

"No, not Miss Holyfield. I ran into…"

Miss Bang interrupted me this time. "Her cousin? I'm sorry about that, my lord. He is a very rude little man."

"No, I…" I thought for a second about how to describe the odd encounter with the old man in the wheelchair, but decided that this wasn't the time to bring up a new mystery. "I'll tell you about it later," I said.

The professor and Miss Bang started walking away from the building. I jogged a few paces to catch up and asked, "You have more experience with this sort of thing, Professor. Do you think the prisoners are going to be in the warehouse?"

He shook his head. "That would be nice, my boy, but I suspect it won't be something that simple. I suspect it is a shipping point, where the parts are received, re-packaged, and then re-shipped to their ultimate destination. But, we may be able to find clues to other facilities the Kindred have." He quickened his pace and we scrambled after him to Bijoy's waiting cart. "First, we need to do some reconnaissance on the warehouse. See how well defended it is, and what avenues are available to get us inside. Even if it is well guarded, we may be able to get in. Perhaps via the sewers! Or perhaps under cover of night we can find a nearby building to use to attack the facility from above. We must go see this property for ourselves! Come on!" He clambered up into the seat of the cart. Bijoy stirred briefly, but continued to lay in the bed of the wagon.

"Harmonious, I'm not sure that's the best use of our time," Miss Bang said.

"What? What do you mean, Titania, my dear?"

"It seems a little too simple. Too easy. And obvious."

"In what way, Miss Bang? Aren't we following the clues that we have?" I asked.

"Yes, my lord. We are. As the Army or the local authorities would. The Kindred obviously have a certain degree of wealth and power at their disposal. They're bound to have considered that if they left any clues behind them that someone would follow them. They will have planned for disconnects. Places where they can easily destroy all evidence of their connection when someone comes investigating. What we need is an intuitive leap so we can get ahead of them before they even know we are there."

"Then haven't we wasted an afternoon, Miss Bang?" I didn't like where this was going. Were we really no closer to finding Aunt Phyllis and the maharani?

"Perhaps. Everything we learn about the Kindred helps us catch up to them. I do think it is worth our time to go take a look at the warehouse, but I don't think we should pin all of our hopes on what we might find there. We need to consider what we're going to do if this turns out to be a dead end. Don't you agree, Harmonious?"

"I think you've got a good point, my dear. We do need to consider our next steps carefully. But there is the possibility that whatever power and wealth these Kindred may have, they may not be that bright. Or this may have been a connection that they missed. We do need to check it out." He stared off in the middle distance for a few seconds. "But if this is a disconnect, as you put it, Titania, where do you think they may be holding the prisoners?"

She shrugged. "I'm afraid I have no idea, Harmonious. While I understand some of the culture from my time growing up in India, there is too much about the local society, the local geography, and the local politics that I don't know. For this, we need help. We *need* a local guide."

"Do you think your cousin might be able to help?" the professor asked, giving her a hopeful look.

Miss Bang drew in a slow hiss of breath between her teeth. "I don't think so. She's only been in this part of the country for a short time. While she may have learned some things about the social structure, I doubt she knows much about the geography. And... I'm afraid Kashvi has never had a head for politics. That sort of thing was always Ranjeet's specialty. And as angry as he is, I doubt he'd be willing to help us." She put one hand to her cheek. "I honestly don't think he'd even give us a chance to explain."

"Not to mention that your cousin may not be willing to risk being set on fire again. Very well, how about..." I said and nodded to the snoozing figure in the cart.

The professor and Miss Bang looked down at Bijoy for a second.

"He does seem to have intimate knowledge of the geography," the professor offered.

Miss Bang crossed her arms. "Do you really think he has sufficient knowledge of the political situation? Social perhaps. It is surprising what can be seen from the bottom up, but I would be surprised if he has the insight into who would be brave enough to challenge the maharaja."

The professor brightened. "Ah! We could use all three. One expert for each!"

"Except Ranjeet won't cooperate with us, Harmonious. And if he has any say in it, we won't be able to talk to Kashvi, either."

"Is he likely to have any say in it?" I asked, remembering how Kashvi locked her brother out of the house when last we saw them.

She sighed. "Unfortunately, yes. Until her husband comes home, Kashvi cannot stand against her brother, and she cannot deny him hospitality. As the eldest male in the local family, Ranjeet would take precedence. She'll have to do as he says. Even if she doesn't particularly like it."

"Then we had better hope that we find a clue at the warehouse, because if we don't, we've lost the scent." The professor looked crestfallen.

I bit my lip as I considered our situation. It was too bad that Aunt Phyllis had been kidnapped. She was exactly the person with the kind of knowledge we needed. I wondered if Uncle Jeremy would know enough to offer us any advice, but Willie had said that Aunt Phyllis was much more astute with political advice. Then it hit me.

"Actually, Professor, I think we know someone who has the knowledge we need."

"Really, my boy? Who?"

"You're not going to like it." I frowned.

"Tell us, please!" Miss Bang implored.

"We need Willie for this."

The two of them pulled back in surprise.

"What? No! Don't be ridiculous, my boy!" The professor put his hands up in front of him, as if to push the suggestion away. "I know he's your brother, but he would never help us. He's under orders from that odious colonel of his to take us into custody if we continue the investigation."

"If we interfere in *his* investigation, Professor. Are we interfering?"

"What? We're investigating for them."

"But are we interfering? Are we hampering their progress?"

Miss Bang looked thoughtful.

The professor dug a hand up under his top hat and scratched his head. "I... I don't know. I have no idea what they are doing. If they're doing anything."

"If we don't know what they're doing, how can we know when or if we are interfering?"

"We can't, of course."

"Remember that."

Miss Bang tilted her head to the side. "Do you have something in mind, my lord?"

"Well, unless I'm misjudging things, we can't have a proper look at the warehouse until this evening. And Willie has to report back for duty in the morning. If we're going to tell him what we've learned, and get him to help us, we've got to tell him now."

"Because if we wait until morning, he won't be free to give us any advice," Miss Bang said.

"Exactly," I replied.

"Then let's not waste any more time standing in the sun talking about it!" the professor said. I helped Miss Bang up into the cart and then climbed into the back as the professor roused the driver. "Up, up, my good man! We need to be back to the house with all haste."

"Back from your sightseeing so soon?" Willie said, glancing up from his book as we walked into the library. "I expected that you'd be out late again."

"We thought so, too," I replied, "but it seems that we forgot something."

"Oh? What?"

The professor cleared his throat. "Um, it would seem, that, what we forgot was you, Lieutenant."

"Me?"

"We need a guide, Willie."

"I thought you had that old man with his horse cart."

Miss Bang came around and sat next to him on the couch. "He's not the kind of guide we need, Lieutenant. We need someone with a more discerning knowledge of the people and alliances, not just the geography."

"I'm sorry?"

"Willie, we've been trying to figure out who kidnapped Aunt Phyllis, and the maharani, and where they are most likely being held." I said as I sat down across from him.

My brother closed his book with a snap and leaned toward me. "You idiot! The colonel told you not to go investigating! Now I'm forced to report you and have you arrested! What were you thinking?"

"Your colonel didn't order us *not* to investigate. He made the professor promise not to interfere with his investigation. *His investigation*. He never said that we couldn't investigate on our own."

"You know that's what he meant."

"He also ordered you not to report for duty until tomorrow morning," I pointed out. "It won't do you any harm to listen to what we've discovered. You can still have us arrested in the morning."

He inhaled to rebut my statement, but instead let it out in a long breath. "Twenty-six years and *now* you finally decide to listen to people."

"Well, after the events in Prague, I've had cause to regret not paying attention." I looked down at my hands, then back up at Willie. "Look, hear us out. If we're on to something, you can take credit for it tomorrow. If not, you can turn us in. We want to figure out where the hostages are being held so they can be rescued. We can't do it without you."

"Very well. I'm listening."

The professor began the tale. "We suspected that the Kindred of Kali might be supported by worshipers of the goddess Kali, so we sought out a local shrine. It did indeed turn out that the priest of the shrine was in league with these Kindred and was using the shrine to drum up support for their cause. They were able to summon a number of supporters on very short notice."

Willie frowned. "You're lucky they didn't catch you. An angry mob can be a very dangerous thing."

The professor hesitated, and I took over before he mentioned that he had been caught and nearly burned at the stake. "It was a near thing, Willie. But we managed to escape with a piece from one of the arm-contraptions that the Kindred wear."

"You what? How?"

"Please, Willie. Let me finish." My brother subsided slightly. "The piece had the Holyfield Industries logo on it, so we went over there this afternoon to see what we could find out about it. Miss Holyfield's staff was able to identify the specific part and determined that a large quantity of those parts were shipped to a local warehouse.

We were going to look into the warehouse, but Miss Bang realized that we were missing something." I gestured to her.

"Simply put, Lieutenant, the pieces didn't fit." Miss Bang ticked off points on her fingers. "The women who attacked us here were high caste, women of power and breeding. The people at the shrine to Kali were all low caste. The priest, as a holy man, is a link between them, but the castes do not mix in this fashion. Whoever is behind this must be someone high caste."

"The caste system is weakening in India," he pointed out. "More opportunities are open to all regardless of caste, and as arranged marriages decline, more foreigners are marrying into Indian families."

Miss Bang nodded. "This is true, but it doesn't change the fact that whoever is behind this conspiracy is someone with wealth and power. At most it slightly widens the pool of suspects."

Willie considered what we had told him. "You're right. It doesn't really narrow the field. These Kindred declared war on anyone who accepted British rule, which includes the maharaja. But whatever their feelings toward the Crown, the local nobles are pretty much loyal to him. They squabble, but when he makes a decision, that is the end of it. I can't think of any of them being willing to move against him like this. Unless..."

"Unless?" We all asked at once.

"What if the kidnapping is a ploy to force the maharaja to cooperate with the rebels? He has troops, resources, and greater standing. If he speaks out against the Crown, even under duress, he'll be the one to go down for leading a rebellion." Willie looked at us, his eyebrows pinched together. "And he might do it if he thought it was the only way to ensure his daughter's safety. He loves her very much."

The professor started pacing. "This makes it that much more imperative that we, that someone, rescues the maharani before her father is forced to decide."

"If his daughter is the lever they're using, how do we know he hasn't already thrown in with them?" I asked.

Willie shook his head. "From what I've seen of the maharaja, he won't cave easily to threats. If they've already given him an ultimatum, he'll bide his time, while doing his best to find his daughter."

"You don't think they would have delivered their demands at once?" Miss Bang asked.

Willie shrugged. "Any communication from the kidnappers is a chance for them to be traced. It really depends on how secure they are in their arrangements. I've been on leave. I don't know what's going on, so I can't say one way or the other."

"Then shouldn't we check out this warehouse? See if it provides any leads?" the professor said.

"It hard to tell. Where is this place?"

Miss Bang recited the address.

Wille shook his head. "That can't be it. Are you sure that is the right address?"

Miss Bang nodded. "That is the exact address printed on all the shipping invoices. Why do you think it is wrong?"

"It's one of *our* warehouses. A civilian facility rented out by the military. We have shipments delivered there for inspection before being moved over to the base. It's a security measure." He scratched along his jaw line. "That means that either those loads from Holyfield are going somewhere else, or someone at the warehouse is working with the Kindred."

"Someone in the military?" I was surprised that Willie would even suggest such a thing.

"Not necessarily. There are civilian contractors there. As warehouse workers and as inspectors. I must admit what concerns me more is that they might have passed dangerous materials on to the base."

"Lieutenant," Miss Bang said, "what kind of connections would one need to have to try to use the warehouse as a staging point? To take materials from the warehouse to another location?"

"You couldn't do it without someone on the inside. There's paperwork for everything. If something is shipped out, we send down orders to put the materials together in a lot, and then lading orders to put that lot onto a particular truck from the right company. The company must have a matching requisition." Willie frowned and slapped the cover of his book into his left hand. "All that paperwork requires Colonel Ticking's signature. It would come through my office. Right across my desk!"

"There's no way an order could be forged?" I asked.

He shook his head. "Military protocol. Even if you could insert a fake order to create a lot, once the lot has been put together, a confirmation is sent back to the office. A little contraband here and there might be slipped in by one of the loaders, but an entire shipment? You'd need everyone at the warehouse to be part of the conspiracy. Even then there are surprise inspections." His frown deepened. "You could do it if you had someone in the office. If they could slip a few extra orders into the pile for the colonel to sign. He doesn't always pay much attention to what I give him. But that would mean someone was slipping these fake orders across my desk and I completely missed it. I'm the adjutant. I collect all the paperwork and organize it."

The professor stopped his pacing. "Perhaps you did see something, my good man. Quite often people see things a little out of the ordinary and dismiss them. That doesn't mean you weren't doing your job properly. Was there anything that seemed a little unfamiliar? It needn't have been anything recent. Perhaps a month or two ago? Possibly farther back than that?"

Willie gave the professor a pleading look. "Professor Crackle, that's an awful lot of paperwork. You have no idea how many reports and orders and requisitions are needed to run a base. It all blurs together after a while. To try to pick out an odd order out of all of that..."

The professor patted him on the shoulder. "Is like finding a needle in a haystack. Exactly, my good man. There's no need to beat yourself up over it. Someone who knows this process better than you found a way to subvert it. There is no shame in being fooled by them.

After all, officers with more experience and rank were fooled as well. All the way up to that colonel of yours."

"I... I guess that is true."

"Of course it is." The professor nodded. "Now, I'm more concerned that this means the warehouse definitely is a dead end. We won't be able to tell the real traffic in and out of the place from anything the Kindred might have arranged. That leaves us no closer to figuring out where these villains are holding your aunt and the maharani."

"Where would they be hiding them?" I asked.

Miss Bang shook her head. "It isn't London, but it is a fair-sized city. With the resources at their command, the Kindred could stash the hostages almost anywhere. Where is the last place you'd look for hostages in a city of this size?"

"The Palace," Willie replied flatly.

"What?" I looked at my brother, wondering if he was serious.

"What's that, Lieutenant?" the professor repeated.

"Given that one of the victims is the maharaja's daughter, the last place you'd expect to find the hostages would be in the Palace. Because that is where she'd be if she was safe and sound. Nobody would even think of looking for her there." We blinked at my brother for a minute. Undaunted by the silence, he continued his explanation. "Then again, if that *is* where they are being held, you'd have to know the place well enough to sneak in two uncooperative women and keep them fed and cared for while they were imprisoned. While you might be able to bribe a couple of soldiers, or bring them over to your cause, the maharaja's guard are all sworn to protect his family. I don't think you could talk one of them into holding a daughter of the house prisoner. Not in her own castle..." his voice trailed off.

"Willie, are you all right?" The odd look in his eye had me worried.

"It's the wrong castle," he said. "The guard is all very loyal. You couldn't smuggle prisoners into the palace. Unless you'd compromised the entire staff, someone would notice and alert the maharaja.

But there is another place. An old fortress, outside the city. Chandra took me out there a couple of times. The family still owns it, although it is seldom used. That place could be held with a handful of men. And you could easily sneak someone in without being seen. She once showed me one of the old escape tunnels. I think I remember where it is. I could get us in." Willie's brow was still furrowed, but he no longer seemed worried. He was determined now.

"Us, Lieutenant?" Professor Crackle asked. "We don't want to get you into any trouble with your commander, if this doesn't pan out."

Willie shook his head. "I'm in. If there is any chance of rescuing Chandra, I'm not going to sit on the sidelines. Besides, you'll never find the entrance if I don't show you. I have to go with you."

"Jolly good!" said the professor.

"Glad to have you along, Lieutenant," said Miss Bang.

"How are we going to get there?" I asked.

The three of them stared at me in surprise.

CHAPTER FIFTEEN
A TRAMP IN THE COUNTRY

W illie said that the fortress was about three-quarters of
an hour's drive away by car. Sitting in the back of
Bijoy's horse cart, it seemed much longer than that.

Given that the old man and his horse were the only manner of
transportation currently available to us, aside from shank's mare, we
moved quickly to get ready. Miss Bang and I hastily changed into
clothes more suitable to the walking and climbing that Willie indicated would be necessary to reach the hidden entrance to the castle.
My brother went off to his room and returned to the foyer with his
service pistol belted on. He handed me a second gun belt with the
9mm that he had shown me this morning. After I secured the gun
belt around my waist, he handed me two boxes of cartridges.

"Sorry," he said, "I couldn't find more magazines for this gun. I
don't think Uncle Jeremy uses it that often. You'll have to reload as
we go, but better to have too many bullets than too few."

Miss Bang came down the stairs wearing a pair of dark, thick
cotton trousers and a matching blouse with a leather cinch about her
waist. Tinka paced along beside her, a ruddy pink color on her
cheeks. I thought at first this was from where the paint from last

night's rescue was scrubbed off, but then realized this was the first time I'd seen Tinka with her face totally clean. Otherwise, Tinka looked her usual self again, dressed in boots, leather pants, a sleeveless cotton shirt that had seen better days, and a leather harness that supported her bosom. She had a dark cloak thrown over her shoulders. A pair of the house servants trailed a few feet behind the women, keeping a respectful distance. This attention seemed to unsettle Tinka a bit.

"Coming with us, Tinka?" I asked. "I would have thought you'd be more comfortable staying here."

She glanced up at me, and quickly suppressed a smile. "Uh, yeah. 'Tanya said you might run into a bit of trouble. I thought I'd better come and keep an eye on you." She fidgeted, and glanced furtively at my brother.

I bowed. "Thank you for looking after me. I'm sure my mother would appreciate the gesture." Straightening, I gestured to Willie. "This is my brother, Lieutenant William Holmes. Willie, this is Tinka, Professor Crackle's adopted daughter, and one of the most capable engineers you are likely to ever meet." I wasn't sure how my brother would deal with Tinka's social anxiety over her appearance, but I hoped he'd react better than I did.

Willie extended his hand. Tinka flinched, then caught herself. She had a moment of confusion as she tried to figure out which of her right hands she should use to shake Willie's outstretched one. She finally settled on using her lower right to shake hands with my brother while she clutched the collar of her cloak with the upper right.

"Pleased to meet you, Tinka. Thank you for volunteering to help." Willie's tone was calm and welcoming. If he had noticed Tinka's additional arms, he made no sign of it and remained perfectly composed.

Tinka shook his hand briefly. "You're welcome," she said in a tiny voice. She drew the cloak together in front of her, using its folds to hide her arms and pulling the hood up to shield her face. She gave

Willie one last glance, then sped past Miss Bang and through the make-shift door of the house.

We followed her outside where the professor waited with the driver and his cart, which was filled with a variety of horse blankets and old quilts.

"Professor, what's with all the textiles? We're not exactly going to market."

"I thought we might need them, my boy. If we find what we're looking for, we may have to evade pursuit, and it will be easier to cover or disguise ourselves than to try to outrun an automobile. Your aunt's house staff was good enough to volunteer some of these quilts," he said, running his hand over a few samples with floral and geometric patterns. "Besides, they provide something to sit on for the ride out."

While I couldn't argue with the logic of having something to use as camouflage, I doubted that the blankets would prove to be comfortable seating after a lengthy ride in the rickety old cart.

Most of the ride we spent in relative silence, with only the clop of hooves, the creak of the tack, and the scraping of the wheels in our ears. Willie gave the driver occasional directions, but we were all a bit concerned about how much we could tell Bijoy. We didn't want him to bolt in fear or force us to tie him up again. Courage was obviously not the man's strong suit. He was nervous enough after seeing my brother and myself with sidearms. I wished we'd realized this was going to be an issue and had loaded them before we came out of the house. Instead, we waited until we were on our way and Bijoy's attention was on the road, and then Willie and I sat with our backs against the bench and loaded our magazines. Tinka curled up against me and pretended to sleep. I could tell she did not like being out among people, and I supposed my presence gave her a bit of comfort.

Willie slid a loaded magazine into his gun, racked it, set the safety, and returned it to its holster. He pulled out a second magazine and began loading rounds into it. I finished loading my own weapon and secured it.

I looked out at the Indian countryside. The area was full of gently rolling, lush green hills. It looked a bit like England, except that the brush looked thicker and greener, and many of the trees I couldn't identify. The smell of petrichor from the road was strong, but I also caught traces of blooming flowers as we rode along. Palm trees dotted the landscape, pushing up through the rest of the canopy. Here and there small areas were cleared where a few buildings stood. Some were modern construction, but in places there were simple huts, or older structures built of stone. Some were still in use, others in ruins.

After a what seemed like a long while, Willie pointed to a structure built into the side of a nearby hill. "There it is." Several towers loomed over a tall wall that ringed the compound and fed back into the hillside. We could see a series of buildings that seemed to be stacked one on top of the other, working their way up to the crown of the hill. The tallest tower was built at the very top of the hill and undoubtedly had an excellent view all around the small fortress.

"How are we going to approach that without being seen?" I asked. "If they have one person keeping a lookout in any of those towers they're sure to spot us miles away."

"We'll go in through one of the escape tunnels." My brother nodded his head towards the far side of the towers. "There is a ravine that curves around the far side. Once we're down there they won't be able to see us. It's too steep, and there are trees for cover."

"If someone spots us heading into the ravine, won't they find that suspicious, Lieutenant?" The professor peered at my brother through the lenses of his goggles. I wished that I had stopped to grab my pair to keep the dust kicked up by the horse out of my eyes, but I wasn't about to ask him for the loan of his other pair. I resolved to make sure I kept a pair on me in the future. The professor was right, they were surprisingly useful.

Willie shrugged. "I don't know. There are a few locals who hunt and gather in the area. If they can't get a good look, they might mistake us for one of them. I'm hoping they haven't run off the locals and are trying to keep as low a profile as possible so no one suspects they are here."

"Is there anyone who should be in the castle, Lieutenant?" Miss Bang asked. "We wouldn't want to mistake innocents for one of the kidnappers." I noticed that she had also slipped on a pair of goggles.

"There are a couple of caretakers who look after the place when the family isn't using it. Two older gentlemen as I recall. I expect they've either been taken prisoner or killed, if the kidnappers are here." He spread his hands. "If not, and we run into one of them, we'll apologize and leave as fast as we can."

"What do these caretakers look like?" I thought it best to have an idea of whom I was looking out for.

Willie gestured to Bijoy's back and said, "Pretty much like that. A bit old and frail. If you see someone looking muscular and robust, they're likely one of the kidnappers."

"I'll try to keep that in mind." I wasn't sure if I was hoping that we would find the princess and Aunt Phyllis or be chased off by the caretakers.

We rattled on in relative silence for several minutes as the road turned to make the fortress on the hill slowly move behind us to our right. I tried to suppress the urge to look back at it to see if we had been spotted, as that was the kind of movement that would draw suspicion down upon us. Instead I looked into the trees as they pulled in against the roadway, becoming a thick green wall to either side.

I thought that we had completely passed the castle by, and we were going to continue to wander out into the country, when Willie moved up next to Bijoy on the bench. "There's a little road, up ahead," he told the driver.

The first sign I had of this "road" was when the cart abruptly turned off the highway and dove into the bush. To call it a cart path would be generous, for the cart scraped branches on both sides and the wheels tilted wildly on the uneven surface. The path was more of a wash created by seasonal rains. It alternated between flat and narrow, and took sharp, winding turns as it careened down the hillside. The horse whinnied in protest at the trail. We bounced roughly from side to side, gripping the sides and having our knuckles lashed by branches with every turn. Waves of insects were dislodged from the trees and rolled over us, chittering angrily. Somehow the driver kept his seat without any difficulty. While we jostled back and forth, he guided the horse through every turn.

After what felt like an eternity of caroming between the trees, we came at last to flat ground where the cart settled down. I looked up through the trees, but only caught glimpses of blue sky beyond the thick foliage.

The last wave of insects leapt from the cart and made for the safety of the bush. We could hear small animals likewise fleeing through the underbrush as we made our way down the trail.

The cart pulled into a small clearing, barely more than a widening of the way and my brother told Bijoy to stop. "We're going to have to walk from here. We can't take the cart any further." He jumped down from the bench and came around around to help hand Miss Bang down.

Tinka sat up and ran a hand through her hair, dislodging some leaves and one last insect that hadn't made its escape yet. "Are we there yet?" She climbed off the back of the cart.

I looked at the trees surrounding us, but as far as I could tell, the clearing was a dead end. "Willie, walk where? The only way out of here appears to be back the way we came."

Miss Bang landed beside my brother. He held her hand for a moment to be sure she was steady, then dropped it and pointed at the trees. "The path is right over there."

I looked where he pointed but didn't see any break in the foliage. "It doesn't appear to be much of a path."

"That's why we can't take the cart any further."

The professor climbed down from the cart. He scanned the trees for an indication of a trail. "It does seem well hidden."

I jumped down, my feet stinging slightly as my boots hit the earth. "All right, Bastard. You're here as our guide. So, guide us."

My brother grinned briefly at my use of his old nickname. He turned to Miss Bang. "It's going to be a bit of rough going, Miss. You may want to wait with the driver." He nodded to Bijoy, who had climbed down from his seat and was seeing to his horse.

Miss Bang cocked an eyebrow at Willie. "Don't be ridiculous, Lieutenant. I wouldn't have come all this way if I intended to sit and twiddle my thumbs. Just because I'm a lady doesn't mean I'm a wilting flower. Please, lead on. I think you'll find that *all* of us are quite up to the challenge of the trail."

He bowed his head slightly. "As you wish, Miss Bang." With that, he walked around to the front of the cart and disappeared into the trees.

Miss Bang followed him and likewise vanished.

Tinka looked up at me. "I thought he was too nice before, but now I see the resemblance. He's your brother, all right." She followed Miss Bang into the greenery.

Professor Crackle and I exchanged a look of mutual confusion for a moment before he turned after them. He pawed at the thick branches for a few seconds, trying to find the gap which our comrades just stepped through without hesitation. At last he declared, "Ah, here it is!" and turned back to me. "Coming, my boy?" he said, then turned and disappeared between two branches.

I grabbed the swinging boughs and pushed them back to reveal the top of a deep ravine, and the backs of my companions as they rapidly descended. I stepped after them and nearly lost my footing. The sides of this "path" were steep and heavily eroded, so the ground crumbled and shifted beneath me with each step. I wondered if this was what Willie meant by "rough going" or if it got worse up ahead.

I reached out to the branches of the trees on either side to steady myself, but the trees quickly gave way to dense bushes with sharp thorns. I looked around and realized that with the cover of the trees and the brambles, it would be difficult for anyone to find this trail as it sank into the soil. If someone didn't know exactly where to enter, they would only find this trail by shoving through the bushes and falling into it.

I followed my companions, bracing my palms against the dirt on either side of the narrow cleft. We descended about thirty feet or so, as the brush closed in overhead. The bright Indian sun managed to find its way down to us, but the light turned a dim green before it reached us. It was dark enough to lose our way, except for the fact that there was no place else to go except forward.

The path wound back and forth for quite a while before we reached a place where it became a flat trench with high steep walls, but level enough for the professor and myself to catch up with Miss Bang, Tinka, and my brother. The three of them appeared to have no difficulty with the uneven terrain and proceeded at a respectable clip. Indeed, the primary reason we were able to catch up with them at all was because Miss Bang asked Willie a question about one of the vines that hung down along one side of the ravine.

We continued in this way for several minutes before the sides of the narrow passage fell away, leaving us walking across a small field of tall grasses perhaps fifty feet across. A broken cliff marked the far edge of the field, rising some fifty or sixty feet above the flat where we stood. Willie led us to the break in the cliff, where a wooden bridge leapt the span from one side to the other.

As we approached, I pointed to the high bridge. "Isn't that path leading towards the fortress?"

Willie replied. "Yes, it's part of another path from the clearing."

"Wait a minute," I said, looking at the towering cliffs behind us, where the fortress lay. "Aren't we going away from the very place we're supposed to be sneaking into?"

"For now," said Willie. "That way would get you to the cliffs, but not inside."

"Don't worry, my boy," the professor cried, somewhat too loud for someone who was supposed to be making a covert approach to an enemy fortification. "It is a secret entrance, after all. There are bound to be a few twists and turns along the way."

"I think we've already had plenty of those."

Tinka snorted.

Miss Bang didn't say anything. She simply hurried her steps and sped ahead of us, forcing Professor Crackle and me to rush to catch up. Tinka seemed to pass us almost leisurely.

We proceeded through the gap beneath the bridge and were met with a glorious view of rolling hills tapering off into the distance. My brother angled back to the left, skirting the wall of the cliff. Several yards along, we came to a hollow in the wall of raw stone that rose over us. The space was perhaps ten feet deep and looked as if a sizable boulder had been removed from the cliff face without disturbing the surrounding rock.

Willie strode to the back of the hollow, squared himself up against the rear wall, then took two steps back and turned to his right. He stepped up to the rock and ran his hands over the surface until he found what he was looking for. He pressed on a round stone, which sank back into the wall. I heard a muffled clack and scrape of parts moving against each other, and then the back of the indentation in the cliff wall pivoted, exposing a dark hole.

"Ah, ha! I was right. A secret door indeed!" Professor Crackle moved over to the gap and peered inside.

"Excuse me, Professor," my brother said, moving past him, and stepping into the darkness. There was a faint rattling, and then a rasping sound and the smell of sulphur. A moment later, a torch flared to life. Willie beckoned to us. "Come on."

Behind the stone door was a small cave that looked half natural and half finished. Most of the walls were rough, but there were several cabinets against one wall, and a barrel next to the door, filled with wooden staves wrapped in cloth that gave off a faint odor of paraffin, torches waiting to be used. Another wall had several floor to ceiling wooden doors built right next to each other. I deduced these must cover the mechanism that controlled the hidden portal, so it could be maintained or repaired as needed.

Willie handed me his torch, then leaned on the pivoting door until it ground shut. We heard a clack of stone on stone from some-where behind the wooden doors next to us. It was eerily quiet in the small space. Only the faint sounds of our breathing and the crackling of the burning torch could be heard.

My brother opened one of the cabinets and extracted an oil lantern and a small candle. He lit the candle from the torch in my hand, then used it to light the lantern. With a flick of his wrist he extinguished the candle and dropped it back on the shelf he'd gotten it from. He grabbed a small leather covered box from the shelf and put it into his pocket.

"How did you know all this was down here, Lieutenant?" Professor Crackle asked as he peered into one of the cabinets.

"Chandra, the maharani, showed me this a month or so ago. She thought it might be good for me to know about the emergency supplies on hand." He set the lantern on top of a sealed barrel, grabbed a pair of torches, and passed them to the professor and Miss Bang. "If we run into anyone, or if you think someone is coming, don't be afraid to snuff out your torch. I should be able to re-light it with the tinder box." He patted the pocket with the leather box in it. He turned back to find Tinka had already pulled out a torch for herself and was comparing its weight to a belaying pin that she had produced from somewhere on her person.

The professor raised an eyebrow at him. "That lantern should provide sufficient light for us to see, Lieutenant. Are you sure we need to carry the torches as well?"

"The lantern will get us part of the way, but when we get up into the dungeons, it will draw too much attention. And if we run into guards, a torch will double as a club." Willie held up a hand as I went to light Professor Crackle's torch. "Save the other torches for now. We've got a bit of a climb ahead of us, so pace yourself. We don't want to burn through the torches too soon, and you won't want to use all your energy too early and run out of steam."

"A climb?" I looked at my brother. "You didn't mention any climbing."

"A secret tunnel to a fortress on a hill? I thought that pretty much came with the territory." He winked at me. "It's not that bad, though. There are steps. There are a lot of them. Quite a lot." Tinka snorted.

Willie grabbed another torch and stuck it through his belt before he picked up the lantern and led us through the tunnel, under the hill where the fortress was built. The passage meandered. In some places it looked like a natural fissure, with oddly slanted ceiling and walls, and in other places it was clearly hewn from the mountain and braced with timbers to reinforce the cut. We passed through several small chambers stocked with supplies of clothing, or weapons, or jugs of water.

As we went, I noticed footprints in the dust on the floor.

"Willie," I said, "someone has been here." I pointed to the foot-prints that appeared to be heading back the way we had come.

He looked down at the floor, then grinned at me. "Those are from when Chandra was showing me the escape root and the supplies. No one else has been here since."

"Do many people know about this tunnel?" I asked.

"No," he said. "Only the family and a few trusted retainers who maintain the supplies."

I drew a finger across a crate stacked to one side of the passage, leaving a trail in the gathering dust on it. I wondered how often these supplies were maintained.

We came at last to a hallway that ended in another stone door. A thick wooden lever jutted from the wall next to the door.

Willie put his hand on the lever. "This is where we leave the tunnel and enter the fortress proper. From here on, there is always the chance that we'll encounter someone, and we may be caught. This is our last chance to turn back." He looked at me, pointedly.

"Don't even think it, Lieutenant," Miss Bang cautioned him.

"I wasn't about to, Miss. Just letting everyone know the score," he lied.

"Why is it the last chance to turn back comes *after* the two-hour cart ride and walking across half of India?" I mumbled.

Tinka poked me in the ribs. "It wasn't two hours."

"You slept through half of it," I retorted. She stuck her tongue out at me.

"Come on, Lieutenant, I'm sure your aunt and the princess are eager to be on their way. Let's not keep them waiting." The Professor winked at me.

"Go quietly, now." My brother pulled down on the lever, and the stone door pivoted slightly. He listened at the door for a moment, then pushed it fully open. We slipped past the stone portal and found ourselves in a broad cavern. The air smelled damp and pungent.

Willie pulled up the rear and sealed the door behind us. The grinding of the door echoed as it shut. I took a few strides forward, holding my torch out in front of me, and had to check myself to keep from stepping in a vast pool of black liquid.

"Oil?" I said and was surprised by how loudly my words echoed back to me in the chamber.

Willie appeared at my shoulder, his finger held to his lips. "Water," he whispered. "Reservoir for the castle. There are wells from above that come down to this level. Don't be too loud or it will echo back up."

The professor looked at the edge of the water and said quietly, "Not a reservoir. This appears natural. Artisanal wells that tap into the aquifer. Very clever."

Tinka looked up into the darkness, and then down to the water. "Isn't that a really long way to lower a bucket for some water?"

Miss Bang shook her head. "Not really. There are artisanal wells in this part of the world that are a thousand to two thousand feet deep. Sometimes more."

Willie nodded. "And there are other reservoirs higher up that are replenished with rain water, or via pumps. It's the back-up water supply in case of siege. Now are we ready to go?"

He looked at each of us. We nodded in turn. "This way," he finished, and moved off along the edge of the pool, his lantern held high. I glanced back at the dark water, and then followed him.

We skirted the edge of the pool and came to a stone column rising up from the water's edge. The column was irregularly shaped, but the exterior was smooth. Professor Crackle put a hand on it and grunted to himself. He murmured "Carved out by water, of course. This must be a harder vein of rock, and this whole space was made through erosion over the ages."

We followed around the edge of the column until we came to a place where steps had been cut into the stone. The stairway wound up around the edge of the column, leaving an outer stone wall or railing that also sloped upwards. Along the inside of the stair's spiral, there was a melted looking stone railing as a handhold.

Willie moved a few steps away and trimmed the wick on his lantern so that it only let out a dim light and then set it on the ground. He then had me light the rest of the torches, and we turned toward the column. The professor raised his torch, and we could see that the stairs wound up and away and into the darkness. In places the rail had been bridged or covered by stone deposits washed down from above. "Stairs, indeed," he commented, perhaps a little too cheerily, and started climbing.

"Professor!" Willie hissed at him.

The professor stopped and turned back to my brother. "Yes?"

"There's a door at the top of the stairs. Don't go through it until we're all with you," Willie said.

"Certainly," Professor Crackle said and resumed climbing.

Miss Bang followed him.

Tinka unclasped her cloak and dropped it near the lantern looking somewhat reluctant about it. She took to the stairs, using all four arms to grab the railings on either side and propel herself upwards.

Willie and I took up the rear.

Willie leaned over and said in a hushed voice, "Your friends are going to be up for this, right?"

I snorted. "I'm not sure that I'm up for this. But I suspect that in ten minutes the professor is going to be wondering what is keeping us all. Tinka is more comfortable climbing than walking. And I've given up predicting what Miss Bang will do. She's full of surprises. But rest assured I expect you to carry your crippled elder brother up on your back."

Willie did not seem reassured by that.

"Carry you? Not a chance. I might have considered it if you'd warned me about the professor's daughter being..." He trailed off searching for the right word.

"A little extra?" I suggested.

He snorted and nodded.

"Sorry about that," I said. "I would have tried to warn you, but I didn't realize that she was coming with us. You probably impressed her more by not reacting, though. God knows you did better than I did when I first saw her." I sighed. "We'd best get climbing." I started up the stairs, with Willie close behind me.

The stone railings felt strange under my hands, but they were necessary with the way the steps had been smoothed out by erosion over time. I was several steps up before I realized that the inner rail was actually a rope that had been mounted to the stone wall and then covered with calcium deposits over time.

As I expected, in a few minutes, Professor Crackle had a sizable lead on us, and Miss Bang and Tinka were keeping up a steady pace, which Willie managed slightly better than myself. The professor and his torch quickly wound up the stair above us out of sight, and the remaining four of us dragged ourselves after him, all breathing heavily from the exertion. My only consolation was the thought that it would be a lot easier to come back down than it was going up.

My brother paused on the stairs and let me catch up to him. "How does he do that?" he breathed.

"Long story. Much brandy. Climb," I panted in reply, and stumbled past him up the steps.

It felt like we climbed for ages, our world defined by the flickering light of the torches, the smell of the burning paraffin, and the damp odor of the aquifer below. I suspect it was only about twenty minutes, but that's a considerable effort when one is not accustomed to that much continuous exertion.

Professor Crackle waited impatiently for us on a landing at the top of the staircase. A steel bound wooden door was set into the wall, and a separate staircase angled off into the rock of the mountain. The professor paced back and forth as we sat down on the bare stone, panting to catch our breath.

Still pacing, the professor said, "I went on up to the top of this staircase while I waited for you, but it ended abruptly. I wasn't able to find any signs of a mechanism to open it, so I thought I'd come back and check on you. You've all taken an awfully long time."

"We don't have your stamina, Professor," I gasped.

"Oh, come now, my boy. Your brother is a soldier. Surely you're not suggesting that I'm more fit than an active duty soldier?"

Miss Bang raised her head. "Harmonious..."

"Yes, my dear?"

"Hush."

Willie and I weakly applauded. Tinka lay on the floor and made three different rude gestures towards her father with her free hands.

The professor's mouth opened and closed several times, giving him the appearance of a freshly caught fish. He then puffed his cheeks and turned and marched up the second stairwell.

"Should we call him back?" I asked.

My brother waved his hand. "He'll be back. There is a hatch up there, but it is a one-way door that leads down here. He can't get out that way. We have to go out this door."

By the time the professor came plodding back down the stair, we had managed to catch our breath and regain some of our strength. He still looked sullen.

Willie pointed to the closed door. "These are the lower dungeons. If they're being held here, they'll be on one of the upper levels."

"Why is that, Lieutenant?"

"Because, Miss Bang, the maharaja who built this castle figured that if his castle was ever overrun and his family held hostage, the enemy would try to humiliate them by throwing them into the lowest dungeon in the castle. So, every cell on this level has a secret escape route. If Chandra was locked up down here, she would have escaped by now."

The professor rubbed his chin. "Sounds like a very clever man. Very forward thinking."

"I'm afraid you're about four centuries too late to chat with him, Professor Crackle," Willie said.

"Is that a well-known fact about the dungeons, Lieutenant?" Miss Bang asked.

My brother shook his head. "No, it isn't. I probably shouldn't have told you."

"Then why do you suppose her captors didn't put the maharani in the lower dungeons?" she replied.

Willie thought about it. "Well, it may be that she's not here at all and I've wasted your day. If that is the case it will be disappointing, but I'll be glad we eliminated the possibility. It could just be that they wanted to keep her close at hand."

"Let us hope you're right, young man," the professor said.

Willie nodded. "All right, let's see if we can make our way up to the next level without being spotted."

My brother threw the latch on the door and motioned us into another dark hallway. He closed the door behind us and led us through a maze of stone cells, the floors covered with a thick layer of sand and dirt. Willie didn't have the surety that he displayed in the tunnel below. We made a wrong turn that brought us to a dead end, and at several junctions he spent a while determining which way to go. But we all knew when we found the stairs leading to the upper level of the dungeons: they were lit by torchlight from above. The next level was clearly occupied. That meant prisoners. And guards.

My brother had us extinguish our torches by rubbing them on the sand floor. "From here on out, we need to be as stealthy as possible." He hefted his torch. "Remember, use these as clubs, if necessary. The last thing we need is to bring a whole platoon down on us with gunshots."

"You're assuming that they're not armed," I said.

"I'm hoping they're not armed with guns. If you get shot at, feel free to return fire. And pray that we're better shots than they are."

Miss Bang nodded her understanding. Tinka smacked her belaying pin into a palm and grinned.

"Don't worry about us, Lieutenant," the professor said. "We'll be fine." He clapped Willie on the shoulder. "Trust me."

Willie did not look reassured.

"Let's go," he said, extinguished his torch, and turned toward the stairs.

CHAPTER SIXTEEN
VOICES IN THE DUNGEON

W e crept up the stairs. My brother took the lead, with me behind him and Tinka at my back. Professor Crackle came next, and Miss Bang in the rear.

We came to a landing which opened out to a new level of cells. A pair of sconces illuminated the hall. Willie didn't spare a glance to the stairs that continued to climb upward, but carefully peeked out into the hallway. I paused at his shoulder and held my breath as he inspected each side of the stairwell and then motioned us on. While the floors on the level below were covered with sand and dirt, these were stone, and relatively clean. There were no convenient footprints or trails in the dust to indicate where the prisoners might have been taken. The rest of the level appeared dark, as far as we could tell. This left us no choice but to search the entire floor until we found the prisoners or were discovered ourselves.

Willie relit his torch from one of the sconces and moved off to the left, gliding over the floor as if his feet didn't even touch the stones. Tinka snaked past me and prowled soundlessly after my brother. I followed more slowly, doing my best to make sure that I made no sound as my soles touched the rock. After taking several steps, I heard a shuffling sound behind me and froze in my tracks. I looked back to find myself staring into the professor's eyes. He stopped and gave me a questioning look. I put a finger to my lips and listened.

Nothing.

Miss Bang appeared at the professor's side. She looked around and gestured a question with one hand. I opened my mouth but caught myself before I spoke. The sound was gone.

I shrugged in apology and turned and followed my brother.

After a few steps, the shuffling came again. I stopped. Silence. Behind me Miss Bang and the professor looking at me questioningly.

Motioning for them to stay put, I crossed to where Willie and Tinka waited, unsure of what was happening. I gestured to Professor Crackle to follow. He moved forward, shuffling his feet along the stone corridor, scraping the soles of his shoes and making a rasping noise. I scowled at the professor. Willie stepped next to me and gestured violently with a finger to his lips and emphatic pointing to the professor's feet.

Professor Crackle looked confused for a moment, but then nodded. He stepped toward us, walking exaggeratedly on his toes. Willie rolled his eyes and resumed the lookout ahead of us.

Miss Bang waited until the professor had caught up to me, and then she drifted soundlessly to us. She gave the professor a scolding look and nodded to me.

We ghosted through the maze of cells, checking them as we went. The doors were stout wood, bound and banded with iron. A small window was set into each cell door with a hatch covering metal bars. Willie opened each one, raised his torch, and looked within as we went. The cells appeared to be dark, but my brother only gave them a quick look. I glanced into a couple of the cells, but without a light source I hardly saw anything other than a few streaks of light on the opposite wall. Willie seemed confident that each cell was empty and moved quickly to the next.

We worked our way down one hallway, finding nothing but empty cells. After working our way to another dead end, I stopped

Willie and leaned close to him, whispering, "Are you sure that they're down here?"

"No," he hissed, "but we need to check all the cells before we head up."

The professor moved up next to us. "Something must be down here, my boy. Someone had to light those torches by the stairs. There must be a reason to come into the dungeons."

Miss Bang appeared at his elbow. "Harmonious, listen." She turned her head slightly.

We all went silent, ears straining for the slightest sound.

The torch my brother carried crackled. I held my breath.

Nothing.

And then, a slight susurration.

The professor opened his mouth to speak, but Miss Bang placed a finger over his lips.

We listened.

It came again. A faint, irregular susurration. A sound that reminded me of...

"Voices," Miss Bang whispered.

The professor nodded.

Miss Bang took the lit torch out of my brother's hands, handing him her own unlit one. She turned and slipped back the way we came. We followed her, moving as quietly as we could. She led us back to the stairs, and then down a different hallway, stopping every few feet to listen for the sound again.

We proceeded in this halting fashion, stopping every few feet to make sure we could still hear the voices. They got louder as we progressed, but we still couldn't make out who was talking, or what they were saying. The hard walls made the sound echo through the hallways, and we caught ourselves making false turns a couple of times, chasing echoes.

Miss Bang came to a stop to listen, but Willie kept moving past her.

I hissed at him. "Willie!"

He turned back briefly. "It's them! The voices are female." He moved forward, one hand trailing along the wall as he moved out of the light from Miss Bang's torch.

I started to follow, but Miss Bang put her arm across my chest to stop me.

"The voices are female, but they're not speaking English," Miss Bang warned me.

"We've got to stop him!" the professor cried and dashed past us into the darkness.

Miss Bang growled after them. "Follow the wall and be careful!" she whispered to Tinka and me as she moved back down the hall, pulled an unlit torch from a wall sconce, and jammed the lit torch in to replace it.

Tinka slid confidently past me into the darkness, the fingers of one hand faintly touching the stones. I put my palm against the wall and stepped after her, trying to find a compromise between speed and stealth as I went. I could hear the professor's shuffling footsteps ahead of me, and a "oof" as he ran into something. That gave me enough of a warning that I slowed down before the wall beneath my hand disappeared. I stopped and felt for the wall. I had come to a corner in the passageway.

I felt more than heard someone move by me across the hallway, and a slight moan from the professor. He must have run into the wall, and Miss Bang was seeing to him. I paused and considered if I should help, or try to stop my brother.

Down the new passage, I heard Willie's rapid steps, and saw him silhouetted against a faint glow of light that lit the hall from around another corner. "Chandra! Chandra!" he called.

His was the only voice I heard.

I started down the hall after my brother, but before I got more than a few steps he turned the corner at a run. I saw him lit up by the yellow light of a lamp for an instant, and then he was gone.

Screams erupted from down the hall, and the sounds of a struggle. So much for stealth. I started to run after my brother, but I was caught up short when a hand grabbed my shoulder and dragged me into a cell. I started to fight back, but a voice in my ear said, "Be still, Sir Richard. We can't help him now." It was Miss Bang.

"Miss Ba..." I started to say but was cut short by her hand clamped over my mouth.

"Quiet," she said. "You, too, Harmonious."

A low moan of assent came from the professor.

I nodded, and her hand withdrew.

Sounds of struggle continued in the hallway. There seemed to be a lot of grunting, mostly by Willie from the sound of it, and flesh striking against flesh. The conflict sounded energetic, intense, and brief.

The voices came again. Much closer. Much clearer.

And definitely not in English.

Miss Bang translated under her breath. "They're wondering where he came from. How they are going to explain him showing up in the middle of the dungeon. One of them..." She paused. "One of them suggested that they tie him up and dump him in a cell without telling anyone about him, but the other one is insisting that they take him to their commander." She listened as the women bickered back and forth. There seemed to be two distinct voices. "They're arguing about who has to carry him."

"We can sneak up..." Professor Crackle started, but his words were quickly cut off.

"No. We let them come to us, then surprise them."

He spoke again, but his voice sounded muffled. She shushed him. "I trust Tinka to stay hidden and know when to attack."

The voices had stopped arguing.

I heard more grunting, a burst of laughter, and an angry retort.

After a few moments, a quieter response, and more sounds of effort.

I blinked as I realized that I could see the faint outline of someone standing in front of me. The light was moving down the hall. We shifted to either side of the doorway and watched as two women came around the corner, a smaller woman carrying a lantern, and the other dragging Willie along with her hands hooked under his armpits.

They moved slowly, the woman obviously struggling with my brother's weight. Both women were dressed in baggy trousers and coarse shirts. It looked like a uniform, but unlike any other uniforms I'd ever seen. Could the Kindred be raising their own militia? With women as soldiers as well as men?

As they came up to the open door of the cell where we were hiding, the one in the lead paused. She raised her lamp higher and pointed to the open doorway. She had barely uttered a word when Professor Crackle rushed past me and grabbed her, knocking the lamp out of her hand, and shoving her face first against the far wall. The lamp fell to the stone floor and shattered, splashing oil over the stones. The other woman dropped my brother to the floor and turned to help her companion. I spurred myself to action, dashing from the cell and grabbing her from behind.

The flame from the lamp caught the spilled oil and spread with a wave of light and heat. The hallway filled with the smell of burning oil.

The woman fought like a demon. She slammed her head back into my face and I barely turned enough to keep her from breaking my nose in the process. She grabbed my arms with both hands and bent at the waist, bending me over her and pulling my feet off the floor. She pivoted forward, throwing me to the floor and landing on top of me. I lay there dazed, unable to maintain my grip on her. She jumped to her feet and turned to face me. My jaw and chest exploded with pain as she rained a flurry of blows upon me.

I pulled my arms in to shield myself from her blows. She swept them aside with one hand and caught me with a right cross, bouncing my head against the floor, filling my mouth with the coppery taste of blood, and making my vision swim for a moment. She brought both hands up to deliver another blow, but instead there was a loud crack and she toppled forward across my body.

I looked up to see Tinka, holding her belaying pin, her face split in a grin that was positively feral. I looked past Tinka to where Professor Crackle still grappled with the other guard. The professor trapped one of her arms, but she was pounding her free elbow into him with remarkable violence, pivoting around the professor and forcing him into the wall. Miss Bang appeared from one of the cells with an unlit torch in her hands and slammed it into the woman's midsection. The professor and the guard both let out an oof and bounced off the wall. Miss Bang followed up with a two-handed strike across the other woman's jaw. The woman collapsed in the professor's arms and he let her tumble to the floor.

I rolled the first guard off me and tried to push myself back up. This action met with mixed results, as I felt the world suddenly spinning around me. Tinka put a hand on my shoulder. "Are ye hurt?"

"Just a bit dizzy," I lied, and tried to pull my legs underneath me.

"Then stop layin' about when there's work to be done," she said and dragged me up to my feet. I lurched to a standing position.

"Thank you, Tinka. I need a moment to catch my balance," I said. My face hurt with each word, and I could feel one eye already starting to swell. "How's Willie?"

Tinka peered at him. "Looks a mite beaten up. 'Tanya?"

Miss Bang came around Tinka, bent down and grabbed my brother under the arms. "Hopefully, he's not seriously injured. We need to move him away from this fire. The oil is still spreading. Tinka, grab the lieutenant's feet. My lord, please help Harmonious move the guards away from the flames." Miss Bang and Tinka lifted Willie and quickly moved him several feet down the corridor, back the way the guards had come.

Professor Crackle shielded his face from the flames with one arm while trying to move the unconscious guard with the other. The flaming oil continued to spread making it hard for him to get a grip without getting burned.

"Professor," I called as I reached down to the guard next to me and nearly fell over myself. "Grab her feet." I hooked my arms under the shoulders and knees of the larger woman and levered her against my chest. I staggered to my feet with her in my arms and stumbled after Miss Bang and Tinka.

The air was hot and thick with the smell of the oil, and my head was still spinning, but I managed to follow them for a couple of yards before I lost my balance and fell to my knees, dumping the woman to the floor. As she hit, something metal clattered onto the stone. It was a pistol. I made sure the safety was engaged, then tucked it into my belt and looked back at the flames of the oil fire.

Professor Crackle stood silhouetted against the flames. He stepped back and grabbed the guard's ankles and rapidly shuffled away from the fire, dragging her behind him. The wall of heat was palpable, burning my eyes as I watched him. I turned my face away and blinked my eyes to wet them again. The ladies carried my brother to the corner, where they were lit by the light of another lamp down the next hallway.

Miss Bang propped Willie up against the wall, and then looked back at us. "That's good enough. Leave them there. We need to find what they were guarding."

"Shouldn't we secure them first?"

"They're unconscious, my lord. If we hurry, we can be gone before they wake." Miss Bang disappeared into the lit hallway.

I got back to my feet and staggered down the corridor, coming to a stop next to my brother. "Is he going to be all right?" I asked. Willie's face was covered with contusions, and one of his eyes was beginning to swell.

Miss Bang called back over her shoulder, "He's taken a bit of a beating, but I don't think anything is broken. I'm sure he'll recover momentarily, my lord. In the meantime, we need to see if the maharani and your aunt are in one of these cells."

The professor came up behind me. "Good idea, my boy. Much as I hate to drag a woman across the floor, that proved the trick for getting her away from the fire." He clapped me on the back.

"Harmonious, did you get the guard's keys?"

He blinked at Miss Bang. "Um, no, my dear, was I supposed to?"

She arched an eyebrow at him. "It will make it much easier to free the prisoners if we have the keys to their cell."

"Ah, yes. Excellent point." He turned and walked back to the unconscious guards.

Miss Bang beckoned to me. "Help me find your aunt, my lord."

I nodded and stood, hanging on to the wall to keep myself steady as the last of the dizziness faded. I followed Miss Bang around the corner.

A lantern sat on a low table flanked by two stools. The table was tucked near the end of a short hallway with doors to several cells on both sides of the hallway. Tinka prowled around the table, looking at the cell doors but not touching anything. Miss Bang walked up to the table. "Hello? Is anyone there?"

There was no answer.

Were we in the wrong place? Or were they not answering because they didn't know if they could trust Miss Bang? The maharani and Aunt Phyllis had just met her and the professor a few minutes before they were kidnapped. They need to hear a voice they could trust.

I moved up to the first door. "Aunt Phyllis? It's me, your nephew. I'm here to get you out."

I heard a faint gasp and the word "Nephew?" from one of the other cells.

"Aunt Phyllis? Where are you? We don't know how much time we have before we're discovered." I moved to the next cell and peered inside, but the darkness beyond the small window in the door remained impenetrable.

"Nephew?" the voice came again. "What are you *doing* here?" A pair of hands appeared grasping the bars on the cell across the hall from me.

I crossed to my aunt, grasping her wrinkled hands through the bars. "We've come to rescue you and the maharani."

Miss Bang stepped to the corner. "Harmonious, did you find the keys yet?"

"Are you mad?" hissed Aunt Phyllis. "If they find you here, they'll kill you. They've only kept me alive so they can use me to threaten Maharani Chandrakanta. Why didn't you talk to William about this before you came? He would have stopped you."

I sighed at my aunt. "We did talk to Willie. He's the one who led us here. Without him we never would have found this place."

"William? William is here?" This voice was not my aunt's and came from the next cell down.

I peered through the window but could only see the faint outline of a person in the cell. "Yes," I replied. "He got knocked out in the struggle with the guards, but he's here."

"He's hurt?" A pair of well-manicured hands gripped the open window in the door. Brown eyes peered out at me with concern.

"Just banged up a bit. He'll be fine. But we need to get you out of there. Professor, have you found those keys?"

"No, my boy. I'm not seeing any sign of them." He appeared at the corner of the hallway. "And I think we'd better hurry. I'm also not seeing any sign of one of the guards."

"Oh, Harmonious," Miss Bang sighed. "You had one job."

CHAPTER SEVENTEEN

OUT OF THE FRYING PAN...

Tinka rushed to the corner and looked down the hallway toward the fire. "Yep, one of 'em's scarpered. And the bloody fire has spread across the hallway. The flames aren't high, but they're too deep to jump over now. We're trapped."

"Miss Bang, you're good with locks. Can you do anything with these?" I beckoned her to me.

She pulled a pair of pins out of her hair as she came to the door. "I'm much better with modern locks, my lord. I don't know how quickly I'll be able to open this one."

"Are you familiar with lever locks?" the maharani asked.

Miss Bang glanced up at her. "I would expect a mechanism this old to be a ward lock. Maybe a more complicated type of ward..."

"They were, but they were replaced when lever locks first came out. Too many skeleton keys floating about at the time. Of course, that was before the new palace was built next to the city center."

"Why do you know so much about the locks?" I asked.

"Part of the family history, Sir Richard. And my father believes it is a useful lesson for the principles of government. One should always be aware of the impact a decision makes upon the people and be prepared in case enough of your people are displeased."

"A very forward-thinking policy, Princess," the professor said.

"And a bit of useful practical knowledge," Miss Bang added as the lock to the maharani's cell opened with a click. "Because you can't tell them apart by looking at the outside of the lock."

The door opened inward, and the maharani appeared, blinking a bit in the light. "William? Where is he?" I pointed, and she rushed to him. She was still wearing her clothes from the party the other day, but she had been stripped of all her jewelry, even her hair pins. Her dress was covered with a dark brown stain of dried blood. Dried blood also clung to her arms in some places, but it appeared that she had done her best to rub most of it off her hands and face. Her long dark hair fell over her shoulders as she knelt next to Willie. "Oh my William! Are you hurt?" She stroked his cheek with her hand, and he stirred weakly.

"Are *you* hurt?" Miss Bang asked, gesturing to the caked blood in the maharani's dress.

She shook her head. "It's not my blood."

"Miss Bang, do you think you can help my aunt now?"

Miss Bang moved to the door in front of me. "It will just be a minute, Lady Griffith-Holmes."

"Please hurry, dear. I am not pleased with these accommodations."

I was stunned. Aunt Phyllis had made a joke.

Aunt Phyllis snapped me out of it with a sharp comment. "Don't just stand there gaping, Nephew. Go help your brother."

"Yes, ma'am!" I said.

"Nephew," she called before I could step around Miss Bang. "Thank you for coming to find me."

"You're welcome, Aunt Phyllis." I crossed over to where the maharani was tending to my brother.

Willie roused at last, with the maharani gently stroking his cheek.

His face was already swelling around his left eye, and it looked like he would have an impressive black eye. I said, "You might want to be careful. It looks like he took a couple of good shots to the face." The maharani nodded.

"William?"

He blinked. "Chandra? We found you!"

She smiled. "Yes. Yes, you did." She leaned towards him but checked herself and kept her distance.

"But we're not out of the woods yet, Willie," I said. "Do you think you're up for more action?"

That seemed to bring my brother around. He blinked and gave his head a good shake. "Where are we?"

"Still in the dungeon. One of the guards is missing and Tinka says that the fire has spread across the hallway. We may be trapped in here."

Willie blinked, and his eyes were clear. "That's not good."

"There's another way," the maharani said. "There's a back entry to the dungeon level. It should be a little farther down the passage."

"Why would there be a secret entry to the dungeons?" I asked.

"There were times in the past when young courtiers were imprisoned for courting a lady who was of too high a caste. Ladies of the court sometimes wanted to visit their imprisoned suitors... discreetly." I thought I saw a slight blush come to her cheeks, but perhaps that was a trick of the dim light.

"And they found builders who are suitably accommodating?" I asked.

She nodded.

"The more I learn about India, the more I'm convinced I know nothing about India," I said.

We helped my brother to his feet. He staggered, but stood, leaning a little bit on the princess. With another loud click, Miss Bang managed to unlock the other cell door, and helped Aunt Phyllis step out into the hallway. She looked both old and frail, and like a storm beginning to build. Her dress also was liberally splattered with dried blood.

"We may have to move quickly, Aunt Phyllis. Are you up to it?"

"Don't try to lecture me, Nephew. I will keep up. Now let's get out of here."

I nodded in agreement, and wisely said nothing.

Willie looked to the princess and said, "Chandra, lead the way."

"Professor, would you escort my aunt?" I asked. "Tinka, guard the rear and warn us if we have company. We don't want to lose anyone." The professor nodded, but Tinka drew herself up and frowned at me.

"An' who put you in charge, Mr. Fancypants?" she said.

"You have a better idea, Miss Rigger?" I replied.

"No, sir, Cap'n." She winked and saluted. "Just wanted to see if you're on your toes."

Aunt Phyllis' eyes widened slightly as she glanced at Tinka, though if that was due to her anatomy or her attire I had no idea. She gave a small snort as Tinka saluted me. It seemed that she had rendered a judgement.

I shook my head. "Willie, do you have your pistol?"

He checked his holster. "No, they must have taken it from me when they knocked me out."

I pulled the pistol I took off the guard from my belt. "Is this it?"

He took the weapon from me, ejected the magazine, and then replaced it when he saw it was still loaded. "Yes. Thank you." He put it back in his holster.

"All right. Let's go. Maharani, lead the way." I grabbed up the remaining lamp from the table, and Willie and I followed the maharani. The professor and Aunt Phyllis trailed us, with Miss Bang close behind, and Tinka bringing up the rear with a lit torch in one hand and her belaying pin and a fresh torch held in an on-guard position. She trailed her free hand along one wall as she followed.

The maharani led us farther down the hallway and stopped at a stretch of blank wall. I held the lantern up so she could see better.

She studied the surface of the wall carefully, and then pressed on two stones a shoulder's width apart. The stones moved into the wall about an inch or so, then the section of wall pivoted, and she slipped through.

Willie grabbed the edge of the rotating wall and squeezed through after her. It was a tight fit for him. This entrance had been built for a much smaller person. I handed the lamp to Willie, and then held the door for Aunt Phyllis to climb through. Professor Crackle paused to let Miss Bang pass ahead of him, and then wiggled his way through with slightly less difficulty than Willie had. Tinka grabbed the door with her free hand and motioned me through with her belaying pin. "Go," she said, "I got this."

I edged through the portal sideways, getting hung up for a moment when the buttons on my vest caught on the door. I pressed my hand down the length of my front and pushed through. On the other side of the door was a narrow, finished tunnel, dusty with age and neglect. The air was dry and stale. Tinka stepped through and let the door slam shut with a thud and a last puff of air to stir the flames of the torch.

The tunnel was almost as narrow as the door, and it made sharp turns that indicated that it was built out of the spaces between other rooms. We moved quickly, going single file through the slim space and up a flight of stairs. At the top of the stairs, the tunnel ended abruptly, at what must have been another secret door.

The maharani turned to face the rest of us. In a quiet voice she said, "Once we pass this door, we'll be in the midst of the kidnappers. They could be anywhere. We won't be able to go back down through the dungeons, or out through the gates. We need to make our way to the courtyard. There is a well there. If we can make it there, we can escape. We must make it to the well." She looked at Willie, who nodded his assent. She looked at each of us in turn.

The professor rubbed his chin. "You're sure there is an exit there, my dear?"

She nodded. "It is hidden inside the well, Professor."

"One more secret of this castle. I see."

"Are you sure about this, Maharani Chandrakanta?" Aunt Phyllis asked. "This sounds very dangerous. Isn't there another way out?"

The maharaja's daughter shook her head. "If there is, I don't know of it. I'm sorry you were dragged into this, Lady Griffith-Holmes. These people wanted me, and they've been using you to guarantee my behavior. We both know that as soon as I'm gone, you won't be safe anymore. This really is the only way. I'm sorry to ask this of you, but there really isn't an alternative."

"Don't worry, my good lady," the professor added, "we'll keep you safe. Titania and I have been in a few scrapes like this. We'll take good care of you."

Aunt Phyllis sighed. "Jeremy always warned me that life with him would be an adventure. I expected some of his posting would put us in danger, but I never really thought I'd end up fleeing for my life. Very well. It is time to do or die."

The maharani released the door, and one by one, we slipped out into the hallway. After traversing the tunnels and dungeons, the natural light coming from the window across the hall seemed strange to my eyes.

It was still day. Indeed, despite all the time we had spent searching and climbing beneath the fortress, it wasn't much past mid-afternoon. We stepped over to the window and looked out. The window overlooked a courtyard paved in flat stones about a floor below us. The yard was wide enough to park five or six lorries side by side. A large gate sat almost opposite us. The walls of the fortress curved around on either side with many balconies and breezeways looking down onto the courtyard. Two large lorries were parked on either side of the gate. In the middle of the yard, a stone well sat, a relatively modern looking roof mounted over it on four stout wooden posts.

Willie moved up to the window, peering down at the vehicles and up at the walls of the fortress. "I don't see any sign of anyone, but if they've got guards up on that wall, they'll have no problem pinning us down as we try to make for the well."

I pointed to the lorries. "Maybe we could find a way around to one of the doors near the vehicles, and use one of them to get away?"

The maharani shook her head. "Even if we could get one of them started without drawing notice, the road down the mountain is narrow and switches back several times. We wouldn't be able to make any speed while descending that, and the whole time we'd be under view of the castle."

"And their guns," Willie added.

Professor Crackle peered over his glasses. "It would seem that our best course of action is to get as close as we can and then make a run for it." He glanced at the maharani and back to the courtyard. "It doesn't look like much."

"It's enough to get us out of here," the maharani said.

I nodded. "Very well, how do we get down there from here? That missing guard is bound to raise an alarm sometime soon."

No sooner were the words out of my mouth than a loud, rapid clanging of metal on metal rang out. The alarm had been raised.

"This way!" the maharani cried, and took off down the hallway. Willie dashed after her, his gun drawn, and the professor and Miss Bang followed with Aunt Phyllis between them. I drew my pistol, and Tinka and I brought up the rear. We sped past a hallway leading deeper into the fortress, and had to skid to a stop to keep from running into Willie and the princess as they abruptly changed direction.

"Back! Around the corner," Willie said in a stage whisper while waving us into the other corridor. I was about to ask why, when I realized I already had the answer: the sound of running feet echoing down the passage ahead of us, coming closer.

We bundled into the side hall and ducked into a nearby room to hide. Willie and I took places on either side of the door and pointed our weapons at it, ready to unleash a deadly volley of lead in case we had been spotted and someone tried to follow us in.

The sounds of boots running down the hallway got louder, and louder, and then mercifully passed by in a thunder, running to answer the alarm. Hopefully, they thought we were still in the dungeon searching for a way out.

We waited for a few moments, the entire room quiet except for the crackle and pop of the lit torch that Tinka carried. Willie nodded, apparently satisfied that we were undetected. We turned to the others and froze.

The room we had chosen for our hiding place was apparently a large storeroom. Shelves lined the walls and barrels were arrayed in groups on the floor. Smaller barrels filled some of the shelves, but the rest were piled high with bag after bag after bag of black powder. Each barrel and bag was marked with warnings in three languages. "Flammable! Keep away from heat and open flame!"

The torch snapped and popped as the dust drifted up across the flame. Dust from a broken bag of black powder that spilled across the floor from where it had fallen from one of the shelves. The air was tinged with a faint smell of sulphur. This wasn't modern black powder, but an older type that put off more dust and was more prone to explosions.

"Time to go," I said. "Willie, get the door. Tinka, back up slowly, please." I glanced upward and saw that there was another laden shelf over the door. "And please lower the torch a bit, we don't want to bump the top shelf."

Tinka held her free hand back to me, grabbing my hand tightly as I took it. Willie quietly opened the door and stood to the side. She stepped backwards slowly, careful not to stir up more dust than was absolutely necessary. She slowly lowered the torch until she held it straight out in front of her, still popping as the warm flame drew the dust up to it. I guided Tinka backwards, pulling the arm holding the torch down slightly to keep the flames from licking at the bottom of the shelf over the door. We backed out into the hallway and Tinka hastily moved to the opposite side.

Willie ushered the others out into the hall.

"That shouldn't be there," the maharani said, fear and confusion showing on her face. "The castle never had artillery. There's no reason for a stockpile of gunpowder here."

"Not unless someone is planning on stirring up a rebellion," the professor said.

"Black powder," Miss Bang corrected. "They must be using older weapons that can't take the force of modern gunpowder."

Willie appeared in the doorway to the room, holding a small bag of black powder under his arm. He closed the door behind him. "Let's move. We can talk it over later."

"What are you doing with *that*, young man?" Aunt Phyllis demanded, pointing to the bag my brother carried. I cringed inwardly, and was glad she wasn't talking to me, for once. "Are you trying to get us all killed?"

"No, Aunt Phyllis," he replied, "but if we're discovered, I think this may be just what we need for a distraction so we can get away. So, keep hold of that torch, but don't get too close."

"No fear o' that!" Tinka said.

"This is no time for a debate," I said.

"We must move! This way!" the maharani said, pointing back to the main hall, but she hesitated. "No, wait. This way." This time she took off down the corridor we were standing in, heading deeper into the fortress.

"Hurry," Willie said as he chased after her, the rest of us following in their wake.

We pounded down the corridor and then down a flight of stairs to a level where the walls were irregular and were scuffed or patched in places. The maharani led us to a door where light shone through a metal grill at approximately head height. She paused and peeked at the room beyond, before opening the door and leading us through.

An array of scents assaulted us as we stepped into the room. Chief among them were smoke, meat roasting, curry, and a variety of other spices that my nose completely failed to make any sense of. The room was a large kitchen. Windows lined one wall, many of them half-shuttered. Several hearths were on one side of the room, two with fires lit in them. The opposite wall was lined with shelves of jars containing herbs, powders, and other ingredients. Two long tables ran the length of the room, with portions of a meal's preparation in progress. The alarm had apparently interrupted the cooks at their work, and they'd paused just long enough to pull food away from the flames before attending to the emergency.

"Well, they're not trained military," Willie said. "Our cooks wouldn't stop cooking unless they were under attack."

At the far end of the room, an archway led into an adjoining space. The maharani led us through this archway into an anteroom. To one side was an open door to a pantry stocked with larger food-stuffs. Opposite that was a pair of double doors leading into the courtyard.

Willie opened the door a crack and peered out at the yard and the balconies surrounding it. After a moment, he pulled his head back in and closed the door. "All right. Out the door to the left there is a rack with firewood. That gives us a little cover, but after that it is a straight shot to the well."

"Shot?" asked Aunt Phyllis.

"A straight run," Willie corrected himself. "I don't see any guards, but that doesn't mean there aren't any, or that they won't be coming back any moment." He pointed at me. "You stay by the wood pile and provide covering fire. I'll lead the way to the well and throw the bag of black powder at the lorries in the yard. Tinka, if we're in trouble, you throw that torch at the bag."

"You better throw it far, mate. That's gonna make a big blast," Tinka warned.

He nodded. "Professor, Miss Bang, you make sure Chandra and Aunt Phyllis make it safely to the well."

"They won't hurt me," the maharani said. "They need me alive to bargain with my father."

"I'm not taking any chances." Willie looked at each of us. "Everyone clear on what they're doing?" We nodded. "Then let's move."

Tinka poked me. "I thought you were in charge."

"I'm delegating to a professional."

Willie opened the door and we had no more time to talk.

CHAPTER EIGHTEEN
...INTO THE LINE OF FIRE

We poured out of the door behind my brother and rushed over to a set of posts driven into the ground with wood stacked high between them. The yard seemed much wider, now that we were in it, than when we had been looking down from above. The gates were almost directly opposite us, and on the other three sides were tiers of balconies and walkways lining the fortress.

Willie stopped next to the wood pile for a second, his eyes scanning the walls for signs of watchers. Then he was in action again, moving out into the courtyard towards the well at its center. "Come on, keep moving." He held his gun high as he went and turned to scan the walls.

Miss Bang grabbed Aunt Phyllis' arm and together they started after him at a fast walk, with Professor Crackle close behind. The maharani followed, moving at a fast clip. Tinka and I both hesitated and scanned the walls one more time before leaving cover, so we were the first to see the gunmen step up to the railing.

"Look out!" I shouted as the men raised their rifles and took aim at our party.

The maharani turned and raised her hands. "Stop! I forbid you to shoot!"

Tinka took off in a dead run, her belaying pin and the lit and unlit torches clattering to the stones. She dove and caught the maharani at the waist, both women tumbling to the ground and rolling away as the gunmen fired, their bullets striking the stones of the courtyard just behind where the maharani was standing.

Willie and I both returned fire as Tinka scrambled to her feet, pulling the maharani up with her. Aunt Phyllis hunkered down in the middle of the courtyard with her hands over her head, apparently too scared to move. Miss Bang grabbed Professor Crackle by the collar and leaned over my aunt, pulling the professor off his feet and using his body as a shield.

"But they're not supposed to hurt me," the maharani said, clearly shaken.

"I don't think they know that!" Tinka yelled and urged the woman into a dead run to the well.

I squeezed off a couple more shots, but they ricocheted off the stone balustrade instead of hitting their targets. I ducked behind the wood pile as one of the gunmen took a shot at me.

"I thought you could shoot!" Willie cried as he fired, backing up to the well.

"It's a little different when they're shooting back!" I replied.

The gunmen were now shooting Professor Crackle, exposed as he was. He grunted with each impact.

"Don't think about it," Miss Bang called to me. "Don't even aim. Just step out and shoot." She looked back at me. "Trust yourself, my lord."

This is madness, I thought, but if I did nothing, Aunt Phyllis and Miss Bang would be pinned down in the middle of the courtyard. I took a deep breath, then stepped away from the wood pile, spun and fired twice.

For a moment, the courtyard was quiet, except for the sound of a rifle as it clattered and bounced down to the yard below. The wood of the forestock was splintered from the bullet's impact. I looked up into the eyes of the young soldier, who stared wide-eyed in disbelief that his gun had been shot out of his hands.

"Go, go, go!" I turned and scooped up the lit torch that Tinka had dropped, and ran to the well behind Professor Crackle and Miss Bang, who had scooped up Aunt Phyllis and carried her between them.

We huddled behind the well, using its stones and the wood roof to provide cover as the remaining rifleman fired on us again.

"Not bad," my brother said.

"I was trying to hit him, not his gun." I panted from the exertion.

"No, I mean you hit the other one. He went down. I think he's just wounded, but he's out of the fight. The one shooting now is the boy that dropped his gun. He grabbed his partner's rifle."

"You boys can congratulate yourselves later," Aunt Phyllis reminded us. "I'd like to see this exit that is supposed to be here."

The maharani nodded. "Of course. We have to..." She stood up to look into the well and smacked her hand on a large sheet of metal bolted onto the stones at the top of the well. "What? NO! We need to get in the well!"

Willie pulled her down as the gunman took another shot.

"Out of time, lads!" Tinka warned. "I hear running feet. They're about to have reinforcements."

Professor Crackle lifted his head up over the top edge of the well.

"Professor!" Willie started to grab him, but Miss Bang stopped him.

"He knows what he's doing," she said.

Another shot rang out, followed by the sound of the bullet bouncing off the metal cap on the well. The rest of us jumped, but Miss Bang only winced.

"There's a hinge!" the professor said. "And it looks like it is only bolted down on one side." He stood up farther and stretched out over the sealed well. Another report and the loud spang of the bullet striking the cover, and Professor Crackle fell backwards, sprawling out on his back. "But I think it is latched down on the other side."

Miss Bang pulled the professor back to the cover of the small roof. Aunt Phyllis touched his arm. "Are you hurt, young man?"

The professor shook his head and fingered the front of his jacket. "Not at all." He poked his finger through a hole and wiggled it. "But I will miss this jacket."

"Willie," I said. "We don't have enough cover here, and we need that distraction now." I shook the torch I carried. "Where's that bag of black powder?"

My brother looked around. The bag was no longer in his hands. He started looking around frantically to see where he had dropped it.

"Oi!" Tinka pointed to where the bag sat on the cobblestones between the well and the wood pile.

"Crap."

"William!"

"I'm sorry, Aunt Phyllis, but..." He sputtered to a halt.

The professor leaned in next to my brother. "I don't blame you, Lieutenant," he said in a low voice.

Miss Bang spoke up. "Will that still serve as a distraction? Is it far enough away that we'll survive the blast?"

Willie looked at the bag of gunpowder. "I, I don't know."

"Too late!" Tinka cried as several men appeared on one of the balconies and raised their rifles. We huddled behind the stone of the well as they fired, bullets bounding off the stones all around us.

"They're going to kill us!" Aunt Phyllis cried.

"No," Willie yelled over the gunshots. "They're keeping us pinned down. Buying time for other troops to make it to the courtyard.

"What should I do?" I asked.

"Throw the torch!" the maharani yelled.

"Do it!" Willie added.

I rolled up on my knees and threw the lit torch overhand. It guttered as it flipped end over end and I silently prayed that it wouldn't go out as it fell to the cobblestones. My heart leapt as I saw that the torch remained lit as it landed on the stones, and then it sank again when I realized that it had landed short of the target. I ducked down again as another volley of gunfire rained down on us.

"I missed, blast it. The torch fell short." I smacked the ground with my hand.

"How far?" Willie asked.

Professor Crackle peeked over the well. "Not by much. In fact, the torch is still rolling towards... Oh, oh dear." He ducked back down and covered his head.

Nothing happened.

Bullets bounced around us to remind us of the presence of the gunmen. The professor raised his head and peeked over the well again. "I could have sworn it was going to roll right up against..."

The ground bucked as the powder went up with a thunderous explosion. The professor went tumbling backwards and the wooden roof protecting the well splintered with the force of the blast.

The world vanished in a grey haze as dust and smoke rolled over us. The smell of sulphur filled my nostrils, and my ears rang from the sound of the explosion. I shook my head to try and clear it, but there was only a painful throbbing as the ringing echoed.

A hand grabbed my shoulder. I looked up and saw Willie through the haze. His mouth moved. He was clearly yelling, but I couldn't hear a thing. He pulled on my shoulder for me to get up.

I stood and looked around. Smoke obscured most of the courtyard, but I could see a divot had been blasted in the cobblestones. Stones were also missing from the side of the well facing the explosion, but the metal cap was still in place. The roof to the well was completely gone. We were exposed.

Tinka helped the maharani to stand, and I went to help Miss Bang and Aunt Phyllis. There was no sign of Professor Crackle. Willie went to the far side of the well and grabbed the metal cover. He quickly pulled his hand back from the metal, which had absorbed a good portion of heat from the blast. He holstered his gun, then wrapping his hands in the cuffs of his sleeves, he grabbed it again and heaved. The cap came up and over, pivoting on the hinge. As it crashed down soundlessly next to us, I could see a lock still attached to the hasp that held it closed, along with remnants of the rock the hasp was bolted to. The metal had held, but the stone had not.

The maharani, seeing the cap open, joined Willie on the other side of the well. I looked past them to the balconies where the gunmen were, but for the moment we were covered by the smoke. But that wouldn't last long.

The princess gestured to Willie and the well, and when he didn't seem to understand, she climbed inside and disappeared.

Willie started, but then his head came up and he gestured the rest of us to come around to his side of the well. I returned my pistol to its holster and Miss Bang and I helped my aunt to Willie's side while Tinka moved around the other edge of the well. The low wall defining the structure had shattered, leaving a rounded gap with darkness beyond.

Willie gestured for Aunt Phyllis to climb into the well, but she shook her head adamantly. She pulled back against Miss Bang's grip and pointed past the well. I looked up to see the professor staggering back to us, holding his head. His cheeks and forehead were smeared with soot, and splinters of wood clung in his hair. There was no sign of the glasses he had been wearing. He walked up and leaned against the well. He said something, but I couldn't tell what because my ears still hadn't recovered.

Miss Bang spoke to him, and the professor nodded as if he understood her. He replied, and Miss Bang nodded in turn. He moved around behind us.

Miss Bang gained my aunt's attention and spoke again. I could tell she was speaking in a slow, measured fashion, but the ringing in my ears blotted out her words. Miss Bang pointed to herself, then the well, then to Aunt Phyllis, and then the well. She made a placating gesture toward my aunt, and then jumped into the ragged opening.

My aunt pulled violently back, pushing against Willie. She fought as we tried to calm her, and almost slipped out of our grasp.

Tinka moved forward. She grabbed Aunt Phyllis in her four-armed grasp and lifted her bodily off the ground. My aunt screamed and kicked, but Tinka simply turned around, stepped up to the well, and dropped her into it. I imagine my aunt still screamed, but I couldn't hear her through he ringing in my ears. Tinka waited for a couple of moments, and then stepped forward and dropped out of sight as well.

The professor suddenly lunged into me, then struggled to regain his footing. He spoke rapidly to my brother and me and gestured to the hole where the others had disappeared. A moment later, a chip of rock danced off a stone as a bullet struck it. The smoke was starting to clear, and the gunmen were shooting again. It was past time to go.

I grabbed Willie and pushed him toward the opening. He jumped and vanished from sight. I stepped up to the edge and looked down. Below me was blackness, and maybe the faintest glimmer of a reflection.

"They say look before you leap, but they never tell you what to do when you can't see anything." I sighed. The professor patted me on the back and said something, but his voice was still only a faint murmuring behind the discordant bell choir in my head. "Here goes nothing," I said, and jumped into the black.

CHAPTER NINETEEN
DOWN THE WELL

W ind rushed by me as I plummeted into the darkness. At first, I could feel the walls of the well rushing by me, but then it opened out into a larger space and it was just me, the air, and the void. With nothing to provide a frame of reference, I couldn't tell how long or how far I fell. I kept expecting to hit something, but it never came. I started wondering if I was going to fall forever when I plunged into water.

The force of the impact knocked the air out of me. I struggled to keep from drawing a breath as my momentum drove me deep beneath the surface of the water. I pushed out to try to drive myself back to the surface. A moment later, I felt a ripple as something large entered the water nearby. I kicked away from it, and felt a burning start in my lungs. My clothes clung to me, their weight dragging me back down, but I kept pushing forward.

I gasped as my head broke the surface of the water, then coughed and spat up half-inhaled water. Treading water, I looked around. A small half circle of light shone high above me. The entrance to the well? It must have been.

Someone sputtered to the surface nearby. The ringing in my ears was fading, and other than the splashing and lapping of water, it was very quiet down here. And very dark.

"Professor?" I called.

"Ah, my boy, is your hearing coming back? Good, good. Where are the others?" I could hear him splashing as he pushed himself in a small circle.

"It's pitch black down here, Professor. I can't see a thing."

"Oh, poppycock. Your eyes need to adjust. Don't look up at the entrance and your eyes will adjust faster." He splashed around some more.

I looked around me, but all I could see was blackness. I could hear him splashing a few feet away from me and a faint echo of our voices, but that was all.

"Where are the others?" I asked.

"Oh, they're here, no doubt. I suspect they're making for the lamp."

"What lamp?"

"That one, over there. Follow me, my boy!" I heard him splashing energetically in the water, and as the sound grew fainter I realized that he was swimming away from me.

Having little choice, and not wanting to lose track of my sole companion, I swam after him, aiming myself to the sound he made as he pushed himself through the water. As I followed, I thought I saw a faint glimmer of a light ahead of us. As we neared it, the light moved, and then flared into brightness. It was a lantern.

In that moment, I realized where we were. The well led to the reservoir under the mountain. The light was the lamp Willie left by the foot of the stairs, turned low so it would last longer. Now that I knew where I was going, I put more energy into my strokes, swimming hard for the shore.

Professor Crackle and I pulled ourselves up onto the rocky edge of the reservoir as Willie held the lantern over his head and walked to a spot further down the shore. As he approached, the light shone on a group of figures on the shore. Tinka and the maharani were tending to Aunt Phyllis, who was very put out about being unceremoniously dropped into a reservoir from a great height. She was loudly scolding about the inappropriateness of dropping someone down a well against their will

The professor called over Aunt Phyllis' rant, "Where's Titania?"

Willie shone the light up and down the shoreline. "She's got to be here somewhere. She was the second one in."

"Titania? Titania?" the professor called, his voice pitching higher as he repeated the name. "Titania, dear, where are you?" He turned back to Willie. "Shine the light on the water, Lieutenant!"

"What?"

"On the water, now!" the professor commanded.

Willie panned the light over the surface of the underground lake. It didn't seem to make much difference. The light bounced off the surface to the far end of the reservoir or was deflected down into the water. All we could see was a vague, rippling blackness.

"Wait. Back up! Over there!" the professor barked. "There she is!" he cried, then dove back into the water. I stared out in the direction the light was pointing. I thought I saw the suggestion of something floating on the surface of the water. Could it be a body?

I fervently hoped it was anything else.

The professor swam quickly out to the object while the rest of us watched from the edge of the water. I shivered as my wet clothing pulled the heat from my body, but that was nothing compared to the chill dread of what the professor was going to find. He reached the object and turned it over. He cried out, "Titania!"

Tinka let out a whimper, and Aunt Phyllis muttered, "Oh, my. The poor girl."

If the professor swam quickly on the way out, he was positively frantic as he turned and made his way back with Miss Bang in tow. After watching for a few seconds, Tinka dove back in and swam out to help him, her extra arms making her a strong swimmer, although with an unusual cadence to her strokes. When she caught up to the professor, she grabbed Miss Bang with one of her lower arms and dragged her back to us.

Willie handed the lantern off to the maharani, and he and I helped pull Miss Bang up onto the shore. Her skin felt cold to the touch, and her weight seemed to have doubled. We dragged her from the water and laid her out.

Professor Crackle scrambled after us. He pushed me out of the way and tilted Miss Bang's head to one side. With both hands he pressed down on her chest, forcing the body to spew up water. He raised her head and kissed her.

"What are you doing, man!" Willie yelled, and tried to pull him off Miss Bang.

The professor shoved him back. "It's a lifesaving technique. Let me be. If I can get air back into her lungs there is still a chance I can save her." He pressed on Miss Bang's chest again, several short strokes with his hands right over her heart. Then he pinched her nose closed and blew air in through her mouth. He repeated the pattern of pressing on her chest and blowing into her mouth. "Breathe, damn it!" he muttered. He repeated the process.

On the sixth repetition, Miss Bang spasmed as he blew air into her lungs, and she turned on her side, coughing and retching. She sputtered, "Why would you do such a thing?" and gasped for breath.

Hands reached down from all sides to help Miss Bang sit up. She coughed some more and regained some of her composure. She also raised one hand to gingerly cup the side of her head. "I seem to have banged my head on the way down," she said somewhat sheepishly.

"Why would who do such a thing?" the maharani asked.

"I'm sorry?" Miss Bang replied with a confused look.

"Just now you said, 'Why would you do such a thing?' as you came back to us. Who were you talking to?"

Miss Bang shook her head. "I don't know." She cradled the sore spot on her head again and winced. "I'm afraid this bump on the head may have scrambled things a bit."

The maharani nodded. "Do you think you're able to travel? This isn't going to be a safe refuge for long. They're going to figure out where we went sooner or later."

Miss Bang nodded, and held a hand out to the professor. "I think so."

The professor helped her up. She was a little unsteady on her feet, but she seemed content to lean on the professor for support. I saw a small grin cross Tinka's face, but she noticed me watching her and quickly put on a look of concern for her friend. I silently wondered how much Tinka knew about the relationship between the professor and Miss Bang.

"Good," the maharani said. "I know that I, for one, could do with some dry clothes."

Raising the lantern, she turned and led us back along the shoreline. She walked up to the rock wall, and pushed on a hidden switch. A seam suddenly appeared in a section of the nearby rock, pivoting outward to reveal a hidden door.

We bundled through the door and Willie pulled it shut again. We stood, dripping, in the center of the chamber, which I realized was part of the tunnels that Willie had led us through earlier. I looked at the pool of water gathering at our feet and asked, "Haven't we left them a track straight to this door? They just need to follow the water."

The maharani grinned and reached into a cabinet to pull on a cord hidden there. As she held it, there was a rushing sound of water nearby. She released the pull, and a second later the sound of water faded. "Not anymore. I released water from a secondary reservoir that washed away any traces we might have left."

"It seems your ancestor considered every eventuality, Princess." The professor rubbed his chin. "I do admire that kind of thoroughness."

"He had a lot of time to think about it, Professor Crackle, and to make preparations." She handed her lantern off to Willie, then moved to another cabinet and opened the door. Grabbing another lantern from inside, she lit the wick from Willie's lantern using a small taper. "Let's go." She led the way out of the small room and into the tunnels.

We moved quickly through the tunnel, retracing our route from earlier that day. We stopped at the first of the storerooms we came to, and the maharani set down her lantern on a barrel and started pulling out clothes from a variety of cabinets.

"I'm afraid you'll have to dress in Indian styles. The clothes are to help us blend in. Western clothing will stand out in the villages. But there are some Europeans who have adopted our mode of dress, so you may not stand out too much." She piled clothing into Miss Bang's arms as she talked. "We'll need to change quickly."

"Oi, you lot!" Tinka said, pointing at Willie, the professor, and me. "Grab your togs and shove off. You're not getting a free show."

Miss Bang shot Tinka a look but didn't say anything. The professor grabbed out a set of clothes and was about to head down the tunnel when Willie called him back and added a pair of slippers to the stack. He shoved a similar bundle into my hands and took one for himself. Snatching up his lantern, Willie led us further along the tunnels.

We stopped at a wide space in the tunnel, some thirty feet or so from where we left the women, and just past a turn so they couldn't see us. Willie dropped his dry clothes by the wall, sending up a cloud of dust in the process, and kicked off his shoes. I looked around for a clean spot to place my borrowed clothing, but there wasn't a surface clear of dust and sand. The professor shrugged and placed his bundle down next to the wall.

My brother dropped his sodden coat to the ground with a loud splat. "Get moving," he said to me. He peeled off his shirt and slung it to the ground with another damp splat and began undoing his trousers.

The professor was already shrugging out of his coat. I picked a spot to place my clothes and scraped my foot across it to clear some of the dust away.

"Is there something I can carry my other clothes in, Lieutenant?"

Professor Crackle asked as he carefully placed his wet coat on the ground.

"We'll leave the wet clothes and send someone back for them later. Our first priority is to get Chandra back to safety."

The professor frowned. "I carry some equipment with me, Lieutenant. I wouldn't want to leave that behind."

"A new harmonic spanner, Professor?" I asked jokingly.

He looked at me disappointedly. "No, not yet. I haven't finished rebuilding it. I thought of a few improvements the other day…"

Willie stepped between us, naked except for an unrecognizable garment in his hand. "Will you stop nattering about your harmonic thingamajig and get changed? We came down the quick way, but that doesn't mean no one else knows about this bolt hole. Or might be willing to come down the way we did. Get changed!" He glared at us and continued dressing.

I dropped my jacket to the ground and unbuttoned my shirt. "All right, Wille."

I peeled off the rest of my clothing without further comment. Shivering, I picked up the bundle of stashed garments. The clothes were a sturdy cotton fabric. Loose pants tied with a drawstring paired with a long sleeved tunic embroidered heavily on the front. No hose, only the short slippers that Willie gave us.

I put on the loose trousers and shirt and felt considerably lighter than usual. The slippers didn't appear to offer much in the way of protection, but they were soft and comfortable.

The professor rooted through his damp clothes, pulling out the contents of his pockets and putting them into a large pile on top of his wet undershirt. "The kurta and pajamas are good choices," he said referring to the loose pants and embroidered long shirt that he now wore. "Fairly common across a wide spectrum of society, so they blend in easily. Roomy, so it is easy to stock clothing that will fit a variety of body types. The only problem is the lack of pockets."

Willie pulled his pistol out of his damp clothing. "These we'll take with us. Did you manage to hold onto yours, brother?"

I dug into my pile and pulled out the gun-belt. The leather was wet from the dunking in the reservoir, but the weapon was still in its holster. "Yes."

"Good. We'll have to find something to wrap these up in. We'll need to give them a good cleaning later. For now, eject the magazine and open the slide. You need to shake out whatever water got into the weapon. Make sure there isn't water in the magazine, too."

A small stream of water splashed on the floor as I ejected the magazine. A few more drops joined it when I opened the slide, dropping a round to the floor. I looked at the magazine in my hand, and was surprised to find it empty. I had shot almost the entire magazine. I checked my jacket pockets for the other ammunition Willie had provided. One of the boxes had fallen out of my pocket somewhere, probably during the fall. The other box fell apart as I pulled it out, spilling shells on the floor. I grabbed up a handful of shells and, having no other place to put them, started pushing them into the empty magazine.

"Shouldn't the ladies have joined us by now?" I asked as I loaded rounds into the magazine.

Willie looked back the way we came. "Good question. Perhaps I should go back to check on them."

"I wouldn't try it, Lieutenant," Professor Crackle warned. "Tinka can be very... belligerent when she thinks someone is taking advantage of one of her friends. And Titania is her best friend."

Willie started to reply, but I quickly cut him off. "I'd listen to the professor. Tinka knows how to handle herself. She's tougher than both of us combined. She'll look out for the ladies. Besides, you wouldn't want to go back and get an eyeful of Aunt Phyllis changing, now would you?"

He grimaced at the thought but fidgeted. "Very well. But what is taking them so long?"

The professor shrugged. "Women's clothing is much more complex than ours, my good man."

"A sari isn't that complex, Professor," he shot back.

"Has your aunt ever worn one, Lieutenant? I'm fairly sure Tinka hasn't." He looked thoughtful. "I'm not sure how well that will work with her additional arms. They may be having difficulty finding her a suitable disguise."

I put the reloaded magazine back into my pistol and holstered it. I looked at the remaining bullets. I didn't want to stick them into the pockets of my wet clothes. "Professor, can we put the ammunition in with your things? I don't have any other place to put it and I don't want to leave it behind."

"Certainly, my boy." The professor took a handful of bullets from me and added them to his undershirt with the rest of his things.

Wrapping the gun belt around the holster, I said, "I'm ready to get moving."

Willie stared to move back up the tunnel but stopped as he saw a light moving in our direction. "Someone's coming."

Maharani Chandrakanta came down the tunnel holding her lantern high, with Miss Bang and Aunt Phyllis close behind her. All three women were dressed in a similar fashion, a long skirt with a drape of cloth that crossed up one side of the body to drape over the opposite shoulder, paired with a short-sleeved blouse. A shawl was draped over Aunt Phyllis' arms and shoulders, while the younger ladies wore sheer scarves wrapped around their necks and draped down the front and back of a shoulder. Tinka brought up the rear, in a different style of outfit. She wore a pair of trousers under a long tunic with a long scarf pulled up over her head and covering her shoulders and arms. Judging by the scowl on her face, she wasn't very happy about it, though.

Professor Crackle smiled as the ladies rejoined us. "You look quite fetching in a sari, my dear." He blinked once and took on an embarrassed look. "That is to say, you all do, ladies."

"Thank you, Harmonious," Miss Bang answered. "It has been a while since I wrapped one. And, of course, Tinka is actually wearing a salwar kameez."

"Yes, of course." The professor nodded and I was sure that he hadn't a clue what Miss Bang had called Tinka's outfit. I know I certainly didn't. I wasn't sure what they'd had to do to it to make it fit her unique anatomy, but I had to admit that the scarf did a good job of hiding her additional arms.

Miss Bang stepped forward and handed Professor Crackle a medium sized bag. "I believe you'll need this to carry a few things, Harmonious."

A huge grin crossed his face as he took the bag. "Yes! This is just the thing." He bent down to shove his pile of possessions into the mouth of the bag.

"Sir Richard, you'll want to put your boots into the bag with Harmonious' things. You'll need them if we have to return to the Argos before we can send someone to gather our clothes from the tunnels."

"What?" I began, but then realized what she meant. "Oh, right." Metal plates were worked into the soles of the boots. I'd need those to keep my feet from sliding out from under me while riding the lift up to the Argos. While the plates were not thick or noticeably heavy, they were needed for the ship's embarkation platform, which used an electro-magnet under the deck to secure persons and cargo and keep it from sliding off the edge of the platform. Especially at the speeds the professor preferred to run it.

Willie grabbed up his lantern and the maharani led us all further down the tunnel. We made respectable progress through the rest of the way, especially considering that Aunt Phyllis wasn't able to move as fast as the rest of us. Although, to Aunt Phyllis' credit, she never slacked the pace or asked for a rest. The maharani knew the path quite well, and she kept giving Aunt Phyllis small words of encouragement. The two of them also shared several small smiles as they went. I wasn't sure what had happened between them during their captivity, but they seemed rather pleased with it. Aunt Phyllis no longer showed any of her foul mood from being dropped down the well, but that may have been a contributing factor to Tinka's sour temper.

When we reached the final chamber in the tunnel, the maharani rushed forward and scrambled up a ladder to one side of the door. She crawled into a space at the top of the ladder.

I gave my brother a quizzical look and he said, "There's a peep hole up there. To make sure the exit isn't compromised."

The maharani backed out and declared, "There's no one out there. It's still light."

Willie handed me his lantern and helped her down off the ladder. I looked at my companions. Our borrowed clothing was all brightly coloured, except for the tan shirt the professor wore. We all had pale complexions, excepting only the maharani. Even my brother's tan seemed pale in comparison. The combination made us all look rather conspicuous. I hoped it wouldn't jeopardize our escape.

The maharani opened the outer door and we filed out into the waning daylight. It was late afternoon, and I suspected it would be fully dark before we were able to make our way back to my uncle's house. The maharani was the last out through the door, pausing only to extinguish both lamps, and place one on a shelf near the door. She stepped out and Willie pushed on the door until it swung back into place, blending into the cliff face.

"Let's go home," the maharani said. Willie smiled.

CHAPTER TWENTY
THE JOURNEY HOME

Whe we emerged from the tunnels beneath the mountain, the air was still warm, but cooling rapidly. We set off along the path from to the cliff face. Willie and the maharani led the way, with the professor close behind. Miss Bang and Tinka followed, helping my aunt make her way over the uneven ground. I brought up the rear.

I quickly warmed through as we walked, and I was pleasantly surprised that the unfamiliar garments kept me from overheating. I didn't think I would be nearly so comfortable in the suit I had arrived wearing.

The path was a long uphill climb, but for the most part it was a low enough incline that none of us had trouble with it. Aunt Phyllis proved to be unusually spry. While her age may have put her past running, a lifetime of habitual evening constitutionals meant she was able to maintain a steady pace for quite a while. Or perhaps she wasn't willing to show us how exhausted she was.

While we rested a few times along the way, we made good progress, and I was surprised how quickly we arrived at the field of tall grasses. We saw no evidence of anyone else as we made our way through the woods. I took that as a good sign.

We crossed the field and came to an area of thick bushes. "Isn't there supposed to be an entrance here somewhere?" I asked. "I don't remember it looking like this when we came through going the other way."

"There is," the maharani answered. "And it does look a little different when you approach it from this side." She walked up to the wall of brambles, turned left, and disappeared. As we followed her, I saw that a screen of bushes hid a turn that led to the covered path we had come down a few hours ago. The thick vegetation formed a roof over our heads and walled us in on either side. A clear, well-trodden path led deeper into the greenery.

The path soon forced us to move single file as it narrowed. Likewise, the slope became much steeper, and we found ourselves walking into a ravine as the ground on either side bounded up much faster than the path. The going got much tougher as the ground sloped upwards and the soil crumbled beneath our feet.

Willie made decent headway by shoving his hands into the bushes to either side and climbing as much as walking along, but the rest of us weren't doing as well, especially Aunt Phyllis.

"Hold up," the maharani said. We stopped. "Give me a moment." She dug her hands into the soft soil in the middle of the path.

After a minute or two of digging around, she grabbed onto something and pulled, and a length of chain came up out of the ground. Professor Crackle laughed and applauded. "It seems your progenitor was very forward thinking, Maharani Chandrakanta."

She grinned mischievously and said, "Well, he was planning an escape route for the entire family, including children and pregnant wives." She pulled on the chain and more of it erupted from the ground running up to where Willie stood. "And he didn't want us to be afraid of getting our hands dirty."

"How did you find that?" I asked.

The maharani shrugged. "The chain lies down the center of the path. When it rains, the dirt covers it. My father made sure I knew all the ways in and out. It was only a matter of digging around until I found it."

My brother grabbed the chain and pulled more of it from the ground. He climbed up the ravine, using the chain to pull himself up the steep incline. The rest of us followed, pulling ourselves up hand over hand. Tinka used her extra hands to help steady Aunt Phyllis and we scrambled up the hillside to emerge from the thicket next to the horse and his cart. The horse raised his head as we appeared from the greenery, then went back to his grazing.

"Why didn't you tell me about the chain, the last time we were here?" Willie asked the maharani.

She laughed. "We didn't need it."

We crossed to the cart and found it much as we had left it. The bed of the cart was still covered with bundles of cloth, although most of them were piled into the middle to form a nest where the old cart driver slept.

"Bijoy!" the maharani cried out in delight when she saw him.

The old man stirred and rose up, blinking at us. He frowned in confusion as he took in our change of clothes. But when his eyes locked on the maharani, his face split in a big smile, and he bobbed his head while speaking rapid Hindi.

Miss Bang angled her head slightly as she translated, "He's very happy that she is well and unhurt, but he doesn't understand what she is doing out here. They haven't seen each other in a long time."

The maharani looked at the rest of us. "He was my father's favorite gardener when I was a child, but he retired years ago." She turned back to him. "I should have expected that you would have led a rescue attempt."

The old man shook his head. "No, no. Bijoy is only simple cart driver. Hired by these nice people." He grinned and bowed his head, showing a number of missing teeth. There was something odd about the old man's story. If he was the maharaja's favorite, surely he would have gotten a significant pension when he retired from service. Why was he driving a cart?

I didn't have any more time to muse over the answer as the maharani laughed. "I can just imagine. But we can reminisce later. We need to get moving. Everyone into the cart. Bijoy will get us home." I helped Aunt Phyllis into the back of the cart, and the rest of us piled on as Bijoy scrambled onto the driver's bench and gathered up the reins.

Willie grabbed up a piece of cloth from the bed and wrapped it around his gun belt. He had me do the same, making sure that I could reach in through the end and draw the gun if needed.

We pulled several of the cloths out and covered ourselves as we huddled in the back of the cart. The maharani sat against the driver's seat, sandwiched between my brother and my aunt. Most of her attention was on my Aunt Phyllis, but the maharani always kept some part of her body touching my brother, as if she wanted to be reassured that he was there.

In contrast, Miss Bang and Professor Crackle sat opposite of me in the back of the wagon. They very carefully made sure that they were not touching each other. The maharani pulled up her scarf and used it to make a hood to hide her features. Miss Bang quickly did the same, and Aunt Phyllis likewise raised her shawl to cover her head. Meanwhile, Tinka crawled under the blanket with me and curled up by my side.

Bijoy tugged on the reins and quickly had the cart moving back up the narrow path that we had come down. He pushed the horse for more speed on the path up, and we bounced back and forth as the cart bumped along the uneven track. Tinka held on to my arm, as we bounced our way along, but I suspect she had more experience dealing with such turbulence than I did.

We burst forth onto the road, crossing to the far side of the road and cutting in front of a steam jitney heading toward the town. The driver of that vehicle jammed on his brakes, his rubber tires skidding on the ground. He yelled a few untranslatable imprecations at us, as

Bijoy turned us into the lane. The other driver re-engaged his gears with a harsh grinding and zoomed around us with an excess flourish of throttle. The cart horse shied from the noise, but Bijoy kept him under control, and urged his horse on to greater speed, following in the other driver's wake.

"Careful now," Willie told him. "We don't want to attract attention."

The maharani patted my brother's leg. "Don't worry about it, William. He knows what he's doing. I trust Bijoy to get us there safely."

Willie gave a doubtful frown, but he didn't say anything further and we all settled in for the ride.

A few minutes later, a lorry rushed by us, going away from town, with several men with rifles clinging to the sides of the vehicle. I considered the vehicle as it sped into the distance. When it disappeared behind a curve, I turned to the professor. "Wasn't that..."

"Yes, I believe so," he answered my incomplete question. "It may well have been one of the vehicles that was in the courtyard."

Miss Bang looked in the direction of the speeding lorry. "The question is, are they looking for us, or are they evacuating, now that they've been discovered?"

I grunted. Willie said, "An good question, Miss Bang. It may very well be a bit of both."

"Then they don't realize that we're heading toward town," I said, feeling a spot of relief.

"Or they sent a car in each direction," the professor said. "And the other one is somewhere up ahead."

We rode in relative silence after that without seeing any more unusual traffic. We had expected to continue along in this manner a lot longer, but Bijoy suddenly turned the cart off onto a side street.

"What do you think you are doing?" Willie barked and half rose from his seat before the maharani pulled him back down again.

"Is faster. You see," was the only explanation the driver gave.

"William, let it go," the maharani chided my brother. "He knows this area better than anyone. If he says this is a faster route, it is."

Willie scowled. "You trust him?"

"Yes," she said. "Like I trust you."

Willie straightened up in his seat and leaned back. The maharani took his hand and gave it a squeeze. She held on to it for a few more seconds before hastily releasing it.

The old driver increased his speed as we traveled down the side road. We bounced along in the back of the cart, holding onto the side rails for dear life. The road quickly transitioned from wooded land to a crowded neighborhood, with children and animals spilling out into the street. Bijoy raised his head and let out a series of loud yells, spooking a number of chickens and spurring the more attentive children to move themselves and their families' livestock out of the path of the madman in the horse cart. We thundered through the streets, narrowly avoiding potholes and one very large pig that didn't see any reason why it should stir itself. Angry parents and the odd unwary pedestrian hurled insults at our backs, and a handful of older children tried to run alongside the cart.

Bijoy swerved to avoid another cart at a cross street, narrowly missing the other vehicle as we rushed past. The road quickly became more crowded as we moved into a busier area. Now instead of children there were carts, vendors, and even the occasional lorry on the road and the old man was forced to slow his pace, but not by much. At one point he swerved between two hand carts moving in opposite directions, clipping and turning them both over in our wake. The owners screamed and chased us for a few feet, before turning back to rescue as much of their wares as they could.

The maharani laughed and called out, "Sorry!" to them as Willie put a protective arm around her. Aunt Phyllis' face wore an expression that indicated the situation was just barely tolerable. The professor looked like an excited schoolboy, and Miss Bang seemed to be similarly enjoying the ride. Tinka snaked another arm around me under the blanket and gave me a squeeze.

My teeth rattled as we took another turn to avoid plowing into traffic on a busy street, instead dodging down a narrow alley barely wide enough for the horse cart. While the driver obviously knew these streets well, he gave no warning as we made sudden turns, slinging us into each other as the cart banked and tried to flip itself. Twice we made turns so tightly I thought one of the cart's wheels was going to break off and send us all sprawling to the ground. On one turn the wheels did come off the ground and we teetered on the edge of going over for nearly half a block before we came back down with a spark and a crash.

I quickly lost my way as the driver dodged back and forth along the city's streets. "Where is he taking us?" it finally occurred to me to ask, as it became clear that we were heading deep into town and not to Aunt Phyllis' country home.

"Home," the maharani answered. "To the palace, of course." Bijoy chose that moment to drive the cart up onto the side of the road to move around a lorry and sedan that were keeping pace with each other ahead of us. We raced down the sidewalk, knocking down two vendor stalls, and sending pedestrians diving into shop fronts to keep from being run down. "We must show my father that I'm alive and unharmed."

"I'm not sure we will be by the time we get there!" I answered.

Our race through the city came to a sudden end as the old driver pulled back on the reins and leaned into the cart brake to bring us skidding up to a heavy metal bound gate in a well fortified wall. Two guards in palace uniforms flanked the gate. They pointed their rifles at us, and several more guards poured out of a nearby sally gate to join them.

"Now, let's everyone keep calm," the professor began as he slowly raised his hands over his head. It was obvious that these guards were on high alert, and given the way we pulled up to the gate, I wasn't surprised.

Bijoy barked something in Hindi to the guard.

The guard seemed puzzled at his outburst. He looked to his

fellows as if unsure what to do. I looked at Miss Bang, hoping for a translation.

She shrugged. "I'm not sure I can make any kind of sense of that."

"But what did he say?" I whispered at her.

She shook her head slightly. "Literally translated? It comes out as..."

Another of the guards said something to Miss Bang, gesturing with his rifle. She prudently became silent. The first guard went to the sally port and called to someone inside the gate.

A moment later an officer stepped out. He was a couple inches shorter than the guards, who may have been chosen specifically for their height and muscular build. The officer wore a turban. He sported a set of very bushy eyebrows that bristled low over his eyes and an equally bushy mustache that served to accent his frown.

The guard who had called to him pointed to Bijoy and said something. Warily, the officer approached the cart. While none of us were Kindred of Kali, I wondered if there were other problems that the palace guard had to deal with. He gave us a measuring look, as if trying to decide if we were a threat or not. He spoke a single short, clipped sentence to Bijoy, who replied with the same phrase he had used a moment ago.

The officer's eyes went wide, then narrowed to slits. He walked up to the cart, standing next to the driver's seat and staring at Bijoy with his hand resting on his sidearm. He talked quietly with Bijoy, who gestured emphatically at the gate several times. Finally, the man stepped back and barked an order at the guardsmen, who pointed their weapons away from us. One of them relayed an order through the sally port and the gate began to crank open.

The gate led to a small yard that looked like it might barely accommodate a large lorry. As soon as the cart entered the yard, the cranks reversed, and the gate quickly shut behind us. The guards motioned for us to stay where we were.

Once the gates closed, they motioned us to come down from the cart and stand in a line in front of the bed. As the maharani rose to move to the end of the cart, she pulled her scarf down, letting the guards have a good look at her face for the first time. One of the men recognized her and straightened. He called for the officer again.

The officer was talking to Bijoy where they stood by the driver's seat. He managed to frown even more as he came around to the back of the cart to see why he'd been interrupted. His expression changed immediately to a look of surprise when he saw the maharani's face. He bowed, then stepped forward to help her down from the cart.

She smiled and let him help her. She talked rapidly and earnestly to the man, gesturing to the rest of us as she spoke. The man nodded several times, then asked a question which she quickly answered. He bowed again and stepped back from the maharani, then motioned two of his men to him. He spoke quickly to each man, sending each guard on his way as soon as he was sure his instructions were understood.

The maharani came over to us as we stood in a ragged line. "Don't worry, my friends. Soon, our escort will take us to my quarters, and my father will meet us there. This will all soon be over."

Tinka stopped giving the guards disapproving looks and turned to the maharani. "Ain't you in charge? What's the point of being a princess or maharani or whatever if you have to wait around for people to sort themselves out."

The maharani smiled at Tinka. "If only it were that simple. Everything in the palace runs by protocol. At times it can feel confining and rigid, but if one works within the process, you can get much more done."

A brace of guards arrived in the small loading yard. I noted that these men wore slightly different uniforms, and two of them were women. When we had seen the maharaja's guards earlier, they wore purple and white sashes and turbans. These guards wore sashes and turbans in a similar pattern of sapphire and white. Willie nodded at them. "I think our escort is here."

The maharani led us over to the guards, who escorted us to her private quarters.

CHAPTER TWENTY-ONE
A TALE TOLD

The maharani's apartments were not a single set of rooms, but a series of connecting rooms for the maharani and her guests. The lounge we were shown to was lavishly decorated with many low couches and tables. We collapsed onto the couches grateful for the chance to finally rest. Bright paintings and complex tapestries covered the walls, but they all looked rather formal. While there were a couple landscapes, most of the artwork were portraits of proud Indian men and women. Warriors and ladies standing against opulent backgrounds. While they were very good, it looked like a collection of official portraits, not like something a young woman would have in her personal rooms. There was also no sign of a bed or other personal items. I deduced those would be found in more private rooms.

Tall windows along one side looked out upon a courtyard garden. The sun was in the process of setting, painting various colours across the evening sky. I wondered if the garden below was the same one where her father had been working. Had it been only two days ago?

"Do you have any idea who it was that kidnapped you, Maharani?" the professor asked. "If we knew who was behind this..."

She shook her head. "The woman was veiled. I never saw her face. But she had metal arms and a steam engine on her back. There can't be many people who could build such a thing. Surely that must make it easier to find the culprit."

The professor sighed. "It would if we could examine one."

"Surely such a device must be unique in the world," she replied.

I shook my head. "There are at least seven. And six of them are still out there."

"Eight," Miss Bang corrected. "The woman that kidnapped your aunt and the maharani wasn't among the ones we saw at the party. And now one of the devices is damaged." She looked at Tinka.

"Eight?" The maharani's face paled slightly. "And you were able to find me by tracking their devices?"

Willie shook his head. "No. We simply went to the last place anyone would look for you. It seems that someone decided they needed a fortress, so they took over one that wasn't being actively used."

The maharani stood up and stepped over to where Tinka sat, putting a hand on the young woman's arm. "I owe you a debt I doubt I will ever be able to repay. Were it not for you, I would have been shot and killed. You saved my life today."

Tinka seemed stunned. "I... I dinna do nothin'. You just weren't watching out is all."

"No, I was being a fool. I thought my value as a hostage would protect me. I was wrong. Nevertheless, as long as I am alive, you need only ask, and you will have whatever aid the house can offer." She squeezed Tinka's arm. "It is the least I can do."

Tinka nodded somewhat sheepishly.

The doors burst open and we stood as the maharaja, clad in a long flowing robe, strode into the room. He rushed over and embraced his daughter. "My jewel, I was so worried about you." He smiled broadly as he hugged her, but then his face changed to a look of concern and he held her at arm's length and looked her over. "Did they harm you? Are you injured?"

The maharani shook her head. "No, Father. We weren't harmed. I'm just tired and a little shaken from making our escape. Bijoy brought me home."

"What? That rascal! I should have known he would not stay retired. It was he that rescued you, then?"

She shook her head. "No, my friends here freed me from captivity. Bijoy only brought us home."

The maharani turned and looked at us for the first time since he burst into the room. He seemed puzzled at first, but then the light of recognition entered his eyes. "You are the ones who told me of my daughter's capture, are you not?"

Willie answered for us. "Yes, Maharaja."

The ruler's expression turned blank, unreadable. "And did I not tell you to leave this matter to my investigators?"

Professor Crackle raised a hand. "Actually, Your Majesty, I believe the exact phrase that you used was that we were not to try and participate in the official investigation."

The maharaja's quirked an eyebrow at the professor. "So, you took it upon yourself to search for my daughter on your own?"

The professor seemed unsure of how to respond. Was the maharaja upset that we had gone against his orders? "Well, sir, I..."

Before the professor could dig himself in deeper, I stepped between him and the maharaja. "I asked him to help me. The professor's not to blame."

The maharaja looked at me. "You did this thing?"

I bowed my head. "Yes. I asked Professor Crackle and Miss Bang to help me find my aunt. Neither you, nor Colonel Ticking would let us help, but I've seen first-hand what the professor and Miss Bang can do. I was worried that the kidnappers might harm her. Aunt Phyllis. Lady Griffith-Holmes, I mean. I... I was sure that if they were holding your daughter for ransom they would treat her well, but I didn't know what they'd do to my aunt."

"*You* chose to defy my instructions?" he yelled, his voice reverberating off of the high ceilings. He took a step toward me, his body poised to strike.

"Yes, Your Highness, I did. If you must punish someone, punish me. Willie, the professor and Miss Bang, they wouldn't have been involved if it hadn't been for my insistence." I stood stiffly, not knowing what he would do.

The maharaja stared darkly at me for a long moment.

Then he stepped forward and grabbed me by the shoulders. "Then thank Vishnu that you did not listen!" He grinned and took me into a fierce hug, then released me with almost equal force. I staggered for a moment and steadied myself by grabbing the back of one of the couches. "Investigators, bah! They were supposed to be the best men in my service. Ha! The fools were running around in circles with no idea where to look." He reached up and grabbed my shoulder. "And I was the biggest fool of all for not accepting your help. You have brought my daughter home safe. You have my gratitude." He shook my shoulder, then nodded to Aunt Phyllis. "And I am pleased to see that you have also been returned unharmed, lady."

She bowed. "Thank you, Your Majesty."

The maharani touched her father's arm to recapture his attention. "Father, I want you to meet Tinka. She risked her life to save mine." She turned to where Tinka stood, half hidden behind Miss Bang.

Tinka's eyes went wide. "Me? No, no. I didn't do anything special."

"She is modest," the maharani said. "Were it not for her, I would be dead."

"Then you shall have our special gratitude, miss." The maharaja nodded to Tinka.

Tinka fidgeted, twisting her hands together behind her back to make it less obvious that she had too many arms.

To the maharaja's credit, he recognized her discomfort and quickly turned to other matters, saying, "As glad as I am to have my daughter back where she belongs, there still remains the matter those who took her from me. Have they been dealt with? Do we know who they were?"

The professor shook his head. "Unfortunately, Your Majesty, they are still at liberty, and their identity remains a mystery."

The maharaja gestured to the couches. "Then sit and let us gather what information we have and see what we can learn of this foe." He turned to one of the guards and told the man, "Bring Sankar. He must hear this." The man took off at a run.

We sat on the couches, which were arranged to form a conversational grouping for a handful of people to lounge and talk. Instead of lounging, we packed ourselves in. The maharani pulled Tinka down to sit with her and Miss Bang. Willie sat next to Aunt Phyllis, leaving me sitting next to Professor Crackle. The maharaja sat on the couch next to his daughter and gave us all a big smile.

About a minute later the advisor, Mr. Chatterjee, arrived, trailed by a scribe with a portable desk. Mr. Chatterjee stalked into the room, eying each of us in turn. When his eye landed on the maharani, he smiled and bowed. "Maharani Chandra, it is so good to see you are home and safe again."

The maharani gave him a tired grin. "Thank you, Uncle Sankar. I am very glad to be home."

Mr. Chatterjee perched himself on the far end of the maharaja's couch, and the scribe set up his desk off to one side.

"Now, daughter," the maharaja said, "tell us what you can of these kidnappers. What happened? Start at the beginning."

The maharani composed herself for a moment. "Lady Griffith-Holmes and I were taking a tour of the hedge maze, and we came to a lovely little contemplation area down one of the paths. We sat down on the bench and we were talking amongst ourselves when suddenly there was this terrible noise coming through the hedge. We looked up and someone was chopping their way through the shrubbery."

Aunt Phyllis nodded. "One moment all was quiet, and the next there were all these flashing blades slashing through my bushes." My aunt shuddered at the memory.

The maharani continued, "In seconds, they cut a hole through the wall of the maze and a veiled woman stepped through."

"A woman?" Mr. Chatterjee asked. "Only one? No one else?"

"Yes!" The maharani nodded emphatically. "A woman with metal arms and an engine strapped to her back. She looked like a spider and like a cobra at the same time. She had swords in her hands, and they were constantly in motion."

Professor Crackle stood up. "One of the Kindred. As we thought." He paced toward the maharani. "Who else was there with you?"

The maharani looked up into the professor's face and she grimaced at the memory, but her voice was calm as she answered. "Yes. Two of my bodyguard were with us. They rushed over to defend us, and the woman cut them down."

Aunt Phyllis put her head in her hands, as if covering her eyes now would shield her from the memory. "It was horrible. She sliced them in two. We were covered in blood." She shuddered again. Willie put his arm around her, and she leaned into him.

"Was there anything unusual about the woman's weapons?" the professor pressed.

"Professor!" I called.

"Is that any kind of question to ask of a woman who has been traumatized?" Mr. Chatterjee interrupted. His muscles bunched underneath him, but he didn't rise from his perch.

"Harmonious," Miss Bang said quietly, "now is not the time. Please let her tell her story in her own way."

The professor didn't seem happy with that answer, but he subsided and stalked away behind the couch.

The maharani swallowed and continued her story. "I... I don't think I would know if there had been something special about her weapons. She was all arms and swords. She cut the first man in half, and split the other guard open." She drew a hand up the center of her body to illustrate. "And he flew back into the bushes and hung there as he died. It was awful." She swallowed several times. "She came toward us then, and I thought she was going to kill us, too, but she told us to come with her. We stood, and she made us go through the hole she had hacked into the wall of the maze. Two men with rifles were on the other side of the hedge. They had scarves tied across their faces. They led us out of the maze, which was cut through in several places, and took us to a lorry waiting at the side of a road. They made us climb into the truck and tied our hands behind us. They sat us down on a bench at the front of the lorry and put black bags on our heads. And then they drove away."

"Was there anything else?" the maharaja asked gently.

"No," she said.

"Yes," Aunt Phyllis said in a small voice.

Heads swiveled to face my aunt. "What else was there?" Mr. Chatterjee asked.

Aunt Phyllis stared into space for a moment. "Before... before they drove off, they put something heavy into the lorry. We had the blindfolds on, but the floor sloped down suddenly."

"Yes." the maharani said. "They were complaining about the suspension. It was hitting bottom."

"Bottoming out," Willie said. "The Kindred climbed into the truck with you, but she was so heavy that she bottomed out the suspension on the back of the truck. Those arms must be really heavy."

"She would have to sit in the middle of the truck to keep it balanced," I pointed out. "Too far back and they'd bottom out. Too far forward and the same thing would happen." I turned to the maharani. "When they drove you away, how smooth was the ride? Was there a lot of bouncing? Rough roads?"

Aunt Phyllis and the maharani considered the question for a bit. "I don't know," the maharani said. "I've never ridden in a lorry before. I don't know how to judge."

"I have. I've had to for some of Jeremy's postings," Aunt Phyllis said. "There were a few bumps and jounces, but it was pretty normal for a lorry."

The professor started pacing again. "Then the truck was near capacity, but not over it. And the Kindred rode in the middle of the vehicle, keeping the weight between the axles."

"They must have planned a route with good roads. Smooth enough and even enough to keep from bouncing around," Willie added. "You think they would take such care with their victims?"

"No," the professor said. "I think they took such care with one of their leaders." He sat down on the end of the couch and leaned toward the maharaja. "Whomever these Kindred are, they have money and influence, and those metal arms are a powerful symbol to their followers. They wouldn't give a set of them to just anyone. That means these women are the leaders of this movement. They're the ones in charge."

"And they wear jewelry into battle," Miss Bang observed. "They're not used to fighting or being in danger. Whomever these women are, they must be high caste. They are used to getting what they want, but now they want to govern, or at least have more control of who is doing the governing." She looked at the maharaja and Mr. Chatterjee. "What women have you offended?"

The advisor drew himself up, scowling at Miss Bang. "What are you insinuating? How dare you accuse..."

"Enough, Sankar. It's only a question. And a fair question at that." The maharaja looked from his chief advisor back to Miss Bang and thought for a moment before answering. "I don't think we've done anything to offend anyone, miss. We are a small, prosperous corner of the Empire. Trade is good. Until this moment there was no unrest to speak of. My people are generally happy and I try to do my best for them. I do not know why anyone would want to come after me this way."

"The Empire." Professor Crackle stood again and stared off into the distance. "This isn't about you, Maharaja. This is about the Empire." He took a step, stopped, gazed into the distance for a couple more seconds, then turned back to us. "When the Kindred attacked your party," the professor pointed at Aunt Phyllis, "they called for the British interlopers to see the error of their ways and go back to their own lands. I don't think they wanted to hurt you, Your Majesty, I think they wanted you to break with the Empire. Instead of tangling with the Imperial forces directly, they called on British subjects to leave voluntarily, and for Indians to stand for their nation again. But the ones they would show no mercy to were those natives who cooperated with the Empire."

"You think they wanted me to pit myself against the Eternal Empress?" the maharaja asked.

Willie automatically replied, "May She Live Forever," but the energy drained out of his words as he realized that he was the only one reciting the response. We all looked at him for a moment. "Sorry," he muttered.

"I believe that is what they wanted," the professor said.

"But that would be madness." The maharani looked at her father. "We have no defense against the Empire's lightning rifles. Such a revolt would be suicide."

The maharaja nodded. "I know. But not everyone sees the lessons of history the same way. Perhaps they believe that if we are prosperous enough and well-ordered enough, we might be able to talk the Empire into letting us go our own way."

"She would never do that." Aunt Phyllis' voice was firm and resolute. "While the Empress is dedicated to doing the best for all her subjects, she does not surrender territory for any reason." She grimaced. "History has given us ample proof of that."

The maharani nodded. "I agree with you, my lady, but it seems that in this case we are dealing with women who have other ideas. And those ideas will prove dangerous to us all if we do not stop them."

The mood of the conversation had turned decidedly dark. Not like a kidnapping was a particularly cheerful subject.

The thought brought me back to where the conversation had split off to follow this tangent. "When your captors drove off with you, did they take you directly to the fortress, or did they stop anywhere else first?"

Aunt Phyllis turned to look at me, puzzled for a second. "I don't know. There were plenty of stops and starts. But that could have been traffic. Or they could have done it to confuse us."

"We were almost in an accident," the maharani suggested.

"An accident?" her father asked.

She nodded. "We were going over a bumpy stretch of road, then we were jostled, and there was this big crash. A second later the lorry sped away. I think we were narrowly missed."

"If you weren't hit, the vehicle shouldn't have been jostled. Could they have driven over something?" I asked.

"Not something, someone!" the professor crowed.

"They hit someone?" I asked.

"No, my boy. They must have stopped somewhere, and the Kindred walked to the back of the truck and jumped out. Each step would have the truck bouncing up and down, and when she jumped..."

"A big bounce and a loud crash," Willie completed his sentence.

"Exactly!"

"Now that you mention it," Aunt Phyllis said, "the latter part of the journey was quieter. Less engine noise."

The professor slapped his leg. "Because the steam engine on the Kindred's spine device was no longer there."

"But where?" Mr. Chatterjee murmured. "Do either of you have any idea of how long you were in the vehicle before this 'crash' happened? Or how long after?"

The ladies sat in thought for several moments, Aunt Phyllis looking down at her hands and the maharani gazing into the middle distance over our heads. Finally Aunt Phyllis spoke.

"It seemed like an awfully long time. I think the whole trip was well over an hour. Maybe two. I'm not sure when they stopped. I'm afraid I can't be much help." For once, my aunt looked uncharacteristically old and frail.

The maharani looked puzzled. "It couldn't have been an hour," she said. "It all happened so fast. A half an hour, perhaps a few minutes more. And the crash was maybe ten minutes before they stopped the lorry and pulled us out and led us down to the dungeons."

Aunt Phyllis shook her head. "No, it was ages."

"Well it couldn't have been both," Mr. Chatterjee insisted.

"Actually, this is quite common," Miss Bang said. "You're dealing with a fear reaction, and sensory deprivation. Experiences of both compressed and expanded time are well known for both phenomena, although time expansion is more frequently related to fear, and time compression with sensory deprivation. Unfortunately, this means we don't have a reliable way to determine how far they traveled before their captor departed."

"Which puts us no closer to determining where the kidnappers are hiding," Mr. Chatterjee finished bitterly.

The maharaja turned to us. "Which makes me wonder how you were able to find my daughter. All the clues we had led to dead ends, but somehow you were able to trace them to where she was being held. Tell me how this rescue was accomplished."

The professor began to give his account of our investigation, with Miss Bang and myself filling in details the professor skipped over, or wasn't present for, but the maharaja's advisor interrupted us every few words. Mr. Chatterjee seemed to be determined to pick at each step of our account as if to catch us in a lie. He claimed that he was trying to pull out details that would help him figure out who these Kindred of Kali were, but he seemed increasingly skeptical.

When we got to the part where Tinka engaged in single combat against one of the Kindred, he stood and growled at us. "You expect us to believe such a flimsy tale? What are you hiding?"

Professor Crackle threw his hands up and crossed the room. "Good lord! The man is worse than that fool back in Prague!"

"Was Inspector Janicek that hard on you, Professor?" I asked.

"Who?" he replied.

"Inspector Janicek. That was the name of the police inspector in Prague that took my statement. Wasn't he the same officer that talked to you?"

"I don't know, my boy. If he gave me his name it was long since forgotten from the indignity of being called a liar multiple times!" The last was obviously directed at the maharaja's advisor.

Mr. Chatterjee stalked over to the professor. "Do you honestly expect me to believe that this, this child, this girl... was able to defeat a steam-powered monstrosity that took down two of our most experienced and trained guards?"

Tinka jumped up and rounded on the older man. "This girl is more than capable of taking you down with her bare hands if you keep talking shite!" She spread her arms wide and shook a fist under the advisor's nose.

Her lower right fist.

The scarf that was draped around Tinka floated to the floor, revealing the loose blouse that she wore, and the slits that were cut below each of the sleeves to allow for her additional arms.

Mr. Chatterjee stumbled backwards into the professor and tripped, landing heavily on the floor. Staring at Tinka from his position on his back, he spoke an oath in his native language.

Tinka's brow furrowed, and her eyes were dark with rage. Her muscles tensed like she was about to fall upon Mr. Chatterjee. I pushed myself up out of my seat and was about to try to talk her down, when she abruptly realized that everyone in the room was looking at her. She went from fierce warrior to shrinking violet and her eyes searched for a place to hide. As I was standing right next to her, she dodged behind me and tried to make herself small.

Miss Bang came up behind me. "It's all right, Tinka. It's going to be all right."

The maharaja looked down at his advisor. "Sankar, I do not believe that anything is beyond this young lady. Choose your questions more wisely."

Mr. Chatterjee swallowed and nodded.

"Please forgive Sankar, young lady. His training tells him to doubt everything, even when he should know better. At times, it makes him a difficult friend, but in most things it makes him an excellent advisor. Know that I admire your bravery and your skill in taking on one of these false Kindred of the goddess."

I felt each of Tinka's hands grabbing my arms as she peeked out from behind me at the maharaja. "You mean that?"

"I do." The maharaja stood slowly. "You have the gratitude of this house, but now I see that you are also due the honor of the house as well." With that he bowed to Tinka and myself.

"Thank you," Tinka said with a sniffle. "You're nice." She pointed at Mr. Chatterjee, still sprawled on the floor. "But he was rude!"

The maharaja looked at his advisor. "Yes, he was, and he should not have been." He looked back at Tinka. "Should I have him removed?"

Tinka looked at the advisor for a long moment. "No. If he leaves, he won't learn nothing about how to behave properly. But if he's rude again, I'll pop him."

The maharaja nodded and smiled slightly. "Very wise. Please, sit." Miss Bang led Tinka back to sit next to the maharani, who held Tinka's hand. I took my seat again, and Mr. Chatterjee scrambled to his feet and stood behind the maharaja. As the maharaja sat down, he said, "Professor, continue your tale."

The professor walked back to the couches, and recounted his own rescue and the discovery that Holyfield Industries had made parts for the Kindred's arms. I described our visit to Holyfield Industries, leaving out the professor's run in with security and my own encounter with the original P. G. Holyfield, and how we determined that the parts were delivered to a military depot, and we couldn't trace the shipments any farther.

"But surely you must have found some connection," Mr. Chatterjee said. "How else were you able to find the hostages?"

"We looked where no one would think to find them," I said.

"What?"

The professor reached for his glasses, which he wasn't wearing since they'd been destroyed earlier in the day. He dropped his hand and screwed up his face. "We came to the conclusion that trying to trace the parts was a dead end. We were sure that these so-called Kindred had resources, social connections, and a good understanding of the area. All things which we lacked. So, we turned to the lieutenant here for help, given his greater experience in the area."

Miss Bang chimed in. "After laying the problem out to him, I asked him what the last place was that anyone would look for the kidnapped maharani."

Willie nodded. "And I answered with the first thing that popped into my head. Here. The Palace."

Mr. Chatterjee frowned. "But you knew she was not here."

"Yes, of course. That was kind of the point. No one would look here because she was supposed to be here. It was a stupid answer, because I knew it would be impossible for someone to convince enough of the guards to hold Chandra here against her will."

The advisor leaned back and nodded his acceptance of Willie's explanation.

"But then, I remembered that this wasn't the only castle in the area," my brother continued. "Chandra had shown me the old fortress about a month or so ago. It occurred to me that it was an ideal space. It only had a couple of caretakers. It was rarely used. Once someone occupied it, it was easily defended with a few men, and no one would think to look for her on one of the family properties when she was so publicly kidnapped."

There was a long silence. Mr. Chatterjee's jaw went slack.

The maharaja leaned forward slightly where he sat on a low couch. "Would you be interested in an appointment to my court, young man?"

Willie's eyes got wide and he raised his head. "I'm flattered, sir, but I'm still an officer in the British Army. I've got several more years commitment to the Crown."

"Think about it," the maharaja said as he leaned back again. "Perhaps after you have completed your service. Or perhaps we can arrange an exchange of officers?"

"Your majesty, I believe we have more pressing business to attend to at the moment." Mr. Chatterjee may have been jealous of the attention that his liege was paying to my brother, but he did have a valid point. There were still dangerous people at large.

"You are right, Sankar." The advisor stood up straight and looked smug, but then quickly deflated as the maharaja continued. "We must have a grand celebration! You shall all attend as my special guests, and you, miss," he pointed to Tinka, "you will be the guest of honor, for your bravery and quick thinking in saving my daughter's life and returning her to me unharmed."

"What? No!" Tinka and Mr. Chatterjee said at the same time.

The advisor rolled on with his protest. "There is a dangerous rebel faction loose in the city! This is no time to be throwing a party! Doing so would only make them bold enough to strike again. You'd be sending a message that you were weak. It would only embolden them to continue their rebellion."

The maharaja regarded his advisor with dark eyes. "And while we prepare to celebrate, you will investigate these rebels, Sankar. Redouble your efforts. If indeed it does make them attack again, I expect *you* to be ready and waiting for them, and to put an end to the threat before it progresses further. I want *them* to take me for a fool, Sankar, not you. Surely you should know me better than that after all these years."

The advisor opened his mouth again... and closed it. "Yes, Your Majesty."

"Good."

Tinka found her voice again. "But I can't be around all those people," she murmured.

The maharani hugged Tinka. "Do not fear. It will be fine, my dear. It will be an evening to remember. You will have a wonderful time." She smiled, but Tinka wasn't cheered at all.

"But... you don't..." she shrank into herself. "I don't..." Her voice got very small. "I don't have anything to wear."

"That's no problem at all," the maharani replied. "I will have my ladies make you a gorgeous gown. My gift to you."

"But..." Tinka ran out of words.

Miss Bang rubbed her back comfortingly. "It will be all right, Tinka. I'm sure the maharaja would never let any of his guests do anything to upset you." She eyed the maharaja as she said this, and from the look in her eye, I thought the local monarch would do well to see that Miss Bang's words proved to be true. "It will be a fine evening."

The maharaja nodded. "You are my guest of honor. To be rude to you is to be rude to me."

Tinka seemed to have run out of protests, but she still didn't look comfortable with the idea. I found it unfair to put her on the spot, surrounded by so many virtual strangers. The fire in her eyes was completely missing.

I stood and crossed over behind Tinka and put my hands on her shoulders. "Don't worry, Tinka. I'll be with you the whole time."

Tinka gave me a surprised look, but then a smile spread over her face. She grabbed my hands and mouthed the words, "Thank you."

The maharaja stood. "The hour has grown late. You shall be our guests here tonight. It is the least that I can do to reward your deeds this day."

"Your majesty," my brother said, "I appreciate your hospitality, but I must return to duty in the morning. A staff car will be collecting me from my uncle's house early tomorrow."

"Then I shall have one of my staff return you this evening. Please give Colonel Ticking my compliments."

"Thank you, sir."

Aunt Phyllis piped up. "Your majesty, as much as I would enjoy your hospitality, I'm sure that my husband is equally worried about me. Please allow me to return home tonight with William."

The maharaja nodded. "Certainly, Lady Griffith-Holmes. I apologize that I did not think to send you home earlier. You have been through an ordeal and your husband has no doubt been worried about you."

"Thank you, Your Majesty. If I could speak to you privately about another matter before I go?"

"Certainly, good lady. Come with me. We shall speak of this private business and then I will see about having you and the Lieutenant returned to your home."

The maharaja gave his daughter one last hug, then gathered Aunt Phyllis and his advisor and left, followed by the scribe who had quietly been making notes through our entire discussion.

Willie stopped by me. "I'll see about getting the guns from the horse cart and see that they're cleaned. I'll be in touch as soon as I can."

"I hope the colonel won't be too mad with you." I shook my brother's hand.

"Well, if he fires me, I still have another job offer."

I laughed.

CHAPTER TWENTY-TWO
PREPARATIONS FOR A FETE

The next week went by very quickly.

Naturally, my uncle was overjoyed with Aunt Phyllis' return. While Aunt Phyllis was glad to see him and to be home again, she was also most definitely up to something. Each day she made trips back and forth to the palace. She wouldn't say what she was doing there, but Uncle Jeremy was convinced that she was helping plan the big party to celebrate the safe return of the maharaja's daughter. Whatever she was planning, she was certainly happy with how things were going.

Willie did not have as easy a time of it.

A staff car collected Willie early on the morning after our adventure. Uncle Jeremy stayed behind because of Aunt Phyllis' return, but he pieced together the details for us later in the week.

Willie reported to the colonel as soon as he arrived on base and informed him that the maharani had been returned safely to her father. The colonel did not take this news well. He was outraged that his own investigation had barely started and someone else had beaten him to the prize. There was much shouting and Willie was grilled for details, but nothing he said seemed to satisfy the colonel or lessen his ire. In the end, my brother was thrown into lockup for disobeying orders.

Willie spent a chunk of the day there, but was released in the afternoon after the maharaja sent a message to Colonel Ticking expressing his gratitude for my brother's part in the maharani's safe return. The note also invited the Colonel, his senior staff, and especially Willie, to attend the celebration of Maharani Chandrakanta's return to be held in a week's time.

Reports from the other members of the colonel's staff indicated that this news did not better the Colonel's mood, but resulted in more shouting, and the occasional broken object in the office.

In the end, the Colonel decided the better part of valor was to release William and put him back on duty. Or, as William put it, on punishment duty. Just about every dirty, exhausting, and demeaning duty that could be assigned to a Lieutenant was suddenly William's responsibility, on top of his regular workload. Daily inspections of the garbage dump. Training troops in digging, cleaning, and filling latrines. With hands-on demonstrations. And other things that neither Willie nor my uncle would describe that they said were even worse.

Tinka stayed at the palace as special guest of the maharani. Miss Bang visited and reported that Tinka was well, but bored and eager to return to the ship. The maharani brought in her dressmakers and they were making a special dress for Tinka for the celebration. They treated Tinka like royalty, and it drove her a bit batty. She wasn't used to so much attention or deference, or being seen by so many different strangers, and was completely lost on how to react, so she fell back on her desire to go hide. This led to several incidents where Tinka disappeared, only to be found hours later climbing back down from a rooftop where she had gone for some peace and solitude.

The professor and Miss Bang visited the palace a few times to be debriefed by the maharaja's investigators, and to visit Tinka when she could be found. The investigators never asked to talk to me, which I found disappointing. I suppose the professor was more than able to fill them in on all the details they required.

The Riggers arrived quite early each morning with a load of lumber and an assortment of carpentry tools and went to work with vigor. This caused a significant racket that defeated any desire to sleep in.

Each morning they removed the makeshift door from the night before and set to repairing and restoring the portal that was smashed by the Kindred. They removed the wooden frame and rebuilt it with surprising craftsmanship, being as faithful to the original door frame as they were able. I was frankly surprised at the quality of their carpentry. I had never seen a finished door being built from scratch before. I went down to "inspect" their work a few times, but they politely informed me that they didn't need me sticking my nose in. I believe the exact wording was, "Look, your nibs, we got work to do. Kindly bugger off until we're done."

While most of the men worked on the front doors, two men applied themselves to removing scarred and broken planks from the hallway floor and replacing them. Another trio rebuilt the doors out into the garden, including carefully cutting and fitting the glass panels into the frame. Before half the week was out, the doors were painted and re-hung; and looked identical to their fellows.

One morning several wagons pulled up and the Riggers assisted the drivers in loading up the last of the wreckage of the various vehicles that remained from the party. The scars on the lawn were neatly repaired, and one had to know where to look to see the signs of the damage caused less than a fortnight ago. The effect this had on my uncle's household staff was remarkable. As the evidence of the destruction was removed, it was as if the event became a dream, a simple night-terror that evaporated with the morning light. They were suddenly going about their work with smiles on their faces.

My time during that week was not as eventful.

I was left to my own devices. At one time I would have spent an opportunity like this exploring my uncle's library. Or his wine cellar. Most likely both.

I hoped to talk to my brother about making sure the pistol was safe to fire, but Willie spent all his time at the base. Instead I broached the subject to Uncle Jeremy while he was waiting for Aunt Phyllis to return from the palace.

On the third day after we had returned to my aunt and uncle's house I got my chance to talk to him. I had just finished eating dinner by myself, feeling a little out of place in the main dining room, when my uncle walked in, following his nose to the food laid out on the sideboard.

I stood up. "Uncle Jeremy, I thought you were going to wait to dine with Aunt Phyllis when she gets back. I didn't mean to start without you." I hadn't dressed for dinner, and I wasn't sure if he was going to call me out for it, as Aunt Phyllis surely would have.

My uncle smiled and gestured for me to sit back down. "Not a problem, Nephew. I am going to dine with Phyllis, but she's been coming back rather late, so I thought I'd pop in and get a bit of a snack." He grabbed a small plate and piled food up on it. "In the army we learn to grab a bite when it is available as you don't know how long it will be until your next warm meal." He looked down and patted his stomach. "I may have taken that advice a bit too often." He grabbed a fork and sat down with me at the table.

"I've been meaning to thank you for the use of your pistol last week. It was very useful in helping us make our escape," I told him.

He smiled broadly. "It was my pleasure, Nephew. I'm so glad it played a part in getting you and Phyllis home safely." He ate with gusto, being in much better spirits since his wife's return.

"I'm a bit concerned about it. We took a dunking as part of our escape, and I don't know if it was seen to after that. Willie said he was going to make sure it was cleaned, but with everything else going on..." I trailed off

"Oh. I didn't realize that. When William came home with Phyllis I was so glad to have her back. I may have missed a few details." The cheer drained from his face. "But now that we've time, we should see that it is well cared for." He thought about it while chewing on another mouthful. "The staff should have returned the gun belt to your room when William got home. Go fetch it, and meet me in the study, and we'll make sure there's no lasting damage, eh?"

I nodded, and excused myself from the table.

When I walked into his study with the pistol, I found that he'd set up a table with a grey cloth covering it, a number of small brushes, and a can of some sort of oil. He sat down as I walked in. I sat opposite of him and when I handed him the gun, he proceeded to disassemble it before my eyes.

He quickly and methodically removed each individual piece and placed it out on the cloth in a precise pattern. The only tool he used was a small screwdriver, which he used to push a metal stud to begin the process and to remove the screws securing the plates on either side of the grip. The rest he did with his bare hands. I sat mesmerized by the whole process.

He picked up and inspected each piece, then administered to it with a brush or an oiled cloth, working from one side of the layout to the other. The scent of the oil filled the air. It was somewhat metallic, but pleasant and somewhat spicy.

When he came to the last piece, after looking it over, instead of putting it back down, he reached for the other pieces and reassembled the weapon in a matter of seconds. I stared, fascinated by the process.

Uncle Jeremy looked up at me and I let out the breath I didn't realize I'd been holding.

"Well, it doesn't seem any the worse for wear, Nephew. I take it you drained it as soon as it came out of the water?" He paused, and I nodded. "Good. If you'd let water sit in there, after a few days you could have gotten a nasty bit of corrosion, especially if it was salt water." He set the safety and put the gun back in its holster. "Still, I'm glad you mentioned it to me. It's always good to check on a gun after you've been using it a bit." He patted the weapon.

"How did you do that, Uncle Jeremy?" I gestured at the pistol in front of us. "It was in pieces and you just pulled it back together!"

He chuckled. "I may be an old officer, but I'm still a soldier. My father was a solider, too. He taught me about taking care of my weapons when I was a boy, and it served me well as a cadet. A dirty gun can blow up in your face, Nephew. We lost a cadet in the academy when his gun exploded. Boy thought he was too important to clean his own gun."

"Can you show me how to do that?"

He laughed, and big grin split his face. "Of course! I'd be happy to."

Over the course of the next hour, my uncle showed me how to take the gun apart and put it back together again. He told me what each part was called, what it did, and how it should be cared for. He showed me where he kept his gun cleaning supplies and ammunition and encouraged me to practice.

I spent a good bit of my time for the rest of the week in target practice.

I found it strangely relaxing.

Each afternoon I would go out alone to my uncle's little firing range, load up my pistol, and let my mind blank out as I fired bullets downrange and disassembled the targets bit by bit. I felt oddly calm even amid all the noise and destruction. I found it relaxing, and I stopped minding the heat of the afternoon. Even cleaning the gun and putting it back together afterward soon became more of a comforting ritual than the simple practice that it started as.

Before I knew it, the week was gone, and it was time to get ready for the maharaja's party.

"Please hurry, my lord! We need to get going soon!" Miss Bang called as she rapped on my door for the third time. "We need to get to the palace."

I grunted in frustration and looked at my mangled bow tie in the mirror. "We've got hours until the party, Miss Bang. Why the hurry?"

Manqoba gently pulled my hands away from the mistreated tie, and deftly untied and re-tied it, pressing it flat against my collar. As he moved away, I glanced at my reflection in the mirror. The tie was perfect. I sighed and wished I could hire him away from the professor as a valet.

"We need to be there for Tinka," she called back. "She's saying she won't go. We need to convince her to make an appearance at the party. Maharani Chandrakanta insists. Do hurry." I heard her shoes clicking against the wood floor as she stalked off down the hallway.

I glanced at the butler as he returned with my vest. "I don't understand why it is so difficult to get Tinka to go to the party. Don't girls... young women, I mean. Don't they like to go to parties?"

Manqoba stopped, and his arms lowered.

He stared at me.

"Sir, you know Miss Tinka is *not* a typical young woman." He spoke softly, and his words rumbled in my ears. "Surely you have noticed she can be most... stubborn, when she sets her mind to something."

I shrugged. "I do know she's got something of a temper, but she isn't mad at the princess, or her father. Why would she refuse to go to a party in her honor?"

His shoulders dipped slightly, and I half expected him to roll his eyes, but instead he pulled his frame back up to his usual posture. "I am sure that you are aware, sir, first-hand, how Miss Tinka is rather self-conscious about her appearance. Normally, she isn't seen by anyone other than the crew of the ship. We have all come to accept and appreciate Miss Tinka's differences. One might expect that she would have some reticence about being seen in front of a number of strangers." He raised one eyebrow at me, then lifted my waistcoat up and held it out for me.

I turned and held my arms out as he slid the garment onto my back. "But this is India, Manqoba! Some people here worship a goddess with eight arms. Surely this is the one place in the world where Tinka would be most appreciated?"

"Would you want people to look at you and treat you as either a god incarnate or a demon from the underworld, sir?"

I looked at him over my shoulder. "I suppose you're right, Manqoba. I must admit that when I first saw her, it gave me a bit of a start." I began buttoning the vest. "Do you think that I've gotten so used to her that I'm not seeing how other people will react?"

He looked at me sharply. "I'm sure that is not for me to say, sir."

Everything about his posture said, 'Yes, you idiot.'

I sighed. "Very well. We need to talk her into making an appearance. Does Miss Bang really think it will take that long? Shouldn't she go ahead without me?"

He gave me an inscrutable look.

"As I said, sir, Miss Tinka does have a well-earned reputation for being stubborn." He turned and picked up my coat, shaking it out.

"She can't be that stubborn."

He paused.

"Sir, it is very rare for Miss Tinka to change her mind after she's chosen a course of action. To my knowledge, it has happened only once. Just once." He held the jacket out for me.

I stared at him, unsure how much to believe.

"You're serious? She's that stubborn?" I shook my head. "If that's the case, I'm sure I won't be any help. I'm not going to be able to change her mind."

"You've done it before," he said, and raised the jacket again.

"What?"

"When you first came on board, she was quite set about seeing you off the ship. Preferably pushed off. From a great height." The butler's voice was calm and matter of fact. The fact that he was telling me that Tinka wanted to kill me, while holding my coat out for me, seemed surreal.

"You're saying that Tinka wanted me dead? Or at the least gone from the ship?" I remembered some painful encounters with some of the Riggers back in Prague. It suddenly seemed all too probable. "But then what changed?"

Of all things, Manqoba shrugged. "We don't know, sir. Miss Bang is hoping that you might tell us."

"Me?"

We stood there, facing each other, for a while. I'm not sure how long. Finally, I shook my head and said, "Let me get this straight. Tinka wanted me dead, but she changed her mind, and you think I had something to do with it."

"Yes, sir."

"And you're hoping I can tell you how I did it."

He nodded. "There are several members of the crew that are quite curious on the subject, sir."

I turned around and stuck my arms into the jacket. Manqoba settled the coat on my shoulders and came around in front of me to make sure that everything was in proper order. He carefully lowered the insignia that identified my rank as a Knight Commander of the Royal Victorian Order over my head and deposited it on my chest. This was a large, white enameled Maltese cross with silver rays extending from it and the Royal Cypher for Victoria in the center, surrounded by a blue ring and topped by a crown. The cross hung from a blue ribbon with red and white edging. He tucked the ribbon along my collar, and adjusted the cross where it hung on my chest. When he was satisfied with my appearance, he handed me my top hat.

I could hear the click of Miss Bang's shoes in the hallway.

"I guess we'd better not keep her waiting any longer."

"No, sir."

"Oh, my calling cards!" I turned to survey the room, trying to remember where I had put them.

"In your inner jacket pocket, sir," Manqoba said.

"Right! Thank you, Manqoba."

He nodded as Miss Bang rapped on the door again.

I called out, "Coming, Miss Bang!" and hurried out of the room.

The car sent to take us to the palace was a wonder to behold. It was long, black, and sleek. It looked like a custom Maybach, with three doors down the side. The middle set of seats faced backwards in the vehicle, creating a private area behind the driver. The sparkling white seats themselves were upholstered in a delightfully soft kid leather. I suspected they didn't import many such cars into India. It clearly cost a fortune.

My uncle stood next to the car, admiring it, as we exited his house. He wore his crimson dress uniform and his polished gold buttons shone brightly. His face was a bit ruddy with the heat and the layers of thick wool he wore, and he fanned himself with his colonial service helmet. He turned and smiled as Miss Bang and I came down the front steps.

The professor had talked the driver into opening the hood, and was staring intently at the engine. Every few seconds he would reach for something, and the driver would step forward and remove his hands from some part of the engine or another.

"I was wondering if you were going to join us," Uncle Jeremy called.

"I'm sorry, I'm sorry," I replied. "Entirely my fault. I didn't fully understand when we needed to be there."

He laughed. "Well, I hope they won't start without us." He took Miss Bang's hand. "You look beautiful, my dear. I'm sure you'll turn a number of heads tonight." He patted her hand paternally.

He was right. She wore a gorgeous gown in a deep blue silk that shimmered in the light. A black lace wrap trimmed in fur covered her shoulders. The dress clung to her curves, and she seemed to flow upwards from the ground like some sort of water spirit made flesh.

"Thank you, Lieutenant-Colonel," she said. "You're too kind."

Professor Crackle's head came up at the sound of her voice.

"Ah, Titania, my dear! There you are! Are we all ready then?" As the professor turned, the driver quickly and quietly closed the bonnet on the car and latched it down. Professor Crackle took a couple steps toward me. "I see you've found a topper, my boy! Excellent choice. Excellent choice. I've always favored them. A very stylish hat and appropriate to almost any occasion." He reached up and tipped his own hat, which displayed his usual two pairs of goggles. The professor certainly stood out from the rest of us. While Uncle Jeremy wore his dress uniform, Miss Bang had on a lovely gown, and I was in white tie, he looked like he had dressed by grabbing clothing at random from a pile.

His cravat was a bright green, the vest was a decent enough navy blue, but it clashed horribly with the red and yellow plaid pants. One boot was brown, the other black. He likewise wore a pair of mismatched spats over them, one with a design that looked like a Chinese dragon motif done up in small stones, the other covered in bright gold studs. The right side of his collar was white, but the left side appeared to be stained a pale pink colour. The cuff of the left sleeve was orange, while the right cuff looked as if someone had dumped a bottle of indigo on it. His coat was made of some kind of beaded leather, but fortunately, I couldn't see it very well because he was wearing a startling white lab coat over top of it. It wasn't entirely white, though. The pocket on the chest sported a large ink stain, and there appeared to be a smear of grease up the back of his right sleeve.

"I believe we're ready to go, Professor, but are you?" I said, gesturing to his mismatched ensemble.

"What?" he said. He looked down at himself and grabbed the collar of the lab coat in one hand. "Oh, you mean the lab coat. Don't worry, my boy, I'll take it off as soon as we get there. It's to protect the rest of my finery while traveling."

I opened my mouth to answer, but Miss Bang put a hand on my arm and spoke in my ear. "No, my lord. Trust me, this is not an argument worth winning. Every garment he is wearing was gifted to him by one notable or another, most of them royalty, and each piece with a lengthy story behind it that must be told to fully appreciate the garment. He sincerely believes these are the best clothes that he has."

"But..." I started to protest.

She shook her head. "I've tried many times. Many. Tonight, we simply do not have the time." She implored me with a look, and I shrugged in resignation.

Instead I asked, "Are we waiting for Aunt Phyllis, then?"

My uncle shook his head. "No, Nephew. She left hours ago. She's helping with the party, so she's already there. I don't know that I've ever seen her so excited for an event. She wants everything to be perfect."

"Oh. Well, I guess we should be going then." I gestured to the car.

Uncle Jeremy opened one of the doors to the back of the sedan and held out his hand for Miss Bang. As he helped her into the car, the professor and I walked around to the other side of the vehicle, where the driver opened the doors for us. The professor sat next to Miss Bang, and I climbed into the facing seat, as my uncle slid in from the opposite side. The doors closed with a quiet thud. The driver slid behind the wheel, closing the door again with a smooth, practiced motion. The engine purred to life. The vehicle made a slow, regal turn, and we pulled out onto the road and proceeded to the palace.

CHAPTER TWENTY-THREE
A FORCE OF NATURE

The streets of Kanpur were decorated with strings of brightly coloured flowers. Bright banners fluttered over the streets, criss-crossing between buildings. Cheerful crowds lined the streets singing and dancing and doing their own part to celebrate the return of the maharani.

"The city certainly seems festive," I said.

My uncle nodded. "The maharani is very much beloved. Both she and her father. It should make a very good alliance."

I looked at my uncle, not sure what to make of his last statement. "If the maharaja is so beloved, is that why the Kindred wanted him to lead their rebellion? Because he would bring the people onto their side?"

Uncle Jeremy opened his mouth to reply but couldn't seem to decide on which words to use. He started and stopped several times before Miss Bang interceded.

"An interesting question, my lord. If he truly believed in their cause, I imagine he would be able to bring popular support behind the movement."

Professor Crackle joined in on the opportunity to lecture. "I hadn't thought of that, my boy. I had assumed that they wanted the maharaja as a figurehead. Someone to take the empire's wrath if they didn't succeed. But you have a point. Many of the Indian people would like the Europeans to pack up and go home. No doubt they feel they could manage their affairs much better if left to their own devices. We are the interlopers."

My uncle bristled. "Now see here! India has been a part of the Empire for over a hundred years!"

The professor nodded. "Yes, and for most of that time we've not been very good landlords. India was a civilized nation for centuries before we came along, Lieutenant-Colonel. In the early days of the occupation of India, Britain ruthlessly exploited the people and the resources of this country. On several occasions the Eternal Empress herself-"

"May she live forever!" my uncle hastily interjected.

"- had to intercede on behalf of the people of India," the professor concluded.

Miss Bang looked at my uncle. "And despite those times she intervened, many of the people still look at her as an oppressor, because she hasn't done more to bring equality to the empire."

"But we *are* equal," my uncle protested.

"Are we?" Miss Bang asked. "My father was half British, but he struggled for recognition in his field because of the colour of his skin. He changed our family name so we would fit in more easily, but he still fought against racial prejudice all his life."

"That might have been true in your father's day, Miss Bang, but we've made great strides since then. Especially with the dissolution of the governors and the reestablishment of local rule." Uncle Jeremy nodded, as if that was the last word on the subject.

Miss Bang wasn't quite ready to let it go. She said, "Even with the new laws and recognition of local rule, British companies are *still* exploiting Indian workers to this day. The Empire was supposed to stop that over forty years ago, Lieutenant-Colonel. As good as things may be now, compared to what they were in the past, it is fairly easy

We're all very proud of you. We'll leave the servants outside for now. Please let us in to talk to you." She spoke in a low voice to the head servant at the door, who nodded, then barked out a single command, and the mass of women moved past the professor and myself and re-formed about twenty feet further down the hallway.

"Who's 'us'?" Tinka asked in a less forceful voice.

"The professor, Sir Richard, and myself, Tinka. I sent the servants away."

"Nobody else?"

"No, Tinka. Please let us in. We just want to talk."

We waited at the door for a few moments, and then heard something large and heavy being dragged across the floor. The sound stopped. We waited a few seconds more, then Miss Bang tried the door. It unlatched and swung open a few inches, stopping again as it came up against an obstacle.

Miss Bang turned sideways and easily slid through the gap, her gown not inconveniencing her in the slightest.

I stepped up after her and saw that Tinka had stacked a number of the room's furnishings against the doors to prevent their use. I like-wise turned sideways and tried to slip through, but found myself jammed between the two doors and unable to move because my honors were too large and were digging into the wood.

I tried to back out and tuck the cross into my coat to protect it, but it kept catching the surface of the door, no matter which way I moved. I put my hands against the door and pushed, but whatever was blocking it was heavy, and not easily moved. I was stuck.

"Um, Professor? A hand?" I squeaked.

"What? Oh. Oh, certainly my boy." He put a hand on the door and leaned against it. It didn't budge. He put his shoulder up against the door, dug his feet in, and we both pushed for all that we were worth. We strained for several long seconds before our efforts were rewarded by a loud squeak of wood against wood and the door moved about an inch or so. This proved to be enough room for me to press my hand over the decoration and still be able to squeeze through into the room with only slightly scraped knuckles.

I moved around the edge of the door to find an eight-foot mahogany armoire pressed up against it. I stood gaping at it as Professor Crackle slipped into the room behind me, his top hat in one hand.

"How...?"

"Low center of gravity, good footing, four arms, and an impressive grip, my boy. Not to mention an exceedingly stubborn disposition." He patted my arm. "Come along."

The rooms were luxuriously decorated, although most of the furnishings had been shoved against the door. Tinka had retreated to the far side of the room and balled herself up on the end of a long chaise. She wore several layers of thin gauze wrapped about her body, but her feet, which were propped up on the lounge, were bare. She hid behind the protection of her arms and legs and peered up at Miss Bang over her knees.

"Tinka," Miss Bang said as she stood over her young friend, "No one is going to make fun of you. These are your friends. They want to honor you and thank you for everything you've done for them."

"It's not them," Tinka replied sulkily. "Chandra and her da are all right. They're kind, and she comes to visit me and talks to me like a person. They're all right. It... it's everybody else. All the fancy people. I'll just be a freak to them. They'll laugh at me. Call me names or make cruel jokes behind my back. I know they will." She managed to shrink further into her ball.

"Tinka." Miss Bang sat next to her on the couch, putting one arm gently behind her friend's shoulders. "I know this is something that you've been struggling with for a long time. It isn't something you can get over in an evening, or a week. But if you're ever going to get over it, you need to try. Do you really think Maharani Chandrakanta would let her other guests mistreat you? You saved her life. She invited you to this party to repay you and to celebrate your deeds, not put you on display."

"No. Maybe. I don't know. I'll feel like I'm on display anyway. Everyone will be looking at me. How's she going to stop them?" Tinka fidgeted with the ends of her skirt.

I stepped up to the back of a nearby chair, and the professor moved by me and sat in it. "You don't think the maharani can make her guests be nice for one evening?" I asked.

She glanced up at me, then looked down and shook her head. "They'll say they'll be nice, but they won't be. They'll be mean. People are always mean. I don't want to put up with mean people." Her voice gained a hard edge with that last sentence. I knew firsthand that it didn't pay to be mean to Tinka.

"Tinka, my dear," Professor Crackle began.

She glared at him and cut him off. "Don't you start in on me, too! You're all ganging up on me."

"My dear," he continued, "I'm your father. I'll support you whatever you decide."

"Thank you," she said in a small voice.

"But I'd still rather have you with me. How often do I get a chance to dance with my daughter at a fancy ball?" He smiled at her.

She gave him a sideways glance, as if judging his words, then shook her head. "No. If you want to dance with me, we can dance on the ship. Durgan has a concertina, and Benji's almost completed her flute. But I ain't goin' tonight."

The professor sat back and looked up at me. I shrugged and said, "Well, I guess that means that I'll need to find another escort for tonight."

"What does that mean?" Tinka asked sulkily.

"It means that I was going to ask you to be my escort for tonight. But I can't do that if you're not going."

"Oh," she said, glumly. Then she sat up suddenly, her feet falling to the floor. "Oh!" Her face brightened as she stared at me. Then her face fell. "No. No, I'm still not going. I won't be a laughingstock." She balled herself back up on the couch and turned her face away from us.

I sighed. Miss Bang looked up at me imploringly.

I considered the situation. Tinka wouldn't go as long as there was a chance she'd be treated like an oddity. I certainly understood that. It had been hard for me to make friends as a boy. It was always much easier for everyone to pick on the boy with the funny name. Fortune gave me the chance to gain a new name, in a fashion, but Tinka would always be the girl with four arms. She couldn't escape that. She needed someone who could help her deal with the unavoidable attention.

The maharani could command her guests to behave, but Tinka was sure they'd disobey her. And she'd probably be right. Even a look would be enough. The maharani and her father were both much loved by their people, but Tinka needed someone who could not only compel obedience, but whom no one would *ever* think of crossing.

"Excuse me," I said. "I have an idea."

I went back to the door of the chamber, pausing only to grab the heavy wardrobe and pull it a little further back into the room with another loud shudder as the feet rubbed against the floor. I opened the door and looked outside. As I suspected, the mob of servant women were still waiting patiently about twenty feet down the hall. I pointed to one of them and motioned her toward me.

I did not expect the entire group to start moving my way at once.

Frantically, I motioned for them to stop, and they halted about ten feet away. I held up a single finger and beckoned again.

The women closest to me seemed confused for a moment, but their leader understood. She approached me, bowing slightly. I told her what I wanted. At first I wasn't sure she understood. I repeated myself, and she smiled, nodded, and quickly hurried away without another word.

I closed the door on the rest of the waiting attendants and returned to my friends. I sat down on a nearby settee and leaned back, crossing my legs.

They all stared at me.

"Well?" Miss Bang said.

"I've sent for someone who I think will be able to help to us," I replied.

Miss Bang looked to the door, and then back to me. "And where is this person?"

"I know she's here in the palace somewhere, but I'm not sure where..." I started, but Miss Bang jumped to her feet and started pacing back and forth impatiently.

The professor tried to help, saying, "My dear, do please calm down, I'm sure that..."

Miss Bang whirled on him. "Calm? I *am* calm." The look in her eyes belied the statement, while brooking no argument.

He nodded. "Of course you are, my dear. I don't know why I said that. What I meant was that we all need to be patient. There are quite a lot of people in the palace, and everyone is quite busy. It is going to take some time to find this person he wants and bring them here, but rest assured once they get his message they'll be along presently. Right, my boy?"

I swallowed. "I certainly hope so."

"See, not a problem at all. We just need to relax until this person arrives." He smiled at her.

Miss Bang did not appear mollified in the least. She turned to me. "You said it was urgent, yes?"

"I did my best. I'm not sure the woman fully understands English, but she seemed to know who I wanted."

"You don't even know if she's actually fetching this person you want?" Her hands balled into fists.

"Well, not exactly, but even if she didn't fully understand, she's bound to come back with someone. We'll get it straightened out eventually."

"Eventually! The ball is tonight, and we still have to get her ready!" She threw her hand out in Tinka's direction.

"I'm not going!" Tinka reminded us.

"We're going to be late unless we can change her mind," Miss Bang said.

Tinka snorted.

"Miss Bang, I'm sure she'll come, but I'm not exactly sure how busy she is right now, so this may take a while."

We all jumped as the door crashed into the wardrobe at the other end of the room.

"What fool put a wardrobe in front of the door?" Aunt Phyllis asked as she stepped inside. She shook her head and stalked across the room. She was dressed for the party, in a black gown covered with silver sequins that reminded me of stars in the night sky. Her brows drew together as she walked, gathering for the storm. "What do you want, Nephew? I'm very busy this evening and I don't have time for any silliness."

I stood as she approached. "Thank you, Aunt Phyllis. I appreciate you coming so quickly. I'm hoping you can solve a little problem for us."

She arched an eyebrow at me. "Stand up straight, Nephew. What kind of problem do you expect me to fix for you that the four of you can't deal with for yourselves?" She looked at the professor and Miss Bang. "I thought you were supposed to be experts at problem solving."

"You remember Tinka, don't you, Aunt Phyllis?" I gestured to the young girl who was laying half-sprawled on the lounge after being startled by my aunt's entrance.

She looked at Tinka and frowned. "Of course, I do. Sit up straight, girl, an extra set of arms is no excuse for poor posture! And what in heaven's name are you wearing? What are you all doing sitting around? She's nowhere near ready for the reception." Tinka sat up on the couch and clutched the loose fabric of her dress around her.

"She says she's not going, Aunt Phyllis," I explained.

"What? Don't be ridiculous. Of course you're going, child. You're being specially honored at the reception for saving the maharani's life. There's no possibility of you not attending."

"They'll all laugh at me," Tinka said in a small voice as she bowed her head again.

"Speak up, girl! Stand up. Look at me when I'm talking to you. Up, up!" Aunt Phyllis barked at Tinka, snapped her fingers. Tinka jumped up and stood at attention, tears streaming down her face. She sniffled. "Now wipe those tears off your face and tell me why you think you aren't going to the reception tonight."

Tinka wiped at her face with the back of her lower left hand, but only managed to smear the tears across one cheek. She sniffed again. "I don't want to go. Everyone will look at me like I'm a freak." Her voice was still small, but it was louder this time.

"Poppycock," Aunt Phyllis snapped. "Is this the same woman who fought her way into a foreign stronghold to save two women she'd never met? And then risked her own life to bring them out again? A woman who dodged a hail of bullets in the process? A woman who threw me down a well when I was too paralyzed with fear to know what was good for me?" She threw a hand towards Miss Bang. "Who pulled this lady out of an underground reservoir when she half drowned herself? The woman who, I am told, stood toe to toe with one of these metal monstrosity Kindred of Kali and not only fought it to a standstill, but won? This is the woman I'm talking to, yes? Am I to believe that you've suddenly turned into a child who's too afraid to stand up in front of a crowd of pampered socialites and let them applaud your achievements? Well, answer me, girl!"

Tinka stuttered. "I, I, yes, no, I... I don't know!"

"Did you do those things?"

"I... yes."

"Then act like it. Stand tall. Chest out. Shoulders back. Be the unstoppable force that you are. Those people mean nothing to you, but you mean everything to them. Your bravery tells them that their lives are worth something, even though they don't do anything with them. Your deeds let them vicariously live the life they always thought was their due, but they were too afraid to chase after. They think they are princes of the world, but *you* will stand and stride across it like a goddess. Do you understand me, child?" As my aunt talked, Tinka slowly straightened and I could see the pride and confidence seeping back into her, right up until that last question.

"But..." she started.

"No buts about it. You can't go into the world second guessing yourself. You've got to stand strong and stand tall. You've got to look the world in the eye and make *it* back down. Don't give them the chance to laugh or snipe at you. You look at them with everything that you've got. Let them know that you see everything they are, and you are *not* impressed. That they're not even worth a response from you. Do this, and you needn't worry about what they might do. They won't dare set a foot out of line." My aunt's eyes were fire as she looked Tinka up and down. Tinka leaned forward, meeting Phyllis' challenge. One corner of my aunt's mouth quirked up. "Can you do that, Tinka?"

"Yes!" Fire met fire as Tinka stared back.

Aunt Phyllis smiled. She put her hands on Tinka's upper shoulders. "Good. Then we'll hear no more nonsense about not going tonight." Tinka nodded. Aunt Phyllis leaned in toward her. "Good. I'm proud of you, young lady." She dropped her voice a bit. I could barely hear her. "My grandmother gave me that advice a very long, long time ago. It has made my life so much richer than I could ever tell you. Remember it."

Tinka nodded. Aunt Phyllis glanced over to me, but I wasn't sure if she wanted to make sure I had heard that last bit, or that I hadn't.

Aunt Phyllis added, "And don't ever give me cause to call you 'girl' or 'child' again. You're better than that."

My aunt stepped back from Tinka and looked at the rest of us. "Now that that is settled, this young woman needs to get ready."

"I don't have anything to wear!" Tinka said.

"I'll get the servants," Miss Bang said as she strode towards the door. "I'm sure Maharani Chandrakanta has come up with something."

"Good. Tinka, go into the next room and get changed," Aunt

Phyllis said. Tinka ran into the next room. My aunt then turned to Professor Crackle. "You're responsible for that young woman, yes?"

The professor nodded. "Yes, my good lady. I've been looking after her since she was a small child."

"Then you are responsible for her appalling lack of social education. I expect you to take better care of her in the future," Aunt Phyllis pointed a finger at the professor. "Or I will have words with you. Understand?"

He blanched and nodded but said nothing.

My aunt turned to me.

"Nephew."

I swallowed, and said as calmly as I could, "Yes, Aunt Phyllis?"

"You did well calling for me. This poor girl needed my help."

Praise from Aunt Phyllis? I did my best to hide my shock and simply said, "I'm glad."

"Go get yourself cleaned up. You look like you've been moving furniture." Without waiting for me to answer, Aunt Phyllis turned and left, moving effortlessly against the flow of servants streaming into the room behind Miss Bang.

CHAPTER TWENTY-FOUR
THE GRAND BALL

I wandered through the public rooms of the maharani's apartment until I found one with a mirror. Inspecting myself in the glass, I saw what my aunt had meant. My suit was wrinkled, and part of my shirt tail had come undone. I set about restoring myself to proper order, tucking in my shirt and smoothing the lines of my pants and jacket. I doubted that it would pass my aunt's muster, but I hoped it would at least be good enough to avoid comment from anyone else.

When I made my way back to the parlor where I'd left the professor, he was staring through the windows into the courtyard below. I joined him and together we watched as the traffic in the courtyard. At first it was just servants finishing preparations for the party, including men moving several very large decorative planters through the courtyard on sturdy wheeled platforms. After a while a few early arriving guests wandered through while they waited. Eventually, a line of dignitaries formed as they gathered for the evening's big event. The professor kept up a steady commentary, as he seemed to find everything going on either interesting or curious, but I didn't listen and now cannot recall a single word of it.

My mind kept winding its way back to my aunt. I don't know if she meant me to hear her words to Tinka, but I did. I wondered how much of the terror I had always felt upon encountering her was my fear, and how much was her own fear of not measuring up as a child, now honed over the years until she had become that person to be reckoned with. And for all that, she saw in Tinka the echo of the small, frightened girl she once was.

I was shaken from my reverie when the maharani arrived. She slipped quietly in through the door, but was quickly spied by Professor Crackle. "Ah, Princess! This is shaping up to be a wonderful evening. I am quite looking forward to the festivities."

I realized with surprise that while I was musing the servants who were not directly attending to Tinka had moved her makeshift barricade away from the doors and put all the pieces back into their assigned spaces.

The maharani approached us. Her outfit for the evening was a dark purple two-piece affair. It featured a short top with elbow length sleeves and a v-neck that was heavily embroidered in silver thread. The designs climbed up her shoulders on either side and branched down the length of the sleeves. The twisting pattern gave me the impression of trees and vines, but seeing as the design mostly covered her blouse, I thought it might not be a good idea to stare too closely at it. Her skirt was long and flowing from the gathered waist down to the hem drifting just above the ground. When she moved it swung around her with a swirl of deep folds. The hem was also embroidered in silver threads that wound around the circumference of the dress. A long, sheer purple scarf with small silver leaves spotting its surface was draped over her arms above the elbows. She wore a pair of long earrings that looked like a silver waterfall studded with small diamonds.

"Thank you, Professor," the maharani said, giving him a look that I took to be a combination of confusion and disgust. "Shouldn't you be making your final preparations, then? I would think you'll want to look your best."

The implications of her statement were completely lost on the professor. He beamed. "I have indeed brought my very best, good lady. Why, this waistcoat was a gift to me from..."

I hastily interrupted. "Now, Professor, you shouldn't be using all your best stories so soon. Save them for the party." I closed to kiss the maharani's hand, saying in a low voice, "Let it go. Miss Bang tells me it isn't worth the argument," and concluded more loudly, "You look lovely this evening, Maharani Chandrakanta."

"Thank you," she replied. "But please, in private, feel free to call me Chandra." She smiled and her eyes lit up with joy and anticipation. "But I was looking for Tinka. Is she ready?"

"Miss Bang took Tinka and a whole squad of servants back to get her ready quite a while ago. We're expecting them any minute now. I have no idea what is taking them so long," I told her.

"She is going to make an appearance, isn't she? She isn't still fighting it?" the maharani asked, looking hopeful.

I shook my head. "No. Aunt Phyllis talked her out of that. And I don't think she'll change her mind back again. One doesn't really cross Aunt Phyllis."

The maharani nodded. "Your aunt certainly is a force of nature."

"I'm sure they'll be along momentarily, Princess," Professor Crackle assured her. "There haven't been any loud noises or calls for help. I'm confident all is well in hand. They'll be along soon, you'll see."

The maharani opened her mouth to speak, but before she could say a word, she was interrupted by a high-pitched squeal from the other room. The sound repeated itself and was followed by peals of laughter.

"I take that as a good sign," I said.

Moments later a young woman came running into the room. She ran in a circle around the room, her strawberry blonde hair trailing behind her. She completed her circuit, and came up in front of us and spun, giggling, with her arms flung out about her. It was at this point that I realized that the young woman was, indeed, Tinka, cleaned and dressed in an elegant silk gown.

Tinka's dress was very similar to the style of the maharani's outfit, as it featured a short, fitted top and a long gathered dress covered with intricate embroidery. While the maharani was dressed in purple and silver, Tinka wore a bright yellow silk detailed in green designs of vines that flowed down her chest from the scooped neckline. Tinka wore a thin green scarf across her shoulders, draped so it flowed down her arms and back. The scarf was thin enough to allow one to see some of the patterns on the back of the dress, but also provided discreet coverage for Tinka's extra arms. Small golden sunbursts dotted the scarf. The effect was stunning. I gaped like a fish as she bounced in front of us laughing with glee.

The maharani smiled. Miss Bang and some of the household servants emerged from the back rooms in time to hear the maharani ask, "I take it you are pleased with the dress, Tinka?"

She squealed again, then sprang forward and wrapped the princess in a hug. As they bounced together, Tinka cried, "It's perfect! Thank you! Thank you so much!"

Miss Bang said. "It is a lovely lehenga choli, and your seamstresses did an excellent job at adapting it to Tinka's frame." She nodded to the servants and several of them bowed in appreciation of the complement.

The maharani replied, "I'm so glad you like it, Tinka. The seamstresses worked very hard on it. They wanted to make sure that it has every feature you would need. Are you ready? My father doesn't want to keep our guests waiting too long. You put too many noble families in one place and someone starts scheming." She grinned at her joke, but I thought it was a bit too close to the truth.

"Well," Tinka said, her former shyness returning, "I do need one more thing." She lowered her eyes and glanced up at me. In a very small voice she said, "An escort."

Recognizing my cue, I stepped forward. Giving my best courtly bow, I tried desperately to remember my childhood etiquette lessons.

I'm sure I looked rather comical, but only Tinka giggled. Extending my hand to her, I said, "Lady Tinka, would you do me the great honor of allowing me to escort you this evening?"

She laughed and said, "I'm not a lady."

"Respectfully, my lady," I said, "there is no doubt in anyone's mind that you are most definitely a lady."

She paused and gave me a long, measuring look. After a moment, she dropped her eyes and said, "Thank you, my lord, I would be happy to have you as my escort this evening." With a small smile, she looked up at me.

I bent my left arm and offered it to her. There was a moment of confusion while Tinka tried to figure out which of her right arms she should use to take mine. After some awkward trial and error, she finally settled on nestling her upper right hand in the crook of my elbow, lightly squeezing my bicep, and her lower right hand draped over my forearm.

I smiled at my partner, then said to the maharani, "I believe we are at last ready to go."

"Excellent," she replied. She directed one of the servants to show us to the entry to the ballroom and then left to make her own way to the hall ahead of us. The professor offered Miss Bang his arm, and we were off to the ball.

Despite the rush to proceed to the festivities, a considerable line of notables was still waiting to enter the ballroom. They stretched back down the hall, couples and a few individuals standing a discreet two paces apart. At the head of the line, a senior usher pounded a staff on the floor and announced each guest in turn, and the line advanced in a stately fashion. As special guests of honor, we were spared the need to stand in line, and were shown by an usher to a private waiting room off the hall.

The room was a small lounge with several low couches. Plates of hors d'oeuvres sat on small tables in front of each couch, and pitchers of refreshments sat on tables near the door. I considered pouring myself a glass of something, but quickly rejected the idea. The last thing I needed before our big introduction would be to spill something on myself.

"That's quite a line of people waiting to be introduced," I said as I sat on one of the couches. Tinka sat beside me and leaned forward to examine the tidbits on the table.

Miss Bang nodded. "Chandra told me that they'd slowed the announcements to make sure we'd have enough time. They should be picking up the pace now that we're ready."

While I couldn't hear any of the conversation in the hallway, I could hear the strikes of the usher's staff as he introduced each couple. I could tell that they were coming more frequently then they had before we sat down.

The wait itself proved to be rather short. It seemed we had no sooner settled ourselves to wait for our turn than another usher appeared to gather us once more.

The professor and Miss Bang led the way back out into the hallway, where the line of notables had vanished. We proceeded up the hall where another usher stopped the professor and Miss Bang. He leaned in to them, and the professor handed the man a card.

"Oh bloody hell," I cursed under my breath and began searching my pockets.

"What's the matter?" whispered Tinka.

"My card! I don't have my bloody card!" I replied as the head usher struck his staff upon the floor twice, and in a booming voice announced, "Professor Harmonious Crackle, and Miss Titania Bang!"

The professor and Miss Bang strode down the stairs into the reception room, the professor still wearing the lab coat he insisted was to keep his other "finery" clean. The junior usher ahead of us turned and motioned us forward. I continued patting my pockets, frantically trying to locate my small pack of calling cards.

"Oi, let's go," Tinka whispered and tugged on my arm.

"You don't understand..." I began, then slid my hand into my breast pocket and felt a second, smaller pocket inside the first. Dipping my fingers into that, I touched the cool metal of the case. I slipped the case out and flipped out a single card. "Oh, thank God," I murmured.

Slipping the case back into my pocket, and the card into my hand, Tinka and I stepped forward to the waiting usher. He leaned in and nodded to her. "Lady Tinka. Sir." He held out his hand and I slipped the card into it. He gestured us forward and padded up half a pace behind us as we stepped to the top of the stairs.

The ballroom was huge. Two of the huge planters I had seen earlier in the courtyard stood at either side of the stairs. Now that I saw them up close, I realized they were huge ceramic vases taller than I was, but the scale of the ballroom made them fit right in. Two more of the planters sat at the halfway points of the room, and directly across from us sat a dais with two large ornate chairs against the far wall. The maharaja and his daughter stood on the lowest step of the dais, chatting with their guests. I spotted Willie near the maharani, carefully positioned a long step away from her. Close enough for conversation, but far enough away to keep from being accused of standing *too* close. The maharani smiled at us over the heads of the various nobles and dignitaries. The crowd itself was a patchwork of black and red military uniforms, mixed among a swirl of colour as western formal wear mixed with the gowns and the colourful dress of local dignitaries. I was surprised by how many soldiers were present.

BOOM!

I jumped as the head usher pounded his staff on the floor right next to me.

BOOM!

It came again as he struck the floor a second time.

BOOM!

He struck a third time.

"MY LORDS AND LADIES!" he called out, his voice filling the room and drawing all eyes that were not already turned to us. I felt Tinka's upper hand tighten on my arm.

"THE LADY TINKA, AND LORD..." The man's voice caught in his throat, and he made a strangled sound. I glanced at him over my shoulder and saw him staring down at the card held in his hand.

My card.

"Oh crap."

I reached back with my free hand and grabbed the card from him. Turning it over, I pushed it back into his hand. As it was, he almost dropped it, and for a moment I thought he was going to storm off. He glanced down at the writing on the back of the card and regained a measure of his composure, although his face had turned bright red.

Clearing his throat, he straightened again and finished my introduction. "SIR RICHARD BLASPHEMY!"

I lifted my foot to step forward and was promptly brought up short by an iron grip on my elbow and forearm. Tinka hadn't moved.

I patted her hand, half to reassure her, half to get her to reduce the pressure on my limb, but she only gripped tighter. I looked over at her. She was frozen, staring wide eyed at the crowd, Aunt Phyllis' advice forgotten for the moment as she looked out at the assembled faces.

From the corner of my eye I caught a movement as the maharani raised her hands. She began clapping loudly. The maharaja and Willie looked at her for a second before they, too began clapping. From there, it spread like a wave until everyone within sight was applauding furiously.

I tried to think of what I could say to bring back the confidence Aunt Phyllis had instilled in her, but my mind remained discouragingly blank.

"Tinka? Shall we go?" I said.

She didn't move. She didn't even blink.

And the words came to me.

I leaned in and said, in a voice just loud enough for her to hear over the clapping, "Come, warrior. Your adoring followers await. Shall we not let them bask in your reflected glory?"

She jumped, as if she'd forgotten that I was there. She looked at me, and I smiled. She grinned back and straightened slightly, lifting her chin. I patted her hand again and she squeezed my arm again before relaxing her grip. She said, "Right. Let's do this."

We stepped forward together and made our way down the stairs and across the floor as the applause continued. Red wool and bright silks rustled as the other guests parted before us. The professor and Miss Bang had stopped a little way ahead of us and turned to watch us enter. Now they parted, still cheering, and let us pass between them and approach the maharaja, his daughter, and Willie. Tinka released my arm just in time for the maharaja to shake my hand, as she leaned forward to hug his daughter. My brother grinned at me and kept clapping.

The applause died off, and the guests slowly turned back to their individual conversations. Tinka quietly reclaimed my arm. While few of the more curious, or ambitious, moved closer, our circle of conversation remained fixed for the moment, with only Miss Bang and the professor joining our little group between Willie and Tinka.

"I am so glad to see you, young lady!" Maharaja Rajender boomed. He wore a dark blue, brocaded silk jacket that was fitted from his shoulders down to his waist, then flared out to end just above his knees. A long tunic of gold silk peeked out from underneath the jacket, and he wore tight-fitting trousers in a matching silk. A deep blue scarf with heavily embroidered edges was draped over one shoulder and tucked into the elbow of the opposite arm. A matching dark blue turban decorated with various bits of jewelry completed his formal look.

"I almost didn't come," Tinka said. "But someone reminded me that I've faced worse than this," she gestured to the other guests, "before." She glanced at me, then at the maharani. "And you made this lovely dress for me." She ran her lower right hand across her stomach and down the side of her skirt. "So, it seemed like the thing to do." She shrugged. "And I got to see you in your pretty dress!"

The maharaja laughed. "You think I am pretty? In this old coat?" He grinned.

"Oh, Father," his daughter chided him, slapping playfully at his arm. "As if you didn't spend all afternoon trying to figure out which was your best sherwani, and then picking out a kurta and chooridar pants to match." She leaned in to Tinka. "He can be such a clothes horse at times!"

"There is nothing wrong with taking care in ones appearance," the maharaja retorted. "Isn't that so?" He looked at us, smiling.

"Nothing whatsoever, Your Highness," the professor agreed, still looking like a refugee from a ragman's cart. The maharaja looked at him and his smile slid down his face as he got a good look at Professor Crackle's attire.

Tinka saved the situation by saying, "I think you look very pretty, um, Your Highness."

The maharaja looked back to Tinka and his smile returned. "Well, thank you, Tinka. You are always welcome here. Consider this your second home." He held out a hand to her and she took it with her upper left. He covered it and squeezed it gently with both hands. "Yes?"

"Thank you," Tinka said, her eyes brimming with tears.

"Thank you, daughter," he answered. "Now, enjoy the party. I must see to our other guests." With that he stepped off into the crowd, moving quickly, and already calling out to someone.

Sankar Chatterjee stepped into the space vacated by the maharaja, along with an attractive middle-aged Indian woman. The advisor was wearing a burgundy brocade robe trimmed with silver embroidery. His companion wore a matching sari over a white top decorated with geometric patterns. Her eyes were bright and very alert. She looked at each of us with the same kind of appraising gaze that my aunt had.

Mr. Chatterjee inclined his head to Tinka. "I hope you realize the depth of the honor done to you, Lady Tinka. Many a soldier serves faithfully for a lifetime, saving their lord multiple times, and is not honored as you have been." When we'd seen the advisor previously he had been aggressive and emotional. Now his face was like a stone, betraying no emotion and giving no hint of his true thoughts.

"Ugh!" the maharani groaned. "Uncle Sankar, this is a party. We're supposed to be celebrating, not depressing everyone."

The advisor bowed. "My apologies, Maharani Chandra, that was not my intention. I wished to impress upon our guests how generous your father has been with his rewards." He gestured to the woman beside him. "May I present to you my wife, Ridhi?"

She bowed her head and gave us a pleasant smile. "It is a pleasure to meet you. Sankar tells me you have had quite a distressing adventure. I do hope you are suitably recovered." She raised her head, looking at each of us with her very intense brown eyes. "I sincerely wish the remainder of your time in India will be more pleasant." Her voice was warm, and somehow familiar, but I couldn't place where I had heard it before.

"Thank you, my good woman! Yours is indeed a beautiful country, and I always enjoy my visits here." The professor bowed deeply.

"You have been here before, Professor Crackle?" she asked.

"To Kanpur, no, but I was in Delhi some years ago for that nasty business with the factories burning. That was a bit touch and go."

"The Lajpat Nagar bomb blast? That was almost twenty years ago. You must have been a child at the time. It must have been quite harrowing."

The professor blushed. "Well, I wasn't exactly a child. I am somewhat older than I look."

"I'm sorry, Mrs. Chatterjee," I said, "but I can't shake the feeling that we've met before. Were you perhaps at my aunt's garden party?"

She pulled back, shaking her head. "No, oh, no. I'm afraid I wasn't able to attend. I'm sure that we have not met before, sir."

"Are you sure, madam?" Miss Bang asked. "Perhaps you were

here at the palace when we brought the maharani back? Your voice seems familiar to me as well."

Ridhi Chatterjee shook her head. "I don't believe so. I have not been at court much lately. Other business has occupied my attention of late."

Mr. Chatterjee smiled. The expression did not look natural on his face. "My wife is very active with local charities, improving the lot of our city's least fortunate."

"Oh, Sankar. You embarrass me. Besides, we shouldn't take up all of their time." She tugged on her husband's arm. "I'm sure they will find some of the younger guests more interesting."

The advisor bowed and followed as his wife dragged him through the crowd. I stepped closer to the maharani to discourage anyone else from trying to join our group.

"Do you remember where you heard her voice before?" I asked Miss Bang.

She raised a graceful hand and tapped her chin with one long finger. "No. No I don't. And that bothers me. Do you remember her, Harmonious?"

"What, of course, I do, my dear. We met her a few moments ago."

Tinka reached across Miss Bang and gave her father a solid thump on the chest. "That's not what she meant an' you know it."

He staggered slightly, but Miss Bang grabbed his arm and steadied Professor Crackle. He said, "Well, ah, ahem. I, uh, I don't believe I've met the lady before tonight."

"But do you remember hearing her voice before this evening?" Miss Bang arched a brow at him.

He tilted his head back and stared at the ceiling for several seconds. "If I heard her speak before tonight, she wasn't speaking in the same calm, cultured tones. Not with that tone and timbre."

"What does that mean?" Willie asked.

Miss Bang nodded. "If she had been calling over a distance, or speaking quietly to avoid being heard, that might be enough to distort her voice to make it more difficult to recognize. Of course, if she tried to disguise her voice, that might throw us off as well."

"Why would she do that?" the maharani said.

"A good question, my dear," Professor Crackle replied. "But it would be one explanation for why she sounds familiar to us."

Tinka shrugged. "She doesn't sound familiar to me."

"Really? How about you, Willie? Maharani?"

The maharani laughed. "I've known her since I was a little girl. She's been around the court for ages. Always pushing Uncle Sankar to work harder and try for the next position that came available."

I looked at Willie. He spread his hands. "I've seen her at half a dozen court functions over the last six months."

Miss Bang looked at the professor. "I'm surprised at you, Harmonious. You don't seem the slightest bit curious about this. I would have thought you'd be as eager as we are to place her voice."

The professor took off his glasses and wiped the lenses with a large handkerchief he pulled from an inner pocket. One side of the cloth was stained an odd brownish red colour, possibly old blood. "Oh, I'm curious, my dear. But I also noticed how much the lady did not want to talk about it. It would seem that Mrs. Chatterjee is hiding something, but it remains to be seen if she's hiding it from us, or from her husband."

"Court is always full of secrets, Professor Crackle," the maharani observed. "Most of them aren't very important, but they are always there. You could say it is in the air. Ridhi Chatterjee has always played the game."

"The game?" I asked.

"Court intrigue," Miss Bang answered. "She seeks to increase her own importance at court?"

Maharani Chandrakanta shook her head. "She has no ambition for herself, but she's very interested in seeing her husband get ahead. She's been a major factor in him rising in the court. And she doesn't give up. He's the highest ranking official in the court, and she's still looking to increase his influence."

"How can she do that? If he's already in the top spot, how can he go higher? A ship only has one captain," Tinka said.

The professor cleared his throat. "But a ship may also have an owner. And some men command fleets of ships. There are ways to add influence, my dear. European history is full of tales of advisors who became more powerful than the kings they served."

The maharani shook her head. "I don't think that's a problem. I call him 'Uncle Sankar' because he's like family. He loves my father. He wouldn't have make Uncle Sankar his spymaster if he didn't trust him absolutely."

Satisfied with the state of his glasses, the professor put them back on and stuffed the handkerchief back into his pocket. "I didn't mean to cast any aspersions on your father's advisor, Princess, I'm sorry if I gave you that impression."

"No offense taken, Professor."

"I hate to put a damper on this festival of speculation, but I'm afraid Mrs. Chatterjee had one thing right. We need to mingle with the other guests. I've noticed Colonel Ticking glancing over here several times." Willie ducked his head slightly. "I think perhaps I should move along before he decides to come over."

The maharani squeezed his arm. "Oh, poor William. I'll save you. You can come with me and get something to drink. I'll see the rest of you later. Please enjoy yourselves." She gathered my brother and headed off to an adjoining room, where a variety of refreshments were laid out upon tables.

Tinka's hand tightened on my arm. "Don't you leave me alone," she whispered in my ear.

I grabbed her hand and squeezed her fingers. "I shall make sure that you're in good company, never fear. Just leave me the feeling in my arm." She loosened her grip slightly.

Professor Crackle looked around the room. "My dear, is that your cousin over there?"

"Oh, I do hope so. Let's go and see." She stopped and grabbed

Tinka's hand before departing. "Don't worry, Tinka. We won't be far."

We watched as they made their way through the crowd.

"So, what do people do at these things?" Tinka asked.

"Well, they talk. They drink. Sometimes there is dancing."

Her eyes lit up. "Dancing!"

I looked at her. "Would you like to dance? Do you know any court dances?"

Before she could answer, Colonel Ticking walked up to us. "Blasphemy. There you are." His tone was friendly enough, but he did not seem pleased to see me.

"Colonel."

"Couldn't leave well enough alone, could you, Blasphemy?"

"I beg your pardon, Colonel?"

He leaned in. "I go and lay down the law to your professor friend, and then you go and grab up all the glory. Very slick, Blasphemy."

I stepped back from him. "I've no interest in glory, Colonel. I wanted to be sure my aunt was safe."

He laughed. "Oh, you don't have to make excuses to me, sir. I understand. We are men of action. We cannot resist the call to battle."

"I'd prefer to leave the battles to you, Colonel. To be honest, I would have done just that if I'd had the option. I didn't really want to stage a rescue as much as make sure that the information we gathered was good. By the time we knew we were on the right track, we were too far into things to back out. I'm sorry if I offended you by searching for my aunt, but I couldn't sit idly by and do nothing."

He chuckled and laid a meaty hand on my shoulder. "No, no, Blasphemy. Think nothing of it. I was angry at first, but when I had a chance to think about it, I realized that I had only myself to blame. I've been in command for so long I sometimes forget that civilians are outside my jurisdiction. I should have brought you in and worked with you. As you pointed out, your companions are accomplished investigators in their own right. I should have listened." He squeezed my shoulder and dropped his hand. "But that's in the past. I'll not make further trouble for you or your brother. I'm going to do what I should have done in the first place: take you into account in my plans. That way I know that I can be there before anything untoward can happen to you. After all, it is my job to look after my fellow British citizens."

I wasn't sure what to say. "Willie will be glad to hear that. He's been proud to serve as your adjutant, and he hasn't liked having you upset with him."

"Well, all that ends tonight." He smiled, but there was something unsettling about the expression. "I'll see you later, Blasphemy." Colonel Ticking stalked off and disappeared into the crowd.

"Who was that git?" Tinka asked, perhaps a bit too loudly.

"*That* was Colonel Ticking, the commander of the local British Army base. He was the one who forbade us from investigating my aunt's kidnapping. Although to be fair, the maharaja said much the same thing." I sighed. "But you're right. He is a bit of a pill."

CHAPTER TWENTY-FIVE

A PACKAGE FOR MISS HOLYFIELD

Tinka and I wandered about the party for a while.

While I had been to many similar events and found them all to be much the same, this was Tinka's first ball. Despite her concerns about feeling like she was on display, she soon was distracted by looking at all the other people. Or rather, looking at their clothes.

The soldiers did look smart in their dress uniforms, but they were dressed the same except for the insignia of rank, and the particular collection of ribbons each man wore on their chest. Likewise, the men in European formal wear were visually boring. Dressed in nearly identical black suits with white pressed shirts and matching waistcoats and bow ties, they tended to all blend in together and disappear. As I made this observation, I realized that I was included in their number. I wasn't sure how I felt about that.

What got Tinka excited was the variety of dresses on the ladies, and the colorful outfits of some of the men. I saw many Indian gentlemen who were dressed similarly to the maharaja, only in darker shades. Some seemed to do so to blend in with the British, but a few were almost defiant in how they dressed. Of note was one gentleman in a black coat embroidered in silver. The coat practically cried out, "You can wear black and still catch the eye!" Another gentleman wore a an outfit in a rich purple velvet that seemed to change shades as he moved.

The ladies were a sight to behold. At balls I'd attended at home, one usually saw variations on whatever particular design was in fashion at the time. All very flattering, but not necessarily interesting. Here, every outfit vied for your attention in its own way. Many of the ladies favored bright, eye catching colors, and everything was meticulously embroidered. Tinka spent several minutes just pointing out different ladies in the crowd and telling me how much she liked their dresses.

I half expected to be mobbed by courtiers hoping to use the evening's brief acquaintance to some advantage, but instead, most of the guests kept their distance. Some were very respectful, bowing from a distance but not approaching closer. I suspect a few avoided us so they wouldn't have to express an opinion on Tinka's unusual anatomy. At times it seemed like people were heading towards us, but were then blocked by a group of British soldiers. It didn't appear deliberate and it may have been a trick of my imagination. It felt like almost half the crowd was in an imperial uniform.

This isn't to say that we wandered completely on our own. Lieutenant Renault and another lieutenant approached us and paid their respects, their uniforms sharply pressed and almost identical, except for the pattern of ribbons pinned to their chests. Lieutenant Renault reached for Tinka's hand to kiss it in greeting and had a moment of confusion trying to figure which of her right hands to kiss. He finally settled on holding his hand out and allowing her to choose. Tinka was puzzled as to why he wanted her hand. She glanced at me and I gave her a slight nod. She gingerly extended her upper right hand which he took gently, raised to his lips, and kissed lightly. Tinka giggled. I didn't think much of it until the lieutenant winked as me as he released her hand. What did the Canadian think he was up to?

After a few pleasantries, they moved on and we were approached by a pair of older women. One was a plump, grey haired British woman, and her companion was a dark-complexioned woman with a mass of dark hair piled into an elaborate style, although she was greying at her temples. They approached us hesitantly and began by apologizing.

"We are terribly sorry to bother you, dear lady, but my friend and I cannot contain our curiosity," the darker woman said.

"Curiosity?" Tinka said warily.

"We do not mean to trouble you." She looked worried and turned to her friend.

The English woman patted her on the shoulder. "Now, dearie, don't turn tail so quickly." She looked up at Tinka. "I'm Essie Tucker. This is my friend, Neha Singh. I'm afraid I'm to blame for disturbing you." She hesitated.

"How can we help, ladies?" I asked.

"We don't want to offend you, but..." Neha began.

"My brothers were Siamese." Essie stated flatly. She looked at us for a moment, as if her bizarre statement had explained anything. Then her hand flew to her mouth. "Oh, I mean, they were conjoined. Conjoined twins. Their bodies grew together in the womb. They were born with three legs and two arms." She blinked and tears ran down her cheeks. "They died when they were only 12 years old." Her friend produced a handkerchief and dabbed at the moisture on her face. She grabbed Neha's hands and held them away from her face. "I know this is terribly rude and I hope you'll forgive me, but seeing you reminded me of them. I loved my brothers dearly and I miss them still. They would have loved to meet someone like you, like them, different, but so confident and beautiful."

Essie opened her mouth, then closed it again. "I guess..." She sniffled. "I guess I wanted to thank you for being here. For reminding me of my brothers. I know it wasn't easy for them, back then. I suppose I also wanted to let you know that there are others who understand, at least a little bit, what it is like being different. And we support you."

Neha nodded. "We both know what it is like moving through the world and being different." She grabbed Essie's hand and held onto it.

I looked at Tinka out of the corner of my eye, unsure of how she would react. By the way her features twitched, she didn't seem too sure herself. I gently took her upper right hand. The unexpected touch startled her. She jerked back for a moment, then relaxed when she realized it was me.

"Are you all right, Tinka?" I asked.

She looked at me, at the two women, then back to me. "I... I don't know."

I nodded. "For what it's worth..." I glanced at the two women. The Indian woman looked deeply embarrassed, but still stood by her companion's side. "I believe her."

While the ladies did seem to be a bit of an odd couple, I wasn't sure what they meant by being different. Tinka seemed to understand, though.

After a moment of consideration, Tinka said, "Thank you. I'm sorry for your brothers. I think I might have liked to meet them. I've never met anyone like myself."

Neha's gaze slid over to me, and her expression changed. She smoothed her face, hiding her emotions behind a mask of politeness. "I'm sorry if we've intruded upon your evening, sir." She avoided looking me in the eye.

"I understand, ladies. If Tinka doesn't have an issue, I don't have a problem." I looked at Tinka.

She shook her head slowly. "I think it is all right."

Essie smiled. "Thank you, my lady. We'll let you get back to your evening. Thank you for your time."

"Thank you. Sorry to bother you," her companion said as they backed away.

"Do people usually do things like that?" Tinka asked.

"No, not really. That was a little odd." I cleared my throat. "Normally in, um, polite conversation, one doesn't talk about the other person's... differences."

"Really?" She sounded skeptical.

"It's usually considered quite rude."

Tinka looked thoughtful. "Maybe I should spend more time in polite society. Most people I've met have been quite rude." She looked piercingly at me.

"I did apologize for that back in Prague. I *thought* you had accepted."

"I'm still considering." She looked away from me but smiled.

"I'm never going to live it down, am I?"

"Probably not." She shot me a grin. "But keep trying."

We grabbed drinks from a passing waiter.

Tinka sipped her drink and made a face. "That is some strange tasting beer."

"That's because it isn't beer. It's champagne," I said.

"What's the difference? It's still alcohol, isn't it?"

"It is, but beer is made with barley and champagne and wine is made from grapes. It gets you a different flavor, and a bit more alcohol. If you're used to drinking beer, you might want to go easy on this stuff."

She sipped her drink again. "It doesn't taste that strong."

"I think that's the idea."

Before Tinka could reply, a woman separated herself from her companion and rushed up to me. She grabbed my arm, nearly spilling my drink. "Sir Richard, can I speak to you for a moment?" She looked at Tinka and added, "Privately?"

"Miss Holyfield?" I said as I recognized the blonde business-woman. She wore a dark blue sequined off the shoulder gown, but her face wore a look of concern. "Is everything all right?"

"Oi! Hands off, missy!" Tinka commanded. Several people nearby turned and looked at the sudden increase in volume. At least one couple started whispering to each other.

Miss Holyfield released her hold on my arm and held her hands up. "Please, this won't take but a minute."

"Who is this?" Tinka asked me.

"Tinka, this is Miss Patricia Holyfield of Holyfield Industries. She helped us in our investigation to find Aunt Phyllis and the maharani. Miss Holyfield, this is Tinka, Professor Crackle's adopted daughter and the head engineer on the professor's ship."

"I don't mean to disturb you," Miss Holyfield said, "But this won't take very long."

"There you are!" Peter Holyfield cried as he ran up to me, pushing an older couple out of his way. Unlike Miss Holyfield, who was at dressed for a formal event, Mr. Holyfield wore a dull grey suit that looked like it had seen better days.

"And her cousin, Peter Holyfield," I added.

"I've got to talk to you, right now," Mr. Holyfield said.

"I saw him first!" Miss Holyfield retorted.

"Yes, but I'm here now. You can go back to whatever it is you do."

"Why you jackass, of all..."

"OI! Can it! Both of you!" Tinka said, putting an end to all conversation in the immediate area. Heads turned to look at our little group. Several people moved farther away from us, distancing themselves form whatever disturbance was about to happen. A British soldier started to move towards us, but his companion grabbed his arm and stopped him.

Mr. Holyfield turned on her. "Don't you tell me what to do you, you..." He paused and made a disgusted face. "What are you?"

Tinka's eyes became hard slits and she drew herself up. Before she could do anything, I grabbed Holyfield by the lapels and lifted him up. "That's it. You're done," I snarled. I turned to Tinka. "Go find Miss Bang and the professor, or my aunt. I'll be back with you as soon as I get done taking out the rubbish."

Tinka stepped forward and cocked both her right hands back.

"Tinka, not here." I released one of Holyfield's lapels and held up a hand. "I'll take care of him. Go find the professor." I pointed at Miss Holyfield. "Take her with you, maybe she can explain this mess."

"Get your hands off of me," her cousin demanded. I shook him to shut him up.

"No, I need to talk to you!" Miss Holyfield protested.

Tinka grabbed Miss Holyfield with her lower left arm.

I turned Mr. Holyfield around and hustled him through the crowd, which parted before us.

"How dare you treat me like this?" Holyfield cried.

"Because you were rude to me and to the lady I was escorting. I can't for the life of me imagine why you thought you could get away with such outrageous behavior."

Two footmen opened the door in front of us and I pushed him out into the hallway.

"Where do you think you're taking me?"

"You said you wanted to speak to me in private. I'm finding some-place private." I grabbed the back of his jacket and dragged him over to a nearby door. I opened it and looked inside. An Indian couple startled at the intrusion and moved away from each other. "Not here," I said, closing the door.

The next room proved to be empty, and I shoved Holyfield inside.

"You cannot treat me like this!" he yelled as I turned and locked the door.

I spun to face Mr. Holyfield.

"Good. I wanted to talk to you," the old man in the wheelchair said.

There was no sign of Peter Holyfield. In his place, Patrick Holy-field sat calmly in his chair, a plaid blanket draped over his lap.

"How did *you* get here?" I asked.

"Oh, the usual way. Don't worry yourself about that. An old man is entitled to have a few secrets. Pull up a chair, boy. Have a seat." He extended a spindly arm towards a nearby armchair.

I was quite prepared to give Peter Holyfield a thrashing over his boorish behavior. Patrick Holyfield's sudden substitution for Peter was unexpected, and emotionally disturbing. I glared at him for a moment, and clenched and unclenched my hands as I brought my temper under control. I took a deep breath. The air in the room was warm, and smelled faintly of jasmine. Old man Holyfield was bundled up in several sweaters, and had a scarf wrapped around his neck. He was not dressed for the heat of India, and he did not seem bothered by it. This fact disturbed me and intrigued me at the same time.

Letting my breath out slowly, I crossed to the indicated chair, and sat down. "What do you want, P.G.?"

"Straight to business." He grinned at me. "I like that about you, boy. Very well. I *had* intended to come to you with a warning about what you're about to be facing, but apparently someone caused a bunch of trouble and they changed the rules on me. Now I'm cut off from my best source of information. I've got no foresight to offer you." He frowned, the expression looking like he had just taken a large bite of a particularly sour lemon.

"What do you mean? What makes you think I need a warning?"

He chuckled. "Too many pages left in the book, boy. Someone's up to something. This story isn't over yet. You need to be on your guard."

"What book? What are you talking about?"

He waved a hand at me. "Don't worry about that. You wouldn't understand. Suffice it to say that I have some insight into your story, young man. You're not out of the woods yet."

"And you've come to call in your favor before I'm killed?"

"What? No! Oh, no. That's not it. Actually, I'm fairly sure that you'll survive for at least a few more volumes. No, I wanted to talk to you because I've been thinking about what you said."

"Mr. Holyfield, you're not making any sense," I said. "What did I say?"

He snorted. "You suggested that I make arrangements to allow some of my grandchildren to pursue paths *other* than my business. After looking at the quarterly statements, I agree that some of them have got to go." He shook his head. "I've had to order demotions and transfers just to keep the Spanish division afloat. I expected with my blood in their veins that they's have some business sense, but that doesn't appear to be the case. Anyway." He pulled a packet of papers out of his jacket and handed them to me. "Pass those on to Patricia. She'll get them through channels, but I wanted her to get an advanced look. Tell her to look at Section seventeen, and to pay special attention to article 35. I had to add a non-compete clause. If one of the children must leave my company, I'm not going to let them try to put me out of business. But if they can be successful doing something else, I won't stand in their way."

I looked at the packet he'd handed me. "This is your will?"

"What? No! I don't need a will. I've found my own way of dealing with mortality. No, those are the updated company bylaws. They allow family members to take a limited sabbatical to pursue other interests and opportunities without forfeiture of assets." He shrugged. "I couldn't cut them off completely, or none of them would take it. It needed to be tough enough to discourage anyone without a plan."

"Why give it to me? Why not deliver it yourself? Why even deliver it in person? Isn't this the sort of thing that is usually handled through some sort of policy announcement?"

"It is. And the announcement has been made, it's just going to take a while to get here. But, as I said, I wanted her to get an advance look, and I wanted you to know that I took your advice." He rubbed his chin. "Most people aren't brave enough to give me advice. This was a new experience." He snorted. "And I took a look at Patricia's story, too. She does a good job, but she's not really cut out for this life." He leaned back in his chair. "I thought she'd appreciate the news. Besides, it'll drive Peter nuts that she got word before he did."

"Peter?"

"Yes. That boy's an ass. He's costing me employees more valuable than he is."

I opened the packet. At thick as it was, the pages inside were almost translucently thin, and the type was tiny. How could anyone read this?

"Anyway. That's it. Deliver the packet and watch your back. I'll be watching you. We'll talk again, Blasphemy."

I looked back at him. "Just like that?"

"Yup, just like that. Don't look at me like that, boy. You've got a young woman waiting for you back in that party. Don't tell me you're fool enough to want to spend it with me." He snorted.

My heart leapt in my chest. I'd promised that I wouldn't leave Tinka alone, but I'd left her with Miss Holyfield, a stranger. I needed to get back. "What about Peter?"

Holyfield snorted again. "He'll find his own way out. Don't worry about him."

"I'm more worried about how he disappeared and you appeared."

The old man smiled wickedly. "Don't worry about it, son. Enjoy the mystery, because you're not finding out tonight. Maybe someday, but not tonight. Now get going."

I sighed, folded the packet back up, and tucked it into my jacket. "Do you ever give a straight answer, Mr. Holyfield?"

He laughed. "Yep, but only to that question. For everything else, I keep them guessing."

I stood up. "Until the next time, then." Giving him a respectful nod, I strode back into the hallway, closing the door after myself.

CHAPTER TWENTY-SIX
SOME UNINVITED GUESTS

When I rejoined Tinka and Patricia, I saw that they had been joined by my Aunt Phyllis. My aunt's presence seemed to have bolstered Tinka's confidence, but Miss Holyfield still seemed preoccupied. Naturally, Aunt Phyllis was lecturing her about it as I approached.

"Heaven's sake, girl. Don't fidget. I would think that a woman of business would know by now that one must never show weakness in an uncertain situation, and fidgeting is a sign of weakness of purpose." My aunt crossed her arms. "*Your* time is always valuable, and even if you must spend some of it waiting, it can always be put to a productive end." She gestured to the nobles and dignitaries milling about. "Observation alone should yield valuable insights to a trained eye." She indicated an Indian couple who were talking to one of the British officers. "What can you tell me about that couple?"

Miss Holyfield swallowed and meekly looked in the direction that Aunt Phyllis had pointed. "Um, well, that's Mr. Mahajan. He owns a shipping company that we sometimes use. He seems quite interested in whatever the Lieutenant is telling him."

"And the girl? What about her?"

"I, uh, I don't know her. She seems..."

"Is she his wife?" Aunt Phyllis pressed.

"What? I don't know."

My aunt clicked her tongue. "No, she is not. She quite clearly doesn't want to be near the soldier, but she is sticking to Mr. Mahajan like glue. She has some sort of designs upon him."

Miss Holyfield turned to my aunt and caught sight of me coming up behind them. "My lord!" She seemed relieved to change the subject.

"Ladies," I said. "I'm sorry to have kept you waiting."

Aunt Phyllis turned. "Nephew." Her voice was carefully neutral, but I noticed a hint of a smile at the corner of her lips.

Tinka cheerfully reclaimed my arm.

"Sir, I need to talk to you, privately," Miss Holyfield began.

I held up my hand and said, "Actually, Miss Holyfield, I have something for you." I handed P.G. Holyfield's packet of documents to her. "I believe you should pay particular attention to Section seventeen, Article 35."

She took the packet and opened it, her brow furrowed and her mouth slightly open in confusion. She read the first few lines and yelped, "How did you get this?"

"Straight from the hand of P.G. Holyfield. For a man confined to a wheelchair, he seems to have an uncanny ability to get himself into places without being noticed."

Patricia's eyes went wide. She glanced around the room as if she suspected her great grandfather to suddenly spring out of the crowd at her. "Is he still here?"

"I doubt it," I said. "I don't know how he gets around, but I suspect he got out the same way as soon as I left him. But he did say that he wanted you, particularly, to have that packet."

"Me?" she squeaked.

"Yes. He wanted you to know that he thought you raised some good points. And that he agrees that Peter is an ass."

"Nephew!" Aunt Phyllis scolded.

"My apologies, Aunt Phyllis, but those were his exact words, and I don't think it is a particular secret at this point."

BOOM!

A herald had ascended the dais and struck his staff upon the raised floor. Conversation ceased throughout the hall.

BOOM!

He struck the floor a second time. Something about the construction of the small stage appeared to amplify that sound, for it was much louder than when Tinka and I had been introduced. We all turned to face the dais.

BOOM!

He struck the floor a third time and drew himself up.

"MY LORDS AND LADIES, HIS HIGHNESS, MAHARAJA RAJENDER YADAV!" the herald boomed into the waiting silence. He then bowed and slid off the side of the dais as the maharaja ascended and turned to face us.

"Welcome, my friends!" The maharaja smiled broadly at the crowd and spread his arms wide. "I am pleased to have you here to celebrate my joy at the safe return of my daughter, Chandrakanta." He gestured to one side where the maharani and my brother stood next to the dais. The maharani smiled and accepted the recognition with good grace, and no doubt much practice.

My brother, on the other hand, stood stiffly, his face devoid of expression. I don't think he was quite at attention, or whatever it is they teach at military school, but he was trying his best to hide whatever emotion he was feeling, which made him more noticeable rather than less. Fortunately for him, the crowd was more interested in the maharani. They erupted into polite applause, and she nodded in recognition.

As the applause died down, the maharaja continued. "I would also like to show my appreciation for the persons responsible for bringing my daughter back to me. First, I would like to thank Professor Crackle, and Miss Bang, whose investigative curiosity allowed them to find clues that evaded my most skilled intelligence officers." He gestured to the professor and Miss Bang, who bowed to more polite applause. The maharaja gave a sidelong look to Mr. Chatterjee, who was standing to one side of the dais. "Even when they were advised to leave the investigation to those trained for it, they continued to pursue every option, and demonstrated a talent that we vastly underrated. To you, my friends, I offer my apologies for not appreciating your skills, and my thanks for your dedication. You shall always find a safe haven here in Kanpur."

More polite applause erupted as the maharaja paused, but he held up a hand to silence it. "Next, I must thank our most honored guest, the Lady Tinka." Now he gestured to Tinka. As the crowd applauded again, she gripped my arm tightly.

"Stand up, girl," Aunt Phyllis said sotto voce. Tinka straightened her spine and held her head higher, but her grip on my arm did not lessen.

The maharaja continued, "Lady Tinka not only helped to rescue my daughter, but when they came under enemy fire, she threw herself into harm's way to save Chandra's life. Thanks to her bravery and quick thinking, my daughter stands here today. I cannot repay such a debt. But this I can do. From this day forward, she shall be counted as a member of my family. A daughter of my house. You shall always have a home here, Tinka." The applause this time was much louder, and Chandrakanta was among those clapping the loudest.

Tinka turned to me. "All this for me?" she asked in a small voice.

"Yes. This is for you." I put my hand over one of the ones on my arm and squeezed it. "They appreciate what you've done, and the risk you took to protect the princess."

Her face flushed, but she turned and said, "Thank you," to the people closest to us.

As the applause subsided, the maharaja continued. "And lastly, I have been in negotiations with Lady Griffith-Holmes, and we have entered into an agreement." He paused, and the room went eerily silent. There wasn't even a rustle of crinoline. "I am very pleased to announce this evening, the engagement of my daughter, Chandrakanta, to the man who rescued her, Lady Griffith-Holmes' nephew!" I glanced over at Willie. He looked surprised, but happy. Next to him, the maharani smiled broadly and took a half-step closer to him. "Sir Richard Blasphemy!"

My hearing filled with a roaring sound. I wasn't sure if it was applause from the crowd, or the pounding of the blood in my ears. Chandrakanta looked shocked, and Willie had put on his emotionless military mask again. Tinka released my arm and retreated to the other side of Aunt Phyllis. My aunt looked pleased with herself.

Smugly pleased.

I needed to think fast. There had to be some way out of this.

I took a deep breath and looked up at the maharaja. He beamed at me, and he was clapping as loud as anyone else.

I took a step forward. The maharaja stopped clapping, and the rest of the room soon followed. I heard a couple calls of "Speech!" from the back of the room, but those people were quickly shushed by their neighbors.

It seemed I had the floor.

I opened my mouth, and realized that I had no idea what to say. What could I say? What would get me out of this without insulting my host? Without making my own brother want to kill me?

To stall for time, I took another step forward.

Say something! Anything. I took a deep breath.

"Your Highness, you do me too great an honor. One of which I am sure I am not worthy."

Lovely. Now he's going to think I'm being pretend humble.

I cleared my throat and tried again. "I have considered the prospect of welcoming your daughter into my family with great joy." Will glared at me, and the maharani gave me an odd look.

Oh, great, that made things worse. Come on, think! How do I get out of this? I licked my lips.

Three's a charm, right? I thought. "But I'm afraid there has been a mistake. As a man of integrity, I cannot accept an honor I have not earned, one that is clearly deserved by someone else." Gasps sounded throughout the room. "While I am sure that all parties entered into these negotiations in good faith, I believe there has been a misunderstanding due to two factors. The first being that my aunt has referred to me simply as 'Nephew' for my entire life. The second is that I am not the only nephew of Lady Griffith-Holmes who took part in the rescue.

"The man who saved your daughter, Your Highness, was my brother, Lieutenant William Holmes. A man who went into danger for your daughter's sake. A man who truly loves her and would give his life for her." I looked over at Willie, who was now flushing, but still tried to maintain his stoic facade. "And a man, unless I am sorely mistaken, that your daughter loves as well."

"Nephew!" my aunt hissed. "It's all agreed."

"You need to start calling me 'Sir Richard', Aunt Phyllis, or there's going to be a lot more confusion." I told her. "This is wrong, for both me and Willie, and we were never given the chance to agree to this."

The maharaja stepped down from the dais and crossed to his daughter. "Is this true?" He lowered his voice to make the conversation more private.

Maharani Chandrakanta took his hand. "Father, I..."

"Lady Griffith-Homes told me that you wanted to marry Lord Blasphemy."

"What? Father, when Lady Phyllis talked to me in the cells about a match with her nephew, I didn't know she was talking about Sir Richard. I've barely met him. I thought she was talking about William."

"This soldier?" He looked at Willie. The maharaja lowered his voice further. "He has no father!"

Mr. Chatterjee approached them and said mildly, "Your majesty, this is not the most ideal place for this discussion."

The maharaja look at him and nodded. "You are correct, Sankar." He stepped up on the dais and said in a larger voice to the rest of the room, "My friends! We have a little bit of confusion to sort out, here. Please, enjoy yourselves, we will return momentarily."

With quick hand gestures, the maharaja indicated that Willie, myself, Aunt Phyllis and Tinka were to come with him. He then had Mr. Chatterjee lead us up the dais through a door, down a short hallway where we were accompanied by two guards, and into a back room with several comfortable chairs. It appeared to be some sort of royal waiting room.

The maharani and her father entered after us, and a guard closed the door from the outside. Tinka crossed to the far side of the room from me and leaned on the back of one of the armchairs, looking daggers at me.

As the door shut, the maharaja turned his daughter to face him and said, "You're telling me you want to marry a bastard?" He looked over at Willie and added, "I'm sorry to say that, Lieutenant, but this is a matter of my family's reputation."

I cleared my throat. "Your majesty, Willie's father and mother are the same as my own. He's true born, but my mother lied to the world, to spare him from our great-grandfather's machinations." I walked over to stand next to my brother. "It is a lie that served a purpose at the time, but it is no longer needed. Right, Willie?"

William's facade cracked and he licked his lips. "No, not anymore."

"And you want to marry the maharani, don't you?" I asked.

He shot me a look, but then turned and faced the maharaja. He took a deep breath and replied, "Yes, sir. I do."

The maharaja gave him a judgmental look. He turned back to his daughter. "This solider is the man you want to marry, Chandra?"

She took Willie's hand in both of hers. I stepped aside, and she stood next to my brother and addressed the maharaja. "Yes, Father. That was what *I* agreed to." She smiled hopefully up at her father. "And what I hope you will agree to, as well."

"But the agreement was for, ah, for Sir Richard to marry her,"

Aunt Phyllis said, stumbling over my new name. "He is the first born and heir. This is an excellent match..."

"Aunt Phyllis!" I said, interrupting her. "Why are you doing this? It's obvious that Willie and Chandra are much better suited to each other. Why are you so bent on trying to get her to marry me?"

The maharaja echoed my thoughts, "Yes. Why *do* you want to marry my daughter to this man instead of the one she loves?" He sounded genuinely curious.

Aunt Phyllis opened her mouth to respond, and her composure broke. She cried and laughed for about a minute. Finally she said, "We all agreed. We all said it was the best thing for you, Nephew." She wiped her eyes and looked at me. "Your parents were very worried about you. Time after time you kept getting into some kind of trouble. Your mother talked about it with us, her brothers and sisters. We all agreed that you needed a wife to make you take responsibility. To help you make something of your life. That's why your parents sent you here."

Aunt Phyllis bowed her head. "I'm sorry, Maharani Chandrakanta, William. I didn't want to drive you apart, but I had a duty to try and find him the best possible match I could."

The maharani said, "Lady Griffith-Holmes, I understand about the necessity of a state marriage, anyone growing up in a royal household does. But why would you think this would be good for either Sir Richard or myself?"

I frowned. "It might be good politically or dynastically, but I don't think anyone was thinking about either of us, Maharani. If I'm the problem they think me to be, they'd just be making me *your* problem. But if I *am* a problem, it has been because my family has been meddling my entire life trying to make me into what *they* want, instead of letting me choose my own path in life. More meddling to take those choices away from me isn't going to make me any better."

Mr. Chatterjee cleared his throat. "If I may, Your Majesty?" The maharaja nodded. "Lady Griffith-Holmes, I know nothing of your nephew before he came to this city, and I will admit that I misjudged his character, and that of his companions, at first. But I have observed that while he may have a talent for finding trouble he has not looked for, he is remarkably skilled at getting himself out of it again. And doing so without having to call on his family's resources or aid. Indeed, his ability to extract himself from difficulty to the benefit of those around him is one of the reasons he's being honored tonight. Are you sure you need to worry about his future?"

I was surprised at the maharaja's advisor speaking on my behalf. Sort of. "Thank you," I said. "I think..."

He dismissed my thanks with a flick of his fingers.

The maharaja asked, "Lady Griffith-Holmes, do you still feel that you have cause to worry about the future of your eldest nephew? Or either of your nephews?"

Aunt Phyllis looked at each of us. "They both have so much potential..."

The maharaja nodded. "But it is up to *them* to unlock it. We can prepare our children to walk their own path, but we cannot walk it for them."

"But I have a duty to my family..." Aunt Phyllis began.

The maharaja stopped her with a raised hand. "And you have discharged that duty admirably. Through your efforts you have arranged a good match for one of your nephews, even if it was not the one you had in mind. We have done what we can on behalf of our respective families, good lady. This is not a matter of state to require a specific outcome. It is time to let the children choose."

The maharaja looked pointedly at my brother and me, and his daughter standing between us. After a moment, I realized that Aunt Phyllis, Mr. Chatterjee, and even Tinka were also staring, waiting to see what we would do.

I looked at my brother and said, "This is your show." I went to stand next to Aunt Phyllis.

Willie looked a bit stunned at first, but then he raised the hand that the maharani was still holding. She turned to face him. "Chandra," he said, but then held his sword back with his free hand and went down on one knee. "Chandrakanta Yadav, will you grant me the supreme honor of becoming my wife?"

Tears glistened at the edge of Chandra's eyes as she looked at my brother. "William, nothing in this world would make me happier." She squeezed his hands. "I will."

The maharaja applauded, and the rest of us joined in. Wille stood up, and the maharaja stepped over and clapped him on the back. He cupped his daughter's face and peered down into it for a long moment as she smiled up at him. At last the maharaja nodded and said. "Then it is settled."

"This is *not* what we agreed to," Aunt Phyllis said under her breath, in what was almost a whine.

"No," I told her. "This is a much better arrangement that will work out better for all parties. This may not be what you wanted, but I'm sure it is for the best."

"Your majesty, you have other guests," Mr. Chatterjee said.

"Yes, yes, you are right, Sankar. We have the whole evening for celebrating, let us return and share this good news with the others!" The maharaja gestured towards the door, and Mr. Chatterjee once more led the way back to the ballroom, followed by Chandra and Willie, Tinka and myself, with Aunt Phyllis, the maharaja, and his guards bringing up the rear.

We spilled down he steps of the dais, with the maharani and Willie stopping at the bottom of the steps, the maharaja stopping at the top, and the rest of us joining the front row of onlookers.

The maharaja clapped his hands twice and addressed the room, grinning. "My friends, thank you for your patience! It seems that I misspoke earlier. But now, we have sorted out, and it is my great joy tonight to announce the engagement of my daughter to Lieutenant William Holmes of the British Army! Please, let us raise a toast to the happy couple!"

A few cheers rose from the audience, some I recognized as coming from other soldiers from the base. Waiters started moving among the guests, carrying trays of drinks and distributing glasses of champagne.

The maharani climbed up a step and hugged her father who had come down to meet her. Then she took Willie's hand again. Smiling, Willie moved up to stand beside her.

The two planters at the far end of the ballroom suddenly burst open with a crash, sending rubble, dirt, and decorative plant in all directions. Screams sounded through the hall, and someone dropped an entire tray of drinks. A heartbeat later, the other two planters at the midpoints of the hall likewise exploded, sending thick chunks of pottery sliding across the floor and knocking guests off their feet. Those who kept their feet scrambled away from the detonations, crowding into the center of the ballroom.

From the remains of the planters, four figures rose, casting off the dirt and debris, and stalking forward into the room. Steel rasped as they drew swords with hands of flesh and metal. Metal arms arced above them, blades pointed towards the guests, prompting more screams.

Chandra started up the dais stairs, dragging Willie with her, only to stop and back down as the curtains behind the thrones were flung back. She stepped backward in horror as two more women wearing the same steam-driven devices stepped into the room, dragging the limp bodies of the two guards who had guided us to the private chamber.

The Kindred had returned.

CHAPTER TWENTY-SEVEN
A TRAITOR UNMASKED

The maharani scrambled backward as the Kindred advanced. Willie moved her behind him and stood his ground, making himself a human shield between the Kindred and the maharaja and his daughter even though he was unarmed.

"Rajender Yadav!" the Kindred leader screamed from the dais. "You were offered the chance to lead us in casting off the invader. Instead, you chose to throw your lot in with them, and to bind yourself to their False Mother. For that, the Divine Mother has decreed that you shall be punished!"

There was something familiar about the woman's voice.

Mr. Chatterjee stepped forward to stand next to the maharaja. "What are you doing?" he cried. "Stop this at once! You will only get yourself killed."

The Kindred leader pointed at him. "This does not concern you. This matter is for your master. Your loyalties will be determined later."

The chief advisor stomped his foot. "Cease this foolishness at once! I would know your voice anywhere, Ridhi! What are you playing at?"

That was it! That was why her voice sounded so familiar. Sankar Chatterjee's wife was the leader of the Kindred of Kali. But why didn't he know that?

"Be quiet, fool! We are doing this for you!" she hissed.

"Treachery!" came a cry from amidst the knot of frightened guests. British soldiers pushed their way outward, forming a barrier between the Kindred and the other guests. Colonel Ticking ran up next to the maharaja, standing on the side opposite of the chief advisor. "You have been betrayed, Your Highness! Your advisor plotted against you, and he brought his own wife into the conspiracy!" The colonel stabbed accusing fingers at Chatterjee and his wife.

"What?" the woman cried. "NO!" Something about Ticking's accusation caught her off guard.

Her husband looked terrified. "No! No, Your Highness! I am your faithful servant. I have no idea what madness has taken over my wife, but I will put a stop to this, I promise you."

Ticking wasn't having any of it. "Don't believe him, sir. This is obviously a plot to overthrow you and your family so Chatterjee can lead an uprising."

The woman reached up and pulled off her veil, the mechanical arms on both sides gesticulating wildly. Ridhi stared furiously at Colonel Ticking. "How dare you?" she screamed. She danced forward, flesh and mechanical arms tracing a fearsome pattern above her and reaching to draw the swords from her back. "This whole thing was your idea!" she yelled as she raised her arms high. On cue, the Kindred behind her drew their own blades, and a cry came from the guests as they drew tighter together, looking for some safe space to go to. Meanwhile one figure, Professor Crackle, moved forward to stand next to the advisor.

The maharaja stepped back as Ridhi and the other Kindred advanced, but the colonel stood his ground. He reached into his jacket, drew a pistol, and fired.

"NO!" Mr. Chatterjee called out as he lunged for the colonel, too late.

Ridhi's scream of anger turned into one of pain. Blood blossomed from her chest as the bullet tore through her. She stumbled and crashed to the ground, sliding down the steps of the dais and coming to a stop on the floor, her swords scattering around her, as the royal party quickly backpedaled to keep from being hit by the blades.

Mr. Chatterjee jumped over the swords and fell to his knees next to the mass of mechanical arms that covered his wife. He grabbed two of the metal appendages and lifted, trying to turn her over, but each limb remained rigid. He couldn't push them out of the way to roll her over, but tried to lift the entire apparatus off of her and flip her like a turtle. He strained at it but couldn't lift the arms more than a foot or so before the weight became too much for him. "Someone help me, please!" he cried.

Ticking pointed his gun at Mr. Chatterjee. "Step away from her, traitor, or I'll be forced to fire on you, too."

"No, Colonel," the maharaja said. "I know this man as I know myself. He is no traitor, though I do not know what may have come over his wife. There has been enough bloodshed here. My guards will take them into custody, and we will get to the bottom of this."

The colonel stepped back from the maharaja. "Brave words to speak of questioning while an armed enemy is in the room, Your Highness. And where are your guards? Were they slain by these women? Or did they let them pass on your orders? Perhaps you *are* the one leading this uprising after all!" He pointed his gun at the maharaja now, and called over his shoulder. "Choose your targets, men."

Around the ballroom, soldiers reached into their jackets, pulled out sidearms, and proceeded to aim them at the nearest of the Kindred.

Willie interposed himself as a human shield, trying to keep the maharani safe from the dual threats of the Kindred and Colonel Ticking, but there was no safe place to go to. Uncle Jeremy went pale. He spun around looking at everything and trying to make sense of the situation.

Rousing from their shock at seeing their leader cut down, the Kindred pulled their arms, flesh and mechanical alike, in front of them with a clash of metal. This created a metal shield around their bodies. Peeking between the blades of their swords, they surveyed the room, but leaderless, they hesitated.

"Son of a whore," Ridhi rasped and spat blood at Colonel Ticking.

"Ridhi!" her husband cried, still trying to get at her past the metal arms that weighed her down. "You're still alive! Don't move, we'll get you help."

She turned her head to glare up at Colonel Ticking. "You came to me, you motherless goat." She coughed again, blood trickling down the edge of her mouth. "Promised that you had a way to help my husband rise to the nobility."

"Your lies won't save you now, woman!" the colonel bellowed over her.

She raised her voice to be heard by the crowd. "*He* wanted to start a revolution behind Maharaja Yadav." She coughed raggedly. "Then he'd quell it for the good of the Empire and make Sankar the hero for putting it down. *You* brought me the damned armor and told me to find the women to fill it!"

"Shut up!" Ticking barked. "No one's listening!"

Ridhi clawed her way toward the colonel and the mechanical arms attached to her back writhed, knocking her husband backwards as metal fingers scraped over the floor but failed to find purchase against the smooth wood. "You wanted a scapegoat. Someone to take the blame for *your* crimes." She coughed again, a sound that gurgled in her throat as she expelled blood, then gasped for breath. "Why? What are you after? You could have started a war..."

"SHUT UP!" Ticking screamed, spit flying from his lips. He pointed his gun at the crawling woman and fired twice. "Die, you bloody wog!"

Stunned shouts came from the guests as they cowered tighter together, and a mournful howl came from Mr. Chatterjee as he crouched over the body of his wife. But before the sound of his grief faded, it was drowned out by an angry scream from one of the Kindred as she charged Colonel Ticking.

The Kindred attacked, and the guests that had clustered together for safety, now screamed and scattered, pushing past the British soldiers who were trying to defend them. Blades flashed high and swung down as they came forward, slashing through soldiers and well-dressed socialites alike. As victims screamed and fell, the soldiers fired. Two of the multi-armed women crashed to the ground as bullets ripped through their flesh. Colonel Ticking fired at his new attacker, but didn't slow her charge. He dived to the side to avoid her blades as she closed, dropping his pistol as he rolled out of the way.

Professor Crackle charged between the colonel and the Kindred, yelling, "No! Stop! Can't you see this is only making things worse?"

Tinka pushed past me, pulling a steel rod and two daggers from pockets hidden in her dress. She stepped around the professor and engaged the Kindred, blocking her strikes as the Indian woman tried to get to Colonel Ticking. Willie grabbed up one of the swords from the floor and took a guarding position over the colonel. I wished that I had brought my uncle's pistol.

The Kindred had reach and strength on their side, but the soldiers were more mobile, although hampered by trying to direct guests to areas of relative safety. More gunfire sounded in the room. The infantry found it difficult to get a clean shot between dodging sword strikes and panicked peers, but one of the bullets found its mark, and the Kindred closest to the garden doors cried out in pain and went down on her back amidst a clattering of metal as the swords she was wielding fell all around her.

Pandemonium broke out in the ballroom, as people tried to flee, and mostly got in the way of the soldiers trying to defend them. Several panicked guests ran to the side of the ballroom facing the gardens, running into the closed French doors. They tried to open them, but more people gathered around them, pushing as they tried to put distance between themselves and the battle between the Kindred and Her Majesty's infantry.

The main doors to the ballroom shuddered as something heavy pounded against them. I'd missed when they were shut, but now someone was making a fair attempt to break into the room. Miss Bang gathered the maharaja, his daughter, and Aunt Phyllis and tried to maneuver them to a corner away from the battle.

Colonel Ticking crawled across the floor and reached for his dropped weapon. I quickly moved forward and stepped on his outstretched hand. Pulling the pistol away from his grasping fingers, I told him, "I think you've made enough trouble for one night, Colonel." I pointed the weapon at him.

The colonel shot me a venomous look. "You have no idea who you're dealing with, boy."

"Actually, I believe we're all in the process of finding that out," I replied.

Glass and wood shattered as the French doors to the garden, and some of the neighboring windows, gave way to the press of the crowd. People spilled through the doors and windows; scrambling and falling over each other in their rush to get away from the fight.

The soldiers vastly outnumbered the Kindred, and were armed with superior weapons, but they held their shots wanting a clear target, as some guests on the far side of the room were trapped behind the remaining Kindred. A few soldiers holstered their weapons to clear wounded guests and their fallen comrades out of the way, risking their lives in the process.

Tinka and Willie engaged the woman who had charged Colonel Ticking. Tinka dodged in and out of the armored woman's guard, blocking attacks with her knives and the metal bar. With her free hand she struck at the woman's body, trying to pull loose the tubing that drove the metal arms. Willie did his best to stand his ground and keep the Kindred from advancing on the colonel and myself, parrying blows as they came, and stepping forward as Tinka drew the Kindred off again.

Uncle Jeremy, red faced and sweaty, took a position a few paces from me, surveyed the room, and startled me with a sudden shout loud enough to be heard over the battle. "Cease fire! Renault! Banks! Fall back to defend the guests. Thomas, someone, open that damn door!"

The line of soldiers stepped back from the three Kindred, guns still trained on their targets, who held their swords in front of themselves as improvised shields while they slowly advanced. The fourth remained locked in battle with Tinka and William. A young soldier broke away and ran to the main doors that were still being pounded on. He unlocked them and they burst open. The maharaja's guard spilled into the room, carrying long spears.

They quickly sized up the situation and spread out to either side, spears pointed at the women, forcing the Kindred into a back-to-back defensive position to protect themselves from the soldier's guns and the guardsmen's spears. One of the women struck at the guard's weapons, but the hafts of the spears were protected by metal plates affixed to the wood and she was unable to strike off the spearheads. More guardsmen filed into the ballroom, spreading out on either side, surrounding the three women, and filling in spaces between the British soldiers.

Tinka and William continued sparring with the remaining woman, shifting back and forth across the dance floor, harrowing her from opposite sides. Blood trickled down one of Tinka's arms from a cut. The Kindred's veil had been ripped off, and a red scratch marked one cheek where Tinka had tried to gouge her eyes. The Indian woman breathed heavily as she glanced back and forth between her two opponents. Tinka crouched, her weight on the balls of her feet.

As the Kindred's eyes shifted back to Willie, Tinka sprang into action. She flipped one of her daggers over to her free hand and ducked under the right-hand blades of her opponent. Grabbing the flesh and blood wrist on that side, Tinka twisted up and out, causing all of the right arms to swing backwards, opening her guard. She struck the woman's left arm with the steel rod, and I heard a pronounced crack. The Indian woman cried out, and Tinka reached forward with her other two dagger wielding arms. She kneed the Kindred, forcing her back, and cutting through the pneumatic lines on both sides of the armor. Bright red fluid fountained out of the severed tubing, and the woman crashed to the ground under the weight of her steam-driven appendages.

Colonel Ticking looked up as the maharaja's guard continued to file in. He pulled at his hand, but I leaned my weight on his wrist, keeping it pinned to the ground. He turned his head and bellowed. "Shoot them! Shoot the Kindred!"

"Hold your fire!" Uncle Jeremy called. Several of the soldiers flinched at the conflicting orders, but none of them pulled the trigger. "Colonel Ticking, you are relieved of duty pending an investigation of your involvement with Mrs. Chatterjee and the Kindred of Kali. I advise you to come peacefully, sir." My uncle stood transformed, his face was drawn and stern, his eyes bright and sharp.

The colonel barked a harsh laugh. "I'm your superior officer, you imbecile. You can't give me orders! Now get this idiot off of my arm!"

Uncle Jeremy looked at me, and his expression softened slightly. He took note of how I was standing on Colonel Ticking's wrist and covering the man with his own gun. "Nephew," he said, extending his hand. "Let me have the pistol, please."

I hesitated, and he gestured with his fingers. I engaged the safety and handed the weapon over to him. He disengaged the safety and pointed the gun at the colonel. "Now step back."

"You're sure?" I asked. He nodded.

I stepped back, releasing the colonel's arm. He jerked his arm back and rubbed his wrist with the opposite hand. Ticking climbed to his feet, puffing loudly. He stood there for a moment, eyes darting around the room. He saw the Kindred surrounded by soldiers and guards, Tinka and my brother standing guard over the maharaja and his daughter, and the other guests watching everything from the garden.

Colonel Ticking puffed up his chest. "All right, men. Let's get these women disarmed and out of those contraptions. Renault! See that the prisoners and their equipment are taken back to the base."

"You are relieved, sir!" Uncle Jeremy snapped. "And you are under arrest."

Ticking snorted and looked at his second in command. "Don't be ridiculous. I'm in command here."

"You *were* in command, sir. You are relieved pending resolution of charges of conspiracy to overthrow civilian authority, murder of civilian personnel, and fomenting rebellion against the Empire."

"WHAT? Don't be preposterous!"

Neither the gun, nor my uncle's voice wavered. "Renault, Sergeant Banks, please take the colonel into custody and see that he is suitably restrained." The two soldiers detached themselves from their positions and made their way around to Colonel Ticking. The Canadian officer holstered his side arm, but Sergeant Banks kept his weapon trained on his former commanding officer.

"Please come along quietly, sir," Lieutenant Renault said, gesturing in front of him. "We wouldn't want to make a to-do."

Ticking eyed the two soldiers and snorted, then said to my uncle, "You know, you won't be able to make any of those charges stick. And then I'll have you up for mutiny."

Uncle Jeremy shrugged. "If that's what the court decides, I'll abide by it, but I just saw you shoot a helpless civilian, and regardless of her crimes, there was no reason for that."

The colonel glared at my uncle, but couldn't muster a reply. Lieutenant Renault gestured for him to come with him and Sergeant Banks, and Ticking reluctantly went with them, grumbling under his breath.

My uncle turned to the maharaja. "Your Highness, might I trouble you for an escort for my men and a secure place to hold Colonel Ticking until I can arrange transportation back to the base?"

"Yes, of course," he replied, then called out a command in Hindi. Four guardsmen fell in with Colonel Ticking and his escort and led them out of the ballroom.

My uncle returned his gaze to the three surrounded Kindred. "Ladies, I recommend you surrender your weapons and come along peacefully. You will have to pay for your crimes, but I assure you that you will be treated well if you surrender now. You'll be remanded into the custody of local authorities while we conduct a joint investigation into these events. But you must stand down now."

Everyone was quiet in the ballroom, although I could hear the low voice of a woman praying outside the garden doors.

The maharani stepped forward, moving up next to Willie. "Please, do as he says. There has been too much bloodshed tonight. Lay down your arms. Do not give your lives for someone else's lies."

The three Kindred stood still, their heads moving slightly as they tried to look to each other without losing sight of the guardsmen and soldiers opposite them. Would they try to fight their way out?

A sword clattered to the floor. Another. Then came a cascade of falling metal as one of the women released all of her blades and raised her hands over her head.

Her companions looked at her, at each other. Neither said a word.

More blades crashed to the floor. The three Indian women stood amid a circle of sharpened metal.

Uncle Jeremy nodded. "Alright, gentlemen. Let the maharaja's men get the women out of those contraptions. We've got civilian wounded who need to be treated. If there are any guests who are doctors, they're in charge. Move!" My uncle clapped his hands and the British soldiers jumped into action. They holstered their weapons and quickly divided into teams. Several men cleared an area to check guests for injuries.

Willie grabbed my arm and passed me the sword that he picked up before joining the other soldiers and helping coordinate the rescue efforts. Miss Bang and Tinka rushed past me to offer their assistance.

Tinka's knives and the metal rod had disappeared again. The room became an oddly directed chaos as the prisoners were removed, and the guests were sorted into the wounded, the healthy, and the dead.

The maharaja called out another order, and six guardsmen ran over. Two of them took position guarding him and his daughter, the other four waited for orders. The maharaja turned to his advisor, who was still huddled over the body of his wife. "Sankar, I will have to take you into custody as well. Just until we sort out what happened."

Mr. Chatterjee did not look up, but he nodded. "That is wise, my liege. I am of no more use to you anyway. How good is an advisor that did not know that his own wife plotted against the throne he serves?" He touched his wife's cheek one last time, and stood.

He stepped carefully over the swords around his wife's body and went with the guards.

The maharaja called out again. "Bijoy!"

Professor Crackle appeared at my shoulder. "Excuse me, old chap, but did he just call out the name of the cart man we hired?"

I nodded. "Well, the maharani did say he used to work here as a gardener."

A small, bald man in a western tuxedo separated from the group of soldiers treating the wounded and ran up to the maharaja. He straightened and bowed.

"Is that..." the professor started.

"It's the cart man!" I finished.

"Bijoy," the maharaja said, "I'm afraid I must ask you to leave your retirement for a while. I will need you to take up your old roles as advisor and spymaster."

Bijoy bowed again. "I am ever at your service, Maharaja."

The maharaja nodded. "Thank you. Now, what happened here? The plan was not for us to be trapped in here with these terrorists."

Bijoy nodded. "The fault there is mine, Maharaja. I did not anticipate the involvement of Mr. Chatterjee's wife, or the method of smuggling these Kindred into the palace. When you withdrew, and the guards did not enter the ballroom, I suspected their orders might have been changed, and agents of the insurgents might be among the guests and would try to slip away if they were unmasked. I surreptitiously locked the doors, which proved a grave error."

The maharaja nodded, and walked away from us, discussing the matter further with Bijoy and flanked by his guardsmen.

The professor watched as they moved out of earshot. "That man is an amazing actor," he said.

I looked at the professor. "Spymaster?" I whispered.

"Well," the professor replied, "He certainly fooled all of us."

CHAPTER TWENTY-EIGHT
AN AUNT'S PRIDE

When we returned to Tinka's quarters in the palace, I tossed my jacket and tie on the back of the settee and dropped heavily down onto it. The recovery from the Kindred attack had taken longer than the party itself. Seven guests had died, along with two of the Kindred. A number of guests suffered small wounds when they were pushed through the doors and windows into the garden, but only one was seriously injured.

Tinka sat down and leaned into me. "That was some party."

I sighed. "It was not the best one I've ever been to. And oddly, not the worst. I'm sorry it was such a debacle for your social debut."

She lifted my arm over her shoulder and cuddled closer. "It wasn't that bad. I was starting to get a little bored with all the chit chat and no dancing. But that cow cut my new dress!"

"Hopefully, our next party will have more dancing and fewer murderous gate-crashers."

She looked up at me with bright eyes. "You mean it?"

I blinked at her. "I'm sorry, what?"

Her eyes got big and she pouted her lips. "You want to take me out again?"

I nodded. "I'd be happy to. It is the least I can do to make it up to you for how poor this outing was."

She squealed and hugged me. Hard. I put my arms around her and squeezed back.

At that moment, the door opened, and Professor Crackle and Miss Bang came in, already embroiled in a loud conversation. I tried to disengage, but Tinka held on. My cheeks began to feel warm, but neither the professor or Miss Bang seemed to notice my discomfort.

"Harmonious, it is entirely possible that she left that particular weapon behind and brought an entirely different sword with her." Miss Bang sounded like she was growing a bit tired of the conversation.

"This is exactly why we must conduct a complete search of the entire castle. To definitively determine if the weapon was on the premises. We must find it for the cause of science! There are definitely strange properties to that blade. We must be able to unlock them in order to understand the nature of my condition." He sputtered. "Um, I mean, to further our understanding of the universe."

"Miss Bang, what is he on about?" I asked, as Tinka released me but stayed tucked under my arm.

Miss Bang sighed. "Harmonious is still searching for the weapon that cut him at your aunt's party. He's been examining all of the swords the Kindred of Kali brought with them, trying to see if one of them was the same blade. When he didn't find it, he started grabbing every blade in sight and trying to cut himself. He frightened a number of people who thought he was going to turn one of the swords on them."

"Oh, poppycock! I would never have tried to harm anyone else."

"Harmonious, you dropped the weapons on the floor when you were done with them. Someone could have been injured." Miss Bang sat down on a couch opposite Tinka and myself. "I was barely able to keep the guards from throwing you in a cell." She adjusted her blood-stained skirts to bring a bit of clean fabric to the top and rested her hands on her knees. She'd had time to wash her hands, but her dress had been ruined treating the wounded.

Despite Miss Bang's objections, the professor continued, undaunted. "Well, I still think it is very important that we find it. That sword is an important clue. I don't see why we shouldn't be doing our utmost to track it down. Who knows what wonders we could unlock…"

"PROFESSOR!" I yelled, loudly enough to shock him out of his tirade. "A lot of people got injured tonight. Some people were killed. We're all tired. It can wait until after we've rested. I know how much this means to you, but for tonight, science can wait."

"But can it, my boy?" he asked.

"YES," we all replied at once.

Tinka was the first to start giggling. Miss Bang quickly joined in. I laughed and the three of us kept looking at each other and laughing again. The Professor stood there, indignant, and unable to see what the joke was. This just made us laugh more.

Finally, he raised his hands and sat down on the opposite end of the couch from Miss Bang. "All right, all right. It's obvious that you're all so worked up I'll never get any useful assistance from any of you." This prompted another round of laughter.

When she caught her breath again, Miss Bang pointed out, "Even if we don't find that particular weapon, Harmonious, we now know that some things *can* hurt you, which is more than we did before. While I don't want to see you harmed, it does give me some hope that your condition isn't permanent, and that someday we'll find a cure. I think that is much more important now. Having hope."

"I suppose you're right," he said. "I just wish I could do something now."

Miss Bang reached over and patted his hand.

I looked at Tinka, still tucked under my arm. She shrugged.

A knock came at the door.

I was about to rise and answer it, when a female servant appeared from the next room, crossed quickly, and answered the door. Uncle Jeremy and Aunt Phyllis came in. "I hope you don't mind the intrusion?" my uncle asked. His face had returned to his usual, jovial appearance. Professor Crackle and I stood as they crossed over to us.

"Is everything all right, Uncle Jeremy?" I asked.

"Oh, I think we've got everything in hand now. I don't see any immediate danger. It doesn't seem likely that they've got many of those machines around, although we still haven't located the one you damaged in that street fight the other week, Miss Tinka." He sat Aunt Phyllis down in an armchair and stood behind her. "And if one pops up now, we know how to fight it."

"No, I meant... we weren't expecting you. Did you need something?"

"Oh, oh, I see." He chuckled. "Well, you do. Need something, I mean. That is, I brought you here, so I thought I'd best see you back when you're ready to go. And since we've done everything we can for the evening, I thought we might as well come here."

"Oh, I'm sorry, Uncle, with everything else going on, it completely slipped my mind that we needed to ride back with you. Do you need us to go now?" I half turned to grab my jacket and tie.

He put his hand out and made a patting gesture. "No, there's no rush. Not on our account. You know your brother is off in a meeting with the maharaja and his daughter right now. I'm rather curious as to see how that turns out, if you don't mind us waiting with you."

Professor Crackle spoke up. "Oh, by all means, do wait with us, my good man. Have a seat!" He gestured to the space next to him on the couch.

Uncle Jeremy shook his head slightly. "I'd rather stand right now if you don't mind. I feel like I've sat for a bit too long, if you take my meaning."

The professor simply nodded in reply. We took out seats again.

Uncle Jeremy continued, "I hear the maharaja has pulled his old spymaster out of retirement to help sort out this mess. A Mr. Bijoy, I believe. He's supposed to be almost legendary in spy-craft."

"Wasn't that the old man with the cart?" Tinka asked.

I nodded. "He was there at the party, in a tuxedo," I said. "He looked almost completely different, but it was him."

The professor looked thoughtful. "I wonder. Was by coincidence that he was the only transportation we were able to find?"

"But why would he want to spy on us, Professor?" I asked.

He shrugged. "Perhaps he thought that we, or young William, would be the ones most likely to find out something worth knowing? I don't know. I don't think we'll ever know." He closed one eye and put a finger up against the side of his nose. "State secrets, you know. Your brother might find out one day, after he's married into the family, but I doubt any of us will."

Miss Bang leaned forward, looking at my aunt and uncle. "You both must be proud of William," she said with a warm smile. "Stepping up to confront one of the Kindred was a very heroic thing to do, even with Tinka's help."

My uncle nodded.

Tinka jabbed me in the ribs. "I thought you were supposed to be the hero."

I blinked at her. "Me? I'm not a hero. I'm just along for the ride."

Miss Bang gave me a slight smile. "Then, Sir Richard, you must be the first person in history to be given a knighthood for being 'along for the ride'."

The professor and Uncle Jeremy chuckled.

I snorted. "You know the whole knighthood thing was just so the Prince could one up great-grandfather's ghost. He was doing it more to prove a point, than to reward anything I might have done."

"My nephew's false humility aside," my uncle said, "I think both he and his brother have acquitted themselves well this evening. I think William will do well in the military."

I noticed Aunt Phyllis giving me one of her odd, intense looks. I looked away from her, hoping to forestall whatever dressing down she was preparing to unleash upon me. "Anyone care for a drink? I'm sure we must be able to get some kind of refreshments."

"No."

The quiet word from Aunt Phyllis shut off all conversation in the room. I turned my gaze back to my aunt, but she faced Miss Bang. "William did as I always expected him to. I have always been proud of him. Tonight was another demonstration of the man always I knew he could be."

Aunt Phyllis turned her head back to me. "But you, Nephew. You said 'No.' Most men would have taken what was offered you tonight. The accolades. The status. Even if you had no interest in the girl, a marriage of convenience would have brought you wealth and power. And you refused it."

I could feel a drop of sweat trickle down the side of my face. I cleared my throat. "Um..."

But she continued. "And you were *right* to do so. I saw an opportunity to settle a troublesome nephew into a good situation, but *you* saw more clearly. You saw what I missed. The bond that had grown up between your brother and the maharani. Despite everything I had done, you took all my carefully arranged plans over months of negotiations prior to your visit, and you handed it off to William with only a few words. Because after only being here a few days you'd seen what I'd overlooked all this time. That William and the maharani were truly in love."

I opened my mouth and tried to phrase some kind of apology.

"I have never been so proud of you in my life."

My jaw hung open as my brain struggled to process what Aunt Phyllis had just said.

"I saw the seed of greatness in you, Nephew, but you always seemed to fall short. To give up. Run away. Until tonight." She paused to wipe her eyes with a handkerchief. "You have great potential, Nephew. I beg you to do more. Try your best to achieve it. And *always* know that I am proud of you."

I sat in silence, my head spinning with what she'd said. She was proud of me?

Everyone else was looking at me and waiting for an answer.

I swallowed.

"Thank you, Aunt Phyllis. I... I always thought I was a disappointment to you. I'll try not to let you down."

She got up from her chair, and I stood reflexively. She walked over to me, and embraced me in a warm, genuine hug. Not knowing what else to do, I hugged her back.

CHAPTER TWENTY-NINE
AUSTRALIA BOUND

I stepped into my aunt's dining room and was greeted by the still unusual sight of my aunt smiling at me. The professor and Miss Bang were already seated at the table.

The faint smell of paint and varnish still lingered in the air from the renovations the Riggers performed upon my aunt and uncle's home. It was the last reminder that there had been any damage to the house at all. The doors and windows all were rebuilt and reglazed, including the main door to the house. The damaged flooring was expertly repaired.

"Good morning, Neph... Richard. Please, come sit down. You're just in time for breakfast." Aunt Phyllis patted the place setting next to her. I counted the chairs arrayed around the table, and noted three extra place settings.

"Are we having guests this morning?" I asked. I pulled out the chair and sat next to my aunt and across from Miss Bang and the professor. I hadn't seen much of them over the past week. They'd been making frequent trips to the palace as Professor Crackle continued his search for the sword that could cut him. We had not been able to dissuade the professor from the thought that the sword must have been there somewhere.

"Tinka came back with us, last night, my boy," he said. "She said she was starting to feel either in the way or completely useless."

"What I said was I wanted something to DO," Tinka said as she walked in. She was dressed in her usual leather pants and harness, and a sturdy white shirt with four long sleeves. Even more remarkably, the shirt was spotless. I started to stand as she entered, but she pushed me back down and slid into the chair next to me. "It's nice to be looked after once in a while, but they were treating me like I was made of spun glass or sumthin'. I'm ready to get back to work."

Tinka pulled apart the folded napkin in front of her with her upper hands, fluffed it out and laid it in her lap. As she did so, I could feel her lower left hand rubbing down the length of my thigh. I jumped slightly in surprise, and tried to cover it by turning to her and asking, "Is the new wardrobe part of getting back to work? I thought you were partial to short sleeves."

She shook her head and fingered the fabric of her new shirt. "Nah, nothin' like that. I just never had any shirts with proper sleeves before. I got hand-me downs from the other crew and had to cut holes in 'em for my lower arms. But Chandra's got some ladies who are right wizards with a needle. Look at this." Standing up, she swung her upper arms up and forward, while rotating her lower ones back and around. Gusseted pockets in the shoulders of the garment opened up, giving additional flexibility without stretching or pulling on the front of the shirt. Tinka moved her lower arms forward, her hands against the table, and pulled her upper arms back. The gussets closed smoothly and while there was a slight tension across the top button, she clearly had full range of movement. "I don't think I've ever had a shirt what fit so well." She dropped back into her seat and replaced the napkin in her lap.

"You haven't?" Aunt Phyllis asked, turning a pointed gaze upon the professor, who seemed completely unaware of her regard.

"Nah," Tinka said. "Once the professor found me, I kinda grew like a weed. It was hard enough keeping clothes on me. Never really seemed worth messing with sleeves, 'cept for my deck coat, and you don't really expect to move much in a heavy coat like that. And there were other things that needed fixing more than my shirt."

Manqoba appeared next to my aunt. It still seemed unnatural how such a large man was able to move so quietly that you never noticed him, and then he was just there.

He bowed and said, "Ma'am, I believe the cook is ready to serve breakfast now. Shall I summon Lieutenant-Colonel Griffith?"

She nodded. "Thank you, Manqoba." He left as silently as he had entered. Aunt Phyllis turned to the professor. "I'd like to thank you again, Professor Crackle, for lending us the use of Manqoba to get things settled here. His presence has helped things run smoothly since the tragic loss of Mr. Singh. I must say I'm tempted to make an offer to retain his services indefinitely."

The professor gestured with one hand. "You're quite welcome to make an offer, Lady Griffith-Holmes. All of my crew are free to come and go as opportunities arise. I'll not hold any man to a contract when destiny might call him elsewhere. But I don't think Manqoba is ready to move on quite yet."

Uncle Jeremy bustled into the room, William trailing in his wake. "Look who I found loitering on our doorstep," he said with a grin. The two of them took their seats, leaving one chair next to Tinka vacant. Manqoba appeared next to the sideboard and rang a bell. A door at the end of the hall opened, and a line of servants entered with platters of food. The smell of sausages and bacon assaulted my nose and made my mouth water, but there were also sliced fruits, eggs, toast, and small sweet pastries. They served us breakfast and filed back out.

"Maharani Chandrakanta won't be joining us today, William?" my aunt asked with an arched brow.

My brother ducked his head slightly, as if dodging a metaphorical blow. "No, I'm afraid that her father has insisted that she remain at the palace for the time being, while he and his temporary advisor review the security arrangements. He's quite rightfully shaken that someone was able to get so close to him." William glanced at Uncle Jeremy. "And I don't blame him. I'm rather chilled at the idea all these troubles were caused by our own commanding officer."

"Lieutenant, you know better than to comment on an investigation in progress," Uncle Jeremy chided him gently.

"Oh, come now, Colonel," the professor interrupted.

"Lieutenant-Colonel," my uncle corrected.

"We were all there when Mrs. Chatterjee accused Colonel Ticking of being the mastermind behind the attacks," Professor Crackle continued. "The man killed her to keep her from saying any more. It is obvious he had *some* part in the whole thing."

My uncle nodded. "I must admit that it has been a bit of a black eye for the Empress's Army. We're meant to be here to keep the peace, not start a rebellion." He forked a bit of egg into his mouth, chewed, and swallowed. "But you must understand that I can't reveal anything until after the official tribunal has cleared it for release. For now, this is a military matter."

Miss Bang paused, holding her tea near her face. "Be that as it may, Lieutenant-Colonel, as civilians, surely we can speculate?"

He nodded. "There's nothing I can do to stop you from developing your own theories, miss. Although I'd prefer you didn't spread them too widely while the investigation is ongoing."

Sipping her tea and returning the cup to the table, Miss Bang said, "Oh, I didn't mean to imply that we would cause any trouble, merely that we can share ideas amongst ourselves. As you said, the commander of the local garrison is entrusted with protecting the citizenry and keeping the peace, it doesn't make sense that he would hatch a plot to foment rebellion in the empire."

"Much less a plan that involved some kind of advanced weaponry," the professor added. "Those Kindred outfits were some very sophisticated engineering. They don't seem like the kind of thing that Colonel Ticking would be able to develop on his own."

"Some secret project? Something developed for the military that he was able to turn to his own designs?" I suggested.

Tinka shrugged and grabbed a piece of toast and proceeded to slather it with marmalade. "It's not really that good as a weapon. I mean, yeah, you can handle a lot of weapons at once, but the movements are predictable, and the person in the thing is completely exposed. They're tough in hand-to-hand fighting, but not much against someone with ranged weapons. Colonel just shot her down as soon as she came at him." She bit off the corner of the toast and chewed. "Mind you, if you got the balance right, they might be handy for lifting and moving cargo."

"Actually, that brings up a good point. Uncle Jeremy, why were you and Willie the only soldiers there who didn't have sidearms?" I looked down the table at the two of them.

Willie swallowed a mouthful of food. "Standard protocol is for officers to go unarmed to state functions, except for ceremonial weapons, as appropriate."

"Then why were all the other soldiers present armed?" the professor asked.

Uncle Jeremy looked down at his plate. "They were ordered to bring their sidearms in their jackets, in case there was trouble." He looked up at the professor. "We never received that order."

Miss Bang frowned. "Why would the colonel want his second in command and his adjutant to go unarmed into a situation where he was expecting trouble?"

Now it was Aunt Phyllis' turn to frown.

The professor shifted in his chair. "Gentlemen, that sounds suspiciously as if the colonel did not want either of you to survive the encounter."

Neither of the soldiers said anything.

Tinka looked at the rest of us. "I don't get it. Why would he want to kill off the two of you? You're not really a threat to him, are you?"

"If Colonel Ticking was trying to stir up the Indian people into rebellion, he might have seen Willie's close relationship with the maharani as an obstacle," I suggested.

"And he really wasn't happy when we went and rescued her after she was kidnapped," Willie added. "Some retribution might have entered into it."

"William," Uncle Jeremy started, but Willie cut him off.

"It's pure speculation, Uncle. I don't have any evidence and I haven't heard the colonel say anything to indicate that was his intent, but he wasn't happy to take me off of punishment duty."

My uncle grunted but didn't say anything.

"But why endanger his second in command?" I asked. "Or did he suspect that the close family relationship would cause you to warn Willie that something might be up?"

"Possibly," Miss Bang said, "but we'd already put a significant crimp into his plans at this point. Perhaps it would all make sense if we knew what his objective was?"

"Aside from rebellion?" I asked.

"But that's really the issue, my boy," the professor said. "What would be the point of a rebellion? Even if he could take over the city, or the region, he wouldn't be able to hold it for any length of time. Once word got back to London, the Empress would send more troops and take it back. A rebellion would ruin him. He'd lose his commission, his reputation, and most likely his life. Along with thousands of people who supported him." He shook his head. "It doesn't make sense."

"Except." Miss Bang grabbed the professor's arm. "Except *he* wouldn't be leading the rebellion. The Kindred of Kali were the ones calling for rebellion, not Colonel Ticking."

The professor blinked at her for a moment, then his eyes widened. "That's right! And they were trying to get the maharaja as their figurehead." He rubbed his chin. "That does put a different light on it."

"How?" I asked.

"Because it wouldn't be seen as a rebellion led by a military officer, my boy, but one led by a charismatic Indian noble, who is much beloved by his people and has a history of ruling well." The professor practically bounced in his seat. "Such a rebellion could quickly spread and become a force to be reckoned with. Once it became established it would take a significant effort to stamp it out. The subcontinent would be embroiled in war."

"Ticking wanted to start a war?" The idea seemed ridiculous to me.

"No." Willie's voice was flat. "He wanted to stop a war. To nip it in the bud. That's why he backed the Kindred. Gave them the suits. He wanted to start a rebellion, so he could be the one to stop it before it grew too big."

"William!" Uncle Jeremy said sharply.

"Still just speculation, sir," Willie replied.

Professor Crackle nodded. "That does sound about right for a man like Colonel Ticking."

Tinka slurped her tea, then asked, "But what would he get out of it?"

"Promotion." We all turned to look at Uncle Jeremy. "Since we're all speculating on facts not in evidence," he said and took a sip of tea before continuing. "If a rebellion broke out, and he put it down, the Army would be hard pressed to find a reason not to promote him to general. He's been passed over twice in the last few years. Each time, he raged up a storm for days. He's got friends back at headquarters who keep putting him in, but they're not placed highly enough to get him past the board. But putting down an uprising? That would do it."

"That's insane!" Aunt Phyllis protested. "To cause all that death and destruction, just to further one's career?"

The professor raised his tea. "Unfortunately, the world is filled with men who would do much worse for much less, my good lady." He sipped from the cup and put it back down. "Sometimes it does seem like the most heinous crimes of passion are committed for the most dispassionate reasons."

"We're all speculating, here, Professor. Do you think that's the real reason?" I asked.

"Hard to say, my boy. It does fit all the facts as we know them. It seems plausible. I guess only Colonel Ticking will ever know the reasons for his actions."

"I don't know about that, Professor Crackle," Uncle Jeremy said as he used a crust of toast to get another mouthful of eggs onto his fork. "He'll have to give some account for himself at the inquiry. He may find that confession is good for the soul. Thanks to you, we do have some physical evidence of what he's been up to."

"Eh?" The professor was clearly perplexed.

"The new suits that were impounded. We've started disassembly and indexing parts. You and William discovered that the parts for them were being shipped to a military warehouse. We've already found some discrepancies in the base inventories. Some of those materials definitely came from our base. And the colonel signed those orders." My uncle put his silverware down on his plate. A footman stepped forward and quietly whisked it off to the kitchens. "So, William, why did you want to join us for breakfast this morning?"

Willie reached a hand into his jacket and pulled out an envelope. "I got a letter from Father at mail call yesterday. I thought you might like to hear some of what is going on at home, Brother." He pulled several sheets of paper out of the envelope. Unfolding them, he scanned quickly down the page. "Father heard about what happened in Prague, and about your knighthood. He petitioned the Lord Lyon for a change of title, in keeping with your elevation, but they denied his request on the grounds that he did not personally earn the honors and one cannot inherit a title from one's son." He looked up as he flipped to the next page. "That's a shame. It would be nice if Father could have dealt with great-grandfather's tricks and had it over and done with at last."

He looked down at the new sheet before him, and grinned. "But, get this! Word got out about Father trying to change the name of the county. The people *loved* it. They didn't care about Lord Lyon's rules. They just started putting up new signs declaring it County Blasphemy. Father even got a strongly worded letter of complaint from a cartography company because the name change wasn't properly registered. It may not be legal yet, but it looks like the name is going to stick." Willie looked at me. "It looks like by the time you get home you'll be Sir Blasphemy of Blasphemy."

"You're kidding me." I stretched out a hand. "Can I see that letter?"

My brother chuckled and handed me the two pages he had read over. I scanned over my father's flowing script, but it was pretty much as my brother had said. Father did note that the Lord Lyon said when I inherited the estate, it would be within my rights to restyle the family title as Blasphemy.

As I read on through Father's account of how the tenants had taken it upon themselves to rename the county as County Blasphemy, somewhat to the dismay of the local vicar, I heard an insistent knocking at the new front door of the house. A moment later, there were loud sounds of many booted feet running through the house and up the stairs. I looked up to see Manqoba appear with a letter on a silver plate. He moved quietly over to the table and presented the letter to Professor Crackle. "A message was delivered to the ship by special courier, sir. The men believed you would want to see it right away." The edges of the envelope were marked with red and black hatching, something I'd never seen before.

The professor grabbed the envelope off the plate and tore into it, removing another page with similar hatching down the right side. He read through the message quickly, then handed it off to Miss Bang. "Lieutenant-Colonel, Lady Griffith-Homes. I'd like to thank you for your hospitality in welcoming us into your home for our time here in India. I'm afraid we're going to have to cut our time a bit short. My men are upstairs gathering our effects. I'm afraid we will have to leave today."

"What is it, Professor," I asked. "What happened?"

"It's a message from one of the agents in my information network..." he began, but Miss Bang took over in mid-sentence.

"There are signs that Lord Scaleslea may be operating out of Australia. A number of mysterious deaths, and some missing shipments of technology." Her voice trailed off as she continued reading.

I grunted in sympathy. "Him again? That's going to be some very nasty business."

"Who is this Lord Scaleslea?" Aunt Phyllis asked.

"A man that I am sworn to bring before the crown. I've been hunting him for a very long time." The professor stood. "This is the first lead on him I've had in a decade. We only stumbled across what he was doing in Prague. If this pans out, we may have a chance of stopping him, or unraveling his criminal empire. Unfortunately, the message is weeks old, after bouncing around from port to port chasing us. To make up that lost time, we're going to have to leave immediately."

Miss Bang folded up the letter, made it disappear, and then she and Tinka rose. "It was a delightful breakfast, Lady Griffith-Holmes. My compliments to your household. I look forward to visiting with you again."

Tinka grabbed a few more strips of bacon, stuck one in her mouth, and smacked me on the shoulder. I looked up, somewhat surprised.

"Coming, my boy?" the professor asked.

"What?" I blinked. "You want me to come with you?"

"Of course, my boy! We wouldn't deprive you of your chance to settle scores with Lord Scaleslea." The professor looked to my aunt and uncle. "Providing you don't have some obligations here that I'm not aware of."

My uncle looked as surprised as I felt at the suggestion. He looked at his wife and nodded.

"Go, Nephew," Aunt Phyllis said with a small flicking gesture of her fingers. "It is clear that you are prospering more in their company than you would in mine. I told you before that you should strive to achieve your potential. You'll do more of that adventuring in Australia, or wherever, than you will sitting in an old woman's parlor. Go. You're supposed to be seeing the world anyway."

I looked at my uncle. He smiled. "I never argue with good advice. I recommend you don't start."

Willie stood up. "I'll help you pack."

I rose from my seat. "I don't want to miss your wedding."

My brother laughed. "I think you'll have plenty of time. I have to get permission from the army to marry first, and that's going to be months going through channels back to headquarters. And I'm sure it will take some time to figure out the details. Keep in touch, Brother, and we'll let you know when you'll need to return in plenty of time."

"Quite right, Lieutenant, a royal wedding is not exactly planned overnight." The professor clapped Willie on the shoulder. "But we'd best get our things together now."

Tinka, Miss Bang, and the professor rushed through the door and ran up the stairs. I paused at the door. "Uncle, I still have one of your pistols. I should return it to you."

Now it was my uncle's turn to heave himself up from the table. "No, no. Take it, Nephew. Keep it. Here, it will sit in a drawer. In your hands, it has a chance to do some good in the world. Besides, I've seen reports of some pirate activity out that way. You may find you need it sooner than you expect. I'd feel much better knowing you had something to defend yourself with. William tells me that you're a decent shot. Put in some practice and you'll get better. I'll put together a cleaning kit for you to take with you." Uncle Jeremy walked over and put a hand on each of my shoulders. "It is a wonderful and dangerous world out there. When I was a young man, I joined the army so I could see it. I understand the allure. I saw many great and horrible things in my time. See the world, but watch your back while you do so. And return to us safe."

"I will, Uncle."

"You had better," said Aunt Phyllis as she came and gave me a quick hug. "Now go, Nephew. You need to pack."

"Yes, ma'am," I told her with a grin, then I went out into the hall and ran up the stairs. The Riggers were going in and out of the rooms, pulling our belongings out and packing them in the hall under the guidance of Tinka and Manqoba. It was absolute chaos, but to me it felt like...

The professor came out of his room with an armful of loose swords. Miss Bang immediately lit into him, demanding to know where he had gotten them and where he thought he was going to put them. Two of the Riggers got into an argument with several of the house servants when they tried to stuff some of Tinka's neatly folded new clothes into a ditty bag. The servants pulled the clothes back out of the bag and shooed the Riggers away as they refolded and packed the clothing into a suitcase.

Tinka put two fingers in her mouth and whistled at me. "Oi! Hero! Get a move on! We got a lot to do."

It was chaos. But it also felt like where I belonged.

I took the stairs two at a time. Rushing headlong back to a family I didn't realize I had been missing and down an exciting path to a new adventure.

The End

About the Author

Doc Coleman has been a blogger, podcaster, voice actor, and writer. His blogs can be found at Swimming Cat Studios (http://SwimmingCat Studios.com). As a podcaster, his voice can be heard on the Galley Table, The Shrinking Man Project, The Writer's Round Table and the Balticon Podcast.

Doc's short stories can be found in The Ministry of Peculiar Occurrences' Tales from the Archives, the Way of the Gun Bushido Western Anthology, the Steampunk Special Edition of Flagship magazine, the Paradise Found, Tales from the Library anthology, and the Forgotten Lore anthology series by eSpec Books. Doc has also published a collection of short stories: The Shining Cog and Other Steampunk Tales.

The Perils of Prague is the first novel in the series The Adventures of Crackle and Bang. *The Kindred of Kali* is the second, and several more books are planned to chronicle the journeys of Professor Harmonious Crackle, Miss Titania Bang, and Sir Richard Blasphemy.

Doc streams the latest video games he's enjoying on Twitch (https://www.twitch.tv/doccoleman) and on Sundays he streams productivity sprints on YouTube (https://www.youtube.com/@DocColeman) with Morgan Hazelwood and Sako Tumi.

When he isn't juggling projects, making a living, or mainlining podcasts, Doc is a gamer, an avid reader, a motorcyclist, a home brewer and beer lover, a fan of renaissance festivals, and frequently a smart-ass. He lives with his lovely wife and a cat in Germantown, MD.

Want to know more about us?

The Author - Doc Coleman

Did you enjoy this story and want to know more? Reading Doc's bio on the previous page wasn't enough? Want the most up to date information on what Doc is working on and releasing? Be sure to check out the web site, and sign up for the mailing list.

Website: https://www.DocColeman.com

Facebook: DocColemanAuthor

BlueSky: scaleslea.bsky.social

Mastodon: @DocColeman

Linktr.ee: https://linktr.ee/scaleslea

Questions? Email him at: Doc@swimmingcatstudios.com

The Cover Artist - Scott E. Pond

Scott E. Pond is an illustrator, artist, graphic designer, humorist, photographer, and author. His artistic and graphic design work can be found in works by New York Times Bestselling Author Scott Sigler, award winning novelist and screenwriter Matt Wallace, Parsec Award winning author Paul E. Cooley, Bram Stoker Award nominated-novelist Jake Bible, Campbell Award winning author Mur Lafferty, Scott Roche, Sue Baiman, Kate Sherrod, M. Jandreau, Escape Artists audio fiction, and many others. You can experience some of his dark and wacky nuggets of wisdom from the mental recesses of his mind in his coffee-table book, *Mental Graffiti*. Want to get the most up to date information on what Scott is working on and releasing?

Website: http://www.scottpond.com

Facebook: ScottEPondDesigns

BlueSky: scottepond.bsky.social

Mastodon: @scottepond

Questions? Contact him at: http://www.scottpond.com/contact

The Editor - Leona Wisoker

Leona Wisoker writes, reviews, typesets, researches and edits, all in glorious chaos. Her short fiction has been published in Abyss & Apex Magazine, *Cats in Space* (anthology), *Galactic Creatures* (anthology), *Sha'Daa: Pawns* and *Sha'Daa: Inked* (anthologies), Andromeda Spaceways Inflight Magazine, and more. She currently has a self-published novel *(Lies of Stone)*, and three novellas out through The Scribbling Lion (thescribblinglion.com).

Perpetually buried in too many projects to count (including an ongoing quest to achieve an Associate's Degree in Horticulture), she updates social media (Mastodon: @lionesslady@mindly.social) and her websites in the rare moments between the completion of one ambitious project and the beginning of the next.

Website: http://LeonaWisoker.com
Writing: http://thescribblinglion.com
Mastodon: @Lionesslady@mindly.social

www.ingramcontent.com/pod-product-compliance
Lightning Source LLC
Chambersburg PA
CBHW050025030726

47506CB00001B/119